THE
Southern
Belle
BRIDES
COLLECTION

7 Sweet and Sassy Ladies of Yesterday Experience
Romance in the Southern States

THE
Southern
Belle
BRIDES
COLLECTION

Lauralee Bliss, Ramona K. Cecil,
Dianne Christner, Lynn A. Coleman, Patty Smith Hall,
Grace Hitchcock, Connie Stevens

BARBOUR BOOKS
An Imprint of Barbour Publishing, Inc.

Print ISBN 978-1-68322-650-5

eBook Editions:
Adobe Digital Edition (.epub) 978-1-68322-652-9
Kindle and MobiPocket Edition (.prc) 978-1-68322-651-2

All scripture quotations, unless otherwise noted, are taken from the King James Version of the Bible.

Scripture quotations marked NIV are taken from the HOLY BIBLE, NEW INTERNATIONAL VERSION®. NIV®. Copyright © 1973, 1978, 1984, 2011 by Biblica, Inc.™ Used by permission. All rights reserved worldwide.

Published by Barbour Books, an imprint of Barbour Publishing, Inc., 1810 Barbour Drive, Uhrichsville, Ohio 44683, www.barbourbooks.com

Our mission is to inspire the world with the life-changing message of the Bible.

Member of the
Evangelical Christian
Publishers Association

Printed in Canada.

Contents

The Belle of the Congaree

by Lauralee Bliss

Dedication

With thanks to Sherry, Austin, and my husband, Steve,
for their helpful critiques and advice.

"Love your neighbor as yourself."
MARK 12:31 NIV

Chapter 1

Looks as if you're about ready."

Am I ready? Is anyone ever ready for anything in life? Especially when doubt comes sneaking in, ready to trip up plans or steal away the confidence that once led to a firm decision. Mason Bassinger glanced at his saddlebags thrown over the croup of his mare Honey, the wool blanket that once adorned Mother's bed, or so his brother Harold told him, rolled up and tied to the back. He was just a lad when she passed away and couldn't recollect things like the blanket on her bed. Harold had been the one to remind him of the past. Harold raised him. Provided for him. Guided him in the things of life.

Now Harold was telling him it was time to leave. But all Mason could envision was falling off a rocky precipice if he rode away.

Harold squinted at him. "It's going to be just fine," he said, trying to alleviate the doubt that sought to disrupt the plans. "You know what to do. We Bassingers have it in our blood to do good. It's a part of us."

Of course Mason knew what to do, but did he want to? Could he construe this mission as something good and godly? "I will go, Harold. But this is the last time."

Harold stepped back, his brown eyes widening. "What do you mean?"

Mason threw his foot up to catch the stirrup and drew himself into the saddle. "Just as I said. I—I need to do other things."

Harold's mouth fell open. "You can't turn your back on what's happening. The business is doing so well. With what I've been told about the land down there in South Carolina after Sherman's march, there's a fortune to be made."

Mason adjusted his hat atop his crop of dark brown hair, gritting his teeth as he did. He wished he could speak the words from the Good Book he'd read last night about the root of mammon and Harold's incessant desire for money. Mason understood where it stemmed from—a life as boys growing up in a ramshackle cabin, with Papa drunk on whiskey and Mother trying to sew for wealthy neighbors to put bread on the table. Harold confessed to him one evening, through narrow eyes and a face red like the sinking sun, that he would never again live the life of a pauper. He would have what he deserved, his castle here on earth. Being ten years Harold's junior, Mason went along with whatever Harold said. Harold had helped him through the difficult times. When they lost both Mother and Papa in a flu epidemic, Harold had been by his side to make sense out of life and provide them food to eat.

Now Harold had made a name for himself by buying up lands ravaged by the war. Many folks called them carpetbaggers. Sometimes scoundrels, scalawags, even scum. To Harold, buying land not only helped him fill his pockets but helped those suffering, which he emphasized as the good part of the business. Mason believed him. He had no choice. Harold had been steadfast and sure in the difficult times of his life when he had no other. He owed his brother a debt of gratitude.

Since turning his heart to Christ a few months ago at a prayer meeting, new feelings had begun to surface in Mason's reborn soul. Almost as if God had now taken Harold's place as the Provider, leading him to new paths for His name's sake. Maybe it was the prayer he'd uttered—looking now to heaven's reward rather than anything here that could turn to tatters. He would rather trust the One who cared not only for his body but also his soul. Especially now, after years of a terrible conflict that saw thousands die. The scars of battle remained on the land and in people's hearts. Except for Harold, whose craving to make money off the misery left Mason to question their business and the profit they made. God's way of thinking looked much more promising and enduring to Mason, and compassionate too. But Harold was kin. Mason pledged to make this one final trip before life took him elsewhere.

"Well, you'd better get going, as daylight is burning," Harold told him. "I'll be looking for your telegrams. You got the map I gave you?"

Mason felt for the square bulge in his pocket that Harold had secured—a map of South Carolina with the place of interest circled. Harold had heard from a contact in Columbia of a rail town called Kingsville in an area once teeming with plantations and good timber lining the Congaree River. "I have it right here."

"And the money?"

He checked the leather purse that jingled under his fingertips before reining Honey about to face southward. "Yes."

"Good. I'll be waiting to hear any news. . . ." His voice trailed off.

The echo of Harold's words reverberated in Mason as if the unspoken words of "or else" were meant to be added. He shouldn't read so much into it. Harold had never been threatening but only supportive. Mason knew well the words in a telegram that would tickle his brother's ears, describing families who'd lost all they had to Sherman's rampage and now wanted a new life. And that meant surrendering property that had been in the family for generations. Mason had with him the gold that would appeal to the sad and depraved families. Gold would speak above the groan of misery from a wounded heart. Harold was counting on it. But at that moment, the purpose of this mission weighed Mason down. He prayed God might yet have the final say over all these plans and release the burden he felt. *What that plan might be, I don't know.*

"Yep. Should do ya right fine."

After a week's journey to this place from New York, Mason already felt worn out but ready to fulfill his duty as quickly as possible. The roguish fellow with a reed poking out of his mouth didn't even look at Mason but only stared at the gold coin reflecting in the light of the noonday sun. As Mason knew it would, money did something inside a man hungering for the feel of wealth after the depravity of war. This fellow was no different. Though right now, as Mason looked over the boat with paint peeling off and cracks running the length of the boards, he had to wonder if the craft would even bear him to where he needed to go. "And you're certain it's seaworthy?" he began.

"Course. Ain't no reason not to be."

Mason watched again as the man flipped the coin back and forth between two dirty hands thick with calluses while his grin grew even wider. "I ain't never seen nuthin' so purty in all my born days." His gray-blue eyes now settled on Mason. "Where'd you get this? Ain't nuthin' like this round here. Only got Confederate money or them Yankee greenbacks, and all worthless."

"I worked hard for it," Mason said, picking up the pair of oars lying on the ground. Though he questioned this particular man's integrity, he was thankful to have found a reputable stableman to board Honey while he went about his business. The town of Kingsville still appeared prosperous, though it had tasted Sherman's wrath, with the burnt-out shells of buildings once belonging to the railroad standing as stark reminders. When he first arrived, the sight of Northern aggression sent trepidation racing through him, and he'd made a decision then to scout the lay of the land by the way of the Congaree

River here in South Carolina. He would take Harold's map and make an inconspicuous sweep of everything. He would write down the kind of timber he found and anything else of value. He would also check out the effects the war had on the area. Harold said property by the river might be valuable. He could imagine his brother's glee when he wired him about several properties secured by the coins he carried, ready to deliver in triumph. Once Mason finished with his mission, he would move on with life.

"So is there good land along the river?" Mason asked the man.

"Sure. Jus' go on down there a spell and you'll see it all. Won't be too flooded neither. Not the storm season." He pocketed the coin. "And there's a mighty fine filly living down there too—sweet looking like sugar candy, but hoo-wee, what a temper. Lost her family's home in the war, you see. Seen her on the river a lot in her pappy's old boat. She owns a lot of land."

Mason was all ears. He reached inside a saddlebag for a piece of paper and the stub of a pencil. "Do you have a name?"

"Ha. I call her the Belle of the Congaree. Hair lak fire with a temper to match. Claims the river's hers, ha-ha. Now if yer lookin' for a quick-tempered, mean-spirited woman. . ."

"I'm not," Mason said hastily. "I'm interested in land."

The man squinted at him "Hey, you ain't one of them Yankee scalawags I hear talk about?" He spit a wad of something brown and oozy onto the ground.

Mason's stomach lurched at the unseemly gift of tobacco. "I am a gentleman of the North and. . ."

"Ha! You must be one of them all right. But never you mind. I lak yer money all the same. Anyways, jus' go on down there a spell and you'll run into her." The man cackled as he withdrew, leaving Mason to wonder if the man had left him to the claws of some unknown evil, whether it be the boat he'd secured or this woman with fiery red hair called the Belle of the Congaree. "What is her name?" he finally asked the man, who began sauntering back to his old donkey hee-hawing in protest as it stood tied to a tree.

"Miss Anderson." He lifted his hat. "And tell her that Chester T. Wilson gives her a mighty fine howdy-do."

Mason twisted his lips, already vowing not to give some nice southern woman a taste of any howdy-do from the rather unseemly Chester T. Wilson. He returned to his task at hand and the dilapidated boat that pitched helplessly under his weight. He hoped and prayed this had been a good idea even as doubts rose over his plan to sneak up the river to where this fiery belle lived. Maybe her family still possessed weapons. He could envision her red hair flying in the wind, her father armed and ready to drive him off their land. Especially if any of them caught wind that he was a scalawag from the North. A bullet could come sooner rather than later.

A half hour went by, and already large beads of sweat were rolling down Mason's face and trickling into his eyebrows, stinging his eyes. Stains appeared on his shirt. He took out a handkerchief to wipe his face, recalling with pain the hot and humid days when he last came to this part of the country. He'd traveled farther south and east then, near Savannah, and there he secured several properties for his brother. He could hardly revel in the open window of opportunity when he saw the lands disrupted by wartime and the helpless faces as people signed over the only homes they ever knew to a carpetbagger from New York. Those were the images that drew him to church and then to the altar of repentance to heal him of the guilt he felt.

Mason heaved the oars, wishing he had more strength. The river was stagnant, with flies swarming around both him and the boat. Trees lined the riverside, veils of Spanish moss drooping over the branches, untouched by war. The area still breathed life and God's favor amid the storm. The vast acreage of timber alone would make Harold's eyes glow in appreciation. Mason fetched his notepad to scribble down some observations. There was much good to be said about this place if not for the sweat that soaked him from the blazing sun and his parched throat begging for moisture. Mason finally took a tin cup from the saddlebag and scooped up brown, tepid river water. It tasted like a freshly plowed field. He poured most of it over his head, hoping not to collapse under the oppressive warmth.

The rowing soon turned difficult as his arms cramped from the relentless battle with the turbid river water. He tried to shift his mind to searching the riverbank for any sign of this fair red-haired belle. He saw no manner of civilization in these parts, no homes or roads or any living thing save the gnarly trees and tall grass in a swampy land.

Mason shifted then and felt a strange sensation as his feet suddenly became nice and cool. He glanced down to see a pool of water forming in the bottom of the boat. "Oh no!" His fear had come true. The boat leaked, and leaked badly. Mason scowled. Talk about scalawags…that Chester T. Wilson was the epitome of one by taking his gold for a leaky dinghy. And now he presumed the miscreant occupied a table inside a Kingsville saloon, laughing with his fellow buddies, showing off the coin while boasting how he bested a Yankee carpetbagger at his own game.

This was a bad idea. Mason groaned. Worse too was his rowing ability that amounted to mere splatters of the oars in the muddy water. He moved his saddlebag to his lap when the bottom of it became soaked from the rising water. Mason inhaled a deep breath and tried with all his might to row to the safety of the shore before the boat sank deeper into the murky depths.

Water soon reached midcalf. His anxiety began to rise. Why hadn't he kept to dry land? Why did he have to act like a serpent and sneak around? *Am I my brother after all?* And so began a list of mortal sins he felt he must have committed to be in this predicament.

Suddenly a voice called out to him. He looked to his right to find another boat on the river, proceeding rapidly in his direction. When the boat drew close, he managed to see the occupant—a young woman, dressed in gray, her large straw hat and veil masking much of her features. She commanded the oars and the situation like a captain in charge of a vessel. "Are you all right?" she called.

"My boat is filling with water," Mason confessed in a strangely calm voice that nowhere near matched the anxiety he felt. "I think it is on the verge of sinking. . . ."

"You must abandon your boat immediately, sir. Hand me your belongings before it's too late."

Mason passed over his drenched saddlebag and his hat.

"Remove any other heavy clothing. I will not look." The woman turned away but added over her shoulder, "Remove your boots also. Nothing must weigh you down, or you will sink along with the boat."

Mason did as she said. He attempted to give her his boots, but the boat lurched and they slipped out of his hands and fell into the murkiness as he fought to stay upright. He sighed but focused instead on the rising water inside the boat. Quickly he entered the river and made his way toward her craft. Thankfully, there was no current tugging him in the opposite direction. He grabbed for the edge of her boat and somehow climbed into it. The craft pitched wildly and nearly capsized but for the woman who shifted to the other side to keep it upright. She never flinched or showed any concern at the thought of being tossed into the water. Even in his predicament, he had to admire her steadfastness and strength. "You—you are a miracle," he sputtered.

"A miracle indeed! Look at you. You nearly drowned."

Mason wiped away streams of water from his face. "Allow me to at least row. I will not have a woman do it."

"I have done just fine, but you may assist me." She handed him an oar, and together they maneuvered the boat to where an old dock still stood with splintered wood toasting in the noonday sun. Mason tried to get a closer look at his benefactress as she rowed, but the veil and hat masked her features. "Tell me how it is you were on the river this day?"

"One must eat." She pointed to the pail of river water with fish floating quietly about as the boat drew near the dock. She threw a loop of rope over a wooden support.

He wondered what else he could offer in the conversation, especially to a woman who appeared to fight every day to live. Only one thing came to mind, given the circumstances he had found himself in. "Thank you. You were sent by God."

The straw hat spun about, the edge of it nearly nipping him on the cheek. Suddenly the woman swept back the veil as if she were by some great marriage altar, ready to greet her groom. It revealed a set of deep green eyes matching the Spanish moss decorating the tree limbs. Ringlets of auburn hair rested beside cheeks colored from either the sun or their conversation. The hair reminded him of what Chester Wilson had said back in Kingsville. He sucked in a breath. No doubt she must be the infamous Belle of the Congaree. He nearly opened his mouth to inquire then shook his head.

"Why do you shake your head like that? Am I so awful to look at?" She laughed as she stooped to pick up the pail of fish.

"Of course not. Please, allow me to carry the pail. I insist."

She left the pail and gathered her skirt in one hand while holding her large hat with the other. She did not look wanting of money or anything else in particular but rather appeared confident and proud as any fine southern lady.

"Do you realize I was introduced to you earlier?" Mason offered.

She glanced at him. "Oh?"

"By a Mr. Wilson in town."

She sighed loudly. "I declare, he is an awful, vulgar man. Why have you anything to do with him?"

"I paid him for use of the boat."

"Ha-ha! What a terrible misfortune for you. I would ask why you are taking a pleasure trip on the Congaree in any boat of Mr. Wilson's. At least you are out of danger."

"Thanks to you. I–I'm glad you decided to go fishing."

"Not a chore a lady ought to be doing, but one I must in order to live. Like everything else here. And I can see, from your clothing and your accent, you are not from these parts. Maybe even a Yankee?"

"I won't deny it. I'm from New York, yes."

"A Yankee from New York, sailing along on our river. I'm sorry, Mister. . ."

"Bassinger. Mason Bassinger."

"Mr. Bassinger. I'm sorry to say, but this does sound like another enemy invasion to me."

Mason swallowed hard as he caught a glimpse of her staring at him, but the veil suddenly fell forward, cooling the otherwise fire in her eyes. He wished then he had heeded his doubts at the very beginning of this venture and refused to come. She was right about one thing. Here in Southern territory, he was most assuredly the enemy.

Chapter 2

Elisa Anderson knew a wealthy and handsome man when she saw one. At least that's how it used to be before the war began. Now the only thing she thought of each day was how to survive. Certainly not by way of a man's good looks, even if this Mason Bassinger had a heap of them in his fine dark hair and molasses-colored eyes. It had not been bad when the war began and she still had time to consider a fine man. She had Father and her younger brother, John. Mother had died many years before, giving birth to an unnamed daughter, who had also died.

And so it had been just the three of them, living a good life. Elisa possessed many dresses, ribbons, hats, and all the finery. She attended balls for the gentlemen and the ladies. Then the war turned deadly. Several of their friends lost sons. John lost his best friend and then took on the fool notion of preserving his right to fight in the name of his friend against the murdering Yankee hirelings. He joined the men in gray over Father's stern objection. A year later they received news of his death at the battle of Chattanooga. Father never recovered from his son's death or the loss of their money in a poor deal he himself had made. He sat long hours in his study, staring at nothing at all. He didn't eat or sleep. Oftentimes Elisa found an empty liquor bottle beside him. A few months later he wandered away, never to be heard from again. After that came the marauding Yankees who stole most all she possessed and then lit fire to the main house. Both family and livelihood had perished.

This was why Elisa had little time for a man, even a handsome one who nearly found himself among the reeds at the bottom of the Congaree. Every day she scraped and fought and did what she must to survive. Elisa sighed as she gazed at the man standing there with river water dripping from his trousers and stocking feet, forming puddles on the hard-packed dirt. She wondered if he possessed some kind of wealth in the way he clutched his leather purse and saddlebag close to him. He hailed from New York, after all.

She imagined how much money he might have in there, so long as it wasn't useless greenbacks. But she was no beggar. Whatever she held in her possession, God had graciously given her. Even when everything had been taken away and final punishment wrought on her family's name through ragtag Yankees who plundered and burned all she held dear, she refused to lie down and die. Elisa had thrown back her shoulders and lifted her head, allowing determination to strengthen the pounding of her flesh. She would preserve the Anderson name, come what may. She would make it.

"Where do you dwell?" the man asked. She thought that a strange question. A more sincere thank-you for saving him from the Congaree's muddy grip would be better. And an explanation of why he was on the river in the first place.

"Not far. I'm here most days, fishing for my food." She pointed to the pail he carried and the small fish swimming about without care, unaware they would soon help strengthen her after a harrowing day.

Glancing now at Mason Bassinger and the way his stocking feet left black imprints on the ground, she had to wonder what in the world possessed a Yankee to be on the Congaree. "So what were you doing?"

He paused. "Doing?"

"Rowing Chester's boat on the Congaree. A rather peculiar place to enjoy oneself. And if you had known how unscrupulous the boat owner is, you would never have paid him a cent. Mr. Wilson would cheat his own dear granny if he could."

She saw the man's facial muscles tighten as if he fought to say the right words. Instantly her skin prickled, and a nervous twitch erupted in her cheek.

"If you must know, I was surveying the area," he said. "I see you have a good timber potential here."

"So you work for some big Yankee boss, eh Mr. Bassinger? Even your last name is fancy."

He suddenly laughed, and she trembled. She expected him to continue fighting for the words to say and not change the mood with the noise of gaiety. No one laughed these days. It proved a startling but pleasant sound.

"Hardly. Older brothers tend to lord it over the younger. I have no say. I go where I am told."

"I never lorded it over my brother, and I was the eldest. He plumb did what he wanted."

"Does he live with you?"

Now it was her turn to look away and sense the heat of a flush enter her face. Tears moistened her eyes. The emotion of John's death in battle still filled her, even though she had tried hard to squelch it with duty and survival. "No. He was killed at Chattanooga."

The pail clinked as it hit the ground, and a certain warmth drew close. When she turned, Mason Bassinger stood but a few steps away, bearing a face that no longer showed the rigid strain of his circumstances but the softness of compassion. Her heart began to flutter, seeing how his eyes softened. The *sorry* whispered from his lips imparted warmth. To have a Northern man care about the death of an enemy seemed contradictory at best, yet she liked it.

"Thank you," Elisa said. "I'm all that's left of my family. Mother and my little sister died in childbirth. Father ran off and is dead, I'm sure of it. He took to the bottle one too many times after my brother John died." She glanced upward, beyond the trees, to the blue sky and the sun's rays streaming through the clouds. A picture of heaven's glory always proved comforting when sorrow gripped her.

"I'm sorry," he said, this time aloud. "I do understand. I lost my parents in an epidemic when I was eight."

"Dear me. Who raised you then?"

"My brother, Harold." Mason Bassinger picked up the pail and continued walking alongside her. "Harold did everything. Made the money we needed so we could live. Did a lot of the work around the house too. He was always the one who could get things done." He sucked in his breath as if to stem anything further from escaping. How Elisa would love to sink a fishhook inside and pull out what he concealed.

"So now you work for him?"

"In a manner of speaking. But I also like to travel and see things. And meet people."

She sniffed. "You can surely meet people here. But there is nothing really to see except a muddy river, swamps, and destroyed property." She stopped. In the distance stood the ramshackle cottage Father had built as a waypoint between the river and the plantation of Cottonwood. Now it was her home. For the first time she saw the feeble structure as Mason Bassinger must see it. These past months the little shanty had been her quaint cottage in the forest. She was happy to be under a roof and within four walls, even if they occasionally leaked, along with what she managed to salvage from the main house. The walls of the small structure sagged. The wood had cracked under the heat and humidity.

Long grass nearly buried the property. Empty windows devoid of treatments showed off the mournful appearance of dirty glass. It all looked shabby at best. She was like a bear in its humble den, thankful for shelter but with a life of foraging for food and drinking stale river water.

"How much further is it to your place?" Mason asked.

Elisa nearly laughed. He had no idea the dwelling before them was her home. "Um, forty paces or so."

He whirled, his mouth forming an O.

"It isn't much, but it suits me just fine."

Mason said nothing, appearing only to stare as if caught off guard. Elisa tried to determine what thoughts might be churning in his mind. No doubt the shabby sight startled his fine Northern senses. He was undoubtedly thinking of a fancy brick residence, with many rooms and floors. But his reaction to her humble abode was not her concern. She had done the best she could with what she had.

"I am but a bear in the woods," she said. "Welcome to my den."

"Hardly. You are a woman of great worth, and God has seen fit to give you a humble castle in His creation."

The answer warmed her heart, more than she cared to admit. "I would ask you in, as my father always had company. . . ."

"No, that would not be proper."

Elisa was already liking this Northerner who portrayed gentlemanly qualities. "The least I can do is bring you some coffee. Or rather a substitute. There is no real coffee here."

"Thank you."

She sighed and entered the shabby surroundings, grateful he would not witness the interior of her so-called castle in the woods. The main room carried the odor of wood smoke and dust. A small woodburning cookstove provided heat and cooking. A braided rug lay on the dirty plank floor. The windows were dim. The only furnishings in the main room were two chairs, a small dining table, and another smaller table. In the back bedroom, a mattress lay on the floor. A rope strung across the room served as the makeshift wardrobe for her few dresses. What would Mr. Bassinger of New York think of her sleeping on a floor rather than a fine poster bed? Or the rags that were her clothing? Or really, any part of this cottage?

At least she managed to save some treasures from the main house. Like her mother's rose bowl. A faded tintype of the family when she was young. A pitcher and bowl that belonged to Granny May. She tried not to think about the night of terror when the Yankees invaded the house. She had snuck out the rear door, grabbing what she could as they plunked themselves down on the nice furniture, their muddy boots staining the thick carpet. Looking back through the windows, she saw them feasting on food rifled from the pantry. No doubt the bread she had made earlier that day was the first to be eaten, along with the doughnuts, the barrel of crackers, and jars of preserves. The cold cellar that held a fair quantity of vegetables and smoked ham did not last long either. Nor did the chickens and the two cows in the barn.

When at last she had a fire going to warm the pot, she brought out a cup of brew to the Yankee man. Mason had found a place to sit on a log. She said nothing when he thanked her but stood to one side, staring off into the woods beyond the cottage.

"You're very quiet," Mason observed.

"I was just thinking about the day the Yankees came and took over."

"They were here?"

"Not here. At Cottonwood. The main house. This cottage is on a corner piece of the property. Father had it built as a place for workers to stay when they traveled by river. I came here after the Yankees invaded."

Mason shifted on the log while staring into the cup she had given him. No doubt his sensitive Yankee nose did not care for the brew made of chicory root and ground acorns. She could only imagine real coffee's flavor and aroma, it had been so long.

He said, "I take it you still own the land."

"Of course. But I have no money to rebuild. I live day to day, you see. Just as we all do in this place."

Mason was silent for a moment. He set down the cup and untied the leather purse he kept close at hand. His large fingers reached inside and removed a gold coin. "It's the least I can do." He held it out.

Elisa stared at the shiny magnificence—really, the most beautiful thing she had seen in a long time. "I'm sorry. I won't take charity, thank you."

"It isn't charity. You have done so much for me this day. Saved my life. You've earned it and more." He pointed to his cup, yet to taste the concoction she thought wasn't too terrible, considering the ingredients. "Buy yourself some fine coffee."

The words made her laugh. "I'm not sure if the general store even has any. But some wagons came by the other day, loaded down with supplies, bound for the store. Folks there are still trying to get the railroad in Kingsville fixed after the Yankees tore it up."

"Kingsville, where I boarded my horse. How far is it to town from here?"

"About a two-hour walk. Though I'm sure you could get a ride with a passerby. Kingsville is the only town in these parts, and even then it isn't much. But we hope one day to make it grand again."

Mason threw the coin in the air and caught it with one hand. "I really wish I could convince you to take this, Miss Anderson."

She watched him toss it again in the air and miss. She reached down to pick the coin up and give it to him when his large hand closed over hers and pushed it away. His dark eyes stared fixedly into hers. "I insist."

"Well, all right." She deposited the coin into the pocket of her skirt beside two rusty fishhooks. "I will ask God what to do with it."

He grinned. "An excellent suggestion. I don't know if I've ever asked the good Lord what to do with my money."

"He has a way of determining things we can't. All good gifts come from above. I think of this as His gift to me, so I need to ask Him." She closed her eyes, and a prayer began streaming from her lips. She didn't know what Mr. Bassinger would think or why she decided to pray in front of a complete stranger, but the words came forth so naturally, she couldn't help it. She prayed for good stewardship, for her needs, and for Mason. When she flicked open her eyes, Mason opened his at the same time, and he smiled.

"It feels good to be in the presence of a God-fearing woman. You're not at all what that fellow in town, Mr. Wilson, painted you to be."

She laughed. "I can just imagine. I've been known to share a bit of my fiery Irish temper with him, especially if he comes nosing around. One must protect one's property and one's virtue."

Mason's eyes narrowed, and he stood to his feet. "It's not safe for you to be out here all alone. Especially with scoundrels around like Chester Wilson."

"Well, Mr. Bassinger, since I've done just fine for myself these many months, I think I can trust the good Lord to send His heavenly angel army to keep watch over a simple southern lady."

"I'm sure you know I meant no disrespect. I only. . ."

He paused, never completing the final thought, though Elisa could imagine what the words might have been. Perhaps—*I only want to see you safe. I want to see you well. I care about you.* Her lips pressed together. Wherever did that last thought come from?

"I should be going." He stared down at his stocking feet with the big toe sticking out of a hole. "I don't suppose you have any kind of shoes? A silly question, I know."

"Oh my. You dearly need your socks darned. But I do have a pair of Father's slippers." She retreated into the cottage and the back room, rummaging through items lying about in haphazard fashion until she found Father's red velvet slippers. Just the sight of them stoked memories of Father nestled in his big chair by the fire, smoking his pipe, the slippers cradling his feet as he read a newspaper. She kissed the slippers and brought them to Mason.

"Perfect." He began untying the leather strings to the purse again.

"No. They are a gift. Use them."

"I feel you have just washed my feet," he said softly. "Still, I would like to pay you for them. . . ."

Elisa shook her head and turned aside. The emotion of it all, from his rescue, to their journey here, to the gold coin and Father's slippers on his feet, spilled over and made her stagger. On the walk here she'd been glad to receive company, but now she could no longer remain in his presence. He was affecting her far too much. "The hour is late, and I don't know how safe it is to be out on the road after dark."

"Yes, you're right. I must be going. Thank you again for everything."

She dared not gaze at him at length for fear another part of her would fall captive to his handsome and gentle ways. "Yes, yes. Do take care. And no more hiring a boat from Mr. Wilson, which I'm sure you already regret."

Elisa glanced out the corner of her eye to see Mason sling his saddlebag over one shoulder, walking funny in the large slippers as he wandered toward the main road. She felt for the coin in her pocket, remembering her tears of last night when she saw the bare cupboards, the empty change purse, and felt the gnawing of her insides for want of food. God had heard the cries of a silent prayer and sent an answer by way of a leaky boat and a Yankee.

She flicked away a tear. *Thank You, dearest God. You sent a stranger to give me what I needed most.*

Chapter 3

Mason could not get the visit with Elisa Anderson out of his mind when he arose the next morning. Just slipping his cold feet into the velvety softness of the red slippers stirred the memory of her relinquishing her father's personal effects to his care and then refusing any payment. How he would love to spend time with her. But for now he stepped out into the sun-filled day to look over the dilapidated town. At one time Kingsville stood as a thriving railway junction near the Congaree River. He could still smell the smoke from the blackened walls of the once busy depot where trains used to come and go, unloading much-needed supplies. Other burnt-out shells of buildings belonging to the railroad bore similar signs of Yankee anger over anything that assisted their enemy's livelihood. Large portions of railway track had also been torn up. He noted the familiar sight of rails bent around the trunks of trees, nicknamed Sherman's neckties. He had to wonder as a Northerner, seeing all this destruction, what on earth he was doing here, attempting to buy up property for his brother. He feared if anyone got wind of his true intent, there was no telling what might happen.

Mason stopped at the stable to check on Honey. He sorely considered riding out of here to somewhere far away. Many were taking to the trails and heading west to find better lives. Then he thought of Harold, the way his brother had cared for him after the passing of their parents, and the look of hurt on his face at the thought of Mason abandoning him without fulfilling his duties. Mason would have no family if he did leave. Harold would never forgive him. He had no choice. If he could just get through these few weeks, maybe find a proprietor or two willing to sell, Harold would be satisfied, and Mason would be free to wander wherever his soul led.

But then came his encounter with Elisa Anderson. She was as striking as any fancy-clad women walking the streets where he came from in New York. She had no fashion, for certain, barely surviving the wounds of war that ripped through her country. She had nothing to her name save her honor. He admired the way she'd forged a life for herself from the ruins of her family's plantation. Elisa was as she said—one bent on survival no matter the cost. How he wished he could do more for her than toss a coin her way. Especially after the red velvet slippers she had given him. When he arrived back in Kingsville, he found a man eager to sell him a pair of shoes to replace the slippers, but her kindness to give what little she had moved him.

He walked along the street then, giving attention now to the people who remained in town, despite the destruction of the railway that had brought supplies to the area. He paused before a large building constructed of clapboards where a few folks rushed in and out. A woman, clad in a blue gown and white apron with a cap on her head, appeared in the doorway. Mason's curiosity got the better of him, and he strode up. "You all seem quite busy here. What is this place?"

"This is the hospital, or it was. We are working to transfer the remaining soldiers to better hospitals. Especially since we can no longer receive adequate supplies. What we can get is difficult because of lack of funds."

Her words jolted Mason, especially when he saw a man carried out on a stretcher to an awaiting wagon, the stump of a leg as a reminder of the grimness of war. It didn't matter to him who the man was or what army he served. He fumbled inside his leather purse, took out several gold coins, and handed them to the young nurse.

She covered her mouth before uttering in disbelief, "My word. Gold coins."

"For the hospital."

Her eyes sparkled. "Thank you, sir. This means a great deal."

A surge of warmth flowed through Mason, though he knew the feeling was fleeting. When he turned about, he suddenly caught sight of a woman striding briskly down the wooden boardwalk toward a small business that served as the mercantile. From the locks flowing out from beneath the straw hat with a fancy blue bow, he recognized at once who it was. He thought of greeting Elisa Anderson before she entered the establishment but held back as she went inside. Instead he hurried to the storefront to hear the proprietor greet her.

"Miss Anderson! I never did see a fine lady looking so cheerful."

"I'm indeed cheerful, Mr. Tanner, and I will tell you why." She showed the clerk the gold coin Mason had given her.

"Hoo-wee, Miss Anderson. Where'd you get that?"

"I earned it. I'm hoping to stock my pantry with much-needed goods. Please let me know what it will buy."

Mason watched through the store window as the clerk laid out several paper bags of goods on the long counter, of what he didn't know. Elisa then took a silver scoop from inside a huge barrel and poured a stream of crackers into another bag. "I've looked at these for so long. Why, even now my mouth is simply watering at the thought."

The clerk laughed. He put a ham and a crock beside the bags as Elisa moved off to look over some bolts of cloth on a shelf. She fingered one pattern in particular, sky blue in color, sprinkled with small yellow sunflowers.

"Thinking about a new dress, Miss Anderson?"

She laughed. "Dresses are not a necessity. I was thinking more of sewing a few window coverings. But that will have to wait. I need the foodstuffs."

Mason shook his head as he instinctively felt for his leather pouch. He dearly wanted to march in there straightaway and buy the fine cloth for her to make the window dressings. But he held back. Maybe it was the fiery look in her green eyes when she told him at the outset she would not accept charity. There was still southern pride, after all. He would think of another way to provide her heart's desire. She'd saved him from a grave in the muddy Congaree. And had parted with her father's fine red velvet slippers.

"Now how do you plan on carrying all this back?" the clerk asked.

"Never you mind. I'm sure there is a willing person to help. Or I will ask around for my dear friend Wilma Parker, as she is always in town." She handed over the coin and suddenly froze in place. Mason wondered what emotion gripped her just then. Were her forest-green eyes filling with tears as she surveyed the banquet of food? Or had some other memory overtaken her, perhaps of her family who frequented the store, happily plunking down the cash to buy whatever they wished without counting the cost?

Elisa began gathering up the parcels, and Mason came to a decision. He returned to his horse, removed the saddlebags, and headed back to the store just as Elisa turned about. Her eyes widened, and her mouth formed a perfect O before words of recognition tumbled out. "Why, Mr. Bassinger!"

He lifted his hat. "Good day, Miss Anderson. I see you have done some fine shopping."

Her face took on a reddish hue, and a tiny smile creased her lips. "I did buy a few things, yes."

"Well as it is, I was about to take to my horse for a ride in the country as I didn't do too well traveling by river. Do you need a ride?"

"Yes, thank you. That would be fine."

Mason began packing the foodstuffs she had purchased into the twin saddlebags. "Do you have everything you need?" he inquired, glancing back at the bolt of blue cloth that had caught her interest. How he wanted to buy the material for her, but he would not cause tongues to wag, especially as several women had just entered the store.

"I have plenty, thank you. Oh, howdy-do, Mrs. Cranford, Mrs. Lewis."

The two women looked at Mason and the bulging saddlebags. "I didn't know you had a suitor, Miss Anderson," one of the women said with a lilt to her voice, staring with large eyes the color of storm clouds.

Elisa glanced sideways at Mason, and the color of her cheeks deepened. "Oh no, Mrs. Lewis. Mr. Bassinger here is just being neighborly and helping me take my purchases home."

Mason lifted his hat. "Pleased to make your acquaintance."

The faces of the women pointed skyward, and they moved forward to conduct their shopping. Mason escorted Elisa into the sun-filled street and to his mare, tied to a hitching post. "Some townspeople are not very friendly, are they?"

"Especially to strangers. Oh, if you don't mind, I must tend to one final errand at the telegraph office. I will return shortly."

"Of course." Mason watched her walk over to the small building on the opposite side of the street. Just then an idea pricked him. He waited a moment or two longer until she had entered the office before dashing back to the store where the clerk was helping the two ladies.

Even if Harold had sent him on another mission of sorts to this area, Mason had a mission too. He silently thanked God for showing him the way.

Elisa believed God guided her in all matters of life. If she didn't, she could never have survived the war and its aftermath that had taken away everything she knew. At least she was grateful God had brought a man like Mason Bassinger into her life. Though the man heralded from the North, he'd been in desperate need on the river. And she'd sensed his compassion from the moment she shared her circumstances until now.

Elisa entered the telegraph office to see Patricia from the hospital there also, wearing a broad smile on her face. "Why are you so happy?" Elisa couldn't help but ask.

"Look at this!" Patricia said in delight, showing Elisa the gold coins she had received from a stranger, as she put it. "He wanted to help the hospital and its needs. Just now I sent out a telegram for more medicine."

Elisa glanced out the nearest window to see Mason's horse still tied to the hitching post, but the man himself had disappeared. "What did this stranger look like?"

"Oh, a handsome man, I must say. Dark hair and the deepest brown eyes. He wore a white shirt and black vest."

Mason Bassinger. Upon this revelation, her heart warmed even more. "That was very kind of him." They talked a bit longer before Elisa turned to why she was there. When the clerk placed the telegram in her hand, she looked it over slowly. Tears filled her eyes. The words said it all. There was no more wondering. The matter had finally been laid to rest.

Patricia laid her hand softly on Elisa's arm. "Sorrowful news?"

Elisa nodded. "I expected it, really. It's news about my father. It says he died. At some boardinghouse in Georgia."

"I'm so sorry."

Elisa sucked in her breath and straightened her shoulders. "It's all right. In my heart I knew all along. But now it's time to think about living." She smiled. "And I'm truly happy to hear of another's giving heart toward the hospital. It's news like this that's much better to think on." She offered a farewell and left the telegraph office, hurrying across the street to find Mason.

"We're ready to go," Mason said when she arrived. He offered her his hand, assisting her onto the horse. "Is everything all right?"

What a perceptive soul. "As much as can be. Thank you for asking." When she had settled herself, he entered the saddle and reined the horse about. Out of the corner of her eye she caught sight of the two biddies from the general store staring and whispering. No doubt everyone had decided Mason was indeed her suitor. *As if that would be so terrible,* she decided, thinking of the generous heart seated before her.

When they rode past the stables, Chester ventured out and gave a loud whistle. "Well now, if it ain't the pretty Belle of the Congaree and the Yankee man."

"You would do well to keep to your own affairs," Elisa shouted back.

Mason cast her a sideways glance. "I think it might be best to avoid him completely, Miss Anderson."

She sighed. "You're right, of course. He gets the better of my nature. For a number of years he asked to court me. Can you imagine? When Father was alive and Chester appeared one night at our doorstep, Father all but chased him off the plantation with his long rifle." She saw Mason's hands tense around the reins.

"I'm sorry to hear he has caused you grief. He seems to have a proclivity for such acts. If you ever catch him around your home, you must tell me."

"Oh, he has only been to the cottage once. Said he had left the river at the wrong landing. I do not take kindly to his telling me tales. I prefer forthrightness. There's too much dishonesty these days." Again she witnessed Mason's hands tense, and when he turned his head to the side, a muscle twitched in the rugged cheek speckled with beard stubble.

"What is the saying by Benjamin Franklin? Honesty is the best policy. Our founding fathers believed in such things when this country came into being." He exhaled a breath. "I am glad we are one country again."

"Are we truly? Fellow countrymen do not burn homes and destroy people's livelihoods. It's a wound too deep to heal, even when generals shake hands and declare the war is over. I wonder if we can ever be united again."

Silence prevailed for a time but for the melodious clopping of hooves striking the hard-packed earth. They rode past acres thick with vegetation. Flies buzzing about soon became unbearable. Elisa took out her fan to swipe at them while holding on to Mason's waist. But the edge of the fan hit the back of his neck, and he flinched.

"Oh my! I'm so sorry, Mr. Bassinger."

"It's nothing. Up north we don't have this kind of heat, although the flies are not welcome guests either."

Elisa quickly put the fan away, not wishing to chance anything else unseemly, though her heart was all aflutter.

"I agree the war caused a great deal of hardship and pain," he said. "Some of the generals thought it better to strike hard and quick to bring the whole terrible affair to an end as quickly as possible."

"And now we are left to fend for ourselves without any means to live." She bit her lip, realizing she was complaining. "Not that God hasn't provided. . ."

"And you have done well with what you have. You are to be congratulated, Miss Anderson, in overcoming such difficulty."

They said nothing more for a time. Mason took to swatting the pesky flies landing on his face. Soon they came to a familiar area to Elisa, a long country lane lined with magnificent oak draped in Spanish moss, leading the way to Cottonwood, her family's plantation.

"Turn here, if you please," she directed.

Mason drew the horse to a stop and wheeled in the saddle. "But is this where you live? I don't recall. . ."

"No. This is where my family used to live. You might as well see for yourself why I think the way I do about this country and a hateful enemy."

Mason inhaled a sharp breath and turned his mount about. Slowly they made their way down the lane teeming with memories, passing each tree with limbs like arms, covered by shawls of earthy moss. Elisa recalled the many times she went for a drive down this lane to go visiting or attend a ball. Soon they came to the stark black columns of the main house, the lone chimneys reaching to heaven as if to inquire why, the silent walls of which one side had collapsed into a pile of rubble. She had been back to visit several times, but for some reason, being here with a Yankee, looking at this hollow shell of the fine home that had once housed the living and brought memories of happy childhood, seemed like a betrayal. Now with the news of Father's death, grief overcame her once more.

Mason sat still in the saddle, taking it all in, or so it seemed. She wished she could read the thoughts circulating beneath his dark brown hair. She imagined his eyes scanning every bit of this place as a sad reminder of happier days. Finally she heard him whisper, "I'm sorry about this."

"Thank you. Before the Yankees left, they set the house on fire. I took whatever I could carry to the cottage, but it was precious little." She slid off the horse and lifted her skirts to approach the shell of the main house. In the front yard were still a few castaways left. Broken dishes. A splintered chair. Then she saw arms and legs and picked up a doll with a dirty dress and a china head. A wee painted smile revealed two tiny teeth. A scratch along the side of the face, the torn dress and blackened shoes, showed the struggle with the destruction that had taken place.

Elisa returned to Mason. "She was mine. I called her Alice." She smoothed out the skirt and adjusted the bonnet over a head of painted brown burls. "She was my best friend. I shall take her home with me where she belongs."

Mason had not stirred but remained frozen in the saddle. Finally he said, "Though the house is gone, this looks like very good land still."

"It is. I'm proud of it."

He opened his mouth as if to say something, but nothing came out.

Instead he dismounted and offered his hand. "I will put your Alice in a safe place. I believe I can squeeze her into a saddlebag."

"Thank you for that." Elisa warmed at his offer, even over such a simple thing as a childhood toy. He seemed to understand. The North had suffered too, she had to admit. Several battles took place on Northern soil. Many families had lost loved ones. He also said he had lost his mother and father, as she had. Maybe he came here seeking solace in the wounds of others rather than the joy of a victorious North.

After she settled once more behind him on the horse, she asked, "Why did you come here, Mr. Bassinger? I don't think you ever did tell me."

"I think it was to come to an understanding."

"An understanding of what?"

"Tragedy. Loss. But victory too. I was uncertain about my trip. But it's obvious now that God wanted me to come, and for a much higher purpose than anything I could have ever planned."

Warmth penetrated her fingertips from gripping his side to steady herself on the mount. Or maybe it was her, feeling the heat of his words and a sense of thankfulness that this man had abruptly entered her life, if just for a short time.

Chapter 4

The house did not appear as dingy to Elisa, and thankfully so, as Mason brought in the saddlebags. The sun shone through the windows she had cleaned with water from the rain barrel. The floor was swept, the braided rug beaten with a broom. She found the doll Alice a proper place in a straight-back chair. She then undid the blue ribbon that held her straw hat in place. "Would you like some coffee? I bought a little today. Did you know the clerk nearly collapsed when I showed him that fine gold coin you gave me?"

Mason stood still, his hands in his pockets, looking about in fascination. Elisa shrugged away his curiosity to concentrate on the goods spread out across the table. She'd never felt such joy at mere paper bags filled with sugar and flour, coffee and a crock of molasses, and of course, the bag of crackers. It all met her starving eyes. "I shall make a molasses cake." She paused. "Except it will take some time."

"What can I do to assist? Start a fire in the cookstove?"

"That would be lovely." Out of the corner of her eye she watched him gather kindling to start the fire, thinking how much they were acting like a married couple. She drew out a big bowl and assembled the ingredients to stir up a cake. There'd been no man to help with the chores since she'd lost her brother and father. Just the sight of Mason's strong arms and broad shoulders made her feel like all would be right in this shaky and devastating world. She shook her head at such thoughts and tried to concentrate on her task.

"Is anything wrong?" he gently inquired

He had observed it all. "I—I am only trying to think of what I must do." She looked over at the saddlebag resting in the chair. "Have we gotten everything? That one still seems full."

Mason said nothing, and she turned to find him buried inside the workings of the stove. "This needs to be cleaned," his muffled voice said.

"I'm sure it does. Look at the ceiling. Black splotches everywhere because it smokes so." She watched him take up a small pail and use another stick to draw out the gray ash and blackened wood left from many cooking fires. "You don't have to do all that...," she began.

"It's no trouble. It will make lighting a new fire easier, and the stove will keep the heat better to cook and bake. Harold had one just like it, and it was my chore to start the fire and clean out the stove every morning."

"Oh yes...Harold is the one who looked after you." She paused, thinking of her own family. At Cottonwood, the family once had a few servants to do the work until Father lost his money in a deal gone bad, and she learned to start fires and cook. The memory of presenting her first newly baked cake to the wide eyes and cheers of her family sent tears welling up in her eyes and her heart longing for just a glimpse of her loved ones. "I went to the telegraph office today. The news was not good. It is as I'd feared. My father is dead."

Mason paused in his work. Black streaks of soot crisscrossed his face and stained his hands. "I'm very sorry for your loss."

"It's a relief, actually. He's been gone so long. He took to the bottle after John died. I knew in my heart he was no longer alive. One has to continue living, even if life takes you on a different path."

"I do understand, having lost my parents. Right now I'm trying to find that path. I need to decide when is the right time to live my own life and not the one my brother has made for me."

"I will say I'm happy your path has led you here." She paused, realizing the words could be misconstrued, even if she was glad to have fallen into his company, what with the gold coin, the fine foodstuffs she was able to buy, and now a working stove. She hastily added, "Though why you would come to this place, I'm not certain. There isn't anything here."

Mason sat on his heels, immovable for several moments, then slowly stood to his feet. He picked up the bucket of ash. She heard him exhale loudly, as if he wanted to say many things but the words remained bottled up inside. Maybe that was a good thing. Father often counseled her on the evilness of words. The Bible talked about the fire of the tongue. And many times she had been caught off guard by words that should have been bridled. Being a man of slow speech was a fine attribute. She would think on that rather than what he might have wanted to say.

A faint whiff of smoke told her the fire in the stove had been lit, and she began mixing the cake batter. A heavy aroma of molasses filled the air.

"It already smells good in here," Mason remarked.

"I still have to add some spices to the batter," she noted, pointing to a few jars on a small shelf. "Mother always believed in a well-planted herb garden, both for cooking and for medicinal purposes. But the spices for this, I'm uncertain where Father got them." Elisa finished mixing the batter and poured it into a small tin while Mason fed the fire a few more sticks. She slid the cake into the cookstove. "It shall be a feast."

Mason found a place to sit at the table and looked at her with eyebrows drawn together in a deep study. "Miss Anderson, may I ask you something? I don't want you to think me presumptuous, but I do want to know."

Her curiosity immediately rose. "Yes?"

"When is the last time you were given a gift of sorts?"

All the busyness of the day, the shopping, the ride on horseback, working together here in her cottage, suddenly disappeared under these words. "When have I received a gift?" she repeated. "I don't rightly recall. You did give me that gold coin, of course."

"That was not a gift. You earned it. I mean, received a simple gift."

"I. . ." Her voice trailed off. Tears suddenly sparked in her eyes. She had passed several birthdays without anyone even knowing the day, save God alone. In her younger days, a birthday was a great celebration, of feasting and a large cake and a gift of a new dress or other finery. She did not think on the past when her birthday came around but tried instead to be thankful for other things—like the cottage spared from Sherman's wrath or the way God had provided for her needs, even when food became scarce. "I'm not sure how to answer. I guess I haven't been given a gift in a very long time. Though the Lord has provided for me many times."

"I saw you were interested in something today." Mason stood and took a package out of the saddlebag.

"What on earth?" Elisa said weakly.

"It's a gift. Nothing more, nothing less." He held it out to her.

"I'm not sure I can accept it. After all. . ."

"Then think of it as a way of God blessing you through others. You can surely accept a gift He is giving you."

"Mr. Bassinger, *you* are the one presenting it. But I will accept that you are His child and therefore can also give gifts to me in His name." She could hardly argue with the way God worked through so many people in times of need. She tried to do her part as well, even to assisting this man from his sinking craft. The more she thought about it, the more she realized how much good had happened since Mason's abrupt arrival. As if he were some heavenly messenger.

She undid the string, trying hard to keep her fingers from shaking in front of him. The paper parted to reveal the material of azure blue with the bright sunflowers that she had admired inside the general store. Elisa stared in disbelief. "Mason...," she began. "I—I mean, Mr. Bassinger. How did you know I wanted it?"

"Well, to be honest, I was watching you through the store window while you were inside shopping. When you went to the telegraph office, I bought it. You deserve to add some color to this place, to make some fine window coverings. And you know I can't take it back, so you must accept it."

Elisa gently stroked the fine fabric, and a tear suddenly escaped, leaving a circular imprint on the corner. She quickly dried away any remaining dampness and heaved a sigh. "This will surely brighten the cottage. Thank you."

"Good. When next I come, I hope to see them." He took up his hat and saddlebags.

"You're leaving? But what about the cake?"

Mason sighed. "Unfortunately, there are duties I must tend to."

She stepped back, embarrassed that her voice betrayed a desire for him to remain. Then her mind began to race about, wondering how she might keep him here a bit longer. She liked the conversation and having a man tend to things around the place. Maybe the loneliness of being a belle shut up in a cottage in the woods had finally caught up with her. But she knew better than to try and convince him to stay when he had things to do. "Of course you must be going. I'm sorry to have kept you so long. I will save you a piece of cake."

"Thank you. That will be worth looking forward to." He smiled and bid her farewell. Elisa hurried to the window soon to be draped in sunflowers to watch him mount his horse. She felt the flutter of her heart and her breathing quicken. Oh, how she wanted him to stay, but she couldn't be selfish. He would return soon, she was sure of it. And when he did, she felt certain God would be ready to show them a new and delightful path.

Mason felt it wise to leave after staring into Elisa's moss-green eyes, the way her lips curled into a teasing smile, the working of her delicate hands in fashioning the cake and then opening the gift. It was all he could do not to scoop her sweet form into his arms and kiss her. Yes, his stomach lurched at the thought of freshly baked molasses cake and a cup of soothing coffee, but virtue must take preeminence. Still, he meandered but a short ways down the road before turning Honey about to look at the faint outline of the cottage nestled among the oak and pine. He enjoyed being with her, helping her carry her purchases home, cleaning out the stove, giving her the material for the window trimmings. He knew there were probably other tasks needing to be done. She could also use other means of food as well, like chickens and a cow for milk. He could plow up some of the land to plant a garden. The ideas came tumbling forth in such rapid fashion, he could hardly contain them. Finally he took a deep breath. *God, help my heart.* He knew he was falling in love with Elisa Anderson, but he couldn't. This place was not his home.

He sighed, turning Honey around to continue the journey back toward town. He passed the country lane that led to the remains of Elisa's family home. He paused at the junction to consider what Elisa and others like her had been through. How could he do Harold's bidding here in Kingsville? How could he ask people to sell the only home and property they had? But the money would help them too, he reasoned. Just the memory of Elisa's glee over a single gold coin to buy a few foodstuffs made him consider its importance. He could make lives better. Surely that was the good Harold had alluded to when he left.

He gently nudged Honey along until he came to another country lane. He rode down it to see a weathered but still standing home at the end. The walls were covered in vines, the roof blackened. He noticed two men in front of it, talking.

Mason inhaled a sharp breath, wondering what he was doing, then thought nothing more of it. "Good day," he called out to them.

They stared. "What do you want, stranger?"

"I was looking to see if perhaps you wanted to sell your place here. Or the land. Times are tough. I know of someone looking to buy and would make you a fair offer."

One of the men flinched. The other grew rigid. "No."

"I can give you a good down payment on it. All in gold." He began to withdraw the leather pouch.

Suddenly the man reached for something at his waist. A pistol.

Chills shot through Mason. His hands squeezed the reins while sweat broke out on the back of his neck.

"Did you hear what I said? I said we're not selling. Now get off my land."

"I'm very sorry to have troubled you." Mason whirled Honey about and, with a swift nudge of his foot, ushered the mare to a fast trot down the lane. *How can I do this?* he thought, recoiling at the memory of the weapon aimed in his direction. He couldn't, even if Harold relied on him. Just yesterday Mason had received a telegram from Harold, asking if he had arrived and to give an account of his activities. Harold remarked that business had been slow, and he could use some good news. Though Mason believed he could no longer do this business, he also did not want to let his brother down. Harold had been there for him, cared for him after their parents died when he might have been sent away to live with others. Harold was counting on him to deliver.

Mason glanced down the road to where Elisa's humble cottage stood but a few miles back. Maybe he should see if she would be willing to part with her family's home and property. Nothing remained of the house, but there were nice large trees, good for timbering. She would have all the money she needed. But she appeared content with her current circumstances, as strange as it seemed. She had become used to the business of survival. Her life was a delicate balance that Mason did not wish to disturb. At least not yet. He would wait, as he should have done with the men he saw. He needed to make friends. Foster a good standing in the town. And then attempt to broach the idea of selling. The people here had been through great loss and difficulty. They were suspicious, and they were hurting. *These things take time.* Harold would just have to be patient.

Mason returned to town and went at once to the telegraph office. He composed a brief message to Harold in the hope of allaying any concern the man might be feeling.

I AM MAKING PROGRESS. WILL TAKE TIME.

He looked it over and felt unsettled. He had not been truthful with the progress, especially having a pistol aimed in his direction. Truth be told, he hadn't pursued anything except the beautiful woman whom he wanted to bless and kiss. Mason crumpled up the note. His heart and mind were engaged in a fierce fight in all the confusion. He must reconcile both before he knew exactly what to do and where to go from here.

The next morning Mason came out of the boardinghouse to greet another sunny day, hoping all would be well. Except he had company waiting for him in the form of Chester T. Wilson, who stood there calmly gnawing on a reed.

"Good mornin', Yankee man."

Mason didn't know what the man could want, nor was he eager to find out. "Good day. And the name's Mason." He began walking in the opposite direction.

"I hears you had a run-in with the Henderson brothers yesterday."

Mason stopped short. Tension ripped through him.

"They said you was trespassin' on their property, demanding they sell it to you."

He turned to face the oily man. "If you mean the property at the edge of town, I merely asked if they were of a mind to part with some of their land. Some folks need money."

Chester stepped closer. "If I were you, I might think about leavin' this here town right quick. Folks are talkin', and they know who you are and what yer doin' in these parts."

"And what exactly is that?"

Chester grinned with stained teeth. "That yer a Yankee scalawag lookin' to do more hurtin'."

"I'm looking to give anyone who wants it a better life."

Chester took the reed out of his mouth. "That a fact? Well now, I might be of a mind to put a good word in fer you with the folks in town, iffen you have more of them fancy gold coins on you. I shore could use a better life like you say." He cackled.

Mason's muscles tightened. "I do not take kindly to bribery, sir."

Chester shrugged. "Ain't a bribe. More like a business contract, which I'm shore you know all about. I only want to help you be neighborly. But you cain't blame anyone but yerself iffen things get rough round here. So you let me know if you change yer mind." He walked off, scuffing up the dirt as he went, whistling a tune. Mason could not help but look around. Had Chester or the Henderson brothers poisoned people's minds enough to want him out of town? Had he only created enemies here?

Mason wasn't about to find out. He returned to the boardinghouse and to his room where he began throwing clothing into one saddlebag and personal items in another. At least Chester had confirmed something for him. He had no business being here.

Just then his gaze fell on his Bible. He recalled a sermon the pastor preached when he was newly saved. How God had not given a spirit of fear but of a sound mind. Mason picked up the Bible and read the passage in Timothy. He thought about his circumstances. Folks did have needs. They needed his gold for certain, just as Chester said. But what they really needed could not be measured in coins. They needed the precious gold found in the words of the book he held. The scriptures that could heal a war-torn soul and give them hope.

I can't give in. I've done nothing wrong, and I won't be driven away. I will leave when the time is right and not a moment sooner. Mason took up his leather pouch of coins and squeezed it. There was something he could do right now to calm it all. He could do the unexpected.

Mason went out onto the street and met with a few townsfolk. Some appeared well in spirit as they talked of working with the railroad. In others he saw the depravity in their eyes and in their words. Some told of mounting taxes on properties or not having much to eat. He met a young boy named Sammy, dressed in rags, who had been a drummer boy in the war. The hollowed look in his eyes moved Mason. To people like this he quietly slipped a coin into their hands. "Remember that God can give you much more," he said. "All this will pass away, but His love does not."

He paused when he caught sight of Chester coming from the stables. He had witnessed Mason placing a coin in the young boy's hand. The man stared with his mouth wide open. "What in tarnation you doin', Yankee man?"

"Being neighborly, Mr. Wilson. The way God would want." With that he plunked a coin in the man's dirty hand. "I don't need any help either."

"Hmmm," Chester said, scratching his head. "Never thought no Northerner would ever part with his money 'lessen he needed somethin' real bad."

"It's a thank-you for opening my eyes. Some of us from the North don't come as thieves out to take from the poor. We want to do what the Bible says. Like love your neighbor as yourself. That's what I believe in."

"Hmm. You know what, Yankee man? I'm a'gonna spend this good. Not on no chewin' tobacco or the bottle but somethin' useful, so's I always remember this day."

"That's good."

Mason returned to his room, his spirit uplifted. He still had plenty of money left to spend a few more days here and make certain Elisa was cared for. Perhaps gain some land for Harold. But he needed to ask God what the future held. And he expected the good Lord to move in ways he never anticipated. Like the idea of giving away gold to those in need in the middle of Main Street. *Whatever You want to do, Lord. . .lead me and guide me.*

Chapter 5

Is it true you're seeing him?"

Elisa tried to hide her dismay when her friend Wilma Parker decided to pay an unexpected visit to the cottage. She had just hung a row of window trimmings she'd made from the material Mason had bought, having stayed up late two nights to finish the sewing. She'd also returned to the family plantation and dug up some flowers that she brought back to plant around the cottage. To her, the new plants and the row of bright window trimmings spoke of hope and life, and all because of Mason.

Now the sun shone bright in her eyes as she saw Wilma standing there with her hands on her hips. "I didn't think you were the kind who listens to gossip," Elisa finally said.

"It's all over Kingsville. You and the Yankee. Some saw you riding with him on horseback a few days ago. Now he's giving money to the townsfolk. That's why I came here, to see if you knew why."

Elisa stared at the tall woman dressed in a fancy ecru-colored gown with hoops. She appeared ready to attend some extravagant ball rather than call on a friend. "What do you mean Mr. Bassinger was giving away his money?"

"He stood right in the street and handed coins to folks in need. Sammy Longbacker told me. He said your Mr. Bassinger gave him a coin after he told him he was a drummer boy in the war. I thought you might know what this is all about."

"I'm sorry, I do not." But the news startled her. She glanced up at the trimmings framing the sparkling glass of the windows. How odd it seemed to simply give away money, but how like Mason too. He had been a strange sort the moment she met him, but now he seemed quite extraordinary. The contrast made him fascinating.

Wilma's voice interrupted her thoughts. "So are you courting? Because if you are, I'd say you picked yourself a mighty fine and selfless fellow.

Even if he is a Yankee."

Elisa stepped back under Wilma's blatant approval. She had to admit she'd thought many times about Mason Bassinger, but his abrupt departure in the midst of preparing him coffee and cake made her wonder if he had tired of her. She had not heard from him in the days since then and thought perhaps he had left the area. Now the news he still lingered in Kingsville made her all the more curious to know what was happening with the handsome man she helped rescue from the Congaree. For months now in the night watches, she would ask God about her future. For so long she had concentrated on surviving day to day. Since Mason's arrival, other thoughts began to invade, thoughts that went beyond this cottage, to a husband and children, maybe even a different home altogether. Things she had put aside under the weight of her family's demise, the destruction of the family home, and the hard life she lived. Mason Bassinger's arrival had somehow opened a new door to hope.

"I can assure you we aren't courting," Elisa said. "But he is generous. He even bought the material for the new window trimmings I just sewed."

"Oh, do show me!"

Elisa led the way into the cottage where Wilma examined the trimmings with a sigh. "How lovely."

"I looked at the material in the store the other day, but of course who can afford such things? He knew it was important to me."

Wilma shook her head. "Dear Elisa, if you allow a man like that to escape, you must be mad."

For the first time Elisa felt a confirmation in her heart that thoughts of a future filled with love need not be so far-fetched but could become reality. A tear entered her eye as she went to put on the kettle. "Do stay for coffee. Real coffee, that is."

"How is it you have real coffee?" When Elisa didn't answer, Wilma added, "The Yankee?"

"You mean Mr. Bassinger. We are all Americans now. We must unite as a country if we are going to survive." She wondered where such words had come from, except for the suffering she and her family had endured at the hand of a divided nation. "Anyway, yes, he did give me money. But only to pay for what I did in helping him on the river."

Wilma sat straighter in her seat and clasped her hands before her. "Oh, do tell."

After serving the coffee, Elisa shared the tale of Mason's sinking boat. Suddenly she heard the neighing of a horse and hurried to the window. Her heart pattered. Mason Bassinger had arrived on his fine sandy-colored mare, his shirt reflecting the sun and black vest a familiar sight. A slow smile spread across her face. A knock came, and she opened the door. "Hello, Mr. Bassinger."

"Hello. I. . ." He paused. "Oh, I'm sorry, I didn't know you were entertaining a guest."

"Wilma's a good friend. She informs me you have been very busy in town making people happy."

"Making people happy?"

"Yes. With your gold coins."

"So you know. I'm not sure about the happiness. At least I feel a weight has been lifted off me. That is, my purse no longer burdens me."

Elisa was uncertain what Mason meant by that. She stepped aside to invite him in. His gaze encompassed the new window trimmings with a grin. He then settled his sights on her guest.

"Mr. Bassinger, may I present Miss Parker."

Wilma stood and extended her hand, which Mason shook. "Pleased to meet you," Wilma said, a bit breathless. "So this is him?" she asked Elisa, who nodded weakly. "How wonderful. I've heard rumors of your good and kind heart with the people here, Mr. Bassinger. Though I'm not certain why you are giving away your money."

"The Good Book says to give when people ask. And to give generously of what you have."

"Maybe, but no one does that."

"It is difficult to give what you don't have. For others, like the rich man, Jesus said it's like going through the eye of a needle. Miss Anderson gave what little she had when I needed it most the other day on the river when my boat began to sink. She didn't even know me. I could have been a scoundrel of the worst kind, but she assisted me and took care of me. Even gave me her father's velvet slippers to wear. One cannot forget such kindness. It's bound to work on a heart."

Wilma's blue eyes grew to the size of silver dollars as she acknowledged Elisa. "How lovely."

Oh dear, thought Elisa. Now that Wilma knew everything, the countryside would abound with talk over what she had done for Mason. She only prayed the conversation would not turn unseemly. "We give when the need is great. Like the slippers. A gentleman barefoot is not fitting." She went to pour him a cup of coffee. "Please enjoy this fine coffee that you helped provide, Mr. Bassinger."

He took a seat at the table, and together they talked about life in Kingsville. Until Wilma asked what kind of work Mason did. Then the man suddenly became tongue-tied and gave only brief details of his travels and working for his brother. Wilma chattered away, sharing about her family as they drank their coffee.

After a time Wilma announced she must be going and thanked Elisa for the coffee. Just before she left, she gave Elisa a broad wink. "He is definitely a fine match for you," she whispered.

Elisa felt warmth creep into her cheeks. She looked aside, hoping Mason would not notice. When Wilma left, Elisa grabbed for a pail and hurried to the door. "I must water my flowers."

Mason followed her outside where she scooped rainwater out of a barrel and carefully drenched each plant. "I don't believe I've seen these plants before. Have I?"

Elisa sighed with gladness at his observant nature. "I dug them up from the plantation and brought them here. There's something about these flowers that made me realize a few things. I've been so busy being sad over life, I tried to make everything look the way I felt. And it was getting quite depressing." She set the pail down and stared at the cottage. "I hadn't done much of anything to make things look nice. I need to make this place a home rather than some cell I'm confined to because of the war." She gazed at Mason. "You helped me realize this, Mr. Bassinger. I feel like God's light now shines here."

Elisa felt a gentle wisp of wind and turned to find that Mason had taken several steps in her direction. Slowly his arms began to enfold her waist. She stiffened slightly, wondering if she should allow such contact with a man she barely knew. But she was right about one thing. Mason did ignite new things in her heart. She wanted to live life to the fullest and not let her losses consume her. She knew when she heard of Mason's generosity that there was much more to life than money or possessions. *It is what one does for others that makes the true riches.*

"I think we're alike in certain ways, Elisa. I too have felt the heaviness of life and wanted to be free of it. Money in many ways was part of that heaviness. Maybe that's why the Bible speaks about having just enough money for what one needs. Nothing more, nothing less."

She laughed. "I'm sure you made many happy."

He chuckled along with her. "They were happy indeed." Slowly his arms drew her to fully face him. "But you have given much too. You showed the true heart of giving by sharing what little you had, even with a Yankee stranger. Thank you."

She saw tenderness in his dark brown eyes. His head tilted. And suddenly his lips were calling on hers in gentle fashion. When they stepped back, her face had gone from warm to blistering hot like the inside of the cookstove. "My goodness. That—that was quite a thank-you."

He grinned. "I can thank you more if you wish. . . ."

"I think that's plenty for now." She noticed Mason's hat had slipped to the ground.

He bent to fetch the hat, sighed, and plunked it on his head. "I must make a decision about what God wants me to do," he confessed. "The reason I came to Kingsville doesn't seem to matter much now. It's difficult to know what's next until one takes a step of faith and finds out."

"You have much to offer." She picked up the pail to gather more water for the flowers.

Mason nodded. "I will return to Kingsville and inquire around. It's time I found meaningful work that will matter."

Elisa wished him well before he mounted his fine horse and took off. The memory of the kiss played over in her mind along with his words of finding something meaningful here in the area. Was he interested in settling down? Could it be a Northerner wanted to forge a new life among former enemies? Could their time together as mere acquaintances be ready to take a serious turn in the road? Was she ready?

Elisa heaved a sigh and poured more water on the flowers. Just like these newly planted posies, Mason was looking to take root somewhere. It amazed her why he chose to do so here, by the swamps and lowlands of the Congaree. And it made her happy too.

Awhile later she heard a horse galloping swiftly down the road. The rider suddenly turned the animal about and rode toward the cottage. Elisa stepped outside to see a stranger astride the horse as the dust cloud settled.

He lifted his hat. "Beg pardon, ma'am."

"What can I do for you?"

"I'm looking for someone. A Mason Bassinger. Have you heard of him?"

Elisa stepped back in astonishment. The man, finely dressed in a short coat with brass buttons despite the heat of the day and the gold chain of a watch dangling out of a pocket, appeared a serious lot. Tailored trousers and polished boots completed the rich portrait. "Yes, I have seen him."

"You have? How long ago? I have heard nothing at all, you see. Not a telegram, nothing. He promised to. . ." The man paused. "Forgive me. Harold Bassinger is my name."

Elisa stared at him. "Why, yes, he's mentioned you. You are the older brother who took care of him."

"So you have talked to him. I represent Bassinger Properties. Mason came here on my behalf, looking for properties to buy for the company."

"Looking for properties to buy for the company?" she repeated, and then she shook her head. "No, I don't think so."

"Yes, he did. He's worked several years for me. Bought me some good parcels down near Savannah. South Carolina was our next area." The man surveyed the property with a knowing eye. "Don't have much here in structures, but your land has some good acreage. It could be lumbered. And there is access to the river for transportation according to my map. No wonder he came here."

Elisa drew a sharp breath, and suddenly anger began to churn within. "Now just a moment. You can't come here expecting to take my land. . . ."

"You misunderstand. I'm not taking anything, ma'am. But I *am* looking to buy. For sure, you won't be able to keep it much longer anyway. I see you have little means of farming. Taxes on property are on the rise. There is something you can do now before it's too late. That is, sell while you can still make a good profit. Lumber is needed for rebuilding and is a highly prized commodity." He lifted his hat once more. "Now I must track down my partner and brother. Thank you for your time, and feel free to come see me in town if you're interested in selling."

Elisa stood frozen in place, unable to believe what she had heard. To suddenly go from the memory of Mason's tender embrace to news that he had come here as a carpetbagger looking to snatch away land felt like a slap. Could this be true of the man she had just kissed? She tried to remember if Mason had ever said anything to her about his real intent in coming to Kingsville. Even when they went to her family's old property, he had not mentioned anything about buying and selling.

Despite this, doubts plagued her. She felt numb as she slowly entered the cottage. All the talk of giving away his money—it could have been a ploy to convince unknowing townsfolk to sell. Her muscles tightened when she gazed at the sunflowers on the backdrop of blue. Had the window trimmings and all he did for her that day in town, coupled with the gold he'd given, also been a scheme to win her heart and then her land?

She stared again at the sunflower trimmings. In a flash she took them down while the tears fell fast and furious. *Dear God, how could this have happened? I should have known it was all too good to be true. I will never trust anyone again.*

Mason couldn't help but smile. Despite the doubt he felt in coming here, his heart now wanted to burst out in song. Especially as he left the tiny shack hastily thrown together for the new railroad supervisor, a paper in his possession giving him the open door to a new job if he so desired. At first he wondered if he was doing the right thing. He'd prayed beforehand, asking that if this wasn't God's will, the door would quickly close. But the man who interviewed him had heard of his generous spirit and goodwill among the townsfolk and was eager to offer a position. "Even if you are one of them Northerners," he added jokingly.

God had been good. The door lay wide open to start a new life. But when the telegraph office caught his eye, he realized he must send some kind of communication to Harold and let him know what was happening. Without a doubt Harold would be very unhappy with the decision. Mason might even be disavowed by his brother. He prayed that would not be the case, that Harold's heart would soften to realize how much Mason wanted to move on with his life. And right now his heart yearned to be with a pretty woman living in a small cottage by the Congaree—a woman who occupied his thoughts day and night. He wanted to provide for her and see about restoring her family's home. If that couldn't be done, perhaps he could whisk her away from these parts altogether, maybe even out West where many had gone to find a better life.

She deserves it all and more, he thought. *She has been through so much. And God, I think I'm falling in love.* They had known each other barely a week, but Elisa had birthed in him strong feelings he could not ignore. She was to be his, he felt certain, and he must take care of her. He wanted to be that bright star in her dark night that guided her and kept her safe.

He began to whistle a merry tune to match his heart. If he could, he wouldn't mind dancing a jig except for the stares certain to come from

Chester Wilson and even some of the ladies like the ones he and Elisa met the other day in the store. He smiled in remembrance of the gift he'd given her. Just the thought of her large green eyes gazing at the flowery trimmings and the flowers surrounding her tiny home made him happy. Already he'd brought light into her life, and it could only continue.

Mason turned toward the telegraph office but stopped short when he saw a man in the distance, talking to a few folks. One of them was Chester, who pointed in his direction. Mason squinted in the piercing noonday sun to see what looked like the familiar form of his brother. "Harold?" he said quizzically. *Impossible.* He must be imagining things.

The face, though grizzly from beard stubble, could not be mistaken when the man came toward him. "Mason. I've been looking for you."

"Harold! What are you doing here?"

"I might ask you the same thing. I have no idea what you are doing here. From what I'm hearing, you've been giving away all our money? And not in a land deal either." Harold's face turned red, and his voice escalated. "Have you lost your mind?"

"There was a need here and. . ."

"I see it is not difficult for you to take our hard-earned money and do with it as you please. You haven't even told folks why you're here. The woman I ran into earlier had no idea you came here to negotiate land deals. What have you been doing, Mason?"

Mason only concentrated on the words that pierced his heart. "What woman did you talk to?"

"I don't know. A fine woman living in a small house in the woods, about four miles back. There is good timber there, I must admit. She didn't seem too eager to sell, but that can change."

Oh no! His heart began to pound in his ears. "You saw Miss Anderson?"

"She never told me her name. But she seemed well acquainted with you. And she appeared to have no idea you were here to do business. So I must ask again, what *have* you been doing since you came here?"

His limbs felt weak, his face turning hot like a branding iron. Dread began to fill him. *Elisa knows. She knows why I've come. Or at least, the initial reason I came.* Even though he had the paper in his pocket from the railroad that revealed his true heart, what would she think of him in the end?

Suddenly he saw his dreams of life and love floating away like brown grass taken up by the wind.

Chapter 6

Elisa wished she could disappear—far away from what she was feeling at this moment. Tears glazed her eyes as she walked about the Cottonwood Plantation, recalling memories and the sense of betrayal that flooded her after the encounter with Mason's brother. Mason had tried once to see her since then, and she shooed him away faster than a broom to a rat. He was like a rodent in that respect. Scurrying about, attempting to look innocent, but on the prowl for things. He thought he could sweet-talk his way into her life, adding to it fineries and then giving gold to others. But he was like any other Yankee. Scalawags. Vermin. Up to evil devices for their own wealth. Ignoring the pain they inflicted on others.

Elisa settled down under one of the larger oak trees with magnificent branches reaching to the sky. She'd often played there as a child, glad for the cool shade the leaves provided when the oppressive summers came. Now nothing seemed able to relieve the heat of disappointment. Everything fell on her in one terrific crash of memories. The death of Mother in childbirth. The day her brother John left to join up with the men in gray, never to return. Father's ensuing despondency and the recent news of his death. The Yankee invasion that led to the ultimate destruction of the plantation. And the day she scurried into the woods to try and forge out a meager life in a dilapidated cottage.

Now came the memory of her encounter with Mason on the river, and the disappointment turned to anger. Mason knew nothing of hardship. He and his Northern friends had everything so nicely laid out for them. Money. Nice clothes. Plenty to eat. Family.

Elisa plucked a handful of grass and tossed it into the air. What did she have? She had the cottage. A few trifles. Some friends like Wilma Parker. Her wits and determination. But she had left out one important detail. Most of all, she had God. He was with her, even through the difficult times in life.

Even when anger now gripped her, He had not given up, and she shouldn't either. Despite the disappointment and grief and hurt, she trusted Him. If only she had not extended a branch of trust to Mason, with all the apparent godliness he portrayed in manner and speech. It was all an act to cover up the real reason for befriending her.

Elisa slowly stood to her feet and smoothed out the faded gown sprinkled with dirt that had rips along the hemline. Like this place and her gown, she was worn out. The plantation showed signs of new life in the form of small plants and new oak trees springing up within the crumbling walls. The wild things were ready to take over, and no one would remember the love and life that once existed here. Nor the sorrow either. Maybe it was a sign that she should do something new. Maybe even sell this place and make some money. But then she glanced again at the wide, gnarly gray arms of the old oak, recalling Harold's words of fine timber. The trees would be cut down for lumber. She would only have the small cottage and barren land to gaze upon. No, she could not part with this place or the woods. It still provided some semblance of life.

I must find her. Dear God, help me.

When Elisa was not at her cottage, Mason strode through the same woods and swamps he did when he first arrived, in stocking feet no less, as his boots were sacrificed to the river. The joy of that initial meeting filled him when he reached the point of the Congaree River and the aging dock where a boat was still tied. She had not left to go fishing. But the vision of that day and her calling to him as his boat rapidly filled with water sparked appreciation. She was a woman in command of the situation. But then he witnessed her vulnerability at the cottage. How she struggled to survive and wished for the nicer things she could never have.

He retraced his way back to the cottage and knocked once more on the door. He stepped back to observe the place and noticed the window coverings were gone. The mere notion she had stripped away the gift he had given her spoke loudly of the emotion raging in her heart. He must find her and set things right. He had to tell her what his heart had been whispering in the wee hours of the night. That he had fallen in love. That he did not care about properties or money, but he cared about her.

Mason returned to his horse and decided to try one other place, the place of her childhood, the home of her family.

Elisa sighed and began walking down the road, away from the failing memories, only to see a rider venturing slowly toward her. Tension gripped every muscle as she recognized the color of the horse from a distance. She no more wanted to see the rider than any other traitorous Yankee.

"Please leave at once!" she shouted.

Mason said nothing at first but simply removed his hat. Then he spoke quietly, "I will, but I must say something, Elisa."

Elisa saw Mason clench his hat in one hand and the reins in the other. She had to admit, even though her heart felt anger, it also felt an attraction for this man. He had come seeking her again. Not to mention the way the sunlight reflected in his brown hair that ruffled in the breeze. Even his horse appeared radiant. "There is nothing more to be said," she managed to say.

"There is much."

Elisa continued walking swiftly down the road, past Mason astride the mare. She heard the sound of him dismounting. Her pace quickened. "Please, just leave me alone."

"I would, except. . .I can't. I love you."

She stopped dead in her tracks and whirled about. "How dare you say that to me!"

"I say it because it's the truth. As God is my witness."

"I'm sorry, but you are gravely mistaken. One doesn't betray the one he loves. Or engage in devious ways."

"I never betrayed you. Nor am I devious."

"Why didn't you tell me the real reason you came here? To buy land off the poor."

Mason hesitated. "Because I knew what the reaction would be. I've seen what the Union army did. The suffering and the anguish. It didn't take me long to realize I wasn't here to buy land but to find out what I'm supposed to do with what I've seen. Yes, I did come here in the beginning at my brother's request. And yes, as one beholding to another. But a sinking boat can change a heart."

Elisa faltered under the reminder of how they met, and she looked away. "I—I don't believe you. Just the other day I heard how you approached the Henderson brothers to buy their land. They were highly offended."

Mason placed his hat back on his head. "I tried a few transactions," he admitted. "It did not work out. And right now, I can't very well pursue much buying with less money in my purse."

The comment reminded her of what Wilma had told her. "Oh, how you gave away your coins in the middle of Kingsville. It makes no sense. What was that all about? To make people trust you?"

Mason shook his head. His eyes glistened then, perhaps with tears, though she refused to believe it. "I can't make anyone trust me. Only God can do that. If you truly believe I was only here for evil purposes and not good, then there is nothing more I can say." He paused. "Except. . . I'm sorry."

With that he mounted his fine mare and, with a soft click, turned the animal about. Elisa watched him as he rode away, his body hunched over, his head hanging low. Even the horse held its head in the same subdued fashion, as if sharing in the sorrow. Mason did not appear like some victorious conqueror looking to take away all anyone had. And those simple words of "I love you" that echoed in her ears also reinforced the doubt forming in her mind.

If only she could be certain of the truth in the things he said. *A sinking boat can change a heart. . . .* Her steps become slow and methodical. How she wished he had not come back. She could have buried him along with what remained of Cottonwood as a dream that was never meant to last. Instead Mason had come, ready to resurrect a relationship that was seemingly dead.

Or was it? Maybe he thought the words *I love you* would repair the breach. Maybe he thought that was all it would take.

Elisa paused to wipe away a tear. His words tripped her like a branch tossed in her path. A part of her wanted to believe that someone cared. That a man wanted to call her his own. But after the demise of her family, she only had God to help keep this shallow life going.

Why did he tell me he loves me? Does he really believe it has the power to overcome the hurt and despair? The rejection and betrayal? Is it powerful enough to restore the joy of life once again?

"I've made yet another mistake," Mason grumbled to himself. He'd prayed hard over this encounter, or so he thought, before he made the ride to see Elisa. He'd hoped to find one in need of strength and care. Instead, the anger that spewed forth startled him. He should have realized it would be difficult for her to learn of his work and then meet him face-to-face upon the very ground where her hurt loomed the greatest. At least he had shared his love.

Maybe God could still soften her heart. But he feared her heart was now encased in cold, hard, impenetrable stone, and he had failed.

Mason made his way back toward Kingsville. His brother had asked if he would check on one of the properties that Harold had gone to see yesterday. Mason had not told his brother he was going to see Elisa, but now that things were in such disarray, he decided to make this one visit. What did it matter anyway? He pulled out a piece of paper to check on the whereabouts of the place and ushered Honey to the next road. Soon they came upon a modest southern home, still intact, surrounded by old oaks. An older woman and her attractive daughter stood on the front porch as if expecting his arrival. When Mason drew nearer, he sucked in his breath, recognizing the brown curls beneath the young woman's bonnet, the blue eyes, and the ecru-colored gown.

"Welcome, Mr. Bassinger," she said, holding out her hand. "I'm sure you remember me. Wilma Parker, friend of Elisa Anderson's. We met the other day."

"Yes, pleased to see you again," he said swiftly, bowing.

Wilma smiled. "This is my mother, Mrs. Amelia Parker. Do come in. Your brother said you would be stopping by today to complete our business."

Mason followed her to the parlor, the droplets of sweat collecting on the back of his neck. He tried to control any nervous tremors. Tea and biscuits were waiting, as well as a familiar document that Harold had drawn up, along with an inkwell and pen. Wilma dutifully poured out tea and handed him a cup.

"We are ready to sign," she announced, taking a seat opposite him, her back straight, her hands folded, looking confident and calm.

Mason set down the cup and took up the document, noting they were selling off a good deal of acreage for timber. For some reason the mere fact made his face heat and his throat clog with emotion.

Wilma stared at him. "Is something amiss?"

"No, no." He handed it back to her. "Thank you for doing this."

Wilma looked at him with arched eyebrows and wide blue eyes. She passed the document over to her mother. "It is as we agreed, Mother," she said.

The older woman took her time reading it once more. Mason tried to imagine what was going through her mind after Elisa's reaction. Did they also hate him for having to do this? Did they think him a scalawag who wanted to rob them of their inheritance? When the older woman continued to hesitate, he said, "This must be hard."

"Actually, this was an easy decision to come to," Wilma said. "We need the money to pay off debts, and your brother was a fair person. Here there is a natural distrust for anyone from the North. But sometimes one must do what is necessary." After the mother signed, Wilma passed the document back to Mason, and he paid them.

Harold would be happy. But Elisa would call him a reprobate or any of the other unsavory titles she came up with, thinking he had duped her good friend. He stood to his feet, wishing he could be anywhere but here. "Thank you again."

Wilma followed him to the door. "Are you quite all right?" she asked.

Mason thought it strange she would ask such a personal question of a stranger. But she was also Elisa's friend. "No," he said. He told her everything that had happened between them and how Elisa found out about his intent to buy land. And how at first he came here to do business but found himself moved by what he saw and especially by Elisa's situation. And then he fell in love.

Wilma nodded. "I told Elisa I thought you were a decent man, Mr. Bassinger. I believe I'm quite keen on such things. But I fear Elisa has been wounded far more than any of us. She has no family and no home."

"But she has God. Everything else will pass way. He is all anyone ever needs."

Wilma stepped back. "Well said, sir. Maybe that's what you need to tell her. Even if she feels lost and alone, God is still with her."

Mason nodded. "Thank you again. I do think, despite all that's happened, that God continues to guide our steps. He did, even to this meeting today with you and your mother. You've given me hope when I thought there was none."

Wilma smiled. "I'm glad."

Mason felt joy at the discovery in his heart. Indeed God had directed his steps. He had done his brother's bidding. Honored the cause. And found a bit of calm in the midst of this storm. Mason felt for the paper in his pocket. All things did work together for good. Maybe this was a sign of good things to come, that God would now work in Elisa's heart and all would be well. He thought of her so often, she felt like a part of him already. How he wanted to ride back and share this meeting with her. Tell her he had the most excellent conversation with a good lady friend of hers, and Wilma had agreed with everything he'd said. But he fought the urge to see her right now. He must give her time.

He nudged Honey to a fast trot, eager to share the news with Harold. He arrived in town to find Harold talking with one of the men Mason had conversed with a week ago, the same one who had offered him a position with the railroad. He tensed, wondering if anything had been said about the job.

Harold shook the man's hand and turned about, his gaze settling on Mason.

"I have the agreement with the Parkers," Mason said, striding up to him.

"Thank you." His brother's voice sounded subdued, without the jubilance Mason expected. Harold walked with him across the street until they reached a few large chunks of split logs where he motioned for Mason to sit along with him.

"Seems to me there is more going on than I know. I talked to Mr. Simpson there with the railroad. He said he offered you a job, and you've basically agreed to take it."

Mason did not know what to say. He looked away, unable to meet Harold's gaze and the words he knew would come. How Mason was abandoning him after all he had done in his life. How he was disappointed in such a decision. How his company would collapse if Mason did not return to help.

"Then I talked to some townspeople. The ones you gave coins to. Several of them now want to sell. They feel it is in their best interest."

Mason stayed quiet, unsure where this conversation was leading.

"I've been thinking," Harold added slowly. "I see now you did a good thing with the money by making it much easier for people to trust us. And I realized something else too. That it's wrong to keep you here in the business."

Mason looked at him, the words sending surprise surging through him. "What?"

"I can find other help. I already hired on a new man while you were away. If you want to do other things, I have no right to say you can't."

Mason could not believe it. He burst to his feet. "Harold, I. . ."

"I just wanted you to know that." Harold stood also. "You've done a good job here. I will make a few more contacts but then I'll leave and allow you to live your life as you feel you should." A crooked smile formed on Harold's face before he placed his hat on his head and moved off down the street. Mason stood frozen in place, unable to believe what had just occurred. He tried to sort this out but instead felt like a caged bird set free. He knew where his destiny now lay. . .in the hand of a mighty God who kept a careful watch over everything.

Now if God could only see fit to bring Elisa into that picture with him, how perfect life would be.

If only. . .

Chapter 7

Elisa tried to concentrate on her tasks for the day, but all she could see was Mason in everything she did. Why his face and words would occupy her thoughts did not make sense. He seemed ever present in her life, despite the feelings she had of distrust and betrayal. Looking over the material he had bought for the window coverings, she studied the sunflowers on the blue background and how happy they appeared. If only she could feel like the flowers looked—bright, beautiful, embracing the sun above. But could anyone be happy anymore? It seemed happiness was only based on something or someone. Some were made happy by the things they possessed. Some by the people they were with. But just as she read in scripture, all these things were passing away. She had witnessed herself the fleetingness of life—when she lost her home and her family, even the despair that gripped Father, enough to drive him away from life itself. None of that brought her happiness or peace.

Maybe she ought to consider a different kind of peace. Like the Prince of Peace, who had given His life so she could experience God's love. She could enjoy His peace and blessing rather than trusting in mortal man.

Elisa frowned. All this seemed well and good, but it still did not erase the fact that Mason had deceived her. His surreptitious activities did not speak well of someone she wanted to know or love. Elisa picked up the pail to fetch water for the flowers. The plants were coming along nicely since being transplanted, sending up shoots of new blooms despite the hot sun. And then she saw the bloom of a new sunflower just beginning to unfurl its pretty yellow petals. Elisa sighed in delight. Could it be a sign?

A buggy came crawling up the road and veered toward her. It was Wilma, all smiles as she alighted. Elisa greeted her and promptly invited her inside where the kettle was put on the cookstove for a little coffee.

"Well we did it," Wilma purred in pride, plopping her beaded reticule on the table and taking a seat.

"What did you do?"

"I signed a contract with your Mr. Bassinger. We sold off a good deal of land. Now we can have whatever we want and do what is necessary. No more living like paupers with bread and water. I can even have a new dress. Isn't that delightful?"

Elisa had picked up the teakettle of hot water but hastily returned it to the stove for fear of dropping it. "Are you saying you made a bargain with the Bassinger brothers? Surely not!"

"Indeed I did. With Mason Bassinger, that is." She sat back in her chair and smiled. "He was very gracious. He and his brother offered good terms. I am very happy with it. And you should be too." Wilma then stared her in the eye in such a way that Elisa stepped back. She could not believe her friend was addressing the very thing she had been contemplating. Happiness.

"What do you mean precisely?" Elisa asked weakly.

"I mean you have a God-fearing man who is in love with you and wants to help. And you swatted him away like he was an annoying fly." She sniffed at a small ant crawling on the table. "I'll tell you though, if you don't want him, then I don't mind inviting him over for cake and coffee. Now that I can buy coffee anytime I wish."

"Why would Mason confide in you?"

"He needed a listening ear. He was burdened. Only a man in love who feels like love has been snatched away for no good reason would act the way he did. I know you've been broken by circumstances, Elisa, but surely you can't go and break the man's heart. He doesn't deserve it."

The words hit her like a plank board with a force that jarred her. She thought on Wilma's challenge, that if she didn't want him, her friend would gladly pursue. "Where is he now?"

"I believe he's still in town. I plan to go there soon myself." Wilma stood to her feet. "As much as I would love to stay, I have things that need tending. But I thought you should know what's going on." She picked up her reticule and strode for the door.

"Wilma, wait!"

Wilma whirled, a grin spreading across her face. "Yes?"

"Are you really going to invite Mason to tea?"

Wilma laughed. "I guess that all depends. Right now I'm seeing Wallace

Greely. But I like to keep my eyes open to what's around me." She added, "So should you. It's very easy to become blinded when we see only ourselves and no one else."

Elisa again recoiled at the words until strength rose up inside her. "I'm glad you came," she finally said in a soft voice.

Wilma laughed. "Dear one, what are best friends for? I don't want you alone and miserable, ignoring the one true gift God planted right on your very doorstep. If I were you, I would head to town this instant and make amends."

The desire to have Mason Bassinger by her side could not be ignored. "Please, can you take me?"

"I thought you'd never ask."

Elisa hastened to the back room to fetch her hat. All this had come about so abruptly, she didn't have time to contemplate what she would say when she saw Mason. She did know she no longer wanted turmoil in her life. God was not a God of confusion but of peace. And He had sent Wilma to restore peace by encouraging her to make amends with Mason. So long as the door hadn't closed.

Elisa hurried to Wilma's buggy and plunked down on the seat beside her friend. "I think I've been a fool, Wilma."

"I think so too. In fact, I know so. But you are doing the right thing."

Wilma urged the horse with a swift flick of the reins, driving the buggy down the dusty road toward Kingsville. Elisa's heart pattered within her like the clopping of the hoofbeats. She only prayed when she arrived she wasn't too late and he hadn't already gone. They drove by the country lane leading to Cottonwood and the last meeting she had with Mason. His look of dejection when she delivered swift accusations sharper than any ax still rang fresh in her mind. Accusing him of misdeeds when he was only there to help. She didn't understand completely why he hadn't told her his reason for coming to this area, but then again, it had never been a topic of discussion. He had never tried to take her land or coerce her. He'd only been respectful and understanding, as much as one can be, heralding from the North. And then there was the money he had given away. The more she thought about it, the more she considered the act in light of the scripture. Money seemed first in everyone's concern. But not Mason's. He made it clear with his actions that he revered other things, and other people, much more than gold coins.

"You're very quiet," Wilma observed.

Elisa sighed. He'd probably told Wilma about their encounter at Cottonwood, but she went ahead and shared about that sad day with her friend.

"I'm glad you're thinking about these things, Elisa. Because I do want you to come with an open heart when you arrive."

"I'll try."

Wilma skillfully directed the buggy along the road. Elisa thought how Wilma had sold off part of her family's land. Maybe that was possible for Cottonwood. To have the means to do what she could only dream of doing seemed the right thing. Then came the vison of Mason handing her the package wrapped in brown paper and fulfilling her desire for beauty. How she wanted to return right now and put the window coverings back up. If only she had not let emotion rule the day but instead had let God's love and understanding flow through the situation. She inhaled a breath, trying to gather her courage for the meeting to come and for words she hoped flowed like honey rather than poison.

Mason was ecstatic after what Harold told him, releasing him to do what his heart desired. But at times the feeling was fleeting, especially when replaced with Elisa's angry face, the sound of her words, and the hurt look that drove him away. He indeed wanted to try and seek understanding. Now that Harold had given him leave to start a new life, Mason went to see the railroad supervisor, Mr. Simpson, to sign the final papers for his new position—coordinating the men hired by the railroad to lay down new track. Mr. Simpson had witnessed how Mason related to the townsfolk with his generosity. He felt there was no one better to bring the men together to rebuild the railroad. Mason liked the idea of North and South uniting as one to see a goal accomplished. They needed this after five years of a terrible conflict that had torn them apart. They could heal while working for renewal in their country and in each other.

He sighed. If only Elisa could be brought into that fellowship of healing. It seemed impossible. She had made up her mind, though he desperately wanted to change it.

Mason walked along the boardwalk, his shoes scuffing, until he nearly plowed headlong into the familiar grizzly face of Chester T. Wilson, chewing on chaw.

"I've been lookin' fer ya," he said before turning his head to spit out a wad of tobacco.

Mason frowned, not wishing to remain another moment in the man's presence. "What is it now, Mr. Wilson?"

"Well, you see, I was in church the other day. I was listenin' to the preacher, y'know. And I got to thinkin'. . . I'd dun some wrong things. Jus' wanted to tell you that I was sorry 'bout the money talk. 'Tweren't right. And about that boat I lent ya. I had no idea it leaked, I promise you, but still. . ."

"Don't concern yourself with it. It actually did me a lot of good."

"Say what?"

"That leaking boat led me to meet the famous and gracious Belle of the Congaree." He did not elaborate on how well they had gotten along until unfortunate circumstances and misunderstandings tore them apart.

"Oh. Well then, I'm guessin' you ain't lookin' fer money then."

"Money?"

"I was guessin' maybe you'd want your coin back." Chester thumbed his new shirt beneath the suspenders. "But I kept it as I shore needed things. I had to show ya, I spent it well here. See my fancy new duds?"

"That's all right, Mr. Wilson. One sows and another reaps." He sighed again. If only that reaping could involve a special woman.

Mason paused, squinting as a fine buggy rolled into town. A woman alighted from it, her straw hat nearly taken away on the breath of a hot breeze, her auburn hair streaming like a banner. He sucked in his breath. Elisa!

She hitched up her skirt to keep the gown from trailing in the dust and marched directly toward him. "Mr. Bassinger, I will have a word with you."

Chester grinned. "Uh-oh. Maybe I got the better bargain after all," he said with a laugh.

"What was that all about?" Elisa asked as Chester walked off, snickering.

"He was worried I'd want my money back for the leaky boat. I told him it was worth that gold coin and more. In so many words."

"I don't understand. You lost quite a bit with all this and—"

"No. I actually gained a great deal. Better than any gold or boots in the river or anything else. I met you."

Her cheeks pinked. She looked away. "Anyway, I did want to tell you, if you still want Cottonwood for the timber, you are more than welcome."

Mason shook his head. He pointed in the direction of the newly constructed railroad office. "I have something to show you." He led the way to the rough-hewn building that still smelled of pine from boards hastily nailed together. Inside was a large desk and a beefy man sitting behind it. "This is my new boss. Mr. Simpson, may I present Miss Anderson."

"Fine meeting you, ma'am," he said.

They exchanged small talk before exiting the building, with Elisa taking hesitant steps. "I don't understand...," she began.

"I'm working for the railroad now. My job is to coordinate the men helping fix the rail line. I was offered the work the other day and—"

Elisa stopped, and Mason thought perhaps further anger would ignite a fire in her forest-green eyes. "You mean you are no longer a carpetbagger?"

"I never meant to be one in the first place. I wanted to help my brother. But he let me go from the business as of yesterday. I've found other work to do here."

Elisa's cheeks now took on a deep, rosy tone. Her lips trembled. "I don't see why you would want to stay here. I acted dreadfully at Cottonwood. In fact, I know now I am willing to let the property go. It's been enough of a burden and turned me into someone I dislike. And I'm sorry."

"Dear Elisa, it also made you who you are. And you won't have to let it go. Not now, not ever." He took her hands in his. Out of the corner of his eye he saw his boss in the doorway of the office, a smile spreading across his face.

"You want me to get the reverend and make it official, Mason?" Mr. Simpson called out with a jolly laugh.

"That might not be a bad idea," Mason said. "In fact, I think it's an excellent idea."

"Mason!" Elisa said, shaking her head and smiling.

He laughed and she relaxed, her laughter joining his. "Don't fret. There's a time and season for everything, as I'm learning. I will get settled here, and then we can talk about some very good plans. In the meantime, I would ask your family if I might court you, but..."

Elisa smiled. "Don't worry. My good friend Wilma has already given her blessing. She's like a sister to me. Her visit today at the cottage helped me see the light."

"Praise God. Since we have witnesses, I think I will give you a kiss to seal a commitment." With an audience of several onlookers gathering nearby and Mr. Simpson grinning from ear to ear, Mason gave Elisa a kiss on the cheek, promising himself in his heart to bestow a kiss on her sweet lips at the proper time. She took his hand in hers and pressed it against her cheek.

The beautiful Belle of the Congaree was his. Soon the bells of marriage would peal loud and clear to match the joy radiating in his heart.

Lauralee Bliss has always liked to dream big dreams. Part of that dream was writing, and after several years of hard work, her dream of publishing was realized in 1997 with the publication of her first romance novel, *Mountaintop*, through Barbour Publishing. Since then she's had twenty books published, both historical and contemporary. Lauralee is also an avid hiker, completing the entire length of the Appalachian Trail both north and south. Lauralee makes her home in Virginia in the foothills of the Blue Ridge Mountains with her family. Visit her website at www.lauraleebliss.com and find her on Twitter (@lauraleebliss) and Facebook (Readers of Author Lauralee Bliss).

Thoroughbreds

by Ramona K. Cecil

Dedication

To my beautiful granddaughter, Gabriella.
May Proverbs 3:5–6 be your guide.

Trust in the LORD with all thine heart;
and lean not unto thine own understanding.
In all thy ways acknowledge him, and he shall direct thy paths.
PROVERBS 3:5–6

Acknowledgments

Special thanks to:
The Auburn Cord Duesenberg Automobile Museum, Auburn, Indiana
The Kentucky Derby Museum, Louisville, Kentucky
The Hagyard Equine Medical Institute, Lexington, Kentucky

Chapter 1

"Oh no, not Clay!"

The sight of him knocked the air from Ella Jamison's lungs as if someone had punched her in the stomach. She stood, transfixed in the center of Lexington's Union Station. The cacophony of voices echoing around the rotunda covered her guttural groan. The impulse to turn and run back through the station to the train car gripped her.

Too late. He'd seen her.

"Ella?" Clay sauntered toward her, giving her that lopsided grin that, even after seven years, still tortured her dreams. Though taller and more muscular—well-defined biceps filled out the arms of his brown leather jacket—the man before her could be no other than her childhood tormentor, Clay Garrett. He tipped his gray wool cap, revealing a glimpse of his curly red hair.

"I thought you were still. . ." The words flew from her lips as of their own volition.

"Still in prison?" His gray eyes glinted, and his grin widened as he pried the leather handles of her valise from her frozen fingers. "Got out last month. Don't worry, I won't murder you on the way to the house."

"I didn't mean. . ." Heat crept up in Ella's face, and the urge to run and hide in a ladies' sitting room tugged hard. This trip that she'd dreaded since getting word last week that her cousin Jared had died of influenza at Fort Riley Army Base in Kansas had turned nightmarish.

The corner of his mouth pulled up in a roguish grin, and Ella's heart made an unexpected flip. "I'm afraid the car is parked out on Main Street. Hope you don't mind hoofing it." His gaze traveled from her wide-brimmed hat to her navy-blue serge suit then down to her sturdy black pumps.

Defiance shot through Ella like an electrical charge. He doubtless remembered how she'd struggled to keep up with him, Jared, and her brother Gavin as a youngster, so he'd parked as far away as he could to tax her endurance.

Clay needed to know that she was no longer the thirteen-year-old girl he'd delighted in teasing. She met his gaze with a glare, and her chin jutted up. "After sitting for hours on a train seat, I welcome a stroll in the spring air."

"Good." He turned and headed toward the front of the building with her valise, and she hurried to fall into step beside him.

"Welcome to Kentucky, by the way." He angled a look at her as they emerged from Union Station into the sunny March day. "Sorry it's not under better circumstances." The somber inflection in his voice sounded genuine.

"Me too." A finger of guilt squiggled through her. She'd seen her cousin Jared—her mother's sister's only child—perhaps a dozen times in her life. Clay, Uncle Davis's orphaned nephew, had lived with Jared like a brother since the age of twelve. "I'm sorry for your loss." The awkwardness she always felt at such occasions fell over her.

"He was your cousin too. . .from the other side of the family, of course." As they traversed the brick-paved, horseshoe-shaped drive that fronted the station, Clay looked toward the grassy expanse to their left centered by a fountain. "God knows best."

The comment caught Ella by surprise. Despite Aunt Vickie's and Uncle Davis's strong Christian example, Clay, as a boy, had struck her as agnostic to the point of irreverent.

"Here we are." Clay stopped beside a handsome apple-green touring car. He opened the back door and put her valise on the seat then opened the front passenger side door for her. "Unless, of course, you'd rather sit in the back with your bag instead of up front with me."

Ella forced a smile. "Up front is fine." Clay Garrett would not intimidate her.

When he took her hand to help her onto the metal step and into the car, his strong grip sent an unexpected surge of warmth up her arm. But by the time he'd rounded the car and situated himself in the driver's seat, she had regained a measure of composure.

"Nice car," she managed, testing the steadiness of her voice. She looked at the oak dash with its assortment of metal buttons and dials including a clock.

"It's an Auburn 6-39, but I doubt you care about that." His smile turned somber. "Uncle Davis bought it last year for Jared." He turned a key on the dash and pressed his foot on a button on the floorboard, and the engine chugged to life. "Green was Jared's favorite color, you know," he said as he adjusted a lever by the steering wheel.

Ella didn't know. Guilt nipped at her heart. Jared's favorite color was but one of many things she didn't know—hadn't cared to learn—about her now dead cousin.

Clay turned the steering wheel, and they began rolling down Main Street. His voice brightened. "This is my first time to drive the car." He shot her a grin. "Guess I have you to thank for that."

Ella opened her mouth to ask why he hadn't driven the car before today then closed it and pretended to smooth down an imaginary wrinkle in her skirt. It likely had to do with his recent release from prison—a subject she'd rather avoid.

An awkward silence fell between them as they wended their way through Lexington. As the city gave way to the countryside, miles of white rail fences bordered rolling green pastures where graceful, long-legged horses grazed. As it always did, the beauty of the sight took Ella's breath away.

"Algonquin Hill has some good-looking horseflesh. Could give Dogwood Farms some stiff competition this year." Clay's glance followed Ella's gaze.

That he'd broken the silence relieved a measure of the mounting tension between them, but at the same time, it burdened her with a need to respond. "So you are back working at Dogwood Farms?"

"Yeah, I'm the trainer now. Sam McFadden left six months ago and Uncle Davis was desperate." He gave a sardonic snort. "He wouldn't have taken me on otherwise. We're here."

His announcement of their arrival swept away the questions his previous comment had raised in Ella's mind. Her chest clenched as they turned down the familiar dirt lane lined with budding dogwood trees. Dread and inadequacy vied for space inside her. As she'd done countless times since boarding the train in Indianapolis, Ella gave a mental fist shake at heaven. It seemed beyond cruel that God had allowed circumstances to require her, the least equipped member of her immediate family, to offer solace to her grieving aunt and uncle. Aunt Vickie and Uncle Davis deserved better comfort than Ella could offer. Mother, Daddy, and even Gavin all possessed a gift for imparting sympathy with consoling grace. With Mother and Daddy in the mission field in New Guinea and Gavin fighting in France, a rising sense of ineptness threatened to engulf Ella.

"And we know that all things work together for good to them that love God, to them who are the called according to his purpose."

The verse from Romans that Mother and Daddy had seared into her brain since early childhood popped into her mind. Bitterness soured in her belly as she fought rising floodwaters of self-pity. *If there even is a God.*

The nagging thought, which she hadn't until now allowed to take shape in her mind, jarred her.

The automobile came to a stop, and Ella's heart shuddered with the car's engine. She gazed up at her aunt and uncle's imposing three-story brick home with its four enormous white columns that stood like sentries across the front portico.

Clay, who she hadn't realized had gotten out of the car, opened the door for her. He took her hand to help her out, and she grasped it like a lifeline. With his strong arm supporting her, she managed to mount the several steps to the porch.

Gwen, the family's housekeeper since Ella was small, greeted them at the door in the hushed tones of a benediction. Her brown eyes sad, she offered Ella a smile. "My, you've grown up pretty, Miss Ella. It's so nice to see you. Ms. Vickie and Mr. Davis are in the south parlor. Would you like for me to take your hat?" Except for a few more wrinkles on her face and more gray in her brown hair, the plump woman hadn't changed in the seven years since Ella's last visit.

With unsteady hands, Ella lifted off her wide-brimmed navy-blue hat decorated with a white grosgrain ribbon and a white fabric flower and handed it to Gwen, who waddled away with it.

"Nice to see you haven't bobbed your hair like so many of the women are doing now." Clay's voice held surprised approval. He grinned, and the teasing tone Ella remembered returned. "There's still plenty of long blond hair to pull."

Yes, this was the Clay Garrett she remembered. Defiance stiffened her spine. She glared at him and pasted on the sweetest smile she could muster. "Odd you should say that. I was thinking of cutting it. Now I'm sure I will."

He gave a little laugh. "I'll take your bag to your room. It's the same one you always stayed in. Do you remember the way?"

"Of course I remember the way." The starch went out of her spine as she realized he wouldn't be joining her to greet Aunt Vickie and Uncle Davis, and a flash of panic struck. "You're not coming with me?" She hated the quaver in her voice.

"No." He glanced down at the parquet floor. When he looked back at her, compassion—an emotion she'd never before seen in Clay Garrett's face—shined from his gray eyes. His gaze locked on hers, and his gentled voice turned encouraging. "You can do this, Ella." He gave her a wink, causing her heart to make a surprising hop, then headed up the curved staircase.

Watching him disappear up the stairs, Ella felt bereft. When she could move again the wood floor echoed beneath her steps, the hollow sound reflecting the emptiness inside her. To steady her nerves she perused the gold-framed portraits of past Dogwood Farms' Thoroughbreds that lined the forest-green hallway walls.

I'm not ready for this. I'll never be ready for this.

Her heart hammered, and her mind fashioned a quick, convoluted prayer for strength and wisdom that surprised her. She'd abandoned prayer months ago. What would she say? What would Mother or Daddy say if they were here?

Her mind remained blank as she walked the rest of the way to the parlor. She stopped at the threshold, her heart breaking at the sight before her.

The afternoon sun bathed the room in a golden glow. Aunt Vickie, dressed in a black-and-gray satin frock, sat on a blue damask wing chair gazing out the south window and twisting a handkerchief in her hands. Across the room Uncle Davis, looking haggard and old, sat slumped on a brown leather sofa.

Aunt Vickie turned and looked at Ella. She emitted a soft gasp, jumped up from her chair, and ran to embrace her. "Oh Ella, I'm so glad you're here." Her words snagged on the ragged edge of a sob, and she dabbed the wadded handkerchief at her brown eyes reddened by tears.

Ella noticed more gray streaks in her aunt's blond hair than she'd remembered. As she returned Aunt Vickie's hug she said the only words that formed in her paralyzed brain. "Aunt Vickie, Uncle Davis, I'm so sorry." Said aloud, the words seemed an insipid cliché, a generic sentiment copied from a dime-store sympathy card and pitifully insufficient.

Aunt Vickie gave her a brave smile and another hug. "At least he didn't die across the sea in a foreign field or in one of those terrible mud-filled trenches they talk about in the papers." She stepped back and looked Ella up and down with a fond gaze. "You've grown up on us. Even prettier than the last picture your mother sent me."

Ella knew that despite her petite form, Vickie Garrett's stature belied her strength. Of her cousin's grieving parents, Aunt Vickie would best weather the gale of sorrow assailing them. Like the supple boughs of a willow, she would bend to the reality, while the resistance of Uncle Davis's hardwood would more easily snap beneath the storm's force.

She glanced past her aunt's shoulder to Uncle Davis, who hadn't moved or in any way acknowledged her presence.

"Davis, Ella's here and all grown up." Aunt Vickie circled Ella's waist with her arm and guided her into the room.

Uncle Davis finally looked up, his face a mask of agony beneath his wavy, graying auburn hair. With slow movements, he pushed himself up from the sofa and stood. His six-foot-three-inch frame looked far less stalwart than Ella remembered. The sparkle she remembered in his blue eyes had gone, and his shoulders that used to carry her as a child appeared stooped. "Hello, Ella. We're glad you could come." No smile touched his lips. "At least we'll have one relative to stand with us." His gruff voice reminded Ella of the growl of a wounded animal. She sensed that his stiff facade masked a fragile interior. At the first misplaced word or too-sympathetic look, she could imagine him crumbling into a heap of broken sobs.

Aunt Vickie walked Ella to Uncle Davis. "Dear, you know that's not true. Clay's here."

Uncle Davis's face reddened. "Not because I want him here."

Aunt Vickie touched her husband's arm. "Now, Davis, it doesn't matter what he did. He's still your late brother's boy, and we raised him like a son since he was twelve—"

Davis swung an angry face to her. "He's an ex-convict, and no son of mine! He brought shame on the Garrett name and the memory of his father. It wasn't my son that doped the horse and caused it to go crazy and kill the jockey. It wasn't my son that spent three years in the state penitentiary for reckless homicide." Trembling, he stabbed his finger toward the large south window. "*My* son is lying in a flag-draped casket down at Ahultman's Mortuary dressed in the uniform of our country." He sank to the sofa as if his legs could no longer support him. "If God had to take one of them, I wish He had taken Clay instead of our boy."

"Davis, you don't mean that." Aunt Vickie shook her head.

"I *do* mean it!" Uncle Davis seemed to grasp at the anger as if it were an anesthetizing drug. "I wouldn't have let him set foot on the place again if it weren't for your and Old Reuben's insistence, and that we were desperate for a trainer after Sam left."

Ella squirmed in the center of the family drama. As much as her heart broke for Aunt Vickie and Uncle Davis, she couldn't help wishing she could magically transport herself back to Indianapolis.

Aunt Vickie wrung her tortured handkerchief. "Clay paid his debt to society and he *is* your blood."

Uncle Davis's voice lowered to an angry growl. "He's a miscreant and a murderer, and I disown him."

At a sound near the doorway, Ella turned her head and her gaze locked with Clay's.

Chapter 2

Clay pressed his thumb on the stopwatch's button as the horse and rider galloped past on the dirt track in front of him. The watch's face blurred in his hand, replaced by another image. Of all the emotions he'd dreamed of seeing in Ella Jamison's eyes when she looked at him, pity was not among them. Guilt at abandoning her when she'd practically begged him to accompany her to the parlor had, against his better judgment, drawn him into Uncle Davis's presence. He had to at least try to rescue her from the uncomfortable situation she'd obviously dreaded by offering her a tour of the farm.

He squeezed the timepiece in his hand as if he might obliterate her expression of minutes earlier now seared into his mind, and swallowed down the wad of emotion gathering in his throat. Uncle Davis's sentiment had not come as a surprise. His uncle had made his feelings clear Clay's first day back at the farm. It was Ella witnessing Uncle Davis's scorn in Clay's presence that had cut to the quick.

"How'd he do?" The exercise jockey's voice yanked Clay from his bitter thoughts.

Clay rested his arm on the top fence rail and managed a stiff smile. "Eight seconds better than yesterday. Looks like he's coming along nicely, but you could turn him loose sooner, I think. He's got more in the tank. I'm sure of it."

The jockey nodded and trotted the horse off toward the barns.

"He's hurting, Clay. I doubt he means it." At Ella's voice Clay's heart bucked like an unbroken colt, and he spun around. His heart bucked again at the sight of her. She'd changed into a brown wool skirt and a blue plaid blouse that matched her eyes.

He prayed his voice would sound casual and that she couldn't hear his heart hammering in his chest. "Yes, he *is* hurting, but he *does* mean it." He had to look away, across the exercise track, to allow him time to get a better grip on his emotions. In a moment, with the Lord's help, he turned back to her, smiling. "Looks like you're ready for your tour."

She grinned and glanced down at her skirt. "Aunt Vickie lent me clothes more suited to touring the farm." Her giggle sounded like music. "The skirt is a bit short, though." She stuck out her brown, ankle-high shoe. "But, if memory serves, that will be a good thing around the barns."

"I expect it will," he said with a laugh that sounded ridiculous. He needed to walk. To his relief, she fell into step beside him.

"Are you training that horse for the derby?" Her gaze followed the diminishing image of the horse and rider.

Clay shook his head, glad that the conversation had turned to a more comfortable subject for him: horses. "No, we don't have a Kentucky Derby entrant this year, but Star Dancer will run in the third race on Derby Day. We do have a yearling I think could be Derby material in a couple of years. Want to see him?"

"Sure." Her smile felt like a sunbeam breaking through the clouds.

As they walked from the exercise track to the barns, the same uncomfortable silence that had grown between them earlier in the car began to build again. He needed to keep the conversation away from Uncle Davis's attitude toward him. "Aunt Vickie tells me that your folks are serving at a mission in New Guinea."

Ella nodded. "Papua."

"So why didn't you go with them?"

The frown that wiped away her smile made him wish he hadn't asked the question.

"Mother and Daddy are cut out for the mission field. Gavin is too, but of course he's in France serving in the army." She shrugged and quirked a weak smile. "I'm kind of the black sheep of the family, I suppose."

Her comment both surprised him and pricked his heart. Half his life, since Ma and Pa died in the train wreck, he'd felt out of place. He'd never imagined that Ella felt the same way. Guilt smote his heart remembering how, as a stupid adolescent, he'd teased her, hoping to win her attention when all he'd accomplished was to earn her disdain and batter her already fragile self-esteem. He opened his mouth to say that they were both black sheep but stopped, fearing it might turn the conversation back to Uncle Davis. Instead he cleared his throat. "So, what do you do in Indianapolis?"

"I'm a court stenographer." Her smile set his heart drumming.

"You're one of those gals who sit in the courtroom and write down what everyone says?"

She nodded. "Using shorthand." A nervous laugh bubbled from her lips. "It was one of the subjects I was actually good at in school."

"Do you like being a stenographer?" A desire to know her better gripped him.

She shrugged. "I suppose I like it all right. With my shorthand skills my choices were to be either a stenographer or a secretary, and I didn't want to be a secretary."

Her melancholy look made Clay want to take her in his arms and tell her she was the brightest, most beautiful creature he'd ever seen, that he'd loved her since he was seventeen, that he'd hardly slept last night knowing he'd be picking her up at Union Station today. But any of that would sound ridiculous at best and scare her off at worst.

The sight of Old Reuben walking toward them saved him from blurting out something embarrassing.

"My, oh my." Old Reuben shook his gray head, and his dark eyes sparkled as they fixed on Ella. "This surely cain't be our li'l Ella. Come here, chil', let Old Reuben git a good look at ya." His grin stretched so wide it nearly smoothed out the wrinkles in his dusky cheeks.

Joy filled Ella's heart as she grasped the old man's dark hands. "It is so good to see you again, Reuben." For the first time since her arrival at Dogwood Farms, tears sprang to her eyes. During her childhood visits to the farm, while the boys roamed the acres of bluegrass pastures, Ella had spent hours with Reuben, watching him tend the horses and listening to his myriad tales of his younger days as a jockey. "You've growed to be a beauty, and that's a fact. Ain't that so, Clay?"

"You know you're always right, Reuben." Clay's voice sounded stiff.

Old Reuben's gaze bounced between Ella and Clay, and an odd look that Ella couldn't decipher flashed across his eyes. The next instant it was gone, and he focused on Clay. "I was 'bout to bring the colt out and exercise that leg."

A relieved look relaxed Clay's features. "Good. We were on our way to visit him."

When Old Reuben had disappeared into the barn, Clay leaned a shoulder against the ancient oak tree in the paddock that Ella had often climbed as a girl to evade his teasing. For a long moment she watched him as he gazed at the barn, his face averted from hers. In repose he lost all resemblance of the mischievous boy who'd delighted in tormenting her. Clad in an ivory cable-knit sweater, faded jeans, and black boots, he looked every inch a man, and a handsome one at that.

A gust of wind played through his red curls that peeked out from beneath the short brim of his gray wool cap, and Ella felt a flutter in her chest. Beyond his good looks, something else about him stirred even deeper emotions in her. His gray eyes held a maturity far beyond that of an average twenty-four-year-old. It reminded her of the look she'd seen in the eyes of boys returning from the war. His tanned face exuded a quiet strength. The many freckles that had covered his features in youth were now gone except for a few light splotches over his nose and under his eyes. Her gaze strolled over his well-shaped lips. *Would they feel as strong and gentle as they looked against—*

"There they are." Clay pushed away from the tree and shot her a smile that sent her heart somersaulting.

Yanked from the startling thoughts skittering through her mind, Ella struggled to regain both her equilibrium and her breath. Somehow she willed her rubbery legs to follow him to Reuben and the young horse.

The late afternoon sun shone on the withers of the handsome dark bay yearling with a black mane, tail, and lower legs. A white horizontal slash on his forehead reminded her of the word *can* in shorthand. The colt shook its head, neighed, and began prancing in a circle around Old Reuben, who held its tether.

"Game's Afoot," Clay murmured, and stuffed his hands in his pockets.

"Excuse me?" Ella shifted her focus from the colt to Clay, and her face warmed when she found him staring at her instead of the horse.

Clay chuckled. "Game's Afoot. That's his name. He should make it to Derby in a couple of years if I do my job right."

Ella giggled. "Aunt Vickie must have named him. I think she's read every one of the Sherlock Holmes mysteries."

"And she sent them all to me during the three years I was. . .away." His voice faded.

Ella focused back on the colt, unwilling to wade into the subject of Clay's imprisonment.

Despite a decided limp, Game's Afoot held his head high as if aware of his worth.

Ella frowned. "I thought you said he could be Derby material. He limps." She began to wonder if Clay *did* know his job.

Clay's smile turned indulgent. "Just a little soreness in his right front leg. Nothing serious." His grin gave her the uncomfortable feeling that he could read her thoughts.

Old Reuben nodded his grizzled head. "This one's special. He's got a sweet disposition and a noble heart. The heart of a Thoroughbred." His dark gaze locked onto hers. "That there's a rare combination, missy."

Ella got the distinct impression that Old Reuben's comment encompassed more than the colt.

The old groom's words replayed often in Ella's mind as she endured Jared's funeral and all that went with the solemn event. The visitation passed in a near blur. Somehow, she managed to mutter appropriate responses to those who came to pay their respects. In the moments when she felt overwhelmed or awkward, her gaze searched, unbidden, for Clay. Each time, he met her look with an encouraging smile or wink that lent her strength. It hurt her heart to see how Uncle Davis went out of his way to avoid Clay. She also noticed several instances of guests huddling together in whispering groups, casting both wary and curious glances at Clay. Marveling at how unfazed he appeared in the face of the obvious snubs, Ella wished she possessed his serenity. His head held high, he reminded her of the Thoroughbreds he trained.

The afternoon of the funeral Ella followed Uncle Davis and Aunt Vickie up the steps to the mortuary. Clay, dressed in a handsome black suit, fell in step beside her. He slipped his arm around hers to help her up the steps then bent and, in a whispered voice, reiterated the words he'd said two days ago in her aunt and uncle's front hallway. "You can do this, Ella. You're stronger than you think."

During the minister's remarks Clay sat with his head bowed and his lips in silent movement as if in prayer, a sight Ella found bewildering.

Later, his presence beside her in the backseat of the Auburn on their way to the cemetery felt at once comforting and encouraging.

"Just a little longer," he whispered as he helped her from the car.

His strong arm lent both physical and moral support as they wended their way through the cemetery to the newly dug grave.

When they lowered the casket into the rectangular hole, Aunt Vickie began to softly sob. Clay handed her a clean handkerchief, earning him an angry glare from Uncle Davis.

To Ella's amazement Uncle Davis, who'd earlier seemed on the verge of collapse, stood dry eyed and stoic through the minister's final words and the military presentation of the folded American flag.

As the crowd dispersed, Clay and Ella followed Aunt Vickie and Uncle Davis from the graveside. Uncle Davis took three steps toward the car, stumbled, and collapsed to the ground.

Chapter 3

I t seems he has suffered a stroke."

A man's voice broke into Clay's silent prayer, and he jerked his head up.

Aunt Vickie sat up from Ella's embrace and emitted a gasp followed by a sob.

"I'm so sorry. I'm Dr. Patterson, by the way." The middle-aged doctor in a white lab coat reached out a hand to Clay.

Clay shook the doctor's hand while trying to process his words. "How bad is it?"

The doctor shook his head. "We don't know yet—won't until he wakes up."

"Will he. . .will he survive?" Aunt Vickie's tremulous voice ripped at Clay's heart.

Dr. Patterson stepped to Aunt Vickie and put a hand on her shoulder. "His heart seems strong, Mrs. Garrett. I'd say his chances for survival are good." He gave her an encouraging smile. "We've called your family physician, Dr. Malloy. He will oversee your husband's care, but I'd say if Davis has no further episodes, he should be able to return home in a couple of days to convalesce."

"Thank you, Doctor." Clay shook the doctor's hand again, his mind spinning with the realization that the operation of Dogwood Farms now lay on his shoulders.

When the doctor left the hospital waiting room, Clay looked over at Ella embracing Aunt Vickie, and his heart swelled. A few golden strands of her hair had pulled loose to brush the shoulders of her black silk frock. She paid no heed to the errant locks as she cradled the older woman's head against her shoulder. Watching Ella take control of a devastated Aunt Vickie at the cemetery, freeing him to deal with Uncle Davis, had felt like watching a flower bloom. The strength he had always sensed in Ella now shone along with the sweet, caring heart he'd glimpsed in her as a young girl. His heart throbbed at the sight of her patting Aunt Vickie's hand and even coaxing a smile from the older woman.

Aunt Vickie looked up at him, her red-rimmed eyes dry. "I'll stay here with Davis. You need to go back home, Clay. The farm needs you. The derby is a few short weeks from now and Star Dancer has to be ready." She looked at Ella. "You go home with Clay, dear. He can take you to Union Station tomorrow."

Ella shook her head. "I'm not going anywhere, Aunt Vickie. My place is here with you until Uncle Davis is well again." Her lovely face held a look of determined resolve. She smiled at Clay, and he had to fight the urge to rush over and take her in his arms.

With a tornado of emotions swirling in his chest, Clay crawled back to the mercy seat of the Lord. *Lord, I know Your ways are mysterious. Please save Uncle Davis and use his illness to build Ella's confidence and reveal the purpose You have for her.*

Clay's prayer remained the same a week after Uncle Davis returned home wheelchair-bound, the left side of his body paralyzed.

"How is he?" Clay's heart leaped at the sight of Ella exiting Uncle Davis's sickroom. As if in answer to his prayer, he'd watched her confidence grow. Over the past week she'd become indispensable to the Garrett household. If not for her tireless work, Clay had no doubt that Aunt Vickie would have collapsed from exhaustion by now.

"Sleeping, thankfully." Her lovely lips tipped up in a grin. "He keeps insisting he wants to see the horses, so that is a good sign I suppose." The dark smudges that shaded the skin beneath her blue eyes concerned Clay.

"So when will you sleep?" While he admired her commitment to Aunt Vickie and Uncle Davis, he'd begun to worry about her health.

She gave him a tired smile. "Maybe after I wash the linens and go over tomorrow's menu with Gwen." Her shrug gave him no confidence that she would actually rest.

A frustrated sigh puffed from Clay's lips, and he took her hand in his. "I know you feel it's your duty to help, Ella, and I don't know how Aunt Vickie could have managed all this without you. Maybe this is God's purpose for you. I have no doubt that all that has happened is part of His greater plan, but—"

"Oh!" She yanked her hand from his, and her brows lowered in a scowl. "I am so sick and tired of hearing how God has a plan for all the awfulness happening in the world! The world is on fire, Clay. Jared is dead and Uncle Davis is half-paralyzed. My own brother could be lying dead this very minute in some filthy, godforsaken trench on the other side of the ocean. My parents could be dead or dying for all I know. So if there even *is* a God, I'm not sure I care to have anything to do with Him!"

She stalked off, leaving Clay feeling like Jack Dempsey had used his heart as a punching bag.

Remorse smote Ella as she neared the barns. Clay didn't deserve the lambasting she'd given him earlier. Since Uncle Davis's stroke Clay had shouldered the business of running the farm on top of his duties as trainer. That he cared enough to take time to inquire about her health touched a deep, sweet place in her heart. She had to find him and apologize for her outburst.

She poked her head into the first barn she came to. The pungent scents of horses, hay, and manure stung her nose as her eyes adjusted to the building's dim interior.

"Miss Ella." Old Reuben emerged from a nearby stall carrying a bridle. A worried look pulled his wrinkled face longer. "Is Mr. Davis worse?"

Ella forced her lips into a weak smile. "No, no, Reuben. He's resting right now, but he keeps badgering Aunt Vickie to wheel him out here to the barns in his wheelchair, so that's encouraging."

Old Reuben gave his grizzled head a sad shake. "I feared Mr. Davis might have an apoplectic fit when I heard that young Mr. Jared had passed." He shook his head again and glanced in the direction of the house. "Mr. Davis thought the sun rose and set on that boy o' his. Blinded him to. . ." He glanced down then looked back up, giving her a sheepish grin. "Pay no mind to me, jist an old man prattlin' on."

"Have you seen Clay? I need to talk to him." The need to unburden her heart to someone gripped Ella. "I said some things to him that I shouldn't have." She gave Reuben a feeble smile. "Overtired, I guess."

Old Reuben brought a chair from beside an empty stall, dusted it off, and motioned for her to sit. When she'd sat, he dragged a three-legged stool from the front corner of the barn and set it across from her chair. He sat and pulled a scrap of oily-smelling flannel from his shirt pocket and began rubbing it along the leather bridle. "Clay's workin' with Star Dancer right now." He glanced out the barn door toward the exercise track. "He'll be back d'rectly. Till then, you sit and rest a spell and visit with Old Reuben." He grinned and went back to rubbing the oily flannel along the leather bridle.

"I don't remember Clay being especially religious as a boy. When did that happen?" Ella had no doubt that Reuben could answer the question chasing around in her mind.

"In prison." Old Reuben kept his eyes on his work. "Ms. Vickie gave him a Bible when he went in." He sent her a glancing grin. "He said it's what got him through." He stood with a groan, walked to a wooden tack box, and picked up an oil can. The can popped beneath his thumb as he applied more oil to the rag. "Clay even started a Bible study group in prison." He shuffled back to the stool, plopped himself down, and went back to rubbing the leather. "Don't know that I'd call Clay religious, but he's got right close to the Lord, that boy has." He looked up and fixed her with a knowing gaze. "Is the Lord what you and Clay had words about?"

There was no sense in trying to evade the perceptive old groom's question. Ella nodded. She blew out a long sigh. "I got angry when Clay said that all this. . .awfulness is part of God's plan. I scolded him and told him I wasn't sure I wanted to know a God that allowed all the terrible things that are happening in the world."

No hint of shock or disapproval touched Old Reuben's features. Instead a kind smile lifted the corners of his wrinkled mouth. "Why, God don't cause the bad things that happen in the world, man does. God allows it 'cause He's give man the freedom to do as he wishes. Trouble comes when man chooses to do bad instead o' good." He gave her a long look, his grin widening. "You should know that, your pa bein' a preacher'n all."

Ella stifled a groan. "I know, I know. Man brought sin into the world. It just seems that a loving God would step in and stop awful stuff like war and disease."

Old Reuben gave a mirthless chuckle. "Why, if He did that, man wouldn't have no freedom to make his own decisions." His voice lowered a decibel. "We'd all be no better'n slaves."

A finger of shame slithered through Ella, closing her mouth to any retort. Reuben had been born into bondage.

Old Reuben shook his head again. "No, Miss Ella, don't you go blamin' God for the war, Jared dyin' o' lagrippe, or Mr. Davis's apoplexy. This old world ain't heaven, and till we git there we gotta hold on to Jesus' hand. He'll git us through the rough patches and take care of us in this life and in the next. God don't never leave us alone." He shot Ella another piercing look.

"You betcha God cares. Alls ya gotta do is look for His love. It's ever'where. And sometimes when we don't think to look, He'll find a way to get our attention."

"Has something happened? Is Uncle Davis worse?" Clay's voice sounded at the open barn door.

"No, he's the same." Ella's pulse sped as she looked up into Clay's anxious face.

Old Reuben rose from his stool and looked at Clay. "I been treatin' the colt's leg with liniment and his limp seems 'bout gone." His gaze bounced between Clay and Ella, and a slight smile moseyed over his lips. He held the bridle chest high and cleared his throat. "Reckon I best git the rest of the tack oiled." With that he sauntered off through the barn.

"I came to apologize for blowing up at you." Ella had to force her eyes to meet Clay's. "None of it is your fault, and I shouldn't have taken it out on you." She grinned, hoping he couldn't hear her thumping heart. "You're right. I allowed myself to get overtired."

A questioning look crossed his face, and he opened his mouth as if he were about to say something then closed it. He smiled, and his soft gray gaze felt like it reached all the way to her heart. "Apology accepted." A ray of morning sun shafted through the barn door, lighting his features and making the faint freckles over his nose and cheeks more prominent. "You want to come with me to check on Game's Afoot?"

Unable to speak, Ella nodded and followed him down the aisle between the stalls.

"There you are, fella." Clay stopped at the stall where the colt with the white "can" mark on his forehead reached his velvet nose out through the open top of the stall door as if begging for a caress.

Clay obliged, rubbing the colt's face from his forehead to his nose. "Old Reuben says your leg is better, is that right?" He opened the door and went down on his knees in the straw-strewn stall and felt of the animal's right foreleg. "Feels like the swelling's down." He rose and brushed the straw and dust from his jeans. He turned to Ella. "Would you like to pet him? You're not still scared of horses, are you? I remember you were always following Reuben around, but you never wanted to get too close to the horses." A challenge glinted in his eyes.

"No, of course not." Glad her voice had returned, Ella stepped into the stall with Clay and Game's Afoot. She decided not to remind him of the times he'd teased her because she refused to join him, Jared, and Gavin horse-back riding.

Clay reached into his pocket and brought out a handful of sugar cubes. He handed a couple to Ella. "Here, give him these and you'll be his friend for life."

Fear spiked in Ella's chest. After having been bitten by a horse when small, she'd shied away from any close contact with the animals.

"Hold your hand out flat." Standing behind her, Clay reached around and straightened her fingers then slid his hand back to cup her forearm. His touch sent delicious shivers up her arm, and she couldn't say if her pounding heart had more to do with his nearness or her fear of Game's Afoot's teeth. "He won't bite you. I promise." His whispered breath caressed her ear and cheek, and she forgot her fear of the horse.

Game's Afoot's soft muzzle tickled her hand as his rough tongue scooped up the sugar, leaving her with a warm, wet palm.

Ella giggled.

"There. See, you did it." A thick-sounding chuckle rumbled from deep in Clay's throat as he continued to hold her arm.

She turned and found herself in his arms. Their gazes locked, and a shared understanding passed between them. As if in a dream she watched his eyes close an instant before his lips found hers. Time had no meaning as she floated in his arms, luxuriating in his kiss as his lips—stronger and softer than she'd even imagined—caressed hers.

"Reuben, I want to see the horses!" Uncle Davis's slurred voice echoed through the barn, shattering Ella's bliss.

Chapter 4

S tupid, stupid, stupid!"

Clay glared into the washstand mirror, myriad emotions roiling in his chest like boiling water in a teapot. He grabbed the towel, wiped the remnants of shaving cream from his face, and threw it across the room. The action did little to relieve his pent-up frustrations.

"Stupid, stupid!" He reiterated the words that had been running through his brain since this morning when he'd succumbed to the temptation to kiss Ella.

He grabbed the edges of the washstand on either side of the enamel pan filled with dirty water and shaving soap. In the mirror, he watched the muscles working in his clenched jaw. The memory of the fright on Ella's face at Uncle Davis's voice and the way she'd pulled away from him and ran from the stall still slashed at his heart.

Despite the stinging regret he felt for putting her in an awkward situation with Uncle Davis, he couldn't make his heart sorry for the kiss. The sweet memory tortured him.

Thankfully, Old Reuben had appeared and walked with Ella to the front of the barn while Clay remained in Game's Afoot's stall. Uncle Davis and Aunt Vickie assumed Ella had come to the barn to ask Reuben to wheel Uncle Davis out to see the horses.

Clay looked for something else to throw. Finding nothing but his razor, he walked to his bed, sank to the mattress, and buried his face in his hands. *Dear Lord, take this feeling from me.* If he thought Ella didn't care for him, he could face that. Until today she'd seemed unattainable. But the memory of her soft, sweet lips responding to his and her arms holding him tight told him otherwise.

A groan emerged from the depths of his soul. What he'd longed for, dreamed about for seven long years, had become real. Before today he could admire her—love her—from afar without jeopardizing her. Now, for her sake, he had to push her away. As an ex-convict he could offer her no future. The moment Uncle Davis found another trainer he'd fire Clay and order him off the farm with no decent prospects for employment. Also, if Uncle Davis were to discover that Ella cared for Clay, he might disown her as well.

His heart felt like a lump of lead in his chest as he stood and put on a clean shirt. Maybe this was God's way of nudging him toward the notion of returning to the penitentiary as a chaplain—something he'd considered before his release.

Hitching up his courage, he headed downstairs. Mealtime at the Garretts' table had proved tense at best since Clay's release from prison. The noon meal today felt doubly daunting. His heart twisted at the thought of seeing Ella. She'd once considered him a cad. Maybe the best thing he could do for her was to try to make her believe that again. But the moment the thought skittered through his mind he rejected it. He couldn't live with another lie. Beyond that, he needed to show Ella Christ's love and do all he could to strengthen her faith in the Lord. During her angry diatribe he'd seen fear in her eyes, fear that had caused her to question God's love and even His existence.

Okay, Lord, if this is the mission You've given me, show me what to do, how to bring her back to You.

Ella struggled to rein in the smile tugging at her lips as she carried a platter of fried potatoes to the table. Her heart pranced at the memory of Clay's kiss. That in less than two weeks' time she'd gone from wanting to run away from him to wanting to run into his arms seemed incredible.

Aunt Vickie wheeled Uncle Davis into the dining room.

Ella allowed her smile free rein. "You're looking well, Uncle Davis. Hope you're hungry. Gwen and I fried up a chicken and a platter full of potatoes."

Uncle Davis gave her a look as close to a smile as his paralyzed face allowed. "That's my girl. We'll make a southern gal of you yet." His voice, while slurred, seemed to have regained its strength. "I think we'll need to keep you."

When Aunt Vickie rolled his chair up to the table, Ella walked to his side, patted his shoulder, then bent and kissed his cheek. "I'm afraid you and Aunt Vickie are stuck with me, Uncle Davis. I telegraphed the Marion County Courthouse in Indianapolis and told them that I would be staying here for the foreseeable future and not to hold my position."

Aunt Vickie smiled up at Ella as she settled herself in a chair beside Uncle Davis. "And we are delighted to have you, aren't we, dear." She patted her husband's gnarled left hand. "And I'm sure your parents will be relieved to learn you'll be staying with us." She reached for the pitcher of sweet tea and poured herself and Uncle Davis each a glassful. "I posted a letter to your mother yesterday, Ella, telling her all that has. . ." Her voice faltered. She paused and her eyes glistened for a moment before her smile returned. Her chin lifted, and her voice grew strong again. "All that has transpired since your arrival here." She shook her head. "I can't for the life of me imagine what Ruth and Thomas were thinking to allow you to live on your own in that boardinghouse for young women in Indianapolis."

"Ella's not a child anymore, Aunt Vickie. She's a grown woman."

At Clay's quiet voice from the dining room doorway, Ella's heart did a little hop.

"My lawyer mentioned that the courthouse in Lexington is always look-ing for good stenographers," he said as he sauntered into the room. His dark red curls still glistened with water from washing up, and he brought with him the clean scent of shaving soap. His muscular biceps bulged beneath the sleeves of his blue chambray shirt that he'd rolled up to his elbows.

Ella's face warmed at the memory of his strong arms holding her, but it was his lips that drew her gaze. "I seem to find plenty to keep me busy here on the farm, so I doubt I will be looking for another position as a stenog-rapher anytime soon." Her voice sounded strange in her ears, and her eyes refused to meet his.

Clay held out a chair for her, and somehow she managed to walk to it on legs that had turned to Jell-O. As he scooted her chair up to the table his hand grazed her shoulder, sending an electric shock through her.

When Clay had seated himself beside Ella, Aunt Vickie smiled at him. "Clay, would you please say grace?"

Clay nodded and took Ella's and Aunt Vickie's hands. Uncle Davis grunted but took Ella's free hand. Beyond giving thanks for the food, Clay fashioned a prayer to rival Ella's father's most heartfelt petitions. He asked for Uncle Davis's healing, continued comfort at the loss of Jared, and safety for Gavin and Ella's parents across the seas. When he finished the prayer by asking that God might strengthen the faith of all at the table, Ella wondered if that request was for her benefit in particular.

A flash of irritation shot through her as he murmured, "Amen," but she couldn't help admiring the depth of his faith.

She slipped her hand from his and thought she detected a faint, parting squeeze, which set her heart twirling again.

"How is Star Dancer coming along?" Uncle Davis shot Clay a critical glance as he speared a forkful of potatoes.

Uncle Davis's gruff tone and refusal to address Clay by name pained Ella. But at least he'd begun talking to Clay again. Perhaps Ella could use her influence with Uncle Davis to soften his opinion of Clay, who, by all appearances, had turned his life around.

Clay swallowed his bite of fried chicken and washed it down with a sip of sweet tea. "He's shaved six seconds off his best time last week. I think he should at least show."

Uncle Davis snorted. "He's the only horse we have in any race Derby Day. He needs to do better than show." He glared at Clay. "If you can't get him there, I'll find somebody who can."

Clay didn't respond and went back to eating. A part of Ella wished Clay would stand up and rebuke Uncle Davis's abuse, but in light of Jared's death and her uncle's stroke, she understood why he didn't. The verse from Isaiah popped into her mind: *"He was oppressed, and he was afflicted, yet he opened not his mouth."*

Ella's heart crimped. If she could do nothing else beneficial while here at Dogwood Farms, she would try her hardest to convince Uncle Davis of Clay's goodness.

Aunt Vickie dabbed at her mouth with her napkin. "Derby Day *is* just around the corner, Ella. We'll need to get you a new frock and hat for the occasion."

Bewildered, Ella set her glass of tea down with a thump. "But we can't leave Uncle Davis here."

"Who said anything about leaving me?" Uncle Davis gave her a twisted grin. "I haven't missed a derby in thirty years, and I don't plan to start now. Doc Malloy says that with some practice I should be walking with a cane by Derby Day." He appeared to attempt a wink, but both eyes closed. "I intend to escort my two best girls to Derby standing on my own two feet." He pounded his good fist on the table, making his silverware jump with a clink.

Since returning home from his hospital stay, Uncle Davis had begun lavishing extra attention on Ella, treating her more as a daughter than a niece.

It seemed, with Jared's passing, he needed an outlet for his paternal attention and had latched on to her to fill that role, which, in her mind, should belong to Clay. Though uncomfortable with the favored attention, Ella feared any rebuke might hamper her uncle's recovery.

An idea flashed into her mind as if someone had switched on an electric lamp. If she could sweet-talk Uncle Davis into allowing Clay to assist her in helping him stand and walk with a cane, maybe she could use her favored status to soften her Uncle's heart toward Clay.

When they'd finished their meal and Aunt Vickie got up and prepared to wheel Uncle Davis out of the dining room, Ella jumped up and hurried to them. "All right, Uncle, if you're going to escort Aunt Vickie and me to the derby, you need to get out of this chair."

"Right now?" Aunt Vickie blinked.

The sadness in Uncle Davis's eyes smote Ella's heart. "I don't know, sweetheart. I'm not sure I can get up by myself yet, and you're not strong enough—"

"Of course I'm not." Ella lifted Uncle Davis's weak arm and laid it across her shoulder. "But Clay is strong enough and he can help."

Clay smiled and gave her a look so sweet it took her breath away, and she wondered if he'd guessed what she was up to. "Sure, I'd be glad to help." He rushed to the right side of Uncle Davis's wheelchair.

Uncle Davis scowled and emitted a sound like a growl. When Clay reached out to help him up, he batted at him with his good hand. "I was wrong. I can get up myself with Ella's help."

Aunt Vickie frowned and fisted her hands on each side of her waist. "No you cannot! Now quit being contrary, Davis, and let the boy help you."

Uncle Davis let out another growl but allowed Clay to help lift him from the chair. Together Ella and Clay managed to walk him the length of the dining room then back to the wheelchair.

When they lowered Uncle Davis back into the wheelchair, Clay folded his arms over his chest and grinned. "Well done! If we do this several times a day from now until the eleventh of May, I'd say you'll be ready to walk with a cane on Derby Day."

Uncle Davis gave a peevish snort. "And you think Willis Kilmer will run that bony gelding Exterminator in the derby. Shows how much you know."

Ella's heart pinched at the scorn, but Clay laughed. "We'll see, Uncle. We'll see."

Over the next six weeks Ella and Clay worked with Uncle Davis three times a day, encouraging him to take more steps every day. In mid-April, Ella and Aunt Vickie drove into Lexington to shop for new frocks and hats for Derby Day, and Aunt Vickie purchased a walnut wood cane with a carved horse-head handle for Uncle Davis. By the end of April he could walk as far as the nearest barn with the help of his cane. Early on derby morning he managed to get himself into the front seat of the Auburn with minimal help from Clay.

"I'm in, I'm in." Grumbling beneath his breath, he gave a huff and settled into the front passenger seat beside the driver he'd hired to drive them the eighty miles to Louisville. "You just see to it that Star Dancer gets to Churchill Downs in time for the third race."

"Don't worry, Uncle. I'll have him there in plenty of time for the race." Clay shut the door and hurried to help Ella and Aunt Vickie into the car's backseat.

As always, Clay's touch sent Ella's pulse racing. She murmured her thanks and followed Aunt Vickie into the car as quickly as her wide-brimmed hat allowed. Once again she felt the now familiar twinge of disappointment that, since the kiss in Game's Afoot's stall, Clay had made no further romantic overtures toward her. It hurt to think he regretted the sweet moment they'd shared. Also, her attempt at softening Uncle Davis's feelings toward Clay seemed a dismal failure.

She gazed at the drops of moisture on the clear ovals of the car's side curtains, her spirit as gloomy as the day. Perhaps it was just as well. However sweet, however good a man Clay had become, she had to question the wisdom of pursuing a relationship with an ex-convict. And with Uncle Davis back on his feet, she should consider making plans to return to Indianapolis.

"Have a safe trip to Louisville." Clay's gaze touched on Aunt Vickie before settling on Ella's face. His lips tipped up in a smile that set a bevy of butterflies loose in her chest. "Enjoy the derby, Ella. I'll see you there."

Ella managed a smile before Clay shut the door. Her face warmed with her throbbing heart. She brushed misting rain from the skirt of her new pink frock and hoped Aunt Vickie didn't notice any heightened color in her cheeks. Her heart pinched. Turning her back on Clay Garrett would be neither easy nor painless.

"Sorry your first derby is a rainy one, Ella," Uncle Davis said as the driver started the car and they began rolling down the long lane. "Jared would have liked this weather, though. He always loved a rainy day at the track." His voice turned thick as it always did now when he spoke of his dead son. He gave a sad chuckle. "From the time he was little, he loved to see the mud flying up from the sloppy track as the horses raced down the homestretch so covered with mud you couldn't tell the color of the horses or the riders' silks." He emitted a soft sob that broke Ella's heart.

Seated behind him, she patted his shoulder and glanced over at Aunt Vickie, who dabbed at her eyes with her handkerchief. Ella realized she couldn't begin to think about leaving Dogwood Farms until her aunt's and uncle's grief had lessened.

The two-and-a-half-hour road trip passed quicker than Ella would have thought possible, filled with Uncle Davis's and Aunt Vickie's reminiscences of past Kentucky Derbies.

Aunt Vickie chuckled as the twin spires atop Churchill Downs came into view. "Davis, do you remember the 1905 derby when Clay and Jared were twelve and ten and snuck into the barns to see the horses?"

"I had to do some fast-talking or we'd all have been thrown out of the Downs." Uncle Davis's voice turned gruff. "That boy was trouble from the minute he came under our roof."

Sadness squeezed Ella's heart at Uncle Davis's disparaging comment about Clay. She was glad when the driver brought the car to a stop.

Over the next few hours the sights, smells, and sounds overwhelmed Ella's senses. From taking in the crowds of people all dressed in their derby finest, sampling treats sold by roving vendors, and thrilling to the sounds of the bugler calling the horses to post, the experiences of Churchill Downs on Kentucky Derby Day swirled around Ella.

She found herself scanning the crowd for red-haired young men wearing gray tweed caps, but her search always ended in disappointment. She considered asking her aunt and uncle where Clay might be but decided against it, fearing her question might invite another mean comment from Uncle Davis.

When the bugler played call to the post for the third race, Ella strained to see past the crowd to the horses prancing onto the muddy track. She saw a horse that looked like Star Dancer, but the man leading it didn't have red hair.

"Mind if I watch the race with you?"

At Clay's voice Ella's heart vaulted to her throat. "N—no." She could scant hear her squeaky voice over her thudding heart.

"Glad to see you made it all right." He gave her the lopsided grin she'd come to love, and his eyes, as soft and gray as the clouds scooting across the sky above them, twinkled into hers. "Are you enjoying the derby?" His always ruddy complexion seemed even deeper in color. As much as she'd like to attribute it to her presence, the brisk breezes were likely the cause.

"I do believe Ella is thoroughly enjoying the derby," Aunt Vickie said, craning her head around Ella to smile at Clay.

Uncle Davis didn't acknowledge Clay's presence but kept his gaze focused on the horses lining up on the track.

"They're off!"

Ella jumped at the announcer's voice and felt Clay's strong, warm fingers wrap around hers. With her heart pounding like the hooves of the horses circling the muddy track, she looked up at Clay expecting to meet his return gaze. But his focus seemed glued to the thundering animals racing around the track, nearly obscured in a shower of mud.

"Come on, come on," Clay whispered. The muscles along his jaw looked taut. When the horses rounded the far turn, he closed his eyes for a moment and mouthed something that Ella read as "Please Lord, let him do it."

Halfway down the homestretch the horse that looked like Star Dancer carrying the jockey wearing Dogwood Farms' yellow and blue silks pulled ahead of the pack. When he crossed the finish line ahead of the other horses, Clay jumped up and let out a loud whoop. The next instant Ella found herself lifted off her feet and swung around while Aunt Vickie clapped and cheered.

Uncle Davis, who'd made no sound, looked over at Clay as he set Ella back down on trembling legs. "Enjoy the win, boy. I just hired a new trainer."

Chapter 5

C lay didn't want to like Jake Teague, but he could find nothing to dislike in the easy smile and pleasant face of the man walking toward
them.

Uncle Davis fisted the horse-head handle of his cane and nodded at the
young man who'd joined them in the stands. "Jake here is the son of the late
Mick Teague, a legend in Kentucky horse training."

Clay experienced a flash of admiration in spite of himself. He had indeed
heard stories of the great Mick Teague and the many winning Thoroughbreds he'd trained.

Uncle Davis gave Jake the beaming smile he used to reserve for Jared.
"He's a bona fide war hero too. Aren't you, son?"

"Don't know about that." Jake's gaze skittered off to the milling crowd.

Clay noticed the empty cuff of Jake's right sleeve and felt a pang of sorrow. The sight also left him unsure as to how to greet the man.

"This is Clay Garrett." Uncle Davis cleared his throat as if Clay's name
left a bitter taste in his mouth. "You'll be working with him. . .for the time
being, anyway."

Jake held out his good left hand.

Clay grasped it with his own left hand. "It'll be an honor to work with
you. Like Uncle Davis said, your father is a legend."

"Well, I'm not my father." Jake looked uneasy and glanced around the
crowd again.

"What branch of service were you in?" Ella's bright voice gave Clay a
slight jolt.

"Army. Eleventh Engineers under General Pershing."

"Oh." The excited lilt in Ella's voice sparked a flash of jealousy in Clay's
chest. "My brother, Gavin Jamison, is serving in the Fourteenth Engineers
under Pershing. Did you meet Gavin?"

"Sorry, ma'am." Jake's smiling gaze rested on Ella's face far too long for Clay's liking. He gave a shy shrug. "Didn't really know anyone in the Fourteenth, but I wasn't there too long."

Uncle Davis introduced Jake to Aunt Vickie and Ella, putting his arm around Ella. "Ella is Vickie's niece, but she's beginning to feel more like a daughter to us."

Jake shook Ella's hand. "It's a pleasure to meet you, Ella." His smiling gaze lingered on her face.

Clay hated the jealousy sizzling in the pit of his stomach. Despite Jake's horse training pedigree, his war-hero status, and his missing hand, Clay might have found a reason to dislike him after all.

A week later, Clay still fought the jealousy Jake's presence on the farm evoked in him—and he knew why. Ella seemed to take special interest in Jake, plying him with myriad questions about his time in the army. While Clay understood her desire to learn more about what Gavin was experiencing overseas in the war, he couldn't help disliking that she spent so much time with the new trainer.

As he approached the barns, the sound of Ella's laughter chewed through his heart like a serrated knife.

I know, I know, Lord. Envy rots the bones.

Still, he couldn't expunge the ugliness curdling in his gut at the sight of Ella sitting on an upturned barrel and gazing spellbound at Jake as he spun his latest army yarn.

"You should'a heard the sarge holler when he opened up the kit bag and all the mice jumped out." Jake raised his arms. "He threw that kit bag so high the Huns shot it three times before it hit the ground."

Ella's appreciative laugh sent another line of irritation zipping through Clay.

"Have you exercised the gray filly today, Jake?" Clay didn't try to blunt his sharp tone. While Jake seemed to know his way around Thoroughbreds, he often seemed more interested in talking to Ella than working.

Jake turned toward Clay and cleared his voice. "Uh, I was about to do that."

"Now is as good a time as any." Clay clipped the words and raised his brows to emphasize his point. "And pay special attention to her left back leg. She seemed to be favoring it."

"Will do, boss." Jake gave Clay a lazy smile that sent renewed irritation scratching down his spine. Jake touched the stub of his right arm to his forehead in a handless salute before sauntering off into the barn's interior.

Ella frowned. "Jake was working. He just stopped to tell me a funny story. You don't have to be so nasty to him. He did lose his hand fighting for our country. If you're afraid he'll take your job, Aunt Vickie told me she won't let Uncle Davis fire you."

Clay couldn't help emitting a scornful snort at her naïveté. "Aunt Vickie's influence only goes so far. Uncle Davis does what he wants, and he has the final say."

Ella's frown deepened, and she fisted her hands on each side of her trim waist. "I don't know why you take Uncle Davis's abuse, Clay. You're a good trainer. Star Dancer won his race, and you even called the derby winner right. No one else seemed to think Exterminator had a chance. Even if Uncle Davis did fire you, you could just get a job on another farm."

The last thing Clay wanted was to quarrel with Ella, but like a car's engine stuck on full throttle, he couldn't stop himself. He crossed his arms over his chest, cocked his head at her, and allowed his voice to go as dry and brittle as a locust's shell. "And just who do you think would hire an ex-convict?"

Her blue eyes glistened with moisture, and her voice flattened. "Maybe you should have thought about that before you drugged that horse."

She stomped off, leaving Clay feeling as if she'd trodden over his heart with cleats.

Ella sniffed and patted her wet face with a towel. She looked in the mirror and groaned. After giving in to a half hour of gut-wrenching sobs, no amount of washing her face with cool water could clear the redness from her eyes. She still cringed at the memory of her scathing words to Clay. Her chest palpitated with regret, pulling another groan from the depths of her being. Frustration at watching him day after day refuse to stand up to Uncle Davis's shabby treatment had built to the snapping point.

She gazed into the mirror, dismay curling in her belly. Clay had spent three years in prison paying for his mistake. Every day Uncle Davis refused to forgive Clay, throwing his past offense back into his face. Clay didn't need Ella's censure as well. She cared for Clay. Despite all attempts to convince herself otherwise, she couldn't deny her growing feelings for him.

Expelling a deep, ragged breath, she headed downstairs. Red eyes or no red eyes, she wouldn't sleep tonight if she didn't apologize and, once again, beg his forgiveness for her thoughtless, hurtful words.

When she reached the barn that housed Game's Afoot, she scanned the aisles of stalls but saw no telltale splash of red hair. Old Reuben had mentioned that Clay used the little walled-off cubby near the front of the barn as an office.

She poked her head into the narrow opening that led into the space. Clay wasn't there, but curiosity drew her into the cramped room. Sunlight shafted through ill-fitting boards on the barn walls and spilled in bright stripes across a dusty, cluttered desk and a three-legged stool.

Her gaze scanned the desk's littered surface and settled on an incongruous object amid the smudged papers and stubs of pencils. A picture of Clay, looking much as she remembered him when she'd visited the farm seven years ago, smiled up at her from an oak frame. Splattered with mud, he held what looked like a newborn colt in his arms.

Ella picked up the frame for a better look and noticed something scrawled across the bottom of the picture. She turned the picture at an angle and read *Clay and Prince's Ransom* written in Aunt Vickie's distinct handwriting. The horse's name sounded familiar. The memory suddenly flooded back, jarring her. Prince's Ransom was the name of the horse involved in the doping incident that had sent Clay to the penitentiary. That he would keep such a painful reminder seemed incredible.

"My, how he loved that colt."

Ella whirled around at Old Reuben's soft voice from the doorway. Heat surged to her face, and she hurried to set the picture back on the desk. "I didn't mean to snoop. I was looking for Clay and. . ." Her itching curiosity begged to be scratched. "Why would he keep a picture of the horse that—"

"I told ya." Old Reuben's expression turned as close to impatient as he ever got. "Prince's Ransom was Clay's horse." He grinned. "He helped birth that colt and even slept in the barn with it the first night of its life to make sure it thrived."

Ella remained confused. "But if he loved the horse as much as you say, why would he have put it in danger by doping it?" She remembered her mother saying that the horse damaged itself so badly in the incident it had to be destroyed. "Was he that desperate for money?"

Old Reuben gave a deep chuckle. "Don't think money ever mattered a whit to that boy." He fixed Ella with a piercing gaze, and his dark forehead scrunched up to the texture of a prune. "You're right. Clay never would've done nothin' to hurt that horse. Why, he'd'a hurt hisself b'fore he ever hurt a hair on Prince's Ransom." His gaze narrowed. "Things ain't always what they look like."

Still struggling to untangle the enigma, Ella opened her mouth to question Old Reuben further when the realization struck her like a bolt of lightning, and she gasped. She felt her eyes grow wide. "Clay didn't dope Prince's Ransom, did he?"

Old Reuben's gaze never wavered from hers. "Like I said, he never would'a done nothin' to hurt that horse."

"So if Clay didn't do it, who did?" The moment the question left her mouth the answer hit her like a physical blow. "Jared."

Chapter 6

I'm sorry, Clay. I shouldn't have said what I did about you doping the horse."

At Ella's voice Clay froze in his work with the pitchfork cleaning out the stall. His heart, far sorer then his back, wouldn't allow him to look at her. While he realized that frustration had sparked her scathing comment, the words had stung. He shoved the pitchfork into another pile of manure-rich straw, his conscience warring with his ego.

Yes, Lord, I know. Forgive and you shall be forgiven.

His conscience won the battle. "You seem to say 'I'm sorry' a lot." He pitched another forkful of soiled straw into the wheelbarrow and couldn't help grinning when, out of the corner of his eye, he noticed her step back.

"I'm afraid I have a temper. I say things before I think." The anguished remorse in her voice plucked hard at his heartstrings.

He continued to work, now managing sideways glances at her. "I know. I used to love goading you just to see you get mad." The desire to look at her grew too strong. He stopped working, propped the pitchfork against the stall wall, and turned to face her. "All right. I forgive you. Happy?"

"But you didn't do it."

An icy bolt shot through his body. Surely she couldn't know. He affected a flippant tone. "Then what do you require to feel forgiven?"

"No, that's not what I meant. You didn't dope that horse, did you?"

Clay felt his lungs constrict. *Please, Lord, let Jake be out at the track exercising Vickie's Pride like I asked him to.* When he could move again, he strode to her and grasped her shoulders. "If you tell that to a soul, then I spent three years in prison for nothing."

Fear flickered in her eyes, and regret pricked his heart.

Clay let go of her. "Reuben shouldn't have told you."

"He didn't. . .exactly." Guilt tinged her lowered voice, and her gaze skittered away from him. "I came looking for you—to say I was sorry—and looked in your office. I saw the picture of you with Prince's Ransom, and Old Reuben told me how you loved him." She looked up at him, her blue eyes welling with tears that gouged at his heart. "Old Reuben didn't have to tell me. I figured it out myself." Her brows pinched together in a look of bewildered pain. "But why? Why did you take the blame for Jared?"

A deep breath whooshed from his lungs. She needed to know, but not here where anyone could walk in and overhear them. "Come, walk with me."

To his relief, she nodded and walked with him out of the barn. A few minutes later they stopped beside the white rail fence that enclosed the pasture where mares grazed with their frolicking colts.

There, in the shade of a dogwood tree, Clay leaned against the fence, resting his arms on the top beam. The horses in the pasture blurred as the painful memories came flooding back. "The spring I was twelve, my folks left me here and took an extended anniversary trip out West. Somewhere west of St. Louis their train derailed and they were killed."

"I remember my mother telling me about it." Ella's touch caressed his arm as her compassionate voice caressed his heart.

"My mother was an orphan and Uncle Davis was my father's only living relative. Uncle Davis and Aunt Vickie didn't have to take me in." He swallowed down the wad of emotion gathering in his throat. "I remember the authorities coming here to the farm. They offered to take me to an orphanage in Louisville, the city where I'd lived with my folks."

Clay glanced at Ella, and his heart warmed at the tears slipping down her lovely cheeks. He paused to get a better grip on his emotions. In the intervening silence a horse neighed and somewhere nearby a blue jay squawked.

The details of the day twelve years ago when he learned that his life had changed forever came rolling back. "I remember Uncle Davis telling the woman from the orphanage that he wanted to keep me. He said I was the only thing he had left of his brother."

He looked at Ella, and the passion he'd felt all those years ago rose in his chest again. "I wouldn't have stayed in that orphanage. I'd have lived on the Louisville streets first."

"I'm glad you didn't have to." Ella's hand caressed his back, and Clay fought the urge to turn and take her in his arms.

"They gave me a good home—a good life. They didn't have to take me in. I owe them." He couldn't help grinning. "But there was never a question as to which boy was theirs, especially with Uncle Davis."

"I always thought Uncle Davis spoiled Jared." Ella stepped to the fence, leaned against it, and looked out at the horses in the pasture. "Old Reuben said Uncle Davis thought the sun rose and set on Jared."

Clay nodded at the accurate description. "Yeah, that was pretty much how it was." He turned and pressed his back against the fence boards. "What happened with Prince's Ransom about killed me." His voice reflected his remembered anger. "When Jared came to me crying and confessing what he'd done and saying he didn't know how to tell the old man, I knew it would kill Uncle Davis to find out. Oh." A mirthless laugh worked its way out of his throat. "I wanted to pound Jared to a pulp."

Not wanting Ella to see the tears gathering in his eyes, he turned away again. "I knew Jared wouldn't survive prison and it would destroy the old man. Aunt Vickie too. If Uncle Davis thought that I drugged the horse he'd be angry, but he could live with it. So"—he held his hands out—"I told them I did it. I was charged with reckless homicide, but because of my age I got off with only three years in prison."

"It seems so unfair. It's you who should be angry with Uncle Davis, not the other way around." Ella's voice trembled with indignation.

"Do you remember the name of the derby winner that year, 1915?"

She shook her head.

"Regret." He couldn't stifle a sardonic snort. "Once I made my decision to take the blame, I decided there would be no regret."

"And you still feel that way after. . .everything you went through?" Her words tiptoed out as if testing the air. They evoked a plethora of dreadful images he shook his head to dislodge.

"Yes."

"But now that Jared is dead, Uncle Davis and Aunt Vickie should know the truth. Uncle Davis wouldn't have such hard feelings toward you and—"

"No!" Clay turned toward her. He had to make her understand. "The only thing holding Uncle Davis together is his pride in Jared's memory. I can't destroy that. It would kill him."

He took hold of her arms and gazed into the watery blue depths of her eyes. "Please, Ella, you have to promise me that you'll keep my secret. Uncle Davis and Aunt Vickie can never know what Jared did, or I spent three years in prison for nothing. Promise me you won't tell. This has to be our secret."

She nodded, sending relief sluicing through him. The tension in his muscles drained away, leaving him feeling limp.

"I promise I won't tell." Her sweet smile started a deep ache below his breastbone. "But I also promise to do all I can to convince Uncle Davis that, as a Christian, he needs to forgive you."

Thank You, Lord! He struggled to control the grin tugging at his lips. "I knew your faith was still in there somewhere."

The tiny crease of a beginning frown etched between her eyes. A freshening breeze played with a sunny tendril of her hair that had pulled loose from the bun behind her head, blowing it across her furrowed brow.

Clay couldn't resist the urge to reach out and smooth the errant lock from her face. "Whether you know it or not, God is working through you, Ella. You've reminded me that I need to ask for someone's forgiveness as well."

Her smile ironed out the frown lines between her brows. "I'm glad you didn't do it, Clay." She reached out and gave his hand a gentle squeeze then turned and headed in the direction of the house.

For a long moment Clay watched her, the ache beneath his breastbone deepening. *Lord, if there is any way she can be mine, let it happen. If not, help me to accept that.*

Expelling a deep sigh, he headed to the exercise track in search of Jake.

He heard the pounding hooves a moment before he crested the hill and caught sight of Vickie's Promise racing down the stretch in a gray blur with Tim, the exercise boy, aboard. Jake lounged against the white rail fence with a stopwatch in his good left hand. As always, the sight of his empty sleeve cuff jarred Clay, and as always, the jolt accompanied a flash of sorrow.

"She's looking good, Jake. What's her time?" Clay forced a casual tone to his voice.

"She's better by four seconds over yesterday." Jake pushed up his cap with the stub of his wrist. A gust of wind caught the cap, snatching it from his unruly shock of brown hair.

Clay bent and picked up the cap and held it out to Jake, who hurried to pocket the watch so he could take the hat.

"I'm sorry I was short with you earlier." Clay shook his head. He needed to do better than that. "Actually, I haven't treated you right since you came to work on the farm. I've come to say I'm sorry and ask your forgiveness."

Jake blinked, his hazel eyes growing wide with bewilderment. A lazy smile crawled across his mouth. "Why shoot, you're not half as tough as most of my sergeants were. Reckon I got used to being barked at in the army."

Clay couldn't allow Jake to let him off that easy. "Well, it wasn't right, and I'm here to ask your forgiveness."

Jake gave an unconcerned shrug and chuckle. "Sure, if it makes you feel better, I forgive you."

"It does." Clay reached out his hand and Jake gave it a strong, quick shake.

Jake's smile faded. "I'm not here to take your job, Clay. I understood I'd be working under you as assistant trainer, not replacing you."

Clay shook his head. "It's not that I thought you were after my job." He gave a mirthless chuckle. "Shoot, Uncle Davis threatens to give me the boot on a daily basis." He looked down. This confession was harder than he'd thought, but Jake deserved to know why he'd acted like such a heel. "The truth is I was jealous of the time you and Ella have been spending together."

Jake gave Clay a sly grin. "I kinda thought that's the way it was." His grin widened. "She's a looker, that's for sure." He turned his attention toward Vickie's Pride prancing along the track, cooling down. "If things were different, you can bet I'd do my best to win her affection." He looked at Clay. "But even if I wanted to, I reckon that train's left the station." He grinned. "I've seen how she looks at you. Her heart's settled." His grin faded, and he turned his focus back to the track. His eyes took on a distant look, and his voice lowered to a near whisper. "And mine is too."

Surprised curiosity muscled aside Clay's joy at Jake's assessment of Ella's feelings. He rested his shoulder against the fence. "What's her name?"

"Simone Marseau." Jake's quick smile returned, wistful now. "She's French—one of the nurses at the field hospital near Cambrai where they took me after I was wounded." He glanced down at his stump. "We fell in love." He turned his face away, but not before Clay glimpsed moisture in the man's eyes. "She wanted to come back with me to America, but the army wouldn't allow it, and Simone's family didn't have money for her passage." He gave his head a shake. "I'm determined to get her here. That's the reason I took this job. I knew I could live on the farm and save all my wages to buy Simone a ticket on a ship to America."

New respect for Jake sprang up in Clay's chest and, with it, a desire to help the man. He put his hand on Jake's shoulder. "I'll do all I can to help you get your sweetheart over here, Jake. I promise you that."

His eyes still glistening, Jake offered Clay his hand. "I appreciate that, boss." He sniffed then turned and looked eastward. A grin moseyed across his face. "Here comes your lady now."

Clay followed Jake's gaze, and his heart leaped at the sight of Ella striding toward them as fast as her heavy wool skirt allowed. He turned to tell Jake that as much as he wished it so, Ella wasn't his sweetheart, but Jake had already headed toward the barns.

"Clay." The concern on her face—rosy with exertion—sparked alarm in Clay.

He reached out and took her hand to help her up the small rise to the track. "What's the matter, Ella? Has Uncle Davis had another episode?"

Still breathless, she shook her head. "No." She paused to pull in a fresh gulp of air. "It's Game's Afoot. I went to give him his sugar treat, but he wouldn't take it." She grasped his arm, tears welling in her eyes. "He's coughing something awful, Clay. I think he's sick."

Chapter 7

C lay fought the panic tightening around his chest like an iron band as he walked with Ella to the barn. Not since Prince's Ransom had he felt such an attachment to an animal. Something about the mahogany bay yearling had latched on to his heart.

"Could it be influenza?" She raised worried eyes to him. "Aunt Vickie said she heard there'd been hundreds of deaths here in Kentucky."

Clay shook his head. "Horses can't catch influenza from people." As they walked he tried to ease his anxiety by telling himself that Game's Afoot had likely snorted up some dust, causing him to cough, and Ella had overreacted. That hopeful reasoning couldn't fend off the dreaded thought of strangles, a contagious and often deadly lung disease in horses—especially young horses like Game's Afoot.

When they reached Game's Afoot's stall, the last bit of hope in Clay's chest withered. The colt heaved deep, wet coughs. A suspicious bulge along his jaw—the telltale sign of a growing abscess—removed any doubt in Clay's mind about what ailed the colt.

"What's the matter with him?" Cold-fisted dread gripped Ella's chest. Over her three months at the farm she'd witnessed an array of emotions cross Clay's face. Until this moment, she'd never seen fear.

His grim expression poured fuel on her fright. He ran an unsteady hand over his mouth. "Strangles."

"Is that bad?" The words sounded stupid, even to her own ears.

He nodded. "Real bad." His throat moved with a hard swallow.

"He could die?" She forced the words through her constricted throat. Until this moment, she hadn't realized how fond she'd become of the yearling colt. More importantly, Clay loved him. What he'd told her earlier had shredded her heart. Now to have this happen to Game's Afoot after all Clay had gone through seemed beyond cruel.

Clay gave another quick nod. "Yeah, he might. What's worse, if it is strangles, it's extremely contagious." He swallowed again. "If we're not careful, we could lose every horse on this farm." His frown deepened as he looked Ella in the eyes. "I have to tell Uncle Davis."

Ella hadn't considered Uncle Davis, how he might react to the news or how it could affect his fragile health. New concerns sprouted in her chest like thorns. "Oh, Clay, I'm not sure Uncle Davis can stand another blow."

"He's dealt with strangles on the farm before." Clay's stiff smile didn't erase the worry in his eyes.

Another, more troubling thought joined Ella's mounting concerns. What if Uncle Davis blamed Clay for allowing Game's Afoot to get the disease in the first place? Visions of him firing Clay and ordering him off the farm sparked new alarm in her. "I'm going with you." Hopefully, her presence in the room would restrain Uncle Davis from doing anything rash.

Clay put his hand on her shoulder. "You don't have to do this. I can handle—"

"I'm not doing it because I have to. I'm doing it because I want to." She took his hand and let her gaze melt into his. "You've had to handle enough on your own, Clay. This time you won't be alone."

They walked together, hand in hand, to the house. Though dread cinched tighter around her chest with each step, her heart thrilled at the warm strength of Clay's fingers wrapped around hers. His revelation of earlier today had refashioned every opinion she'd ever had of him. The verse from John 15:13 had flashed into her mind: *"Greater love hath no man than this, that a man lay down his life for his friends."* The man holding her hand personified those words. Her heart throbbed with a longing she wasn't yet prepared to name.

Once inside, he let go of her hand, and they shared an encouraging gaze before heading into the parlor where Uncle Davis spent his afternoons reading the newspapers.

"Uncle Davis." Clay pulled off his cap as they stepped into the room together.

Uncle Davis looked up from his paper and peered over the top of his reading spectacles. "What is it?" His bushy brows lowered in the aggravated expression he always wore when greeting Clay.

Clay cleared his throat, and Ella longed to take his hand in hers again but dared not in Uncle Davis's presence. "Ella noticed a problem with Game's

Afoot. It looks to me like strangles."

Uncle Davis's expression turned serious, and he put the paper down. He took his spectacles off, and Ella noticed a slight tremble in his hand, but his voice remained gruff. "It could be something else. We'll need to call Doc Hagyard for a definite diagnosis. But if it is strangles, you'll have to put the horse down."

Stunned and horrified, Ella gasped. She'd never once considered that Uncle Davis might want to kill Game's Afoot. She ran to his side, ignoring the tears now streaming down her face. "No, Uncle, please. You can't kill him."

Uncle Davis gave her a sad, paternal smile and patted her hand. "I'm sorry, sweetheart," he said in his slurred speech. "I know this must be disturbing to you, but these things happen from time to time on a horse farm." He glared at Clay, and his voice lowered to a near growl. "Clay shouldn't have brought you in here. Should have known it would upset you."

Ella crouched beside Uncle Davis's chair. "Please, Uncle Davis." She clutched his hand and raised her sodden face to his. She needed to use every ounce of influence she had with Uncle Davis to save Game's Afoot. "Surely there is another way."

Uncle Davis gave his graying head a sad shake. "You don't understand, sweetheart. Strangles is contagious. I plan to run Vickie's Promise in the Latonia Derby next month. If our farm has strangles, they'd scratch her from the race."

Ella couldn't give up. All his life Clay had had to fight alone. If there was a chance she could save his favorite colt, she had to try her hardest. "Can't we keep Game's Afoot away from Vickie's Promise and all the other horses until he gets well? Please, for me?"

"If Doc Hagyard says it's strangles, the Latonia Derby is gone anyway." Clay's voice sounded remarkably calm considering the turmoil Ella suspected he must feel. "We can't consider taking any of the horses off the farm before the Falls City Handicap at Churchill Downs September 30th."

Uncle Davis's deep sigh and long pause gave Ella hope. "I hate to admit it, but you're right. We've managed before to keep the strangles from spreading with quarantine. I suppose we can do it again."

Ella expelled the breath she hadn't realized she'd been holding.

"All right." Uncle Davis's expression turned stern. "But if one more horse comes down with it, we'll have to destroy them both."

"That won't happen. I won't let it." Clay's determined voice behind Ella made her believe him. "I'll tend to Game's Afoot exclusively. Jake, Old Reuben, and Tim can handle the other horses."

Uncle Davis nodded. "I'll have Vickie call Doc Hagyard. The sooner we know for sure what we're dealing with, the better."

"Thank you, Uncle Davis." Overcome with gratitude, Ella hugged Uncle Davis's neck and kissed his cheek.

He patted her hand then gave her another stern look. "Stay away from the other horses if you've been with Game's Afoot."

Ella nodded and followed Clay out of the room. An hour later they stood together in Game's Afoot's stall as Dr. Hagyard, the veterinarian, inspected the yearling.

At last the doctor, clad in a white coat, rubber apron, rubber sleeves, and rubber boots, patted the horse's neck and turned toward Clay. "I'm sorry to tell you, you are right, lad. It is strangles. Your other horses need to be moved out of this barn, and no horses on or off the farm until I determine that this one is free of the disease." He bounced a stern gaze between Clay and Ella. "Wash up and change into clean clothes before entering the other barns or dealing with the other horses."

Clay nodded. "I've already had all other horses moved from this barn. I will care for Game's Afoot while my staff tends to the other stables."

Ella's gaze slid from the doctor to Clay. "*We* will care for Game's Afoot." Clay needed to know that for once in his life he had an ally.

A smile so sweet it made her chest ache crawled across Clay's lips.

"Good, we need to keep this contained." Dr. Hagyard gave an emphatic nod and headed out of the stall. "When the abscess ruptures, keep the wound cleaned out with alcohol or peroxide. Other than that, all we can do is to wait and see how he does." Outside the barn, he walked to the bench where Ella had earlier left a pan of hot water and soap and began cleaning up. When he'd divested himself of the apron, sleeves, and boots and finished washing his hands, he turned a grim face to Clay. "If the horse gets worse or any more horses show signs of the disease, call the office."

"Will he make it, do you think, Doctor?" Ella managed to articulate the question throbbing in her brain.

Dr. Hagyard gave her a kind smile as he rolled down his shirtsleeves. "Only the Almighty knows the answer to that, lassie, but he seems strong otherwise, so I reckon I'd give him a better than even chance."

When the veterinarian had left, Clay turned from watching the truck roll down the lane. "Ella, I know what you told the doc, but no one expects you to help—"

"But I want to help." She glanced back at the barn. "I love Game's Afoot too. And. . ." Her mind flew back to the kiss they'd shared in the colt's stall, and her gaze refused to hold his. "In a way, I feel like he is *our* horse."

Clay's smile that sent her heart tumbling told her he understood. "Yes, I feel that way too." His brow furrowed. "But this won't be easy and, like the doc, I can't promise he'll—"

"Game's Afoot will make it." She grasped his hand as determination solidified her resolve. "We will pull our horse through this together."

Clay grinned and squeezed her hand. "I wouldn't bet against you."

To her aunt and uncle's chagrin, Ella spent much of June in the barn helping Clay—who'd taken up residence there—care for Game's Afoot. Besides bringing Clay his meals three times a day, she helped to mix and carry buckets of the sloppy mash that Game's Afoot could more easily swallow. She and Clay took turns applying hot compresses to the growing abscess on the colt's jaw until the day it burst, spilling vile-smelling pus over Ella's now red and roughened hands. Fighting back the urge to gag, she'd walked to the bucket of hot water and washed her hands while Clay poured alcohol over the colt's wound. She soaked rags in alcohol to clean the pus from the open sore on Game's Afoot's neck.

As tiring as her days in the barn were, she knew that Clay, who rarely left the yearling's stall, endured near exhaustion. Still, he found the time and energy for prayer. Most mornings when she brought him breakfast she'd find him reading his Bible. Despite her doubt that God listened to prayers or cared to intercede in any earthly concerns, she daily joined Clay in praying for Game's Afoot's recovery. She'd promised to help him care for the ailing colt, so even though her heart wasn't in it, she bowed her head and held Clay's hand in support.

Clay always began his prayer by reciting Matthew 18:20: "For where two or three are gathered in my name, there am I in the midst of them."

Her diminished faith caused guilt to nip at Ella's conscience, and she wondered if she could be counted as one of two gathered in Christ's name. Still she clasped Clay's hand, bowed her head, and joined him in finishing each prayer with a strong "Amen," wishing she possessed a fraction of his faith. In those moments Daddy's voice reciting James 5:16, "The effectual fervent prayer of a righteous man availeth much," rang in her ears, assuaging her guilt. Whether or not God counted her as one of two gathered in His Son's name, Clay's prayer alone should avail, for she'd never met a more righteous man than Clay Garrett.

By the first week of July, Game's Afoot had ceased coughing, the abscess wound had begun scabbing over, and the colt even started taking sugar cubes from Ella's hand again. So when Dr. Hagyard returned to examine the yearling, Ella held her breath waiting for the doctor's verdict. The anxious look on Clay's face suggested that he too watched with bated breath.

Finally the veterinarian gave the colt a pat on the neck and turned toward Clay. His mustache bristled with his smile. "I can find no sign of the disease, and the wound on his jaw is healing nicely. I feel comfortable declaring this farm free of the strangles."

Tears of relief filled Ella's eyes as she expelled the breath she'd been holding.

"Praise God." Clay grasped Ella's hand and gave it a gentle squeeze. His tender gaze set her pulse racing.

While the doctor instructed Clay how to disinfect the stall, Ella walked to Game's Afoot and pressed her face against the horse's neck, something she would never have considered doing four months ago. A happy giggle bubbled from her lips as she ran her hand down the animal's forehead to his velvety nose. "Now I know why you have the word *can* on your face. You can survive the strangles, and one day you can run in the Kentucky Derby."

Game's Afoot replied with what sounded like an affirmative neigh, evoking another giggle from Ella.

"I believe he will." Clay walked to her as the distant sound of the doctor's truck engine sputtering to life wafted into the barn. He took both her hands in his, and his voice thickened with emotion. "Thank you, Ella. I don't think I could have done this without you."

"He's our horse, remember?" Her nervous giggle sounded silly to her ears.

"Yes, he is." Clay let go of her hands and slipped his arms around her waist. His voice lowered to a husky whisper. "You are the most amazing woman I've ever known."

Ella's heart pounded so hard she feared it might beat out of her chest. His gaze held hers in a mesmerizing grip. She felt like she was sinking into the soft gray depths of his eyes until the moment they closed. When his lips met hers, she knew she'd found where she belonged. It was as if she'd slipped into the niche in the universe carved explicitly for her.

At last he let her go, jarring her back to earth. Still holding her hands, he went down on one knee.

"Ella Jamison, I love you. These past weeks have made me realize that I want you—I need you—by my side for the rest of my life. Will you marry me?"

Ella's breath came in short puffs as her spinning brain struggled to grasp what was happening. The man she'd detested four months ago and had now come to adore was asking her to marry him. Joy burst like fireworks inside her chest, unleashing a cascade of tears down her face. Yes, she loved him too. *I love Clay Garrett!* The world might as well have ground to a halt on its axis and begun spinning in the opposite direction. The revelation struck her like a two-by-four across the face. Yet she couldn't deny the truth burning in her chest. Life without Clay had become unimaginable. Knowing she wouldn't have to face such a future made her giddy.

"Well, will you marry me? Will you be my wife?"

The anxious look in his eyes reminded Ella that she'd left her darling on his knee without an answer. She fought to suppress a giggle as the mischievous thought to keep him waiting another moment skittered through her mind, but her head had already begun to nod. "Yes," she managed through a deluge of tears, "I will marry you. I love you so much—"

Clay sprang to his feet, took her in his arms, and smothered her words with his kisses. When he finally let her go, his forehead puckered in a worried frown. "Are you sure? Life with an ex-convict might not be easy."

She smiled up into his troubled gaze. "My mother always told me that everything worthwhile in life is found down rough roads." She cupped his dear face in her hands. "I'm not looking for easy, Clay. I'm looking for worthwhile." Planting a resolute foot on the rougher road, she stepped back from him and grasped his hand. "Come. Let's go tell Aunt Vickie and Uncle Davis our news."

"No." Clay didn't budge at her tug, and his frown returned. "As much as I would love to shout the news of our engagement to the world, you know how Uncle Davis feels about me. If we tell him we plan to marry, he's liable to throw us both off the farm." His frown deepened. "How will I provide for you if I can't get a job?"

Ella couldn't help grinning. "I thought you were the one with the rock-solid faith?"

At his shamefaced expression guilt smote her heart. She took his hands in hers again. "But I agree it might not be a good idea to blurt it to Uncle

Davis out of the blue. We'll need to ease him into the idea gradually."

A look of relief smoothed out the worry lines on Clay's forehead. "So we're agreed, we need to keep our engagement secret for now?"

A shuffling sound drew their attention to the aisle outside the stall where Jake stood grinning.

Chapter 8

Jake held up his hand, palm toward them. "No worries, lovebirds. Your secret is safe with me. Like the flyboys say, I've got your six, I'll protect your back."

"Thanks, Jake." Relief washed through Clay as he reached his hand out to Jake, who took it and gave it a firm shake. "Things between me and Uncle Davis aren't good right now."

Jake nodded. "Old Reuben told me most of it, I reckon." He brought his fist to his mouth and made a turning motion. "My lips are locked, boss. None of my business anyway." His smile returned. "The veterinarian stopped down at the third barn and gave me the good news about the colt."

Clay experienced a rush of gratitude. "And I have you to thank for that, Jake. Game's Afoot might not have made it without round-the-clock tending. If you hadn't been here to take over the training duties, things might not have turned out so well, and Old Reuben tells me you're doing an outstanding job with Star Dancer and Vickie's Promise." He grinned and shook his head in wonder at the merciful hand of God. Jake's hiring, which Clay had viewed as a threat back in May, had proved a blessing. "And we know that all things work together for good to them that love God."

Jake laughed. "You sound like my Simone. She was always reciting scripture to me."

At Ella's puzzled smile Clay told her about Jake's wish to bring his sweetheart to America.

Ella put her hand on Jake's arm. "Oh Jake, I would love to write to Simone if it's all right with you." She grinned. "I'll tell Aunt Vickie about you and Simone and, knowing Aunt Vickie, the minute this awful war is over, she will move heaven and earth to get Simone here."

Jake's eyes turned watery, and his voice thickened. "Thank you, Ella." He flashed a broad smile. "There might be all kinds of weddin' bells ringin' round here."

Ella put her finger to her lips.

Jake held up his hand again. "Not a word, I promise."

As they watched Jake mosey toward the front of the barn, Clay looked down at his beloved, and love and pride filled his chest. "That was very kind of you." He couldn't help chuckling. "I believe you're right about Aunt Vickie. She loves nothing more than championing a cause, and if romance is involved, all the better."

Ella's smile melted his heart like sunshine on a lump of butter. "I'll work on sweetening up Uncle Davis so we can give them our news as well." She cocked her head, and her expression turned thoughtful. "I think I'll begin right now when I tell him the good news about Game's Afoot." Her cute nose wrinkled up in an impish grin. "I'll let him know that he has you to thank for saving Game's Afoot and keeping the disease from spreading to the other horses." She bounced up, hugged his neck, and kissed his cheek. "I'll be back in a bit with your breakfast."

Clay shook his head. He couldn't let her fight for him alone. "Now that Doc Hagyard has declared the farm free of strangles, I'll take my breakfast in the house after Jake and I disinfect this stall and I wash up."

With a parting smile and nod she headed out of the barn.

As he watched her go, doubt and fear gnarled around Clay's heart like choking weeds. *Dear Lord, let me have done the right thing.* He loved her so much, but would love prove enough? He'd spent a sleepless night in prayer petitioning God's guidance as he wrestled with the decision of whether or not he should propose marriage to Ella. He couldn't ask for a better help-mate. He'd marveled at her strength and determination in the face of conditions that would cause most women to faint or flee. Day after day he'd seen her brought to tears by his prayers for the colt's healing.

His heart told him that he and Ella belonged together. He felt certain that the ember of faith still burned within her and, with a breath, the Lord could restore it to a bright flame. But could he trust his heart? As the Lord warned in Jeremiah 17:9, "The heart is deceitful above all things." All night he'd begged God to take away his desire for Ella if she was not the woman he should marry and to give him the strength and peace to turn away from her. The first rays of sun shafting through the cracks in the barn's timbers had found his heart still throbbing with love for her. When he first opened his Bible, his gaze had fallen on Psalm 21:2: "Thou hast given him his heart's desire, and hast not withholden the request of his lips."

At that moment he'd felt God's blessing on his decision to propose to Ella. But now the demons of doubt slinked again from the recesses of his mind. Should he have waited until God repaired Ella's tattered faith before he proposed marriage? What if they married and he found himself unable to provide for a wife whose faith remained tenuous? He prayed he'd made the right choice.

All the way back to the house Ella felt as if her feet never touched the ground. Happiness filled her chest like helium, and she longed to shout the news of her engagement to the world. Keeping her joy corralled seemed an impossible task. Still, she knew Clay was right to insist they keep their engagement secret for now. Uncle Davis's initial grief at Jared's passing had, in recent days, seemed to have abated and, she hoped, with it his anger at Clay.

She stepped into the dining room, unable to suppress the smile that stretched her face so wide it made her cheeks ache. At least she had Game's Afoot's recovery as an excuse for her elation.

Uncle Davis and Aunt Vickie looked up from their breakfast plates. "Well, young lady, have you decided to take your breakfast in here with us instead of in the barn this morning?" Though his tone sounded gruff, Uncle Davis's blue eyes sparkled at the sight of her.

"Game's Afoot is all well," Ella blurted. "Dr. Hagyard left a little while ago. He declared the farm free of strangles."

"Praise the Lord." Aunt Vickie's words puffed out on a relieved sigh.

"That's good news," Uncle Davis mumbled around a bite of scrambled eggs. He gave an approving nod. "By the Falls City Handicap at the end of September there'll be no question as to the health of our horses."

"Thank you for not insisting that Game's Afoot be put down, Uncle Davis." Ella's smile softened. She walked to his side and kissed his cheek.

He patted her hand on his shoulder. "I'm glad he recovered. I've seen plenty that didn't."

Ella sat down in the chair beside him. This was her chance to begin softening his heart toward Clay. "Clay saved him, Uncle Davis. You should have seen him. He was wonderful. He never gave up on Game's Afoot, even when the horse's temperature rose and he took a turn for the worse. And because of Clay's actions, the strangles didn't spread to the other horses."

Uncle Davis frowned, gave a harrumph, and went back to eating his eggs.

Dismay filled Ella at his derisive reaction to Clay's name. She had to try harder. "I do wish you could find it in your heart to forgive Clay as the Lord requires of us, Uncle Davis. He's a good man, and all he wants is a clean start." Ella couldn't stop the tears gathering in her eyes. To her alarm Aunt Vickie, seated at Uncle Davis's other side, perked up and gave Ella a quizzical smile. Ella would need to be more cautious around her astute aunt.

Aunt Vickie patted his gnarled hand. "Ella is right, dear. Since Clay returned home, he hasn't set a foot wrong, and I honestly don't know how we would have managed these past months without him. He at least deserves a chance to show he has changed." She gave Ella a wink and a knowing grin that sparked another flash of alarm. "And you know the preacher's sermon last Sunday was on forgiveness."

Uncle Davis had the grace to look ashamed, buoying Ella's hopes. He huffed out a resigned sigh. "All right, all right. As long as he keeps his nose clean, he'll have a job on the farm." He gave Ella and Aunt Vickie a perturbed frown though his mouth twisted in what now passed as a smile on his paralyzed face. "Now, can a man enjoy his breakfast without being pestered by females?"

Ella giggled and gave him another hug. "I'm sorry, Uncle Davis. I didn't mean to upset your breakfast."

"Speaking of breakfast." Aunt Vickie dabbed at her mouth with her napkin, covering her expression, but Ella noticed a sparkle in her aunt's brown eyes. "Will you be taking Clay his breakfast again this morning?"

Ella shook her head. "No, he said he'd take his breakfast in the house today after he and Jake disinfect Game's Afoot's stall." With the mention of Jake she remembered her promise to tell Aunt Vickie about him and his Simone. Also, news of Jake's sweetheart might keep Aunt Vickie's mind busy, lessening the chance for dangerous speculations about Ella and Clay. "Aunt Vickie, did you know that Jake has a sweetheart in France?"

"Why no, I did not." Aunt Vickie perked up.

Ella told her about Simone and how she had nursed Jake back to health after he was wounded and how the two had fallen in love. "He is desperate to get her to America. Her family can't afford the ship passage. That's why Jake took this job—to earn money for Simone's passage to America."

Aunt Vickie clasped her hands on her chest. "Oh, that is so romantic. As soon as the sea lanes are safe, we simply must see that she gets here."

As July gave way to August, Ella found keeping her and Clay's engagement secret easier than she'd first feared. With Clay and Jake working long hours to prepare Star Dancer and Vickie's Pride for the Falls City Handicap race at the end of September, she saw little of her fiancé. Aside from a rare stolen kiss when she visited Game's Afoot's stall to give the yearling his daily sugar cubes, she and Clay spent scant time alone together. She lived for mealtimes when she and Clay could manage a surreptitious touch of their hands and exchange loving glances.

As she'd promised Jake, she wrote his sweetheart, Simone, a letter of introduction and encouragement. Aunt Vickie latched on to Jake and Simone's cause with gusto, researching passenger ship lines that docked at ports closest to Cambrai, France, and generally began planning the couple's nuptials. Ella and Aunt Vickie often spent the early autumn afternoons perusing the fashion magazines for wedding wear. When her aunt would point out a particular gown as perfect for a southern bride, Ella couldn't help imagining herself as a southern bride, dressed in one of the lacy gowns and exchanging vows with her darling Clay.

By mid-September her hopes to finally announce her and Clay's engagement began to rise. Uncle Davis, who now walked well with his cane, visited the barns several times a day. Ella's heart lifted to see him and Clay engaging in conversation and even sharing an occasional laugh as they were doing now outside the first barn.

She gave the two men a smile and a wave as she headed down the long lane to check the mailbox. Clay sent her a wink, sending her heart soaring like the hawk making lazy circles in the pale blue sky over the nearby pasture. Perhaps this would be the day Clay would feel confident enough in his mending relationship with Uncle Davis to announce their engagement.

A freshening breeze snatched a crimson-tinged leaf from one of the dogwood trees above her and deposited it on her head. Giggling, she plucked the leaf from her hair and flung it back into the wind, which carried it to the thick bluegrass along the lane.

As she stepped to the mailbox, Ella realized she loved this farm. The thought of living here with Clay for the rest of her life filled her with anticipation for her wedding day.

She opened the metal box and pulled out two envelopes. At the sight of her brother's name on the top envelope her smile evaporated, a sickening ache started in the pit of her stomach, and she began to tremble. Fearing she'd fall, she sank to the grassy bank beside the mailbox. She drew in deep breaths as she fought the panic threatening to overtake her. She'd heard that if the news was bad, the envelope would be edged in black. This envelope had no black edging.

Somehow she managed to get a trembling finger beneath the glued flap and pry it open. If the news was bad, she'd rather read it alone before sharing it with Aunt Vickie, or even Clay. The paper shook in her hands as she unfolded the grimy pages. Dread's icy fist released its grip on her chest as she began to read her brother's words.

Dear Ella,

I hope this finds you well. Got Ma's letter about Jared. Rough news. Hard to believe he's gone, but I've lost a lot of friends in the past few months. I hate to say I'm getting used to it, but I guess I am. As for me, I could use a hot bath and one of Ma's roast chicken dinners, but other than that, I'm doing all right. Most days we sit around in the mud, bored. Things did get interesting last week though. June 6th we got cut off from the other American and French forces in a place called Belleau Wood. The enemy was closing in and it looked like we were done for. Just before we ran out of ammunition a company of marines showed up and chased off the Huns. Learned later they'd got lost, weren't even supposed to be in our area. God was sure watching out for us that day, little sister. Praying He's doing the same for you. The sergeant's hollering, so it looks like we have to pick up and start marching again. Take care of yourself and God bless. Hope to see you soon.

Love, Gavin

Ella blinked away the tears and wiped the wetness from her face. Sniffing back fresh tears, she folded the letter and returned it to the envelope then brought the second envelope from beneath it.

Excitement vied with disbelief when she saw Mother's name. When she'd decided to stay on the farm after Uncle Davis's stroke, she'd contacted her post office in Indianapolis with a request to forward her mail here. Until today her mail had consisted of magazines and advertisements. That she'd gotten letters from both her brother and her parents on the same day seemed beyond remarkable.

She opened her mother's letter with steadier hands and began reading.

Dear Ella,

I cannot tell you how much Daddy and I miss you and Gavin. We pray for both of you continually. I'm so sorry we were not able to be there with you for Jared's funeral, but we are so very proud that you went on your own. Knowing how you hate funerals, I'm sure it couldn't have been easy. Our hearts ache for Vickie and Davis, but we are comforted in the knowledge that they will see their boy again when they too go to be with the Lord. Vickie told me about Davis's stroke. We are thankful he was spared and are praying for his full recovery. We are proud and relieved that you have volunteered to stay and help your aunt and uncle. Your aunt Vickie tells me that Clay is back on the farm. I hope he is no longer pulling your hair.

Our work here has harvested many souls for Christ, which is a great blessing. Influenza has found this place though, and there is much sickness, with many going on to be with the Lord.

The war too is a worry. As long as Palau stays in British hands we are safe. Of course, we worry about Gavin fighting on the front. He is always on my mind, but a few days ago, on June 6th, God burdened my heart with him. Daddy and I together with all our Christian brothers and sisters here began bombarding heaven with prayers for Gavin's safety. We've heard nothing, but Daddy says no news is good news.

Praying you are well and happy on the farm. We know you are a tremendous blessing to your aunt Vickie and uncle Davis, especially at this difficult time for them. We are still planning to return to the States next spring if the war permits.

May God keep you and hold you close to Him.

Love, Mother

Ella's gaze flew back to the date June 6, when Mother said she'd felt burdened to pray for Gavin. She folded her mother's letter and slipped it back into the envelope, then opened Gavin's letter again. As she reread it, her whole body began to shake. Tears sprang into her eyes, and sobs that rose from the depths of her being convulsed her. Had God put it on Mother's heart that Gavin needed help? If so, why did Mother, Daddy, and their congregation have to pray to save him? Why didn't God just save him without them needing to pray for it?

Somehow she managed to push herself up on shaky legs. For once, she was glad for the long driveway. It would give her time to compose herself, dry her tears, and stop shaking.

At the sight of Clay standing alone outside the first barn, her steps quickened with her heartbeats. "Clay, you will not believe what came in the mail."

"A thousand dollars?" He gave her the lopsided grin that made her heart flutter.

"Better." She pulled the letters from her skirt pocket.

His expression turned serious. "Good news, I hope."

She nodded and exhaled a breath she hadn't realized she'd been holding. "Everyone is all right." The need to share the amazing coincidence with him overwhelmed her. She handed him Gavin's letter, which he perused with a narrow-eyed frown.

Clay blew out a low whistle. "God *was* looking out after them. Praise the Lord for that."

She handed him Mother's letter. "Read this."

He began reading, a baffled look drawing his brows together. He glanced back at Gavin's letter in his other hand, and his eyes widened. He looked at Ella, then back at Gavin's letter. "Praise God." The words puffed from his lips on an incredulous whisper.

The question that had scratched at Ella's mind since reading the letters blurted from her lips. "If God did send those marines to save Gavin and his company, why did Mother, Daddy, and their congregation have to pray for Him to do it? Why didn't God just step in and save Gavin without involving them?"

Clay frowned and handed the letters back to Ella. "Why are you here, Ella?" He waved his hand at the letters. "Why did you share these with me?"

Ella felt a painful stab near her heart. It hurt to hear him sound disinterested in her concerns. Fighting tears, she stuffed the letters back into the envelopes and gaped at Clay. "Because I love you, and you love me." She didn't try to disguise the tone of hurt confusion in her voice. "We have a relationship. Don't we?"

A tender smile graced his lips. "Yes, we do." His expression turned thoughtful. "In the same way we want to share things like these letters with one another because we love each other, God wants us to pray for. . .everything, because He loves us. He wants us to love Him and have a close relationship with Him. Yes, God could have stepped in and saved Gavin and his company without your parents' prayers, but God *wants* us to ask." His smile turned to a grin. "I also think God is trying to get your attention." He folded his arms across his chest, and one rusty eyebrow quirked up. "If you had received those letters even a day apart, you might not have noticed the June 6th date in each letter." His grin widened. "God went to a lot of trouble to make sure you got both those letters in your hand at the same time."

"Maybe so." She couldn't help a chuckle. "Old Reuben says God finds ways to get our attention."

"And Old Reuben is always right." His gaze softening, he slipped his arms around her and drew her into the barn and a wedge of shade cast by the barn door. His mouth found hers, and she returned his sweet caresses with equal ardor.

A soft chuckle intruded on her bliss, and they sprang apart.

Old Reuben ambled toward them wearing a knowing grin. "I seen the Lord knittin' you two together way last spring." He gave another chuckle. "Wondered how long it would take you to get there."

With his arms still around Ella, Clay turned to Reuben. "Ella has agreed to be my wife."

Old Reuben's gray brows shot up. "What does Mr. Davis think o' that?"

Clay gave Ella a squeeze. "We haven't told him. Or Aunt Vickie. We're waiting until we feel Uncle Davis might be more accepting of our news."

Ella felt no alarm at Reuben's knowledge of her and Clay's secret. She'd never known anyone more circumspect than Old Reuben. He had kept Clay's secret about the horse doping for the past three years.

Old Reuben nodded, confirming her confidence in his silence. "I do b'lieve Mr. Davis is warmin' back up to you, Clay. But he'll hear it first from you, not from me." His old face lit with a mischievous grin. "But ya best take care sparkin' in the barn. Yer li'ble to catch the place afire." With a parting grin, he ambled outside.

Tiring from the effort to keep their engagement secret, Ella sighed. "When do you think we can tell Uncle Davis and Aunt Vickie? Aunt Vickie already has Jake and Simone's wedding planned. I'd love for her to start planning ours as well."

Clay's brow furrowed. "I know, darling, I'd love to tell them too. If Star Dancer does as well in the Falls City Handicap as I think he will, Uncle Davis should be in high spirits. What do you say we give them our news that evening?"

Joy effervesced inside Ella. At least now she had a date to look forward to. Unable to speak, she answered by hugging his neck and kissing him again.

The two weeks leading up to the Falls City Handicap at Churchill Downs dragged for Ella. When the day finally came and the men spent the day at the racetrack in Louisville, she and Aunt Vickie hosted a group of women from the church for a knitting party making cold weather garments for the troops. When Aunt Vickie regaled the women with plans for Jake and Simone's wedding, Ella had to press her lips tight together to keep from blurting the news of her own engagement.

When the last of the guests had gone, Aunt Vickie gathered the fruits of their labor. "I'd say we did quite well," she said as she piled up the knitted mufflers, mittens, and socks. "I'd have rather used brighter colors than black, brown, and olive green, but it is for the army."

The sound of an automobile chugging up the driveway in front of the house interrupted her musings.

"One of the ladies must have forgotten something." Ella abandoned counting a pile of socks and stepped to the window. At the sight of the Garretts' green Auburn her heart leaped in her chest. "It's the Auburn. I thought the men wouldn't be back until dark."

Aunt Vickie's forehead scrunched in a look of worry. "They shouldn't be. I hope nothing is wrong."

The next moment they heard the distinct *tap, tap* of Uncle Davis's cane in the hallway. When he finally appeared in the doorway, the scowl on his face set alarm bells clanging in Ella's chest.

Ella ran to him. "What has happened, Uncle Davis? Where is Clay?"

His scowl deepened, matching the anger in his voice. "Upstairs packing. I fired him four hours ago."

Chapter 9

C lay stuffed his few possessions in a leather valise, too numb to feel anything. *This can't be happening again, Lord. It can't.*

When the track authorities came to him and Davis before Star Dancer's race to inform them that the horse had been scratched from the roster, Clay thought it must be a mistake. Then when the man told them that they'd found a hypodermic syringe in Star Dancer's stall with traces of stimulants, Clay felt as if his blood had turned to ice. Though the man didn't accuse them of the deed, he promised there would be a full investigation of the matter.

Of course Davis accused Clay and fired him on the spot, unwilling to listen to Clay's pleas of innocence.

As the numbness began to abate, the pain set in. Uncle Davis had ordered Clay off the farm before nightfall. Clay's concerns about where he might lay his head tonight paled beside the thought of breaking his engagement to Ella. But with no job and a possible indictment facing him, he couldn't in all good conscience keep her tied to him.

He'd rather be drawn and quartered than face her tears, but leaving without saying goodbye felt intolerable.

The past few hours had tested his faith like never before. The verses from Psalm 34:17–18 that had encouraged him during the darkest days of his incarceration gave him strength to face what lay before him. *"The righteous cry, and the Lord heareth, and delivereth them out of all their troubles. The Lord is nigh unto them that are of a broken heart; and saveth such as be of a contrite spirit."*

He'd never felt so brokenhearted. He picked up the bag and headed downstairs.

When he reached the parlor, the sight of Ella's crumpled face drenched in tears scourged his heart.

Ella ran into his arms and sobbed against his chest. "Tell Uncle Davis you didn't do it. Tell him!"

"I have, Ella, but he doesn't believe me." Her every sob felt like a lash across his heart.

She tore away from his embrace and strode to Uncle Davis. "This isn't fair, Uncle Davis. Clay didn't dope the horse."

Uncle Davis blew out a long sigh. "I know you want to believe that, Ella, but he did it before. Why wouldn't I think he did it again?"

She clenched her fists. "Because Clay didn't dope Prince's Ransom! Jared did. Clay took the blame so Jared wouldn't have to go to prison and your opinion of him wouldn't be tarnished! If you don't believe me, ask Old Reuben."

Clay froze in disbelief. His heart seized then shuddered at the stricken looks on Uncle Davis's and Aunt Vickie's faces. Ella might as well have plunged a knife into his chest.

Dear Lord, let this not be happening.

Aunt Vickie sank to the sofa and sobbed into her hands while Uncle Davis's face turned an unnatural purple.

Uncle Davis pounded his cane on the wood floor with such ferocity it sounded like a shot. His voice lowered to a near growl. "Get Reuben in here."

Ella turned and strode from the room.

The next minutes felt like an eternity as Clay, numb to all emotion, stood mute before Uncle Davis's angry glare.

When Ella returned to the room with Reuben, Clay prayed his old friend would refute Ella's words. That prayer withered at the anguished look on Reuben's face. Clay had never known the man to speak anything but the truth.

Uncle Davis focused his narrowed glare on Reuben. "Reuben, did Jared dope Prince's Ransom?"

A visible swallow moved the old man's wrinkled throat. "Yes sir, he did."

The light went out of Uncle Davis's eyes. Leaning hard on his cane, he slumped out of the room without saying another word. The moment he crossed the threshold into the hallway, he collapsed.

The sight of his uncle in a heap on the floor jarred Clay from his paralysis. Fearing the worst, he sprinted to his side. He knelt and touched his uncle's throat. The faint throbbing of a pulse beneath his fingertips sent relief sluicing through him.

The next hour passed in a blur. Clay, with Reuben's help, moved Uncle

Davis to the room across the hall that had served as a bedroom for his aunt and uncle since Uncle Davis had his stroke last spring. Ella phoned the family doctor, who rushed to the farm. After an examination, Dr. Malloy determined that Uncle Davis had suffered a mild heart attack.

Clay and Ella followed the doctor out of the room, leaving Aunt Vickie to sit vigil at her husband's bedside.

The doctor closed the bedroom door behind them. "I've given him a sedative and left digitalis pills with instructions. No excitement and plenty of rest." He shook Clay's hand. "Call my office if anything changes."

As they watched the doctor leave, the anger Ella's betrayal had kindled inside Clay grew to a simmering fury. Since her outburst he hadn't spoken to her for fear of what he might say.

"I'm sorry, Clay." She reached out for his hand, and he drew it back, unable to bear her touch.

Her teary apology released the pent-up hurt and anger stewing inside him. "Yes, Ella, I know. You're sorry. You're always sorry. You promised me you wouldn't tell, and now Uncle Davis may pay for your betrayal with his life." He averted his eyes from her quivering chin and tear-drenched face. His heart felt like a stone inside his chest. "A marriage has to be built on trust, Ella. If I can't trust you, I can't marry you."

Three days later those words continued to play through Clay's mind in torturous repetition like a scratched phonograph record. The look of shock and anguish in Ella's eyes and the sound of her wrenching sobs as she ran from him after he broke off their engagement still shredded his heart.

Since that moment she'd treated him like a stranger—not speaking to him, refusing to meet his gaze, and seeming to avoid him when possible.

In the far back corner of the first barn, Clay sat hunched in the empty stall where he'd taken up residence. Though no longer employed by Dogwood Farms, he couldn't leave while Uncle Davis teetered between life and death. The news yesterday that the jockey slated to ride Star Dancer in the Falls City Handicap had confessed to doping the horse came as cold comfort.

His gaze fell on his Bible peeking out of the leather bag beside him that held his belongings. The sight pricked his conscience. He hadn't opened it since his world shattered three days ago.

"The LORD *is nigh unto them that are of a broken heart; and saveth such as be of a contrite spirit."* The words from the psalm beckoned.

Expelling a sigh, he lifted the book from the bag and opened it. It fell open to one of the many pages he'd marked with a scrap of paper. His gaze fell on the thirteenth chapter of 1 Corinthians. *"Charity suffereth long, and is kind; charity envieth not; charity vaunteth not itself, is not puffed up. . .is not easily provoked. . .rejoiceth in the truth."*

Charity. *Love.* He loved Ella. He would always love Ella. Soon he would leave this place, but he could never outrun the truth.

He closed the book, put it on the stall floor beside him, and went to his knees. As far as he knew, Ella remained distant from God. Though the thought of living the rest of his life without her felt excruciating, perhaps he should leave things as they were. "All right, Lord, what am I supposed to do? Just tell me what You want me to do."

"Love her."

Clay lifted his head, and his eyes flew open. The words had sounded as clear as a loud whisper in his ear.

Tears blurred his view of the barn's interior beyond the stall's open door. *"Rejoiceth in the truth."*

The truth he'd avoided for three days hit him like a kick in the gut from a stallion, convicting his conscience. Ella had broken her promise out of love for him just as he had lied three years ago out of love for Jared and Uncle Davis. He'd allowed his wounded pride to sit in judgment of her when he had no right to judge her. Whether or not they would share a future together didn't change the fact that he needed to ask her forgiveness and tell her that he forgave her and that he still loved her.

Guilt flayed Ella's heart raw as she sat at Uncle Davis's bedside. An excruciating tangle of sorrow and despair rolled through her like a ball of barbed wire.

She looked at Uncle Davis's pale countenance, and another dagger of remorse twisted inside her. She'd done this. Clay was right. In her zeal to save Clay, she'd sacrificed Uncle Davis, Aunt Vickie, and Clay's love for her.

Aunt Vickie's hand on her shoulder sent fresh tears cascading down Ella's face. "It's not your fault, Ella. I think, in my heart, I always knew Jared had doped that horse. I just didn't want to face it."

Ella sniffed back tears. "But I promised Clay I wouldn't tell, and I did." As despair gripped her, she lifted her sodden face to Aunt Vickie. "Now Uncle Davis might die and Clay hates me."

Aunt Vickie directed a tender look toward her husband. "Your uncle

Davis is strong. Dr. Malloy says with rest he should recover." She bent and embraced Ella. "Clay doesn't hate you, Ella." She pressed Ella's head against her shoulder and patted her back. "Why, he's in love with you, child. I see it in his eyes every time he looks at you."

Stunned, Ella pulled away from Aunt Vickie to look into her face.

Aunt Vickie gave a little chuckle. "Oh, I've known you two were in love for a long time. Maybe even before you knew it."

Ella tried to smile, but her lips wouldn't support it. "We were engaged. . . secretly. But when I broke my promise to Clay, he broke our engagement." She buried her head in her aunt's shoulder again. "I can't stop loving him, Aunt Vickie. I don't know what to do."

Aunt Vickie patted her back. "Have you talked to the Lord about it?"

Ella pulled away, shook her head, and looked down. "I'm afraid the Lord and I haven't been on speaking terms for some time."

Aunt Vickie put a crooked finger under Ella's chin and lifted her face to look into her eyes. "Maybe *you* haven't been on speaking terms with the Lord, but He's always been there waiting for you to talk to Him. He wants you to bring your troubles to Him."

Ella wiped the tears from her eyes. "I don't know if I know how to talk to God anymore, Aunt Vickie."

Aunt Vickie sighed. "When I really need to talk to the Lord, I like to go to the place where I feel most at peace. Do you have a place like that here?"

Ella nodded. The place that came to her mind was Game's Afoot's stall. When she went there each day to give the colt sugar cubes, she felt the happiest—the most at peace.

Aunt Vickie squeezed Ella's hand. "Then you go to that place and ask the Lord for peace and for His direction." She gave her a caring smile. "Just talk to God like a friend and tell Him what you told me."

Minutes later Ella entered the first barn with a contrite heart, eager to crawl to the mercy seat of the Lord.

Game's Afoot stuck his nose over the top of the stall. He gave a neigh and thrashed his head, begging for the expected treat.

Ella dug the sugar cubes from her pocket. She tried to smile through her tears as she offered the horse the sweets. "I need to talk to God, Game's Afoot. I need His help."

She dropped to her knees. Her heart rent, and her words tumbled out like apples from a torn sack. "Lord, I need You. Please be there. Please hear me.

I've made a mess of everything and I need to know what to do." She sniffed back tears. "I am so sorry I betrayed Clay's trust, and I don't blame him for not wanting to marry me now." She had to pause to choke back a sob. "But please, Lord, heal Uncle Davis. Don't let him pay with his life for my mistake. And please don't let Clay hate me. Help me know how to live without him if that is Your will, but please, please just let him not hate me." Her words dissolved into gut-wrenching sobs.

The next moment she felt herself lifted in strong arms.

"I love you, Ella. I'll always love you. Please forgive me." Clay's voice sounded husky, and his breath felt warm against her cheek as he embraced her.

Ella surrendered to another spate of sobs as joy filled her chest, pushing out her sorrow. "Thank You, Lord. Oh, thank You, thank You." She drenched Clay's flannel-clad shoulder with her tears. At length she pushed away. "But you're not the one needing forgiving. I am."

He leaned back to look in her face but kept his arms around her waist. "And I do forgive you, but God reminded me that I don't have the right to judge you. You acted in love for me, just as I acted in love for Jared and Uncle Davis three years ago. At least you told the truth." His voice sagged with remorse. "I broke our engagement out of hurt and pride, and that was wrong."

He took her hand and went down on one knee. "Ella Jamison, can you forgive me for putting my pride ahead of my love for you? Are you still willing to be my wife?"

"Yes, yes," she managed through her sobs. "You are my darling. My champion. My Thoroughbred."

Clay stood and wrapped her in his arms again. "Good," he whispered. A mischievous look glinted in his gray eyes. "I was afraid I might have to pull your hair." He pressed his mouth to hers, stifling her giggle-laced sobs as he sealed their promise with a lingering kiss that sent her heart soaring.

At the sound of someone clearing his throat, they turned to see Old Reuben wearing a sheepish grin. "Now that we have that settled, Mr. Davis is awake and asking for both of you."

Ella and Clay exchanged smiles and, hand in hand, followed Reuben to the house.

They stepped into Uncle Davis's room still holding hands.

Uncle Davis, looking better than Ella would have imagined, eyed them with a narrowed gaze. "Is there something else you two need to tell me?"

"Ella and I are engaged to be married, Uncle Davis." Clay squeezed Ella's hand.

"Praise the Lord." Aunt Vickie breathed the whispered prayer from her spot beside her husband's bed.

Uncle Davis looked down as if studying the patchwork quilt covering him. When he looked back up, he focused on Clay. "Thank you for what you did for Jared. . .and for Vickie and me three years ago. We owe you a great debt." His broad forehead crumpled with a look of pain. "I'm sorry I repaid that debt with unkindness. I ask your forgiveness as I've asked the Lord's."

Clay shook his head. "It was my debt to pay, Uncle Davis. You and Aunt Vickie gave me a home when you didn't have to. Three years was a small price to pay for the life you gave me."

Ella's heart sang in love and pride for her beloved, her champion with the heart of a true Thoroughbred.

Aunt Vickie wept, and Uncle Davis's blue eyes turned watery. He harrumphed as if to clear the emotion from his throat. "Son, you have a home and a job here as long as you want." His gaze slid to Ella, his mouth twisting in a crooked smile. "Our little Yankee gal will be a southern bride with the biggest, most lavish wedding this county has ever seen."

Epilogue

Ella gripped her father's arm, her filmy veil fluttering in the early May breeze laden with the scents of lilac and dogwood blossoms. Joy filled her chest to near bursting. The Lord had answered her every prayer and showered her with blessings more abundant than the white blossoms adorning the many dogwood trees that dotted her aunt and uncle's lawn.

Good to his word, Uncle Davis, who had both survived and thrived after his heart attack last fall, had gifted Ella and Clay with a wedding beyond their wildest dreams.

"Are you ready, honey?" Smiling, Daddy patted her hand resting on his arm.

Ella returned Daddy's smile. "More than ready." She sent up a silent prayer of thanks that God had spared her parents from the deadly influenza outbreak that had ravaged Papua, New Guinea, and had brought them safely home.

The orchestra Uncle Davis had hired began playing "American Wedding March," setting off a bevy of excited butterflies in Ella's stomach.

As she and Daddy traversed the white carpet runner spread over the lush Kentucky bluegrass lawn, Ella searched for a bright splash of red hair among those gathered beneath a flowering dogwood tree several yards ahead of them. Her heart thrilled when she found her darling standing beside his groomsmen Jake Teague and her brother, Gavin, who looked dashing in his army uniform.

She caught her brother's eye and he gave her an encouraging wink. *Thank You, Lord.* Two more blessings: the war's end and her brother's safe return.

Across from them stood her new friend and matron of honor, Jake's wife, Simone. Looking stunning in her French blue frock and hat, the dark-haired, dark-eyed beauty sent Ella a bright smile before her gaze slid back to her husband's face.

The sight of Old Reuben beaming from his chair on the front row beside

Uncle Davis and Aunt Vickie reminded Ella of his sage words of a year ago, that God finds a way to get man's attention. A year ago she'd shaken her fist at heaven, wondering why God had allowed the events that brought her here.

As she took the last several steps toward her future, the answer smiled at her from soft gray eyes brimming with love.

Thank You for getting my attention, Lord. Thank You for bringing me here to Clay. Her grateful prayer winged its way heavenward as her darling's face blurred through her happy tears. When she finally stepped beneath the canopy of white blossoms and Daddy handed her off to Clay, Ella grasped her beloved's hands knowing she'd found her home.

The minister cleared his throat. "Dearly beloved, we gather here today to join this man and this woman in holy matrimony."

The pounding of Ella's heart in her ears drowned out the minister's words until Clay gave her hands a gentle squeeze, slowing her heartbeats to a canter.

Somewhere in the distance a horse neighed as she and Clay exchanged vows and he slipped a gold wedding ring on her finger to join the diamond engagement ring he'd given her last Christmas.

"With the authority invested in me by God and the state of Kentucky, I pronounce you man and wife." The minister grinned at Clay. "You may kiss your bride."

Clay bent and pressed a tender kiss on her lips to seal their vows then whispered in her ear, "My southern bride."

Ella giggled. Clay Garrett would not get the last word. She whispered back, "My Kentucky Thoroughbred."

Ramona K. Cecil is a wife, mother, grandmother, freelance poet, and award-winning inspirational romance writer. Now empty nesters, she and her husband make their home in Indiana. A member of American Christian Fiction Writers and American Christian Fiction Writers Indiana Chapter, her work has won awards in a number of inspirational writing contests. Over eighty of her inspirational verses have been published on a wide array of items for the Christian gift market. She enjoys a speaking ministry, sharing her journey to publication while encouraging aspiring writers. When not writing, her hobbies include reading, gardening, and visiting places of historical interest.

The Marmalade Belle

by Dianne Christner

Chapter 1

December 31, 1894
Ocala, Florida

In Maribelle Sinclair's midnight dream, the highly sought-after bachelor, Virgil Agnew, sank to the knees of his tuxedo trousers and asked the coveted question, displaying more duty than love and pinning her sleep-mummified body to the sheets with foreboding. There were particular expectations surrounding his marriage proposal because Daddy had already planned how he would implement the finances available to Marmalade Plantation from their alliance.

Time-frozen moments afforded her to do what southern ladies normally did not risk, and she studied Virgil's mouth, full lips parted in expectation beneath a thin mustache. Even on his knees he was virile, physically powerful as well as financially. She felt vulnerable. And chilled to the bone. For once they wed, he might do whatever he wished on a whim, such as whisk her north away from her family. Any place north of her beloved Sunshine State would be as frigidly welcoming as the Arctic Circle. She couldn't leave her sunny plantation nor the crystal-clear waters of Silver River.

"I'm waiting for your answer, dearest." His closely spaced blue eyes glittered like dancing ice, and his cheek flinched with impatience.

She opened her mouth to do her southern duty, but the words didn't form and her surroundings momentarily hazed, giving her a dream-within-a-dream-like impression. She noticed her clothing. She was adorned for the New Year's Eve party. Her gown was green with gold lace, which Mama claimed showed off her hazel eyes and black hair. A stray thought struck her. *I'm dreaming in color.*

"Maribelle? What game is this you play?"

It was Virgil again. His wavy brown hair was parted in the middle, and one strand tickled his thick brow, emphasizing the intensity of his gaze. "I'm sorry, I can't," she blurted.

"Why not?" He frowned.

"Because I'm in love with someone else." Shock struck her that her dream was taking such an odd twist, until an instant later when she followed this new and fascinating rabbit trail. She loved someone? Her mind sought a face, and a vision manifested, revealing a slim masculine silhouette. Just beyond him an orchestra played. She started across the room, pushing through the throng, when he turned. Oh no! Not *him*? Of course, it had always been him. But he didn't count. Yet she was drawn to him. He smiled.

Once again, she was the skinny child, basking in his attention, until Virgil's voice broke dreamland's spell.

"What? What kind of nonsense is this?" Virgil's tone came fast and sharp, as it sometimes did with his northern accent, and to her dismay, the smiling man faded along with the music.

With growing frustration, she narrowed her eyes at Virgil. "I can't." Even as she spoke, she braced for his response. It wasn't the way things were supposed to transpire. She knew it. Virgil knew it. He rose. She desperately tried to conjure up her hero's likeness again. But it had dissipated. Only Virgil remained. He clutched her shoulders.

"No!" Maribelle gasped, sitting upright in her cane bed of carvings and opulent swags. She unwound her arms from their death grip on the sheets. Her heart raced, and as she slowly awakened, she shivered violently and clutched the covers. Virgil would never behave unseemly or hurt her. He was kind and generous, the perfect gentleman for a Northerner, if not a bit passionate at times. Everyone claimed she was fortunate to be the woman of his choice. And though only a dream, the engagement would soon be genuine. She shivered again. Where was her lady's maid? Bundling herself in her blanket, she bounded from her bed and padded across an icy wood floor to the hearth. Its coals had not been stoked before the servants retired. Highly unusual. She wondered if Milda was ill.

Then she heard noises also unusual for the midnight hour. Maribelle strained and recognized Mama's and Grandmama's voices. She groped for slippers and a wrapper and tossed her blanket on the bed. Moonlight brightened the way as she padded into the hallway.

She followed the noises downstairs to the blue parlor and found the women huddled close to the fire. "What is going on?" she asked with chattering teeth.

"Come warm up, dear," Grandmama urged.

She moved to the elderly woman's wheelchair and repositioned a shawl around Grandmama's bony shoulders. "Where are the servants? What's happened? The fire's gone out in my room."

Mama gushed, "Oh Maribelle, it's most dreadful. Your daddy. . ."

The manner in which Mama kept their home was blameless. Mama was not considered a ninny by any means, but the woman—whom Maribelle closely resembled except for a few wrinkles and graying at the temples—could be overly melodramatic, so Maribelle glanced at the older, more sensible woman to judge the gravity of the situation.

"Is Daddy ill?"

"No. He's in the grove saving the fruit. All the servants are enlisted, even the cook."

A sudden cold spell? A dreaded freeze! Maribelle snatched up a lamp and started back to her room.

"Where are you going?" Mama managed.

"To the grove!"

"But—"

"Let her go. She aims to help," came her grandmama's stern, age-strained voice.

Maribelle hurried upstairs and scrambled into her riding habit then snatched a short cape, thankful for the moonlight as she ran for the stables.

In the daylight, under normal circumstances, Marmalade Citrus Plantation was a perfect southern spectacle of beauty, everything a young belle came to expect and call home. A white two-story house with stately columns and a wide beckoning veranda trailed with jasmine and nestled into the shade of magnolia and cypress. Birds singing and crickets chirping. A perfect life, at least before Virgil Agnew came along with his courting plans and gold-filled pockets, luring Daddy into bigger dreams for Marmalade.

Mama's pet pink camellia hedge, which had been blooming and nodding playfully beneath a Christmas sun, shone rigid and grotesquely spooky in the moonlight. Maribelle quickened her mare's pace. Beyond the manor and stables was Daddy's pride—four hundred acres of neatly spaced rows of orange trees.

"Oh no," she moaned, leaping off her mare and banging her knees on the frozen ground. Painfully, she raised her gaze. The ground was littered with perfect, nearly ripened citrus. Their family's livelihood scattered across the hard-crusted earth. She'd never witnessed anything like it. She plucked up an orange and inspected it, frozen solid and cold through her gloves.

Stumbling to her feet, she made a complete, slow circle. Everywhere trees drooped pitifully, though some fruit peeked from inside the shelter of the branches. Only a day earlier the limbs were verdant and laden with fruit, and now they were wilted. Voices from the west drew her attention where Daddy worked alongside the servants.

"Daddy," she gasped. "Are we losing the crop?"

"We may." Weariness lined his leathery, tanned face and sorrow darkened his blue eyes. "If we'd only had a warning, we could've saved more."

More? Hope burgeoned. "The fruit on the trees is good?" She observed how the servants were scrambling to harvest it. However, most of the crop was on the ground.

"I'm counting on it. And the trees will survive. So there's that." Daddy was a strong man, and his optimism always counterbalanced Mama's fretful nature. "Don't worry, Junebug. Just a slight setback, is all. We'll use Virgil's loan to get us through another season and put off my expansion plans." He gave her a strained smile. "Wouldn't hurt to encourage him along with his proposal at the party."

He and Mama were in agreement over the engagement, and Mama claimed Virgil was going to make it official at the upcoming New Year's Eve party his uncle Walter was hosting. Knowing it was not the time to add to Daddy's problems, she wanted to assure him she would do her best, but instead the cold rattled her teeth. A wind flurry swirled brittle citrus leaves. She shuddered.

"You aren't dressed warmly. Scat back to the house, Junebug."

"Work will fix that." She spoke to the nearest servant, one hired to tend the groves. "Please. I aim to help."

Daddy nodded. "All right. Pick low. I don't want you climbing trees." He turned back to his work.

Maribelle spied Milda and copied her, quickly learning how to snap the fruit off the limbs and gently place it in baskets. As the baskets filled, she helped tote them to the wagon and cover them with hay. Warmth quickly spread through her body, but her toes went numb. She noticed Ebony Rose, named for her sleek black coat and white rose patch, nosing an orange close to the wagon. She marched to her mare. "Stop. Those aren't good for you." Ebony Rose looked up at her with soulful, adoring eyes. She patted her nose. "Sorry, I'm not mad at you." The black servant who would take the wagon to the barn dipped his head and shyly grinned. "Miss, I'll take her wit' me, if ye wish. Back ta the stable."

"Thank you."

Together, she and the frizzy-haired Milda worked silently to fill their baskets. Then her servant urged, "Miss, your arms be shakin' from tired. Best ye let us finish. Your mama wouldn't want you turnin' sick for the party."

"I'm not quitting. You aren't used to this kind of work either."

"Meybe, but I be paid fer it."

Maribelle lifted her chin. "We can't quit."

The servant acquiesced, and they turned back to the trees. When at last the grove was plucked clean as a Christmas turkey carcass, someone brought her horse back to her again. Mounting, she sank exhausted in the sidesaddle. "Home, Ebony Rose. Let's go home." She'd every intention of pitching straight into bed, but upon reaching the house, the pleasant aroma of bacon drew her instead. She followed it into the kitchen and stopped in surprise. "You're cooking, Mama?"

Milda helped Maribelle off with her boots and brought clean wool stockings for her feet. Mama brought her a cup of tea and wiped her hands on her apron. "Yes. And I enjoyed it. How bad is it out there?"

Before Maribelle could reply, the house servants started to reassemble, and Mama turned away to talk to the cook. Everything was in disorder, for at the same time, the butler announced a messenger had arrived. Mama left the room and returned with a crestfallen expression.

"What is it?" Grandmama asked.

"The New Year's party's been canceled because of citywide devastation of crops. Everybody's got to tend to their affairs." She cast Maribelle a hard expression.

"Surely you don't blame me."

Mama shook her head, coming to her senses. "No. Bless your heart. I'm just sorely disappointed."

Maribelle certainly wasn't. In fact, if she weren't so weary and weren't a lady, she'd dance a jig around the table.

Grandmama Sinclair fairly read her mind. "There are more important matters at hand." She clasped wrinkled hands on her lap. "More important than a canceled New Year's party or marriage to a Yankee."

Maribelle bit off a smile.

"Heavens to Betsy," Mama snapped, pushing back a strand of black hair. "If we've lost the crop, it's more important than ever that Maribelle marries Virgil."

"Have we lost it?" Grandmama asked.

"Daddy says most is gone," Maribelle verified wearily. She closed her eyes and enjoyed the warmth from her cup. Her fingers felt sore, possibly blistered, in spite of her gloves. Though she was miserable for Daddy, she snatched at the small reprieve to stay unwed. She wasn't in love and was perfectly happy with her current station in life.

Virgil Agnew was a charming suitor. Maribelle had no complaints there. Her dream must be the source of her newfound butterflies. Only a day earlier she'd been quite receptive to the idea of marriage. Virgil was pleasingly handsome in a rugged way, and if she turned him down, another woman would win him away. But as Grandmama continually pointed out, he wasn't a southern-bred gentleman. Would her parents approve of Virgil if he wasn't the nephew of one of the wealthiest men in Ocala? Walter Agnew owned half the town, including the largest bank. Grandmama claimed it was a shame the way the war had changed the world and manners in general.

When Maribelle's head bobbed so that her nose touched bacon, she jerked upright and excused herself. In her room, she glanced out her bedroom window to see if there was any sign of Daddy. Through the pane, she heard the dim honking of flamingos flying pink against the sunrise. She'd never grow weary of such a marvelous sight. Her heart filled with resolve. This was the South. It wouldn't stay cold forever. It was the nature of things, just like she wouldn't be able to ward off Virgil forever. One day soon, she'd marry for the sake of Marmalade. She'd grow to love him. They'd have handsome boy babies, and her girl babies would be pretty belles and she'd instruct them to speak in a melodious southern drawl. She'd raise them on Mama's marmalade and sweet tea. She vowed, for Grandmama's sake, that much should never change.

Chapter 2

Indeed, the Florida sun did blaze again, bright and warm and prickly on the neck. Within a week, budding leaves created new life in the grove. Ever since the cold snap, Mama's prattle about the upcoming dinner party grated more and more on Maribelle's nerves. She didn't care which brooch she wore or if the weather would be perfect for her new kid slippers or if she was the envy of all the other belles. Well, maybe Willa Fay Carroway, a little bit.

She couldn't blame Mama for thinking it was her personal duty to wed her to Virgil, especially under the latest circumstances. It wasn't Virgil, of course, Mama aimed to impress at the party. Nor Willa Fay. It was always Daddy's childhood friend, Walter Agnew.

But at present, the fair weather beckoned, and Maribelle set out to ride and let her worries fly away like flamingos. She could feel the magical marsh smooth her troubled brow as she took the bridle path that led to the crystal-clear springs and the private, hidden spot where she could watch nature and an occasional tourist-filled glass-bottom boat glide along the river. It was where she went to be alone with her thoughts and pray. It was where she'd gotten her first kiss, even if it was a mere peck on the cheek. Dipping her head, she passed beneath a canopy of cypress dripping of Spanish moss. When she was a child, the ride was a secret and grand adventure, one of watching for snakes and gators and battling dastardly villains and fire-breathing dragons. Now it was home both to her and Ebony Rose.

She kept a vigilant watch though, for lately she'd been noticing bear scat. As isolated as the path was, she couldn't let down her guard, or she could land in serious trouble. When the glimpse of white sand appeared, she slid to the ground, allowing Ebony Rose to graze on her own as was their custom. Maribelle perched on her flat prayer rock, dangling her feet in a small clearing, allowing the rock's warmth to seep through her clothes. Overhead, clouds floated soft as buttermilk biscuits. She happily smoothed her riding skirt, settling in to have a serious and long overdue chat about Virgil and her obligations, when she caught a silver glint. Curious, she craned her neck and looked toward the river.

A small, green, shabbily painted boat bobbed in the reeds just a few feet from the shore. She watched the back of a slim man seated and fiddling with fishing gear. If she was quiet, he'd never notice her and soon be gone. But she was curious, for she hadn't seen anyone use this spot for many months. She frowned. There was something familiar about the set of his shoulders.... But her thoughts abruptly aborted when a beastly grunt bristled her skin. Instinctively she knew the creature crashing behind her was the bear she'd been hoping to avoid. Ebony Rose snorted, and she turned to see her mare galloping away, at the same time catching a glimpse of mottled black fur. Another closer grunt, and she shot up and sprinted, splashing through the knee-deep water, jerking her skirt free from the reeds and lurching recklessly into the stranger's boat with much thrashing and disarray.

"Row!" she cried, flailing her arms for something to steady herself in the careening boat. She dug her nails into the startled man's arm. "Bear!"

He shot a look over her shoulder, scanning the shoreline. Disentangling his arm, he gently directed, "Sit. Or you'll dump us both into the water."

She hit the seat and clutched both sides of the boat. "Please, sir. Row."

Her back remained to shore, but he maintained an advantageous view of the beach, seemingly unmotivated as he leisurely dipped his arm into the river and retrieved a soggy fishing pole she most likely had knocked into the water. "Better not have ruined my reel," he mumbled, now drawing his brown gaze to the pole to check its mechanics.

"Is that all you care about?"

He cast her a somewhat agitated glance and must have read the fright in her expression, because he sighed. "Very well. I was about to set sail anyway." Of course, there was no sail, and the ship she'd chosen was nothing more than a shabby rowboat, more likely than not to sink. He mocked her with a lingering perusal, his soft brown eyes moving from her sopping boots to her black hair and misshapen equestrian hat. His lip curled. His face was unshaven, very thin with a masculine ruggedness. He wasn't burly like Virgil, but his arms easily set the boat into the water with a few quick strokes of the oars.

Once a significant expanse of water separated her from the grunting predator, she dared a glance over her shoulder. A small cub stood on its hind legs, batting a blackberry bush loaded with green berries. What? That little fellow couldn't have made the menacing grunts that had her writing her eulogy and her mare bolting in fright. Well, in truth, Ebony Rose was skittish. Had dumped Maribelle more times than she could count, but she kept her because of the horse's soulful gazes. She scanned the glimmering sand and tangled brush for another beast, one worthy of her fears, but absolutely nothing manifested. The man easily brought the boat around broadside so they could both witness the cause of her growing humiliation.

She straightened her hat and sat rigid. "There's another bear out there. Besides that cub. I'm sure of it."

He arched a dark brow, and the corner of his mouth curled up again. "Mmm-hmm." He had a calmness about him. "Where?"

"Someplace. I'm sure—" She gestured and quickly grabbed the side of the boat again to keep her balance. "Cubs just don't go around on their own."

"Neither should young women. You could get into all sorts of trouble." It was the tone of his voice that gentled his strength and the softness of his gaze, even in mirth. His mannerisms were oddly familiar. "Especially those afraid of bears."

His eyes were straight from her dream. Her breath caught. If nothing else, she should've recognized the crusty old tub. Her cheeks grew hot. Mama would be proud to see her now. She'd been pressing Maribelle for ages to practice the art of blushing. Her mouth went dry. It was Jackson Taylor—at least an older, more hardened version of the young man who'd rescued her from a gator when she was ten. She'd had a mad crush on him and even wrote him a love note. At the time, she hadn't known he was married, because spying on him at the beach was a secret place. She never told her parents about him. How foolish she'd been to carry a crush for a married man. Then when she was old enough to fill out her corset, she learned there'd been a scandal and he'd enlisted in the cavalry. But she'd been too young to be privy to the details and too devastated to stir up her heart with questions.

Now she wished she had. It was eerie dreaming of him and shortly afterward encountering him. Good sense cautioned her not to reveal her identity, especially since he took her for a foolish, frightened female. She watched him set the oars aside and retrieve a rag from his wicker fishing basket. He wiped down the cane pole as they lazily drifted with the current. His presence was overwhelming for such a trim physique. She closed her eyes against the power he possessed over her and turned her face to the sunshine, basking in its warmth. How many times had she dreamed of being afloat with the man she idolized? The only time she'd ever been this close to him was when he'd swooped her up in his arms that day there really was a threat, a need to be rescued. She remembered the strength of his arms.

She opened her eyes and pulled off her gloves to drag her fingers through the translucent blue water. "Look." She pointed toward the shore. "A turtle. I'm glad he survived."

It slowly pulled itself onto a bank of lush subtropical vegetation sheltered by majestic trees.

"The freeze," he said with understanding. "He appears to be a tough old fellow." He rubbed his stubbly chin, and his voice held a hint of accusation. "What were you doing on my property?"

Skirting the question, lest she let her identity slip and he discover she was the one who penned that ridiculous love letter, she snapped, "You own the river? I suppose you are rich from collecting dues from all the tourists who frequent the glass-bottomed boats?"

He arched a brow and answered patiently, "The beach where you trespassed and hijacked my boat. Yes, miss. That's mine."

She wished she could argue. Ever since he'd left for the military, she'd thought of that stretch of beach as her own little oasis, even though she knew it was part of the Taylors' cotton plantation. "I was riding." She fumbled. "The path is romantic, and I've been here before without running into bears."

"Romantic?" He grinned, suddenly interested. "Go on."

His gaze was unashamedly admiring her. "Never mind. I shouldn't be here alone with you. We're drifting. And I should return."

He motioned. "Ah, but you are a romantic. And this is a perfect place among the pond lilies."

"Flowers or not, we both know I shouldn't be alone with you. Especially with the way you're looking at me."

"You noticed that? Not very gentlemanly of me, is it?" He shrugged. "I admit, I'm not harmless either."

Blushing again, she replied, "My point exactly."

"But I don't wish to return to the beach empty handed. On the other hand, a swim would be restorative. And. . .romantic. A tale for your friends."

"I don't tell tales. Anyway, most gentlemen would help a woman in distress."

"Hmm. This presents a problem. We've established I'm not a gentleman. You aren't safe here with me. And the beach isn't safe with prowling bears. The choice is yours."

"Take me back to the beach."

"But you forget that I came to fish."

"And I didn't. My boots are soaked, and my horse is waiting back there."

He cast his fishing line and shrugged. "Soon as I've caught my supper, I'll take you back, and I suppose I can give you a ride home." At her instant ire, he continued. "Your horse is long gone. Name's Jackson Taylor. And where will I be taking you, Miss. . . ?"

She huffed. "Oh, bliss and blazes! I'm to be stranded the entire day so you can attempt to catch your dinner?" She knew it wouldn't be the entire day. She'd lost count of the fish he'd caught while she'd spied on him as a child.

"First-name basis. I like a woman who knows what she wants. Well, Bliss, call me Jackson then. Look! See those fish swimming around eager to be caught."

She gazed over the side of the boat into the clear river and caught sight of several large fish. "An unfair advantage."

His eyes narrowed. "On second thought, Miss Bliss, how do I know you aren't the dangerous one? Perhaps you jumped into my boat to set a matrimonial trap. Yes, I believe that was your intention all along." He laughed bitterly. "Don't get your hopes up on my account. I'm not in the market for marriage. . .unless you're interested in. . ." At her incensed look, he shrugged. "Me either. Not anymore."

"How dare you?"

She felt her cheeks flame to think she'd been holding him in such high esteem all these years. The hint of scandal came to mind. He must have cheated on his poor wife. It was time to employ her good southern graces and put an end to this madness. "This river is too serene for raised voices. And your brooding face is frightening the fish away. I'm sorry I interrupted your sport. But please. Take me back to the beach and then you can drift around in manly solitude."

"I did come here for a bit of peace and quiet. It's settled, then." He retrieved the oars and set their course back to the beach.

They rode in silence until the tip of the boat gently nudged the shore. In an instant, she leaped out and sloshed through the water again, jerking at her skirt to plow through the reeds.

"Hope your daddy didn't pay too much for those boots," he remarked.

Ignoring him and the sandspurs that stuck to her wet clothing, she whistled. Thankfully, Ebony Rose immediately appeared out of the brush, unscathed by the ghostly bear.

He crossed his arms and stretched out his legs as if happy for her absence. "Well, what do you know. A devoted animal. That's almost as surprising as a woman who can whistle. But can it find its way home?"

"We can both find our way home." She cringed, wondering if she'd divulged too much. Oh, it didn't matter if he learned her identity—later, when she didn't have to face that infuriating smirk.

"Well, if you're sure you aren't lost?"

One last peek. His handsome face was a picture of mockery. "Of course not."

He tipped his hat, considering. Then shrugged. "All right. I hope you don't run into any more bears, Miss Bliss."

Her toes squished in her boots as she hoisted herself into the saddle. She used her gloves to bat off as many sandspurs as possible. "And I hope you brought a lantern, Mr. Taylor. I'm sure you'll be fishing far into the dark to catch your supper. The fish can see you too, you know." She nudged Ebony Rose to the edge of the vegetation, which now looked more pathetic from the freeze than when she'd first arrived, if that were possible. She paused to look over her shoulder. His back was already toward her, his black hair curling long around his neck. The nerve! He really didn't care a whit if she made it home safely or not. And to think Virgil could never measure up because she'd been subconsciously pining for this infuriating, unfaithful man all these years. She hadn't prayed, but God knew her soul. Today's encounter must be His way of healing her childish heart and changing her mind about Virgil.

Jackson cast his line and looked back toward the beach just in time to see the intriguing brunette belle disappear into the mossy forest. He lay back his head and laughed. She was the best amusement he'd enjoyed in a very long while. Though the little belle caught him unawares when she'd launched into his boat, throwing her small, curvaceous body against him and nearly dumping them both into the water, his instincts quickly kicked in to avoid the danger.

He'd noticed the bear scat too and even caught a glimpse of its black fur disappearing into the woods after she'd jumped into the boat. He knew mama bears could be dangerous, so he'd kept them adrift to be sure to give it time to leave the beach. He shouldn't have provoked the little belle, but she'd been on the defensive from the start and he'd enjoyed the tease. He wasn't good with women, didn't trust them, and didn't have anything to do with them unless he was weak. He'd also wanted to observe her, for there had been something oddly familiar about her, if not intriguing.

Huge hazel eyes like hers left a mark on a man, soulful, trusting, deep. In all honesty, he'd stalled on the water longer than necessary because he'd been mesmerized. He knew if he could but take time to explore those eyes, he'd find mysteries like mischief and dignity, so much was there open for observation. It was like looking through the glass-bottomed boats and watching the aquatic life. Something about her made him feel nostalgic. But he couldn't place it. Her face was common, roundly pleasant, but the mouth was what would get him in trouble. Hers wasn't a prissy mouth or a grim one, but expressive, supple, and naive. He'd kept his eyes away from her lips after that one long glance.

Drat, he'd snagged his line daydreaming. He rowed to the spot where the crystalline waters showed it hooked on a rock. He was able to maneuver until he freed it. Startled orange-and-green sunfish darted away from their river castle. She was right. They could see him too. Who was she? It wouldn't be long before he knew. It was a small community, and he'd figure it out soon enough.

As intriguing as she was, he needed to clear his mind of her. He had no intention of getting entangled with a female again, not after his wife had cheated on him and trounced on his heart. He'd been crushed to discover all in one fell swoop of her unfaithfulness and also her fiery death. He'd been young and foolish to run away and invest so many miserable years in the cavalry.

He wasn't cut out for fighting Indians or defending railroads for all those bloody years his heart longed to return to the land. The cotton. The river. His father. In order to remain here, he needed to make peace with himself. But, he vowed, he would never allow himself to become vulnerable again. No woman would wield power over him, the power to break him into a million worthless pieces. A sudden tug on his line commanded his attention. As he brought a plump bluegill into the boat and watched it flop helplessly, he thought, *And that, gentlemen, is what happens when you take a woman's bait. No sir. Never again.*

Chapter 3

"You look stunning," Virgil said as he tucked Maribelle's gloved hand in the crook of his arm and led her toward his awaiting carriage.

"You're too kind." She moved gracefully in her long green gown of fitted bodice and ruffled skirt that fell in eloquent folds, and held her head in a regal posture fitting of her glittering tiara. "And I'm sure all the ladies will envy me, Virgil, for you are in excellent form." He wore a stylish tuxedo suit with white shirt and white tie that gave a contrast to his dark good looks.

He whispered huskily in her ear. "With eyes only for you. It's going to be a special night for us. Watch your step. The rain made things a muddy cesspool. I guess perfection is too high an aim, except for you, sweets." The air was saturated with the musty smell of decaying foliage.

"I'm sure your uncle has done everything necessary to make the evening perfect. Only look at the full moon."

Virgil glanced upward. "I don't think he's responsible for it. But it is beautiful, you're right. The night is young, and we have each other." He helped her inside and spoke some private words to the footman. She caught something about going extra slow. He joined her, and the rig lurched and set into motion. Before the carriage had left Marmalade Plantation, Virgil moved to sit next to her on the scarlet padded seat. Taking her hand in both of his and resting it upon his knee, he stammered a bit, which was unlike his nature, something about the moonlight and her beauty. Strange for Virgil, to still be prattling on about the moon.

"The moonlight's dreamy, isn't it?" she agreed, smiling, hoping to calm him. Mama had warned her that he might propose on the way to the party so that his uncle could announce it to the guests. There would be plenty of time, as the road went past the citrus grove and wound through a subtropical forest before it entered Ocala, where Virgil resided with his uncle Walter on an acclaimed boulevard dotted with affluent town houses. She was instructed to encourage him in his endeavor, for Mama claimed men often needed help with these types of things. The biggest event of her life was happening at this very moment, and yet she wasn't nervous or giddy, simply resigned.

He massaged her hand. "Your smile makes everything easier. That's why I need you at my side. Want you. Forever. What I'm trying to say, sweets—"

Maribelle gasped as the carriage careened violently then pitched sharply to the right. *Bliss and blazes!* "Ouch!" She rubbed the side of her head where it had banged against the carriage.

"Are you all right?" Virgil asked, looking quite startled.

"Yes, I think so."

She heard the driver cursing and suddenly found her hand brushed aside as Virgil swung open the door and leaned out to shout at him. "Is this how you carry out my instructions?" The night air rushed inside the coach. With a groan, Virgil eventually popped back in and apologized. "The footman claims it's the wheel or axle. He's checking."

"Virgil, you're making the carriage even more unstable."

Now glowering, Virgil settled onto the opposite seat and folded his arms. The sudden distance added to the unpleasant situation.

"I'm sorry. I didn't mean to upset you."

"No, sweets, it's not you. Just disappointed," he replied.

The footman knocked on the door, and Virgil opened it.

"Sir, we're stuck and the axle's bent. But the other carriage can take y'all."

At this pronouncement, Virgil leaned out and waved at another carriage then ducked back in with a more optimistic expression. Maribelle appreciated the way he quickly rebounded. One thing for sure, whatever his mood, it was always passionately displayed. Now he was overplaying the gallant. "Prepare yourself to be swept off your feet. I will carry you to the new carriage."

"What? But surely there's another way?"

He shook his head. "Not in those slippers. I aim to get you to safety."

She nodded reluctantly.

"Excellent. I'll jump down first, and as long as I don't disappear into the muck. . ." He winked. "Just trust me."

"Oh, I do." She heard the sucking sound of his boots, and the humor of their situation hit her so that she couldn't help but giggle.

With the carriage at such a crazy tilt, she leaned forward and fell easily into Virgil's arms. He clutched her close and secure. She didn't know where he obtained such a muscular form, since he worked with his uncle at the bank, but it was one of his endearing features. "This really *is* turning into a special night," she said, laughing.

"You mock me." He grinned back.

Once they reached the road and the sucking boot noises subsided, she turned her attention to their rescuers. Two obliging men, dressed formally, stood on the road waiting for them. The closer they got, the surer she became that her fate had taken an even crazier turn.

The older of the two gentlemen stepped forward in good spirits. "I see you're in a bit of a pickle. We are headed to your uncle's and happy to give you a ride."

"And we're happy and grateful to accept," Virgil replied, still playing gallant.

She tugged on Virgil's sleeve, reminding him to set her down, but he paid her no heed except to hold her in a less possessive manner.

The older man, James Taylor, introduced his son Jackson to Virgil—the veritable Yankee newcomer to the community—and while Virgil extended a friendly greeting, Jackson's manner was decidedly cool. It remained evident that Virgil was the true gentleman of the two.

"And the lovely young lady?" Jackson asked his father while giving Maribelle a mischievous glance.

"Oh. You don't remember? This is our neighbor, Maribelle Sinclair."

"Gentlemen," she acknowledged with as much grace as she could muster. "I believe I can walk from here."

"Not on my watch," Virgil replied. "You know how I fear your mama, and I'll not allow you to muddy your shoes."

"Well, then. After you." Jackson motioned while curving the corner of his mouth.

She knew exactly what he was thinking and gave him a quelling look, hoping he would keep certain information private.

Virgil stopped just outside the carriage and glanced forlornly at the footman's seat.

"Oh, don't worry about your boots," Mr. Taylor said, shooing them inside.

In a few moments, Maribelle sat next to Virgil, facing the other two men, one eyeing her with far too much interest as she straightened her skirt and tried to regain her composure. She could barely breathe, the interior was so crowded.

"Bliss. . .hmm," Jackson said, studying her.

Virgil frowned.

Before Jackson could elaborate, she blurted, "It's a blessing you came along when you did. Are you visiting here, sir?" The jig was up, but she tried not to let him unnerve her.

"No. I'm home to stay."

Virgil eyed them curiously.

However, Jackson's father beamed. "Yes, I'm happy for him to ease into the business of running the estate. I'm delighted for your uncle's invitation, which will be a good way for him to renew our connections."

The dinner party was to be a small group of a dozen or so couples, many of whom were Walter Agnew's business acquaintances. Maribelle could tell her near intended was picking up on Jackson's flirtatious glances when he replied, "I'll be sure Uncle Walter knows how you rescued us tonight." He smiled possessively. "He's very attached to *our* Maribelle."

Jackson's brows arched. "How blissful." He settled back into his seat, remaining sullenly silent.

Virgil eyed him crossly, no doubt well aware that was one of Maribelle's bywords.

When they reached the Agnew town house, Virgil quickly excused himself to change his boots and muttered something about speaking to his uncle, promising to return hastily.

Maribelle sighed and looked about the stately room. Furniture had been pushed to the perimeter and small tables were scattered about, eloquently decorated in white and gold with green bough remnants of the holiday season and laden with hors d'oeuvres and drinks. A huge chandelier sparkled from the town's electricity—which had not reached Marmalade yet. In the corner, a handful of musicians played soft music.

"Feeling deserted, little belle?" Jackson asked, stepping forward seemingly out of nowhere and smoothly guiding her to the edge of the room.

"Somewhat. Thanks for not exposing my antics of the other day."

"You really owe me now." He studied her. "Seems you make it a habit of throwing yourself in a fellow's arms."

"It would seem that way, yes, but it's hardly true."

He offered her a glass of punch. "Why didn't you tell me who you were the other day?"

"Because I already looked foolish enough in your eyes, and that would have made me appear even more foolish."

"Yes, I remember the gator. But that was a real threat. And worse, it would have made me twice the hero."

"Exactly. I could tell you already carry a high enough opinion of yourself and didn't need my praise, so I kept my peace." She looked about the room. Papa was in a corner speaking with Walter and some of their old friends. Mama was talking to Willa Fay Carroway and Mrs. Carroway, and from the restless look in Willa Fay's eyes, it wouldn't be long until she made her way to Maribelle. It was peculiar to be having this private moment with the phantom from her past. "I'm glad you're home, as long as you don't deny me my favorite beach spot."

"I'm home and ready to do my duty now. Though the cotton harvest is past, I'll probably still be too busy to do much fishing, so go ahead and use my beach."

She couldn't help but wonder what had happened to his wife. "The other day you made a big point about not getting married again. Isn't that part of your duty?"

"I meant what I said. Surely you aren't planning to entrap me again?"

"Hardly."

"What about you? Has Virgil spoken for you?"

"No, but I'm expecting it."

"I see." He got a glint in his eye. "Being the romantic you are, I suppose you didn't miss tonight's full moon, and I imagine you nearly swooned when he carried you over the mud."

She laughed. "Not at all. I could hardly keep from laughing."

And they were laughing together over the ridiculous scene when Mama appeared with a puzzled frown. "You remember Mama?" Once she renewed the introductions, Jackson excused himself from their presence.

"What was that about?" Tonight Mama looked beautiful with her hair in a sleek twist, but she eyed his departing back as if he carried the pox. "Where's Virgil?"

Maribelle quickly explained as Mama's eyes widened more and more.

"Don't panic, Mama. The night is young. And so far it's been exciting. Certainly not dull."

"Sometimes dull is the better option. Let's go talk to Willa Fay and her mama. I'm sure Virgil will find you as soon as he can."

Maribelle wasn't fond of Willa Fay because, in the other woman's eyes, they'd once been—and probably still remained—rivals over Virgil. But Willa

Fay seemed to be thrown into Maribelle's life right now since her daddy also had connections with Walter Agnew.

"Hello, Maribelle. I'm surprised you didn't arrive with Virgil. I wonder what's keeping him, do you know?" Willa Fay asked.

"Actually, we came together, but his rig got hung up, so we switched carriages and came with Jackson Taylor and his father. I suppose Virgil is changing his boots or something." She patted Willa Fay's hand. "Which gives the two of us more time to catch up."

The redhead gave a fake smile. "Delightful. Who is Jackson Taylor?"

"He's our neighbor. He was serving in the cavalry for many years but he's home again."

"Then you must introduce me. You can't have all the men to yourself." Glancing around the room and opening her fan, Willa Fay frowned. "Most of them are ancient."

"Well, if you don't like older men, Jackson Taylor might not suit." Maribelle tapped her forehead as if thinking. "On the other hand, he's older than us, but not ancient." She leaned close and whispered, "And rumor has it, he's returned to take over his rightful duties. And you know what that means." Maribelle felt more justified than guilty, putting Willa Fay on a false scent.

"Is that so?" She peeked over her fan, gazing about the room. "Is that him by that palmetto palm in the corner?"

"Yes."

Willa Fay's green eyes widened. "Not ancient at all. Very good looking."

"There you are." Virgil advanced, looking immaculate and charming, perfect in every way.

"Good evening." Willa Fay lowered her blackened lashes and raised them again. "I was just telling Maribelle I haven't met Mr. Taylor yet."

"I'll introduce you at dinner. May I escort you ladies now?"

The table was set with many forks and gilded tablecloth and place cards. Three centerpieces of exotic fruits and greenery set off the glowing candles and sparkling goblets. After introductions, a freckle-cheeked Mrs. Carroway began at once to acquaint Jackson with Willa Fay's many assets and abilities. He gave Maribelle a quelling look from his place across the table. She shrugged and hid her smile in her napkin. While Willa Fay sat on Virgil's left, Jackson's left was flanked by Mrs. Whitman, the wife of a buyer, who was listening to Mrs. Carroway with a pinched expression. Jackson noticed her interest and spoke something pleasant to her, but she shook her head.

Meanwhile, Willa Fay asked, "What spurred you to return to Florida?"

Jackson's brown gaze got a dreamy, faraway look for an instant, and then he replied, "Actually, it was last year's Oklahoma land rush."

The footman brought in a second course and, once he'd moved past, Willa Fay replied, "I'm not familiar with it. Was it good or bad?"

"It was the most amazing thing I've ever witnessed. The government was giving away Indian land, and it was the most riotous event you can imagine. A land race." Jackson was now gesturing with his hands. "People came from everywhere and camped out, ready for the event. Everybody lined up on horses and in wagons, some on bicycles and some afoot. There was even a train. At the cannon's blast right at high noon, the race started. All the people had to do was claim their land."

"Why, I've never heard anything like it," Willa Fay exclaimed.

Beside Jackson, Mrs. Whitman, who was in the motherly way, was turning positively green. Perhaps she found it as ghastly as Maribelle did.

Virgil blotted his mouth with his napkin and placed it back on his lap. "I'd like to have seen it."

"You can. They're planning another one this year in Oklahoma."

"Oklahoma." Virgil tasted the word.

If possible Mrs. Whitman appeared even paler.

"I imagine it's cold in Oklahoma." Maribelle frowned. The last thing she wished to do was leave her beloved South. Surely Virgil wasn't open to such a crazy venture.

"It sounds exciting," Willa Fay replied, her green eyes sparkling. "I would love to see something like that. Are you going back?"

Jackson replied, "No. I watched people risk getting stampeded for a chance at something I already possessed. I decided when my term was up, I would head home. Seemed sinful to neglect such a gift."

"How poetic." Willa Fay sighed.

Poetic? Did the girl not know how to identify sadness? It cut Maribelle's heart to catch a glimpse of pain in Jackson's soft brown eyes and wonder what could have happened to push him away in the first place. He must have come to a point of regret over the way he had treated his wife. Whatever it was, the glimpse into his soul made her sad for him now. She looked up at him, and he held her gaze, most likely reading her thoughts.

Virgil winked at Maribelle. "So what do you imagine these settlers do in Oklahoma?"

"Raise hay and beans and children," Jackson replied.

Mrs. Whitman blushed, and Maribelle was heartened to see some color return to her face.

"Sounds enticing," Virgil said.

"Doesn't sound so different than here," Willa Fay said. "Only we raise oranges and cotton."

"And we don't have to freeze while we're doing it," Maribelle added just to be certain Virgil was catching her position on the matter.

He lowered his voice to a whisper. "I know you don't like cold weather, and I don't plan to whisk you away to Oklahoma, but I hope you'll spare me a few minutes in the garden during the musical. I didn't get to finish what we were speaking about when the carriage interrupted us."

She could feel her eyes widening and tried to remain unaffected under the gaze of their fellow guests. "Yes, of course."

"I promise to keep you warm," he nearly purred.

She lowered her lashes. It seemed he understood her, and if he was so determined, they might as well get it over so everyone could relax again.

After supper the women were led to a brown-and-mustard-colored parlor with intimate seating and a pianoforte, also decorated with more candles, holly, and oranges. Mrs. Whitman disappeared, and Maribelle became the sounding board for Willa Fay's ramblings about how dutiful and handsome Jackson was. Willa Fay prodded her with questions about how Maribelle thought Jackson felt about her. Maribelle was grateful when the men returned and the room was arranged for the musical. When Mrs. Whitman entered the room and drew a bit of attention to herself, Maribelle used the opportune moment to slip away to meet Virgil in the patio garden. Cobblestone walkways were lit with electric lanterns. The familiar scent of citrus trees and magnolias filled the air and moved to calm her.

"There you are." Virgil slipped his coat over her shoulders. "I promise we won't go to the Oklahoma land race. I'm sorry I teased you. You're not mad?"

"Of course not, but Mrs. Whitman didn't seem to enjoy the conversation either. Do you think her husband has plans—"

"Shush now." He led her to a wooden arch decorated with holiday greenery. "We only need to concern ourselves with our own plans. Plans I've been trying to make all evening now. I hope you know I'll do everything in my power to make you happy, to take care of you."

"You did a wonderful job of that tonight."

"I did, didn't I? And I hope to always have that privilege. What I'm try-ing to say. . ." He took both her hands in his. "If you'll just put me out of my misery since I'm botching this magical moment and say you'll wed me, then Uncle Walter can make the announcement tonight after the musical, and I promise I'll do a better job of professing my love in the future. A very long and happy future, I might add."

His expression was not at all like he'd had in the silly dream. She'd been scrutinizing for any sign of harshness, but none was exhibited. Exasperation, perhaps, over some of the events of the evening, but he was a passionate man. Now, if anything, he appeared humbled. Although it was a blundering proposal, she opened her mouth to put him out of his misery when they were once again interrupted.

"I say, Virgil!" a voice called, rather forcefully. Footsteps could be heard on the cobblestones coming in their direction.

"Whatever the. . ." Virgil's shoulders sagged and he snapped an irritated gaze toward the house. "Over here," he called.

Jackson came upon them and abruptly hesitated. "Oh, I'm sorry to inter-rupt. It's just that Mrs. Whitman—forgive me for my bluntness—is having a baby. Her husband's a puddle of nerves and someone should send for a doctor."

Virgil gave Maribelle a weak smile. "This is madness."

"Don't worry. We'll finish this later. You better go." She slipped off his coat. "You may need this. I'll be right behind you."

He left her, mumbling something about why his uncle hadn't taken care of the matter or sent a servant.

The instant Virgil's back was turned, Jackson draped his own coat over her shoulders. "Did I interrupt that something special you were expecting?"

"Yes. You certainly did." She shook her head in disbelief of their unfortu-nate circumstances. "He was waiting for my answer. You see, the reason he's so frustrated, he told Daddy he planned to propose at the New Year's Eve party. Then the party was delayed because of the freeze. Then in the carriage he was in the middle of it when we broke down. And now again. Three times. Mama's not going to believe this. She'll think I'm sabotaging it on purpose."

"And why is that?"

Maribelle shook her head. "You obviously don't know Mama."

"Hmm. You're right about that. As a casual observer, may I offer an observation?"

She tilted her head and shrugged.

"Could it be fate? Three times, that's daunting. Are you sure you want to marry?"

"I don't believe in fate, but I do believe in prayer. And I assure you I've been praying and will continue to do so. That's why I went to my rock the day we met."

"Your rock?"

"Very well, your rock on the beach is my prayer rock."

"And you were interrupted that day too. Hmm. All coincidences?"

"I..." Maribelle grew quiet. Though her prayers had been interrupted that day, God knew her heart. Could it be that He was giving her a sign?

All evening his protective instincts had reared up in Maribelle's behalf. At first because she was the same woman who'd needed his help from the gator and the bear, and next because it seemed she was headed for a marriage with three counts already against it. If only he could keep her from the heartbreak he'd experienced. He sensed something flighty about Virgil. But mostly, he owed Maribelle. The note she'd given him all those years ago had sustained him through some dark days. Its message of heroics and overcoming had wiggled its way into his brain until he almost believed it. The note had become a lucky charm as he carried it next to his heart through battle. When he'd told Willa Fay about the reason he'd returned home, he'd left out the most important part. He'd become a believer in Jesus.

His newfound faith was something he didn't entirely understand, but he knew it was real. Now he longed to tell Maribelle about it and should have when she mentioned prayer. Maybe she would have some of the answers to his questions about his faith. As he contemplated this, he noticed her sudden silence and wondered if he'd offended her. He wished to make amends and thank her for writing the note. But tonight was not the time for it. "Forgive me for prying. Let me make it up to you with a ride on the glass-bottomed boat. As friends who share a beach."

"Friends?"

"I'd like to be friends."

She smiled. "I'd like that too, but maybe we can discuss the boat ride another time, when it's not so cold."

As he retrieved his coat and led her back inside, he ignored the little tug on his heart. *Just friends who share a beach. Surely there's no danger in that.*

Chapter 4

The next morning Maribelle awoke with a headache and lay abed staring up at the six-foot headboard and wrestling with her thoughts, blaming herself for not having secured an engagement. She'd gone over it repeatedly. Why hadn't she given her acceptance at once? Was it because Virgil hadn't gotten down on his knees to give her the proposal of her dreams? It may not have been the time to announce the engagement, given Mrs. Whitman's situation, but at least she wouldn't have to endure yet another attempt. She hadn't even refused Jackson's invitation. She'd been fighting the image of glass-bottomed boats all morning. There was no reason to think about him. He was no gentleman and held no honorable intentions. Why, Virgil was more of a southern gentleman than the man who'd been bred to be one. She should have turned the rascal down on the spot. Friendship?

There was a tap at the door.

"Come in."

Mama entered with a look of concern. "Milda said you're suffering this morning."

"I've a headache, probably from hitting my head on the carriage. It was such an eventful evening I pushed it aside, but I awoke feeling like I'd been hit with a club."

"Where is it?" Mama examined the spot. "There's a small bump. Shall I send for the doctor?"

"I don't know. Maybe it's just my thoughts giving me a headache."

"Tell me what happened."

"Twice Virgil proposed and twice we were interrupted. He tried once in the carriage and again in the garden, but then Mrs. Whitman went into labor. On the ride home he was silent and surly."

"Oh dear, I wonder what that could mean? Surely he's not having second thoughts? Is that what you think?"

She frowned. "I don't know."

"Let's invite him for supper. Since he's already asked, you can give him your answer."

"I have a headache, remember?"

"Oh yes. I'll get you something for that." Mama rose. "If it doesn't go away soon, we'll send for the doctor."

"Mama, let's allow Virgil to take the lead. If he's the man I need him to be, he'll figure it out."

"Just rest, dear. I may go back to bed myself." She started toward the door. "Oh, Mrs. Whitman had a boy. Everything is fine."

"That's good news." The door closed, and she berated herself for not even praying for Mrs. Whitman.

The following day Maribelle spent the morning persuading Mama to allow Virgil to call at his own will. A man like Virgil didn't toss a proposal into the air without following it to its end. However, Jackson was the first gentleman to arrive. They walked together along a path edged in gardenia and hibiscus. "It's sad how the freeze has ruined them. Usually, they bloom all year."

He scrutinized her with his soft brown gaze and a hint of a smile. "You're not fond of cold weather, are you?"

"Of course not. Are you?"

"No. Yet another reason for my return."

"I don't see how anyone can move north after they've lived in the South. Sometimes I worry that Virgil will want to do that after we're married. He doesn't seem settled. Daddy says that's ridiculous, because he has his financial connections here, that he'd be foolish to abandon them. I wish I could be sure."

"Why don't you ask him?"

"I have. He asks that I trust him."

They sat on a bench between two gardenias. "Not sure I'll ever fully trust again." His expression took on a faraway look. "You gave me a note once."

She cringed. "I'd hoped you'd forgotten it."

"Why?"

"Because I didn't know you were married and I'm pretty sure it was inappropriate."

He smiled. "You were only a child. I went through a dark time after I lost my wife, and I carried your note in my pocket. I didn't know God then. I sorely needed the encouragement it provided."

It was flattering to discover the note held meaning for him. "What happened to your wife?"

"You don't know?"

She shook her head.

"The big fire caught her. . .in her lover's bed."

Maribelle gasped. "I'm so sorry. I had no idea."

"I'm fine. It was a long time ago."

To think she'd assumed he was the cheater. It all made sense now, and he was far from fine. She touched a gardenia stem.

"Don't look so sad, little belle. The garden will bloom again."

"I love Marmalade Plantation. Daddy has grand expansion plans. Virgil's already promised to see that he gets the money he needs. Daddy's always trying to prove himself. His family thought he was crazy to pull up his Carolina roots and grow citrus instead of cotton. Anyway, the freeze lost Daddy a lot of money, but Virgil will keep us afloat. You see, I have to marry him for the sake of Marmalade." She wondered how it was that she could speak so freely to Jackson. Perhaps it was all the imaginary conversations they'd had when she was a child.

"I'm sorry. But maybe it's better if you don't love. Then love can't be taken from you."

She thought about that a lot after he left. And she was still thinking about it when Virgil arrived.

The family left them alone in the parlor, and Maribelle could only hope there weren't any ears pressed against the wall.

He sat next to a small table with an oil lamp. "I apologize for ruining everything the other night."

"Why, none of it was your fault. None of it could be helped."

"Are you religious?" he asked, his blue eyes intense.

"Yes, I believe in God and His Son, Jesus. Do you?"

"Yes. I keep wondering why He's allowing this to happen to us."

"I wondered about it too. Are you retracting your proposal?"

Virgil looked surprised. "No. Nothing like that. A few jitters perhaps."

"I've sensed your restlessness. If we marry, do you plan to leave Ocala?"

"I can't promise you we won't. The nation is in financial straits right now. Who can predict the future?"

"But your uncle is well planted, isn't he?"

"Yes. And as long as he holds the purse strings, I must fall in line with his wishes. As you know, he wants me to fit into his community. My restlessness comes from deciding if it's worth it. But if you agree to marry me, I'll do what is best for our happiness. Trust me, please. I know you will make everything I must do worthwhile."

They broke off the conversation as they were served tea and cake. Once again he'd failed to persuade her of his affections. She wondered how long this virile man could be happy remaining under his uncle's thumb. He looked the type to be doing something far more dangerous than learning how to become a southern gentleman. She thought about the implications a breakup would have for Marmalade. It wasn't only the possibility of Virgil's uncle withdrawing the loan, but he and Daddy had old connections from their roots in South Carolina, roots strong enough to redeem Virgil's northern ways. She traced the rim of her teacup. "I confess I'm feeling the jitters too. I was ready to say yes, but now I wonder if we are both being forced into this marriage—"

He placed his cup back on the side table. "I spoke too freely and gave you the wrong impression. Any man would be mad to spoil his chance with you. I know you are a free spirit, and I'm sure we'll be a perfect match whatever the future holds. So please don't say anything unless it's yes." He stood and went to her. "Please say yes, sweets."

"Yes."

He kissed her hand. "Thank you. I love you."

He looked relieved to have it settled. "But. . .I'd like to go slow," Maribelle said.

"Of course, darling. I understand. I'll leave all the details to you."

He left her with a smile on his thoughtful face. Were his shoulders a tad too rigid and determined for a man in love? It reminded her of her Daddy's stance when he braced himself for an unpleasant task.

Jackson found the prayer rock and used it faithfully. There was always an endless list of requests as he eased into his position on the family's cotton plantation. For the first time in a decade he was sure of his peace with God, and yet there was still an unsettled feeling. For instance, after prayer there was always that desire to pull out Maribelle's note. A grown man shouldn't need a child's note, but the closer he grew to God, the more attachment he felt to it. He withdrew it now from its place inside his shirt. Sometimes he merely patted the hidden pocket to be sure it was there; sometimes he handled it and relived his days in the cavalry. Today he carefully unfolded it and read the childish handwriting.

> *Dear Jackson,*
>
> *Thanks for saving my life. I thought that old gator was going to eat me alive. But you scooped me up and protected me. You are so brave. I never felt so safe before. Sometimes at night when I'm afraid of the dark, I think of you and then I can fall asleep. I wonder what this means. I know one thing it means, you are a hero and willing to sacrifice your life for others. I will always remember how fearless you were to rescue me. I'm counting on you to remain dauntless and when I'm sixteen I hope to claim a real kiss and not on the cheek. Maybe we can ride the glass-bottomed boat together.*
>
>

Yours truly,
Maribelle
P.S. I'm ten years old, and my birthday is February 1.

He hadn't seen her after that because of the terrible fire. He'd never had an opportunity to explain he was married and often wondered if she'd even thought about him when she turned sixteen. He'd certainly thought about her often enough, remembering her round, trusting eyes. After using the note to scrape up the courage to face each day, he felt an odd connection with her and knew he needed to see her again and make sure she was going to be all right if she married Virgil Agnew. Hard as he wished, he couldn't deny the affection he felt for the curvy little brunette belle.

Over the next few weeks, Mama began preparations for the wedding even though Maribelle kept reminding her that she and Virgil had agreed to take it slowly. Mama couldn't understand why she didn't want to share her joy with the world, and Maribelle soon fell in line with the family's wishes. Her doubts faded until the day a note was handed to her by Milda. Jackson wished to meet her at the glass-bottomed boat dock on the morrow.

Chapter 5

Maribelle stood on a shaded dock, watching the expanding ripples from a pair of wood ducks, thinking how strange a turn her life had taken with Jackson back in Ocala.

"Happy birthday, little belle," he said softly, stepping up beside her.

"Thanks." She was surprised he knew it was her special day. "I probably shouldn't be here. Virgil wouldn't approve, nor Mama." She disapproved of her own actions, which could possibly stir up the old feelings, yet here she was like a moth drawn to the flame.

"Why are you here?"

She shrugged, trying to disguise the longing in her gaze. The sunlight filtered through the trees, casting silver glints around them. She tucked in the tresses that escaped her small wool equestrian hat. "This river has cast a spell over me." She sighed. "But I need to grow up and put aside fanciful notions."

She let her gaze wander to his stubbly chin so masculine, but his tone was gentle, even flirtatious. "It's not fanciful to feel a pull to such a beautiful place. I confess I used it to my advantage. You mentioned the glass-bottomed boats in your note, and I didn't think you could resist the romance."

"Oh, bliss and blazes! I don't see romance on every corner, I assure you. In fact, I'm taking a practical stance for my future."

"Then you've changed." She hadn't, and he knew it. It upset her that he always seemed to have the upper hand. She drew from the hurt she had experienced. "After I gave you the note, do you know how disappointed I was when I never saw you again? I came today to close that last door to my childhood." So that she could push it from her mind once again and turn her attention to Virgil and their future.

The river's soft breeze lifted the ends of Jackson's hair, a bit too long and shaggy for current style. He fastened his gaze on the ducks. "It was Theresa's death. Her betrayal. I couldn't cope with it and fled without thinking through the consequences, especially for my dad. I was glad Mom wasn't alive to see it. I was in a dark place and owning nothing but my own despair."

Maribelle turned away from the railing. "I often returned to the beach, waiting. I didn't know anything about your marriage or your departure at the time. I thought I'd frightened you away with my confessions. It was a blow to my ego." More than that, he'd broken her heart. She met his soft brown gaze. "I know now that my childhood crush was nothing like the pain you felt. I'm sorry you had to experience it."

"Thanks." He gave her more of a grimace than a smile and changed the topic. "I'm here now and I've got tickets. Ready to enjoy the moment?"

His face was lean and angular. The strength in it was nothing like Virgil's brute power, but it was sensually masculine. A face that could entice women and yet maintain a smug control against their charms. She knew she was smitten, had always been. And though she could at last forgive him, she shouldn't have come today. How would she ignore these feelings? "Yes."

A large rowboat fitted with a glass bottom, a canvas canopy, and a tour guide who would serve as their oarsman awaited them. Once seated, she tucked her green riding skirt in close to peer into the water visible through the glass window in the middle of the boat. She couldn't help but feel a childlike delight to be able to see into the aquatic world. Large clumps of tall grass waved with the current and provided places for the fish to feed and hide. There were a few other passengers, winter tourists but thankfully all strangers, which provided them the privacy to continue their conversation in low tones.

She looked through the crystal-clear waters at the swimming creatures. Sitting beside Jackson brought back so many childhood memories. "I spied on you back then."

"I know."

"You did?"

He nodded. "I should've told your father to keep a better watch on you, but I didn't want to interfere."

"They've always allowed me a lot of independence. I'm sure once I marry I'll never enjoy such freedom again."

"It's official, then?"

The sun beat hot, and she loosened the top buttons on her jacket and straightened the neck of her white blouse. "Yes. As I told you, Daddy and Walter have old ties. Virgil's attending my birthday supper tonight. Everyone's pressing for us to set a date."

He watched her attentively. "I see. I think you're wrong about one thing. Virgil would be a fool not to fall in love with you."

"That's sweet." His eyes were filled with kindness, and she knew he wasn't speaking as a contender but as a guardian, and she wished it were different. "I'm not a little girl anymore. I don't require your protection."

His smile widened. The corners of his mouth dimpled beneath the shadow of a day-old beard. "I'm aware of that."

She pouted her full lips. "Are you?"

"Yes. I'm aware of your womanly charms, but I won't let my mind dwell there. I warned you, I have no plans for a relationship. And since I've become a Christian, there's no place for anything inappropriate either. Even if you weren't engaged, I don't think I could ever trust another woman. I mean, you admitted Virgil wouldn't approve, and yet here you are spending the afternoon with me." He shook his head and threw up his arms. "Women are so fickle."

He could be infuriating. Wasn't he the one who'd invited her? "That's hardly reasonable, so I'll disregard your insinuations. As your friend, I hope you'll change your mind and love again. Of course, I'm not talking about me, but I want to see you happy. You just need to forgive Theresa first."

They glided past thick trunks and twisted cypress roots. Pond lilies floated on the surface. So tranquil, and yet her heart raced from his nearness. And her pulse quickened from her lies, the way she covered her feelings.

"I didn't have a chance to forgive her before she was gone. To be honest, it wasn't all Theresa's fault. I was pretty restless in those days. I got married too young and I wasn't ready for all the responsibility of the estate. I loved her, but I didn't give her the devotion she needed."

Tears stung the back of Maribelle's eyes, but she was able to keep them at bay. "Virgil is restless too."

"Then you'll have to be patient with him. Stay true to him until he comes to his senses."

"While everything he says and does is quite proper, there's a wild glint in his eyes, and I don't want to hold him back. I don't want to settle for second best either. And I certainly don't want to follow him on some grand gallivant across the country." Or would it be better to get away from her past, her memories, this man whose very nearness set her nerves on edge?

The guide allowed the boat to drift a bit, offering them fish food to toss over the side. Bluegill, bass, and fish she couldn't identify darted around the boat to snap up the food. "Who would want to live anywhere but here?" she asked, verbalizing her struggle.

"Not me," he admitted. "I'm praying for you to make the right decision."

"Thanks. I'm going to pray that you'll be able to forgive and give everything to God, including your fear of women."

He laughed out loud, and she arched a brow. The other passengers pointed to the water, and they turned their attention to watch an otter's antics.

When the tour ended, he helped her off the boat and guided her to a private area behind the cover of some low-hanging acacia trees. "It's a blow to my ego and a bit ironic to hear you name my fears after I've carried your note all these years to remind me of my courage."

"It will be our secret. As well as our prayers for each other."

"God knows."

"Yes, He does."

He took her hands. "I like that. It seems the right way to continue our friendship. I was glad you came today because I wanted to fulfill your requests, the ones you wrote about." She felt her cheeks warm. She knew exactly what she'd written to him all those years ago. He pulled her close. "I missed your sixteenth birthday. You must be about twenty today?"

"It's ungentlemanly to speak of it," she said.

"I'm surprised you haven't married."

"There were offers. I just couldn't." At his intense gaze, she knew he understood and hated herself for admitting it.

"If you'd still like to claim a *real* kiss, I'd be happy to oblige."

She stared at his lips. His smile was taunting and knowing, as if he understood her desire and mirrored it. She wavered but kept her head. "Someone has beat you to it." She saw his disappointment. "So I must decline. But our discussion has helped me decide to break off my engagement with Virgil." There was no *real* in that relationship. "Now please be a gentleman and put some distance between us so I can breathe again." There was a dark flicker in his eyes, and for a moment she thought he was going to kiss her anyway. She would have welcomed it, but he nodded and released her hands.

She took several deep breaths.

"Well done, little belle. I've rescued you three times now. So even without the kiss, we are good now?"

"Especially without the kiss," she replied. "Yes, we are good now." She held out her hand. "In fact, you can give me back the note now."

He shook his head and laughed. "That's never going to happen."

She groaned.

"Let's get you to the stables."

Jackson watched his little brunette belle ride away and disappear into the subtropical forest before he went for his own mount. His heart burgeoned with gratitude. She'd handled him perfectly. She must know how confused he felt, wanting to grant a little girl's dreams while knowing he couldn't make the woman happy.

He would have kissed her given the slightest provocation because he was weak and their bond was strong. Her black hair had glistened playfully all afternoon, and her lush lips had laughed and tempted. But could he ever be faithful to those trusting hazel eyes without breaking both their hearts? She knew he couldn't, and she also knew what he needed to do. Forgive. She once believed the impossible about him, and now it seemed she did again.

He didn't know how to forgive. The best he'd been able to do was harden his heart and put it behind him. He'd given Jesus all that he had to offer, and it was up to God to heal, wasn't it? He'd thought returning to Ocala would help, but he was still as resentful as ever. The only difference was that he now knew running wasn't the remedy.

For now, he'd made his amends with Maribelle. According to her, he'd kept her from entering a loveless and possibly troubled marriage. That is, if she followed through with her plans to end it with Virgil. He thought about her birthday supper. Would she wait until afterward when they were alone or break the news in front of her parents? No, she was too kind to humiliate Virgil like that. He imagined how he would feel if he were Virgil. Would he fight for her? He shook away his musings. He needed to immerse himself in the estate and forget about her. He hoped she didn't come to him for reassurance after she'd broken it off with Virgil. If she did, he didn't know if he would have the strength to resist her. Falling in love again wasn't in his plans. He squeezed his knees against his horse's flanks. "Let's go home."

Maribelle's birthday supper was an intimate affair. Her older married siblings usually didn't attend her birthday parties since her birthday chased the holidays, when they'd all been together. But Grandmama, Daddy, Mama, Virgil, and Walter were included. However, Walter got a cold and couldn't attend. One less to witness her humiliation, and Virgil's. Mama made sure to serve her favorite dishes: crab cakes, roasted turkey, seasonal vegetables, and orange marmalade.

They took dessert in the parlor, which had been stripped of its holiday doodads except for some red berries and burgundy damask on side tables and hearth. Mama thought they suited the month of February. After cake, Grandmama was a living dichotomy when she parked her wheelchair beside Virgil, telling him incidents about Maribelle's childhood, all the while flashing him judgmental frowns. It seemed a shame Grandmama's stilted efforts were wasted.

However, upon watching the elderly woman and the intimate setting around her, Maribelle questioned her own intentions. Should she really turn away such a catch just because he hadn't gotten down on his knees to propose—on any of his three attempts—or just because his love proclamation sounded pat or because of his birthday gift? It wasn't the book of poems he'd given her that disappointed, but the dull inscription. At least he could have bookmarked something.

To her relief, the evening eventually wound down and Virgil asked her to see him to the door. He was probably going to press her about setting the date again. It had been hinted at from the family earlier. Her heart racing, she dismissed the butler at the entryway door. "May I have a word with you before you go?"

"Of course, sweets. It's your birthday. You may have anything you desire within my capability."

"I'm sure I'm the biggest fool who ever breathed, but. . ."

He touched her arm. "What's wrong?"

"I can't marry you."

His hand fell to his side. "But I thought we'd gotten past our doubts, that this was settled. Except for the date, of course."

She glanced up at the coffered ceiling and down at the geometric foyer tile in shame. "I thought so too, and the only reason I can give you is that I don't believe we suit each other. In the end we would make each other miserable."

His brows arched, and he said passionately, "Everyone else seems to think we suit."

"Only because we fit into their expectations and plans. Think about it.

What do you want, Virgil?"

His passion abated. "I believe you know. But I can't let you do this. Your parents and Uncle Walter will never forgive you."

"Oh, surely they will someday."

One side of his mouth curled. He was ruggedly handsome, and she inwardly chastised herself for pushing him away. "You're so brave." He placed his hands on her shoulders. "Look at you. I've never loved you more."

She cupped his face. "It's the right thing. We both know it."

"Very well. We won't marry. And I'll say it was all my doing. I'm sure in a way, it was. You were able to read me so thoroughly."

She nodded gratefully. "I want you to know, I saw your good intentions and don't fault you. Will you leave Ocala with your newfound freedom?"

"Not now. Uncle Walter's too fond of me. But I will do things my way in the future."

"I hope it doesn't dissolve Walter's friendship with Daddy." *Or Marmalade's future,* more to the point.

"That remains to be seen. Goodbye, Maribelle." He bent and kissed her cheek.

She stood in the open doorway, watching his retreating back, wondering if she'd done the right thing or if she would regret this some future day when she was old and lonely and unmarried. Flamingos honked in the distance. She shuddered and went to face the family, who no doubt were expecting her to return with a wedding date.

Grandmama broke the silence, squinting her eyes. "He will do, I suppose."

"I know you tried to like him. But I fear he won't do, after all." Maribelle braced herself when all eyes shifted to her face. Meeting Mama's wide, alarmed eyes, she explained, "We just dissolved our engagement."

Mama gripped the blue fabric of her tufted chair. "You can't mean it."

Daddy asked harshly, "What is this?"

Squaring her shoulders, Maribelle replied, "Virgil and I have agreed we don't suit. He's not ready to settle down. Surely you know he's an adventurous sort being forced into a cage, and he's tired of his uncle stifling his opportunities."

"I'm so sorry, dear." Grandmama's voice held a sad tone, but her blue-gray eyes twinkled beneath her gray brows.

"It's fine." Maribelle smiled. "It would have been a loveless match. Looking in his face has been like looking in the mirror and seeing my own regrets.

My pain comes from disappointing you all."

"What is love?" Daddy asked in a booming voice then, at Mama's alarm, patted her arm. "I'm sorry, I didn't mean it like that."

Mama softened. "It's true, we didn't love each other at first, but now we do, and you shall too, Maribelle. Don't hold that against Virgil."

"Well, I never liked him," Grandmama stated, poking at a pearl pin in her white chignon.

The room silenced, and Maribelle read their grim minds. "What's to become of Daddy's plans for Marmalade Plantation? Although we're in agreement on the matter, Virgil plans to tell his uncle he broke it off. He's accepting the blame. He was very gallant and determined to protect me, but I had to tell you the truth. It was mutual. This whole situation has forced me to be untrue to myself and others. I can hardly pray anymore."

"Maribelle! Don't say such things," Mama chided.

"Maybe Walter will still finance Marmalade." She turned to Daddy. "You are old friends."

"This isn't about a loan, Junebug," Daddy explained. "It's about alliances and a secure future."

"I'm sorry to disappoint."

Mama wiped her eyes. "You'd never disappoint us. Let's not talk about it anymore. It's your birthday."

A stark reminder to all. Twenty years old and turning down another marriage proposal.

Chapter 6

Another unusual cold spell moved in, even worse than the first one, while Maribelle moped about the house grateful Mama left her to her own devices. Only her daily horseback rides brought any peace. She'd ventured to the beach hoping to run into Jackson, but he was nowhere to be found. In a moment of weakness she even wrote another note, this time telling him that she'd ended the engagement with Virgil, how he'd taken most of the blame, and how everyone was disappointed and downcast. She asked him to meet her at the prayer rock the next morning, if he could. She knew it was unseemly, but she asked Milda to see that it was sent discreetly to Jackson.

The next day she awoke early, anxious to see him. She donned her favorite blue riding habit and set out with cheese and wine inside her saddlebag. Bracing against the bitter cold, she went against her better judgment and rode toward the beach. The wind howled. Even the river was choppy. She fetched a blanket from her saddlebag and huddled on the frigid rock, hugging her knees. After miserably waiting past the designated hour, she realized Jackson wasn't going to show. With distress, she imagined he was intentionally avoiding her. What had she been thinking to snatch at hope, repeating history and tempting fate with yet a second note? Lifting her chin, she jumped down and threw together her belongings. She must let him go too. So be it.

Jackson paced before the hearth in his new town house, reading and rereading the little belle's letter. Finally he crumpled it and tossed it in the fire. As the flames blackened the paper, the decision was made. He wouldn't encourage her. Though it pleased him immensely that she wouldn't be wedding Virgil, he had nothing to offer her either. He wasn't in the market for a wife, and if he continued a flirtation with Maribelle, marriage would be the inevitable outcome. Yet, with a pang of conscience, he remembered how she'd felt when

171

he hadn't responded to her childhood note.

There was a good excuse for not meeting her. His father had bought this town house intending to rent it out to Northerners who wintered in Florida, and Jackson had been staying in town getting it up to snuff. Interestingly enough, it was directly across the street from the Agnews. But it would be better not to give her any excuses or touch on the matter at all. Reluctantly, he penned his reply.

The next morning Milda's curls were wilder than usual and falling out of her cap when she brought Maribelle Jackson's note, saying, "There be a ruckus downstairs. Better I fix your hair while you read. Best not waste time."

"Of course." She thrilled to hold a missive from Jackson. "But it's so cold. Let's sit by the fire."

"Yes, miss, but hurry."

Hardly hearing or caring about Milda's babbling, Maribelle tore open the missive.

> *Little Belle,*
>
> *I applaud you for following your heart. Seems Virgil turned out to be the gentleman, and I know how you appreciate a proper gentleman. Not like me, for once again I stood you up. The estate keeps me busy, and there isn't much time these days for fishing or dallying about with neighbors. I do wish the best for you.*
>
> *Jackson*

Her heart smote her. No mention of meeting at another time, this was a brush-off, if anything. Not even a hint of fondness in the signature. "It's finished then," she muttered, knowing she'd been hoping for so much more from him.

"Almost, miss. One more pin."

Maribelle glumly descended the stairway, feeling worse than when she'd broken it off with Virgil. Downstairs, the atmosphere was dismal. Searching the forlorn expressions, she wondered if they'd heard from Virgil's uncle. With trepidation, she ventured, "What's wrong?"

"A hard freeze," Mama explained. "Again. And there's no indication it's going to warm."

Maribelle glanced at the frost on the windows. "Oh no."

Daddy stood and paced. "If this doesn't let up, we'll lose the entire grove. The trees were already vulnerable and budding, but this will kill them."

"What can be done?" she asked.

"Nothing, Junebug." He ran his hands through his silver hair. "There's nothing I can do."

"We can pray," Grandmama offered, tapping the worn Bible on her lap.

Many prayers all across Ocala were lifted up, but the Lord allowed the freeze. Night after night, until there was no longer hope for Marmalade or any of the neighboring citrus groves.

One afternoon, while already feeling guilty for her part in ruining Marmalade, Maribelle was summoned to a family meeting. She stepped into the blue parlor filled with the scent of freshly polished mahogany to see the others already assembled.

Daddy stood at the hearth facing them. He squared his shoulders. "I've spoken to Walter and he won't finance replanting, and of course it would take half a decade to rebuild Marmalade even if he did. So I've decided to sell out and move south."

"What!" Maribelle gasped. "But who will buy Marmalade?"

Grandmama answered, "No doubt, Northerners will prey on our bad fortune."

Daddy nodded. "We'll look for a small grove and expand. The southern bankers will be more willing to loan money for citrus because they don't have the threat of cold weather. We need to be one of the first to take advantage of the situation, as there'll be a big shift, with everyone dashing to make the best of the new opportunities, including those who want to sell down south."

Maribelle exclaimed, "Bliss and blazes! Why can't everyone see this is a fluke? It never gets this cold." She looked at Mama. "Tell Daddy. It never gets this cold."

Mama remained silent, probably already having discussed this with Daddy.

Grandmama smiled, her creases lining her face. "Thank you for sharing the details with us. I'm fortunate to have a son who takes the time to explain business matters to his family." She gave Maribelle a stern look. "It makes sense to me. We'll make it through this and draw together with purpose." She turned her chair to face Maribelle more squarely. "You adore the sun, and it's even warmer down south."

"And rainy and swampy," Maribelle replied with twisted lips.

"Not so swampy anymore," Daddy corrected. "And we won't be alone. A lot of the citrus farmers are moving south. Why, we may even keep some of our same neighbors or be able to divide up a larger parcel to get started."

"The Carroways," Mama said cheerfully. "Such good friends."

"That's not selling the idea," Maribelle replied. Didn't Mama know anything about her own daughter's relationship with Willa Fay? "I understand the need and the common sense, but there's only one Silver River. What about that?"

"You spend too much time at the river," Mama admonished. "It's time you put such girlish things behind you."

"It's settled." Daddy strode across the room, his voice fading. "I have many things to do. I'll see you at supper."

Maribelle watched him depart, her heart sinking with the knowledge of her actions that had slammed the door to Walter Agnew's investment in Marmalade. She'd caused all the sorrow overwhelming the family. With growers moving south, this would have provided Daddy with his golden opportunity to expand.

"Maybe you'll meet a young fellow who will capture your heart," Mama said hopefully. "I feel this is going to be a good move for all of us."

"I'm sure I won't!" *How can I when it's already engaged? How can they all be so optimistic?* "May I be excused?"

Mama looked startled. "Why, of course."

In her room, Maribelle dismissed Milda and fell upon her bed. Being uprooted was worse than marrying Virgil. She tried to convince herself that southern Florida would be pleasant and she'd grow accustomed to her new surroundings and maybe even like them. Utter foolishness. She despised her situation. The only hope for her was to formulate a redemptive plan. The idea that arose went against all her southern training and would be most humiliating. If it worked, it would be worth it. If it didn't, she'd never see him again anyway. The family must not discover her intentions, or they would stop her.

Chapter 7

Maribelle tried not to showcase the butterflies she felt in the pit of her stomach. If anything, she overcompensated with cheerfulness. As the supper dishes were cleared, Grandmama backed her wheelchair away from the table. "You're feeling better. I'm glad to see it."

Joining the older woman as she wheeled toward the parlor, Maribelle replied, "I'm dwelling on what will be best for the family." She was really trying these days to be truthful.

"Such times can be looked at as seasons. When you are as old as I am, you'll see what I mean. Better times are ahead. You're young; you'll see."

"Yes, Grandmama." Maribelle hoped to escape to her room before the rest of the family joined them.

"Your father will be taking a trip, going south to get the financials in place and scout property before we begin packing up the estate."

Her heart leaped. "When does he leave?"

"Day after tomorrow."

Relief flooded over Maribelle that she still had time to implement her plan before Daddy secured the money and set them up with a future that would change their lives forever. "I'm going to my room early. Will you make my excuses?"

"Why so? Have I distressed you?"

"No, I plan to read a bit."

"Of course, dear. What are you reading?"

Maribelle replied guiltily, "The Bible."

In her room, Maribelle pulled out her Bible and read a few verses, trying to meditate on them, but it was impossible. She prayed for her safety and for his heart to be prepared before she arrived. Then she quickly donned her riding habit, forgoing a hat for a hooded cape, and pried open the window. She turned out the lantern and stepped onto the veranda roof, creeping carefully across the frosty surface until she found the pillar that supported the trellis. She carefully tested it and descended to the ground. The dank smells reminded her of when she used to sneak off to the stables at night when she couldn't sleep. The grooms-man never reported her. . .that she knew of, and she was sure he wouldn't betray her now. Of course, back then, she bribed the plump man with cookies.

Fortunately, he was nowhere in sight. Perhaps eating with the other servants. Ebony Rose, however, seemed reluctant to leave her comfortable stall. Maribelle had long ago let the animal have its own will, but couldn't give up the attachment even though over the years Daddy had tried to persuade her to choose a more reliable animal. Maribelle had remained stubborn, and now she saddled the mare and led her from the stables into some dark shadows before mounting. Ebony Rose nickered and sidestepped nervously.

Maribelle leaned forward and spoke softly. "It's fine. We'll give your eyes time to adjust. See, there's plenty of moonlight." Over a month had rolled by since the full moon the night of the New Year's dinner. So much had happened in such a short while. "Okay, girl. Let's go." She led the mare beside the magnolia trees to the road and kept to the side, heading into town at a moderate clip. She slipped into the trees when a carriage approached and kept out of sight until she reached the edge of town where there was too much traffic to avoid being seen. She could have been even more improper and donned men's clothing, but it was too late for that now, and it wouldn't have made a very good impression on the young man she hoped to influence.

Her heart pounded as she went through the shady district. A man yelled something obscene, and she kneed Ebony Rose to pick up the clip. Finally, the boulevard widened with grand magnolias on either side. She slowed and rehearsed her spiel until she entered Virgil's influential neighborhood.

Arriving outside his house, she dismounted and guided Ebony Rose around the back to a manservant, explaining she wouldn't be long. Then she squared her shoulders and marched up to the front door. Pushing back her hood and patting her hair in place, she knocked. A tall butler with immaculate posture answered the door, recognizing her at once and stammering a bit. "Wh—what can I do for you, Miss Sinclair?"

"I'd like to speak privately to Virgil, if he's home."

"Certainly, won't you come in?"

"No, I'll wait here."

The butler arched his brow but gave a bow and disappeared. Maribelle moved to the shadows, and it was only a few moments until Virgil appeared, looking ruggedly distraught. "Maribelle! What's wrong?"

"Nothing. I mean, everything. I just need to talk."

"Of course. Come inside."

"I'd rather not face your uncle."

"He's gone. Please," Virgil urged, his thick dark brows making a V on his forehead.

She let him lead her inside past the stunned but stoic butler and into a small parlor. He hesitated then left the door ajar.

"Let's sit by the fire." Virgil smiled compassionately, if not somewhat nervously.

She noticed a book on the small table between them. *Kidnapped* by Robert Louis Stevenson. She touched its cover. "I wish I was such an adventurer. Then I wouldn't be here asking for your help."

"Just say it. What can I do?" he implored.

She lifted her gaze from the novel to Virgil. "I suppose you know this last freeze has ruined Daddy's groves."

"Yes, I heard. He wasn't the only one who lost everything."

"I know. It's terrible." She gathered her courage and went on. "Daddy has decided to move south. Pick up and start over."

Virgil touched her hand. "I'm sorry. I know how you feel about Ocala. But how can I help?" Then his eyes widened, and he withdrew his hand, rubbing his thighs. "Have you changed your mind about us, then?"

The nights grew long for Jackson at the town house. At first it was enjoyable to live the single life, but the servants stayed to themselves, and he missed the card games and lively debates he enjoyed with his father since he'd returned to their estate. Now that the remodeling was finished and routines had been established with the hired help, he was free to return to the estate. He planned to leave on the morrow.

Only, after the gossip he'd just heard, his plans were unimportant. Now there was a decision to make. He took tea onto the small veranda attached to the front of the house, where he worked at his thoughts while stargazing and listening to crickets. In the quiet, he mulled over the problem and how it related to the letter he'd recently sent Maribelle.

Nights like this, he often ached of loneliness, remembering the beginning of his marriage and what it had been like to be happily wed. Was he foolish to turn away the only woman besides Theresa who had burrowed into his heart?

Could he allow himself to give Maribelle a chance? What if she was the one who could make him happy? Or was Jesus the only one who could do that? Was his restlessness a sin, a shortcoming in his relationship with God?

And so his thoughts swirled. When he'd written the note, he believed it was the right thing to do, and he'd also believed he could change his mind at any time before she found someone else, someone more worthy. But after today's news, this option had changed. The Sinclairs were moving away. That's when it hit him how desperately he wanted her. How he needed her. And he must act fast.

"Have you changed your mind about us, then?" Virgil asked.

Maribelle perceived the bluntness of the question in an instant, for Virgil's facial expressions struggled. He didn't want her back, but he would play the gentleman card.

"No, I haven't changed my mind about us, and I can see you haven't either."

He brushed away an errant lock of hair from his forehead. "I'm sorry if I'm behaving like a cad. I don't understand."

"I'm hoping somebody else will change his mind."

His expression slowly comprehended. "Uncle Walter."

"Can't you convince him to help his old friend? I shouldn't ask and put you on the spot like this, but I can't bear to move away. I'm so humiliated to come to you, but I had to. For all that we've shared, is there anything you can do to help us?"

Virgil took her hand again, "Oh, sweets. Don't you realize I've already pleaded on your behalf?"

"You have?" she squeaked.

He nodded sorrowfully. "I've gone to him more than once about the situation. Uncle Walter claims he's been hit too hard by the freeze and the money's not there to give. Citrus has become a gamble." He rose and faced her. "Aside from that one way."

"What?" she implored.

"If we married, he'd be honor-bound to help."

"Oh," she said sadly, clasping her hand and looking down at her lap.

A noise awakened Jackson, and he realized he'd nodded off on the porch. He noticed some activity across the street and, ever scrutinizing his competition since he'd taken board in the town house, his curiosity drew him to his feet. Until the present, nothing unsavory about the Agnews had been revealed. Now he saw two figures in the front. He watched as Virgil leaned close to a woman's face and pulled up her hood, hugging her and standing near.

"What is this? Surely he hasn't entertained a woman in his very own home?"

Then a horse was brought around. When it stepped through a patch of light from the streetlamp, his heart sank with dread and disbelief at the white rose on the beast's flank. Maribelle's horse? As his neighbor helped her mount he realized without a doubt, it was indeed her. He moved closer, behind a newly painted pillar, to try to catch their conversation. But they were being discreet. Virgil held her hand, kissed her, and sent her on her way. Unscrupulous! The least he could do was see her home safely. As Jackson watched her ride away, the taste of bile crept into his throat and he stormed into the house, into the dark masculine parlor, and stood seething before the ebbing fire in the hearth.

It was as if he'd gone back in time to that other night, another fire and another discovery, when Theresa had betrayed him. He tried to calm his anger, but it engulfed him all anew. Had Maribelle changed her mind after they'd lost the groves? Maybe she'd gone to beg Virgil's forgiveness. Fickle. Deceitful. After the embrace he'd witnessed, it was undeniable there was a bond between the couple. He didn't want to believe she could be as low as Theresa had been, as wanton. Whatever was going on between them was undesirable if they had to sneak around at night.

Taking the poker, he stirred up the coals until the fire flamed and crackled. Then he took the note he'd carried all these years and crumpled it. If he was to move on, he needed to rid himself of it as well as every woman who had hurt him. He would cut himself off from Maribelle once and for all. Thank goodness he hadn't made the mistake of telling her how he felt. Hardening his jaw, he tossed the paper into the fire.

Maribelle turned away from the town house and started home, allowing the tears she'd been holding back to flow free and blindly. It was more than her humiliation. It was horrible to ruin one's family's life and dishonor a young man once, but she'd been cruel enough to do it twice. And if word of it got out, it would ruin her reputation, and her family would leave in disgrace. So overwhelmed with despair, she let Ebony Rose have her head and wasn't paying attention to their whereabouts. There was no warning when a dark figure darted across the road. There was only that startling moment when her mare reared, the sensation of falling, and overwhelming darkness that sucked her into nothingness.

Chapter 8

Jackson only had about an hour to grovel in his misery that night. Not enough time to work through his despair when there was a hard knock at his door. "Wake up, man!"

He flung open the door and glared at the intruder, the man causing his pain. "What do you want?" It flashed into his mind that Virgil must have seen him on the veranda and had come to beg him to keep his peace about the matter. Well, he'd let him grovel.

Instead the visitor lowered his voice, conspiringly. "Maribelle's in trouble. I didn't know who else to get."

A flurry of images went through Jackson's mind. Virgil's frightened expression sent tremors through his body. In trouble? Still unable to tamp down his emotions, he demanded, "Out with it. What's happening?"

Virgil grabbed his arm. "She came to see me tonight. I was a fool not to see her home, but her horse just returned without her."

Anger flooded over him anew to hear the other man blatantly admit that she'd been to *see* him. At least he'd the sense to keep the matter discreet. But then his anger changed to fear for her safety. "I'll get my coat."

As soon as he had his mount, Virgil lamented to him, "I was a fool to let her leave alone. I knew better."

"I won't argue with you."

"She's braver than any other woman I've ever met," Virgil said. "She just didn't love me enough."

"Then how could you abuse her?"

"What? I haven't done anything of the kind. Except let her leave unattended."

"You allowed her to risk her reputation," Jackson argued, needing to blame someone for his distress.

"I didn't allow anything. She came to me for financial help, but I couldn't help her unless she agreed to marry me. She turned me down again."

As the situation became clearer, Jackson's anger dwindled. He hadn't behaved any better. He remembered letting her ride home alone that day she'd jumped into his boat. The woman was willful and sometimes infuriating.

"Don't blame yourself." What hurt the most was the fact that he could be losing the woman he loved. How many men had the good fortune to love two women and the bad fortune to lose them both? More determined than ever not to let her go, Jackson gripped the reins hard. Desperate to find her, he scanned the shadows along the road. When they reached the outskirts of town, he saw a dark lump in an overgrown ditch.

"Look!" Quickly guiding his mount, he leaped down. "It's her." He gingerly moved her onto her side and felt her neck for a pulse. "She's breathing."

Virgil hastily reached them and brushed dirt from her face. "I'll get her home and explain what happened. Will you ride for the doctor?"

"Why not take her there? It's closer."

"Because it could start a scandal."

Jackson hesitated, unwilling to give her up or risk her life, but Virgil's plan made sense. Virgil was the one who should explain to her father what had happened to Maribelle and why. He nodded and held Virgil's reins as Virgil mounted. Then he carried Maribelle to Virgil and placed her carefully upon his lap. "I'll send the doctor, then. And send word to me as soon as you can."

"Of course. Thanks."

Adrenaline pumped through Jackson's veins as he hurried into town and jumped down to run to the doctor's door.

The elderly man appeared disheveled as if he'd been asleep. "Yes?"

"There's an emergency at Marmalade Plantation. Maribelle took a spill on her horse, and I was sent to fetch you."

"At this hour?" The doctor sighed. "Very well. I'll go at once."

His part done, Jackson went home to wait.

Virgil rapped on the door of the plantation house, holding Maribelle in his arms. The butler appeared, frowning at receiving callers at the late hour until he recognized the bundle. He threw open the door, leaving Virgil standing outside while he raced to his master's salon. Virgil followed a few steps behind.

Maribelle's parents burst from the room in their bedclothes, donning wrappers, and her mother let out a frightened shriek. "In here, place her on our bed." She instantly began to work over her unconscious daughter.

"Explain yourself," Mr. Sinclair demanded.

"The doctor's on his way. May we speak in private?"

Mr. Sinclair led Virgil to his study, motioning toward a pair of leather chairs, from which the story unfolded.

Mr. Sinclair rubbed his hands through his hair. "I had no idea she was taking this so hard, foolish Junebug."

"I'm sorry I didn't accompany her back home," Virgil replied. "I asked, but she wasn't having it, but that's no excuse."

"No, it isn't!" Mr. Sinclair glared then softened. "But I know how stubborn Maribelle is and how used to having her own way she's become. It's easy to spoil the youngest. I guess we can share the blame in this, but I only hope we won't have to live with our mistakes. I—" Mr. Sinclair cut off to answer the soft rap upon the door. "Doctor's here," he exclaimed, leaving Virgil to wait alone.

Chapter 9

In town, Jackson found himself on his knees. At first his desperation muddled his thoughts. But once he confessed his fear to Jesus, it was as if the Holy Spirit opened a spiritual tap. Hidden motives and stuffed emotions, every evil thing he'd tamped down, flowed outward in confession. He remembered the event of Theresa's death and was able to own a portion of the blame. While he wasn't the betrayer, he'd driven her away by his cold attitude. He regretted how he'd continued such harmful behavior even knowing he was acting unloving toward her. After that, he lay on the carpet by the hearth, weak and numb, feeling reproved and low and so very wicked.

"You're forgiven."

The idea welled up in him, but he didn't feel deserving. Yet his heart wanted to explore the scrap of hope. He thought about when he'd asked Jesus into his heart. How he'd felt God's unconditional love. How he'd clung to it.

"It's true." He knew it was so, and he felt more love toward his Savior than ever before. He was forgiven, and because of it, he could forgive Theresa too. He rose, stoked the fire, and sat in his chair, contemplating this new discovery. *Please, Lord, heal Maribelle so that I can tell her.* He touched the charred remains of the letter that he'd retrieved from the fire and basked in her words of encouragement and in the spiritual truth that he was forgiven and loved. He continued to plead with the Lord on her behalf. Surely God had placed her in his life to help bring him to wholeness.

When the knock came, Jackson wiped his eyes and hurried to the door. Virgil stood there looking as disheveled as he felt. The man's mouth broke into a smile. "She woke up. The doctor wouldn't give us his word, but he has hope she'll fully recover."

"Thank God." Jackson felt relief flood over him.

"The family was gracious enough, all considered."

"I'm glad." He felt a strange kinship toward his neighbor for the first time since they'd met. "Come in for a drink?"

"No, thanks. I'm tired. You must be too." He gave Jackson a lopsided grin as if he read his feelings for Maribelle. "Appreciate your help tonight."

"Night then." Jackson closed the door. "Thank You, Jesus," he praised as he strode toward his bedroom.

❦

Maribelle awakened the next morning with a pounding head. She'd been in and out of sleep and vaguely remembered Mama's cool touches and soft encouraging words.

"She blinked," Mama declared.

"Well, go to her," Grandmama ordered.

"Are you awake?" Mama asked, stroking Maribelle's forehead.

Forcing her eyes open, Maribelle croaked, "Yes."

"She sounds like a frog. Give her some water," Grandmama urged.

"Simmer down," Mama said. "I know what to do for my own daughter."

"Really?" Grandmama replied. "Since when?"

Mama sent a servant for a fresh pitcher of water, and Maribelle flinched as she was raised higher on the pillow and took the glass. The room spun, but she was determined. "I can do it." But Mama hovered, eager to help. Maribelle drank deeply then returned the glass. "I don't remember what happened."

Mama's eyes widened in alarm, and she exchanged a glance with the older woman.

"That's as expected," Grandmama soothed. "They brought you in unconscious."

"Who did?"

"After you fell off your horse, Virgil brought you in," Mama explained.

It was Maribelle's turn to feel alarm, and she sank back under the covers in shame. "Virgil," she squeaked.

But before she could be set at ease, Daddy strode into the room. "Is the Junebug awake?"

Maribelle felt a great burden pressing upon her chest, so heavy was the guilt she bore. "I'm sorry, Daddy. So sorry."

Mama sniffed.

"Now, now. Virgil told us everything, and we understand."

"You do? But it's all my fault, don't you see?" She hiccuped. "He told you everything?"

"Yes, I believe he did. And we all share the blame now. We shouldn't have pushed you into the engagement."

"You tried to tell us," Mama agreed.

Daddy said sternly, "We are fortunate Virgil is honorable and guards your reputation."

Maribelle nodded then flinched at the pain. "Yes. But there's nothing he can do to help you, Daddy. Unless I marry him."

"And we're finished going down that dead end." Grandmama reared up in defense.

Mama rolled her gaze toward Maribelle's high headboard. "Yes, we all know how you feel about it." Then she looked down at her daughter. "In the future, I promise to pay more attention to your feelings and not force you to get married. Even if it's in your best interest."

"I've a promise to make too," Daddy interjected. "I'm going to quit coddling you. As long as you're in this house, there'll be no more secret meetings and gallivanting all over the place as you please."

"Yes, Daddy. I'm grateful for all your understanding, but can we talk about this later? I'm not feeling well."

"Of course," he replied, nodding at Mama before leaving them.

Mama kissed her on the cheek. "I'll send Milda in."

Grandmama wheeled to her bedside. "Is the fuss over now? It's time you got on board with your Daddy's plan, you know."

"I know. Love you, Grandmama."

After that, Maribelle's headaches waned a bit as each day passed. Even though she'd come to terms with the family's move, and knew Mama had been right about needing to grow up, and Grandmama about fitting in with the family's plans—marriage notwithstanding—her dizzy spells kept her in her room to brood. Mourn, one might say, for all she would be leaving behind.

Two weeks later, Mama told her Daddy had found a parcel of land with a thriving citrus grove and he planned to purchase it, partnering with Mr. Carroway. Willa Fay had asked after Maribelle when word got out that she'd fallen off her horse, and she planned to visit soon.

"Mama, I'm not up to visitors yet." She especially didn't wish to face Virgil.

"Of course, dear. You'll let us know when you're ready. We don't want to be rude to our friends." And in spite of the fact that there had been forgiveness and promises all around, Mama didn't tell her who had called and been turned away. Visitors were never mentioned again.

Chapter 10

Once Maribelle recovered, she volunteered her usefulness and was put to the task of helping to oversee the packing. There was so much to be done that she didn't have time to think about herself or even taking the luxury of riding Ebony Rose, who must feel she was being punished. Then one day, Mama asked if she wanted some time to make calls. She agreed it was time, and they took the carriage to call upon Willa Fay first and then Virgil. Afterward, she asked, "Can I take Ebony Rose to say goodbye to the river?"

"For heaven's sake, you still want to keep that horse?"

After receiving a short lecture on riding "that awful mare" again, Maribelle was feeling the wind in her hair. She leaned close to Ebony Rose's ear. "I'm sure it wasn't your fault. You're just as spoiled as I am, that's all. We are meant for each other, so don't worry about it."

The mare didn't seem worried at all but rather was content to head to their familiar haunt. There were no fresh signs of bear, and everything else appeared fine until they burst through the opening that led to the beach. Then Maribelle saw the human intruder. She pulled Ebony Rose up short and sat still for a moment, taking in the scene.

There sat Jackson, his back to her and his long hair curled on the collar of his shirt. His legs were stretched out before him, and his back was hunched, as if in prayer. She slipped out of the saddle and let go of the reins. "Hello. I hope I'm not interrupting."

He snapped his head about and jumped up. "Maribelle! I can't believe you came."

"I wanted to say goodbye." She saw the hope well up in his eyes and quickly added, "To the river." She lifted her arm and gestured. "My favorite place in all the world." She tried to sound nonchalant. "I don't know if you've heard, but we're leaving Ocala."

"I've heard. Why do you keep turning me away?"

"I've been ill. I fell off my horse."

"I know. I was with Virgil when we found you. I'm the one who went after the doctor."

She was sure her slackened jaw gave away her shock. "I didn't know. I hadn't talked to Virgil until this morning. I've been recovering, getting used to the idea of moving, packing." She shrugged. "I suppose you are privy to my humiliation then."

"I did see you that night, and I admit I jumped to some wrong conclusions, but in the end I came to all the right ones."

"That's good to hear," she said. "Thank you for calling the doctor."

His face appeared different, relaxed and peaceful, his brown eyes seeking. "I came here as often as I could, waiting for you."

"Waiting?"

"Yes, I have so much to tell you, but you never came."

She thought bitterly of the irony that he was the one waiting for her.

Maribelle's world was flip-flopping. She felt confused. How could she be unaffected by the words that would have stirred up hope a few weeks earlier? Mama would be pleased. She must have grown up at last. "Well. . ." She glanced around for her mare, but she was no place in sight. *Bliss and blazes!* "Where is that horse?" she asked grumpily. She had a hundred questions to ask, and she needed to get out of there before she started to ask them.

"She'll probably come at your whistle, but I hope you'll give me a chance to explain first."

Maribelle crossed her arms. "You won't say anything upsetting or reproving. I'm not up to it today."

His voice was low and soft. "I forgave her. I forgave Theresa."

Maribelle's defenses instantly melted. "Oh." She ventured forward, touching his arm. "I'm so glad."

"That night, praying for you, God brought me around. I see everything so clearly now."

She withdrew her hand, smiling. Now she understood the difference in his countenance. "I'm happy for you. And thanks for praying, and getting the doctor. It seems everything is turning out for the best. The way it should be. Or has to be."

He gripped her shoulders. "It will if you allow me to come calling. I want to see if everything you told me is true, about loving again."

She squared her shoulders. "And you've been waiting here every day to ask me that?"

"I have." His eyes looked more hopeful than she'd ever seen them.

"You want to call on me?" she clarified.

"I do; please say yes."

"It seems you shall get your just deserts for all the heartache you've caused me. Because I say yes. Yes!"

Laughing, he pulled her into his strong embrace. "I've been a fool."

"And how long do I have to wait for a real kiss?" she baited, breathless, staring into the face she loved above all others.

"Not a moment longer."

She knew in her heart that he would be able to love again, but she wanted to do everything right. When they drew apart, she said, "Let's not rush."

"Of course I'll court you," he whispered.

"But how? I'm moving with my family. They need my help, and I've nowhere to stay here."

"I'll come to you. It doesn't matter how many trips it takes."

"You will? So we can take time to make sure we're suited for each other?"

"Yes." He put his arm around her waist. "Whatever it takes, little belle, whatever it takes."

In her heart she already knew they would be perfect for each other.

Dianne Christner lives in New River, Arizona, where life sizzles in the summer when temperatures soar above one hundred degrees as she writes from her air-conditioned home office. She enjoys the desert life, where her home is nestled in the mountains and she can watch quail and the occasional deer, bobcat, or roadrunner. Dianne was raised Mennonite and works hard to bring authenticity to Mennonite fiction. She now worships at a community church. She's written over a dozen novels, most of which are historical fiction. She gets caught up in research, having to set her alarm to remember to switch the laundry or start dinner. But her husband of forty-plus years is a good sport. They have two married children, Mike and Rachel, and five grandchildren, Makaila, Elijah, Vanson, Ethan, and Chloe. She welcomes you to visit her website at http://www.diannechristner.net.

Debt of Love

by Lynn A. Coleman

Chapter 1

Palatka, Florida
1868

Miss Edwards, I'm sorry, but you are incorrect. I have the promissory note at the bank. Your father secured a loan for ten thousand dollars before he left for war. The plantation was used as collateral. Unless you can come up with the entire amount by the end of this month, I will be forced to foreclose on your property."

Adeline closed her eyes and counted to ten then opened them. She focused on the blue flames emanating from his eyes and narrowed her gaze. "I do not believe you, sir. I've heard no mention of this loan. And to come to my home and claim it so with no prior letters of intent from your establishment..." She paused. "Well, I'm sorry, sir, but you appear to be a charlatan."

"I resent your accusation, Miss Edwards. As I said, you are more than within your rights to come to the bank and look at the actual documents. You shall see for yourself that it is your father's signature. I trust you know your father's signature."

"Of course I know my father's signature. He kept immaculate accounting records."

"I'm certain he did. I do not wish to speak poorly of the dead but..." He paused and scanned the room. "You've maintained a good home here. Perhaps one of your brothers can answer this question."

Adeline took in a deep breath and held it for a moment before speaking. "You are talking with the owner of this plantation. My father and brothers were killed during the war. I have maintained this property and kept it going without slaves for the past three years. I have seen a marginal profit each year, and the property is in the black." She squared her shoulders and stepped toward the front door. "Now, if you will excuse me, I will come to town tomorrow and view those records. And I will prove that they are false."

Mr. Phineas George Hamilton III nodded before turning and stepping off the front porch. She watched with fascination. In this part of the country, a man with red hair and fair skin tended to burn from the intense rays of the sun, and yet he seemed to not be affected at all.

She closed the door. Was he correct? Had Father taken out a loan before he went to fight the North? If so, where did the money go? There were no records of income or loans from that time period. And he didn't purchase ten thousand dollars' worth of cattle before he left to fight. She doubted there was even two thousand head for sale in the entire state in '63. She glanced out the window to the far pasture where several cattle stood munching on the grass. Replenishing the herd had been one of her primary goals. The troops, both North and South, had taken most of their stock.

Adeline shook off those unwelcome thoughts and hustled back to her father's office. Even though she had inherited the ranch, the house and all, it still felt like her father's space. To make it her own, she had brought in some lighter colors to brighten the heavy wood-grained furniture and walls.

"Miss Edwards, what was all that shoutin' 'bout?" Mammy said, running into the office and wringing her hands on a dish towel. Mammy and a few former slaves still lived and worked the plantation with Adeline.

"Apparently Mr. Hamilton from the bank says Father took out a loan before he left for the war. I've never run across such a thing. I believe Mr. Hamilton III"—she nearly choked on the title—"is one of the many charlatans that have come to my door since the war ended." Adeline huffed. Folks had shown up saying they owned a piece of the plantation. Others saying they were kin and she was expected to provide for them. She would return to the fact that if she hadn't heard of or seen them prior to the war they were no kin of hers.

Mammy looked down at the floor and continued twisting the dish towel in her hands.

Adeline took in Mammy's posture. "Mammy? Is there something I should know?"

Mammy shook her head.

"You know you are free to speak your mind with me."

The older woman looked up with her rich chocolate eyes and smiled. "Yes'm. I knows."

Mammy lived in her own house along with her husband and their three children. When the war ended, giving Mammy and Jimmy their own house had seemed the right thing to do. He worked the stables and land and helped run the plantation. There wasn't a better cracker in a hundred miles. He knew the land and the cattle. Paying him wages and a percentage of the profit from the sale of stock had been a beneficial arrangement for all.

Adeline thought about all she'd learned from Jimmy about caring for the herd and the horses. Her mind flittered up to the closet full of fashionable gowns in her bedroom. That world seemed like a dream. She looked down at her hands, worn and strong, a cowgirl's hands. Adeline sighed. She missed the carefree days she'd known as a child.

She snapped back to the present. Mammy was looking at her expectantly. "What did you say?"

"Was the loan Confederate dollars?" Mammy asked.

Adeline smiled and wrapped Mammy in a hug. "Thank you, I hadn't even considered that. If so, there is no debt, right? Those dollars are worthless."

Mammy smiled. "If you says so. You best be gettin' ready for dinner at five. The crew is coming in after the branding. I'm fixin' to feed the hired hands."

Adeline dipped her head in agreement. "I will be the first in line."

She grabbed the ledgers from behind the desk and plopped them down. "I will go over these again and see if I missed something."

"Y'all will figure it out, Addy."

"Thank you, Mammy."

After Mammy left, Adeline settled down behind the desk and started going through the journals one at a time. Her father wouldn't have taken out such a large loan, knowing he was going to fight. He couldn't. . .wouldn't. . . would he?

"Phin, how'd it go?" Randall Ferguson asked as Phineas walked into the bank.

"Not well." Phin placed his wide-brimmed hat on the tree stand. "Miss Edwards does not believe her father borrowed the money."

"It is of no consequence whether she believes it or not. He did, and the plantation is ours if the debt is not honored by the end of the month." Randall Ferguson was a hard man. There seemed to be no grace in him for anyone.

"She claims she never received a notice from the bank concerning the debt." Phineas tempered his voice. He was beginning to have his doubts about Randall's integrity. He'd come from the North, which was the first warning sign. The second was his treatment of people when grace needed to be extended. He felt the losses from the war were of no consideration. "If there was no notification, the loan will have to be extended until proper notice and time is given."

Ferguson snorted and shuffled back to his office, mumbling that he had given her notice.

Phineas went to his desk and pulled the original loan papers from his drawer. The papers were in order, and Mr. Edwards's signature appeared to be identical to the ones on earlier documents. Then he looked up the Edwards Plantation bank records. He ran his finger down the deposit and withdrawal columns and paused as he saw a shift in the records once Adeline Edwards took over running the plantation. She'd made a small profit each year, even after losing her slave labor. How?

He worked long into the evening on other bank matters, having set aside the Edwards account. Phineas had been hired by the bank owners in Boston to go over the branch records and determine why the bank continued to show losses after the war ended. His one advantage was he too was a southern gentleman, with his family hailing from the Savannah area. The owners felt he would be accepted and trusted by the bank customers as one of them. Which brought him back to the Edwards file. He'd found the loan—a substantial one—unpaid, and Ferguson immediately jumped on the foreclosure process. However, ten thousand dollars, while a hefty amount of money, did not nearly account for the losses Ferguson had reported for the past three years.

A gentle knock on the glass window caused him to raise his head from the papers. It was too dark outside his door to make out anyone. "Can I help you?" he called.

"Sheriff Brill, Mr. Hamilton. Y'all workin' late again?"

Phineas chuckled. "Afraid so, Sheriff. Come on in." He unlocked the door. "How are you this evening?"

"Fine, fine. A paddleboat just came to port."

Steamboats did a brisk business up and down St. John's River, and Palatka was one of the largest ports. Prior to the railroad coming in, Palatka did more business than Jacksonville. Even though the railroad had come to Palatka, cattle, crops, and people still loaded on at various points along the river. There was a thriving business district on the riverbank as well. A few of the local bars were known to be open late, pouring out beer and spirits. The inn hosted folks from the North who came down to experience the warmer temperatures.

The sheriff reached into his coat pocket. "I was given a telegram for you this afternoon." He handed the folded piece of paper to Phineas.

Phineas scanned the note. It was in response to a letter he had sent to his superiors last week. They were happy with his findings and encouraged him to ask the sheriff to investigate Mr. Ferguson. "Did you read it?"

Brill shook his head as he sat down.

"What do you know of the Edwards Plantation?"

The sheriff shifted his weight on the leather chair in front of Phineas's desk. "Liam Edwards was traditional, died in '64 during the war. Both his sons were killed too. He must have had at least fifty slaves, if not a hundred, workin' the plantation. Not to mention a dozen crackers."

"Crackers?"

"Florida cowboys."

Phineas nodded.

"The plantation runs about a couple hundred head of cattle each year. Liam raised the grain for the cattle as well. He had a large chicken operation too, but his daughter hasn't been raising many chickens, at least not from what I've seen. She does all right takin' care of the place though. She probably has about twenty of their freed slaves who continue to live on and work the plantation. Which is a pretty good number, given all that happened. Not many folks, white or black, like takin' orders from a woman, much less a southern belle who wears pants and rides a horse like the best cracker."

"She works the cattle?"

Sheriff Brill smiled. His day-old growth marked the line of his double chin. The sheriff wasn't overweight, but he wore a double chin that could flap in the breeze. "Yup, a family member has to these days. Gone are the formal parties and the introductions of available southern belles. Gotta give Adeline credit though; she has kept the place together and pays her free slaves and crackers. Can't say that about all the old plantations."

Phineas knew that to be true. Which again made him question why Ferguson was demanding a quick foreclosure on the property.

The sheriff rubbed his chin. "Why do you ask?"

"She has an account here at the bank," Phineas stated without giving too much information.

"It's either this one or First Savings on Lemon Street."

This was true. Old Boston and First were the only two banks left in Palatka. At one time there had been more, but the South was struggling. Phineas didn't doubt the pluck of a Southerner. They would survive. "Right, thanks for the information. Is there anything else I can help you with, Sheriff?"

"Nah, just checkin' on ya."

Phineas stood and walked the man toward the front door. "Good night, Sheriff. Always good to see you."

A group of men swayed down the street, singing. Sheriff Brill put on his cap. "Guess I better get to work."

Phineas chuckled and glanced at his desk. Dealing with folks was part of his job, but fortunately, dealing with ones who indulged in spirits was not a common occurrence for a bank manager. He waved the sheriff off and sat back down at his desk. He opened the note.

> *Mr. Hamilton,*
>
> *We are hoping you will come to a conclusion soon. Investors want answers. Randall Ferguson does have debt here in Boston and an outstanding loan.*
>
> *We expect a report by the end of the month.*
>
> *Sincerely,*
> *J. C. Wild*

Phineas swallowed hard. It wasn't often he heard from the president of the bank rather than the cashier, Mr. Gunderson. Which meant they wanted answers now. He rubbed the back of his neck. If Ferguson had cheated the Old Boston Bank, he had done an excellent job of hiding it. Phineas closed the ledgers and put them back in their cubbies. He needed to rest and have fresh eyes on the problem. There had to be proof, somewhere. But where? He blew out his oil lamp and locked the doors behind him.

An image of Adeline Edwards flickered through his mind. Her brunette hair accented her sun-kissed complexion. A smile crossed his lips. Perhaps the day hadn't been a total waste. He loved the sparkle that ignited in her hazel eyes when she was standing her ground. He was intrigued.

Adeline tried to stretch her tired muscles after a restless night's sleep. Mr. Hamilton III's visit kept her up to the wee hours trying to track down the loan and what her father could have purchased with it. The overarching problem of losing the land to the bank at the end of the month had her running figures of what she could sell to possibly raise such capital in a couple of weeks. There was nothing. She might be able to raise three thousand dollars.

But ten. . .that was impossible.

She guided her buggy to a stop in front of the bank. She didn't have time for this nonsense. There were chores to do on the plantation, important chores.

If he was a flimflam man, he wouldn't even be at the bank today. A smile inched up at the thought. As she stepped down from the buggy, her foot caught on the step and she started to tumble to the ground. If she hadn't had to wear a dress and boots with heels, she wouldn't be in this predicament.

Someone caught her just before she landed on her backside in the mud. "Are you all right, Miss Edwards?"

The warmth of the man's voice smoothed her ruffled nerves. She turned to thank her rescuer and frowned. Mr. Phineas George Hamilton III stood there with his flaming red hair and sparkling blue eyes.

She held her tongue and mustered up all the civility she could gather from the extensive training she'd received from her mother, which ended when she was thirteen. "Thank you, Mr. Hamilton."

A slight nod of the head and he turned toward the bank's door offering his elbow, a gesture any proper southern gentleman would make to a southern belle. She took his elbow. She could do this. She had to do this. There could not be any signs of weakness, not now when her entire future rested in this man's hands. If his assertion was correct.

He opened the door and held it for her to pass before him. He'd been trained as she had. Proper manners were a thing of the past. She hadn't had anyone treat her with respect since her father and brothers went off to fight. She closed her eyes for a moment and stepped into the bank. A sinking feeling grew within her. Somehow she knew he had the proof. Her father must have taken out a loan. But why? And why so much? Where did he spend the money?

"Please come with me to my office, Miss Edwards."

"Good morning, Mr. Hamilton." Randall Ferguson stood behind the teller window. He had a narrow gap between his eyes and a pencil-thin nose. He'd always been kind to her, but Adeline didn't know him apart from a few transactions at the bank.

"Good morning, Mr. Ferguson. I shall be in my office with Miss Edwards."

Randall acknowledged his words with a slight bow of his head and went about his business.

Mr. Hamilton led her to the office on the left side of the lobby. She stepped inside. She'd never been in here before. She'd never had a need.

"Take a seat." He motioned to the chair across from his desk. The desk was dark mahogany, no doubt harvested from southern Florida.

She sat down as he pulled open a desk drawer and drew out a folder. He opened it on his desk. The wooden chair creaked when he sat down. Adeline's palms moistened. He took out a single sheet of yellowed paper. "You'll see this is the original debt, and if you look on the bottom you'll see your father's signature." He pointed to the paper and passed it across his desk. "I have compared your father's signature with the other paperwork we have, and it is a match."

Adeline's hands trembled as she took the paper. She closed her eyes then forced them open and scanned the document. She closed them again.

"As you can see...," Mr. Hamilton continued.

She tossed the paper back on his desk. "If this was signed in 1864, then he was paid with Confederate money. The current value of Confederate currency is less than a nickel on the dollar. What would my actual debt be? Five hundred or less?"

Mr. Hamilton frowned. "I'm afraid it is still ten thousand dollars."

"That is impossible. How can I fight this? I don't believe my father borrowed this money. I have no record of it in the plantation's ledgers. There were no purchases around that time. Nothing. This can't be true." Adeline felt the heat of her anger. She was upset, not only with the bank but also with her father. What could he have done with ten thousand dollars, and why would he borrow it if he was going off to war? It didn't make sense.

"You are free to send a letter of complaint to our main office in Boston, if you wish, but I'm afraid you will not have a positive result."

She pulled the paper toward herself again.

"As you can see, that is your father's signature."

"Yes, but who witnessed it? Who gave him the loan? Mr. Ferguson?"

"No, Mr. Ferguson wasn't working at the bank then."

"Can I speak to someone who worked here in 1864 when Father supposedly borrowed this money?"

"I'm sorry, no one presently on staff worked at this branch of the bank in 1864." Phineas stood up and walked to the front window with his hands clasped behind his back. "If you trust me, I'd be happy to look over your father's accounts. Perhaps I could find something you may have missed."

Adeline's temper rose another notch. "You presume because I am a woman I do not have a mind for numbers?"

Mr. Hamilton turned. "I am merely offering my service to assist you. I can extend to you an additional month to raise the money, if that will help."

"You could offer me an entire year. There is no way I can pay ten thousand dollars. Nor do I believe I have to. I shall see you in court, Mr. Hamilton." Adeline stood and marched out of the bank. If he wanted a fight, she'd give him one. She'd been raising cattle and working the land for three years. She could handle Mr. Phineas George Hamilton III.

Chapter 2

Phineas put the papers for the Edwards account back in the file and into his desk drawer and locked it. Miss Adeline had a couple of valid points. If her father borrowed Confederate dollars, did she still owe the same amount? He knew what the officials back in Boston would say, but they would also be flexible and negotiate a settlement with her. The other was the lack of records in her father's account ledgers at his home office as well as the fact that the loan was not recorded in the bank ledgers, at least not the ones he'd gone through so far. To say the bank's records were incomplete would be putting it nicely. Of course, the attack on Palatka in '64 could have something to do with the missing records.

Phineas glanced out the window of his office to where Randall Ferguson worked in the lobby. Things weren't adding up. In fact, more questions were rising about Ferguson. He silently prayed for wisdom and guidance. *Father, help me discover the truth.* He paused for a moment then added, *And Lord, if You would, provide for Miss Edwards so that she doesn't have to lose her family's plantation. Thank You.*

He pulled out the ledgers for 1865 and started going over the figures, checking and rechecking every entry. Somewhere in these pages were the answers he was looking for. If the loan wasn't recorded in these pages, did Adeline Edwards even owe the money to the bank?

"Phineas," Randall said as he tapped on the office door.

Phineas lifted his head. "Yes?"

"I'm going out for lunch. Can I bring you something?"

"No, thank you." Phineas stood up and stretched his back. "I'll take care of the front."

Randall exited the building as quietly as he walked around the bank. Phineas went to the main lobby. No one was in the room, but then again, it was Friday and almost the lunch hour. Folks would be coming in soon to deposit and withdraw their funds while on their lunch break. Phineas walked behind the teller's desk and counted the money in the drawer. He glanced at Ferguson's accounting of the drawer. He was off by one dollar in the bank's favor. Phin set the dollar aside and noted it on the ledger sheet. The bell above the door jingled, and Phineas greeted the woman who entered. "Good afternoon. Can I help you today, Mrs. Stewart?"

"Oh, I hope you can. I've been searching all morning. I lost a dollar after I left the bank."

Phin glanced at the dollar he had set aside. "Did you count the money when Mr. Ferguson gave it to you?"

"My gracious, no, child. He counted it right into my hand. But somehow"—she started looking around the floor—"I must have dropped a dollar."

"I just went over the accounting of the drawer, and it is off by one dollar." Phin handed her the extra bill. "Mr. Ferguson must have seen you drop it and picked it up for safekeeping."

"Oh my, I'll have to thank him," Mrs. Stewart gushed. "Will you tell him if I don't see him first?"

"Of course. Have a wonderful day, Mrs. Stewart."

She folded the dollar and put it inside her change purse. "The good Lord and you have made it a wonderful day."

The hour went quickly, with customer after customer coming in. When there was a lull, he looked at the ledger where the day's figures were tallied and noted an extra dollar in Mrs. Stewart's account. *Interesting.* Was Randall Ferguson skimming from the bank a dollar or two at a time?

Randall walked in and smiled. "Good afternoon, Phin."

Phineas didn't enjoy hearing his nickname from Ferguson. "Afternoon. You'll be happy to know that Mrs. Stewart came in and retrieved the dollar she was missing."

Randall paled then smiled. "Oh, marvelous. I found it on the floor after she left. It was in the drawer."

"Yes, I counted the drawer. Also, I corrected the error in your accounting of the ledger. Apparently you added a dollar to her deposit as well."

"I'm so sorry, Phin. I don't know how I could have made that mistake."

Phin nodded. "It's an innocent mistake, but please be more careful."

"Yes, sir. Absolutely."

"Oh, I also heard from the main office. Your loan is due. I'm happy to receive your payment."

"Marvelous," Randall said again then paused. "I'll write you a check."

"Cash will suffice. I'll give you a receipt."

Randall leaned over the drawer, pulled out forty dollars, and handed it to Phineas, then made a note of it in the ledger, forty dollars out of Randall Ferguson's personal account, all according to procedure.

Phin smiled, took the cash, and put it back into the drawer after noting in the bank's record that Randall Ferguson made his loan payment. "I'll send them a statement that you are current."

"Thank you, sir."

"You're welcome." Phin went back to work in his office. He watched Randall and saw the plastered smile on his face as customers came in. Something was definitely wrong with this man. Perhaps Ferguson was responsible for the bank's losses. But stealing a dollar or two a day wouldn't amount to the hundreds of thousands missing from the bank's ledgers. Something wasn't adding up.

He worked for another hour then exited his office. "Mr. Ferguson," Phin said. He always used the proper address when customers were in the bank.

Randall lifted his head and looked in his direction. "I'll be gone the rest of the day," Phin said. "Would you please lock up today?"

Ferguson smiled. "Yes, sir."

Phin said goodbye to the customers and strode toward the door. He was working on giving Randall Ferguson a false sense of security, letting him think Phin trusted him, and hoping that the man would let down his guard and make a mistake.

The bright Florida sun baked down on Phin as he left the bank and walked toward Lemon Street. It was time to have the sheriff fill him in on Randall Ferguson. Where did he live? Whom did he associate with? Was he a gambler? Was he a thief? He had worked at the bank for a year before Phineas was called to come in and help balance the books. Was there someone else involved? The losses had been going on for three years. But who? And how? He needed to find the former employees of the bank, but where were they?

Adeline brushed the dirt and grime from her blouse and pants. It had been a long day branding the cattle, but it had been good to get her mind off the meeting at the bank. How could Father have borrowed ten thousand dollars and not record it anywhere? What had he purchased with that much money?

She had to find out what he'd purchased and where. Then perhaps she could sell whatever it was and recoup enough to settle with the bank and work out a payment schedule for the rest of the debt. There was no doubt in her mind that the loan had been Confederate dollars. There had to be a way to reason with the bank. Addy banged her hat against her thigh. A plume of dust fell to the ground.

It had been hot and dry all day. She glanced to the sky to see if the afternoon Florida rains were coming today. Off in the west a buildup of dark gray clouds was emerging.

The creaking of springs brought her focus to a carriage making its way up her road. The buggy had a roof and open sides. The man driving the carriage had brilliant red hair. She hadn't had time to meet with a lawyer after visiting with Mr. Phineas George Hamilton III. She did not want to talk with the man, not again. Once a day was more than she could handle.

He waved as he came closer. Instinctively, she waved back, then groaned. Why was she being civil to him? She turned and marched up the steps and onto the front porch. From this position she'd be taller than him. She placed her hands on her hips. "Why are you here?" she said as he pulled to a stop.

"Pleasure to see you too, Miss Edwards." He dipped his hat as he climbed down from the buggy. "I was hoping you would reconsider my offer to go over your books. Perhaps I can help find the missing money." He stepped onto the first step and lowered his voice. "I wish to help you. I don't want to see you lose this plantation to the bank."

She relaxed her stance for a moment then remembered that if she gave him access to her books, the bank would have full knowledge of the plantation's finances. "No, sir. I do not wish to accept your offer."

His smile dipped. He nodded and looked down at his feet. "I understand, Miss Edwards. My desire was merely one of assistance." He turned to leave.

She hated what she was becoming, no longer trusting anyone. But this man represented the bank that would take this plantation by the end of the month. She couldn't waver. She wouldn't.

He turned back to her. "Whereas this may be the last time we shall speak, I do wish to say, I admire your ability to maintain the plantation these past three years. You've done a wonderful job under such hard conditions. I'm afraid not many have done quite as well."

"Then why are you trying to take my plantation?"

"Miss Edwards," he pleaded, "I am not trying to take your plantation. I am merely doing my job as a representative of the bank."

"Is it because I'm a woman?"

"Pardon?"

"The reason for no notice and only a couple of weeks to come up with ten thousand dollars."

"Mr. Ferguson assures me he has given you written notice of the debt and the payment due date."

Adeline puffed up her chest. "Mr. Ferguson is mistaken. He has never mentioned the debt to me, nor has he sent correspondence on the matter. Your arrival was the first I heard of this erroneous debt. I'll grant you that was my father's signature but—"

He leaped forward and took her hand. "Let me help?"

She yanked her hand free. "No, sir. I am not a lawyer, but I know for a fact that a lawyer would not be happy if I were to show you the books before our trial." She narrowed her gaze. "Is that why you are here? Trying to convince me not to take legal action?"

He stood up straight and placed his hat back on his head. "I do not fault you for wanting to secure legal assistance in the matter. However, if you wish to impugn my integrity. . .I will bid you adieu."

Adeline raked her dusty hair with her fingers. She needed to change or she would become a harsh person. Did running a business make men harsh? Did she have to be?

Mammy came out on the porch. "Miss Addy, there's a bad one comin'. Ya best get in the house."

Addy didn't question Mammy and her weather predictions. Over the years the woman had been right at least 98 percent of the time. "What's about to happen?"

"Driving rain, perhaps a twister, air's right." Mammy said.

"How much time?" Addy asked.

"Thirty minutes, so ya better hurry." Mammy's bones were never precise but still well worth listening to.

Addy sprang into action. "Forgive me, Mr. Hamilton. I have work to do." She placed her hat on her head and ran toward the barn and into the corral. She rounded up the horses and sent them to the open range. They would have a fighting chance out there. There was no telling if the storm would hit the barn. In the field they could run to safety. Then she penned up the chickens and pigs, praying they would not be hit by the storm.

From the corner of her eye she saw Phineas George Hamilton III releasing his horse from the buggy. "What are you doing?"

"Do you honestly think I can outrun a storm?" he yelled.

She couldn't decide if he was yelling at her or simply raising his voice over the rumble of thunder now closing in on them. "Perhaps not."

A loud crack of thunder charged the air, then the rain began to pelt them. "Come on," she hollered at Mr. Hamilton, and ran toward the house. By the time they made it to the front door they were soaked from head to toe.

Phineas slipped out of his suit jacket and hung it on the hanger that Miss Edwards provided. "I'll be happy to wait on the veranda, if you wish."

She held his gaze then turned away. "You may stay in the house until the storm passes."

"Thank you."

She pointed to a wooden chair in the front room. "Sit. I'll fetch you some tea."

What he needed was a dry pair of slacks and a dry shirt, but he would never be so presumptuous as to ask for them. He might catch his death sitting in his wet clothing. He knew she was fighting herself for even letting him into the house.

Phin sniffed. Someone could cook, and he'd venture to say it wasn't Miss Edwards. Probably the former slave, Mammy. Why had so many of her slaves stayed?

The front door opened and a man, perhaps thirty—maybe forty—walked right in. Phin stiffened. He wasn't used to a former slave thinking of himself as having the right to walk into the main entrance of the plantation house. Weren't they supposed to use the servants' entrance? Phin caught himself thinking in terms of the old South. It was a new era, and it demanded that a man think differently than how he was raised.

"Is that your buggy out there, mister?"

"Yes."

"I ain't responsible if it gets broken to bits."

"No, sir. I am."

"Yes, sir." The black man marched toward the kitchen. He was followed by a stream of former slaves of all different shapes and sizes. At some point, Miss Edwards came out and brought him a tall glass of iced tea.

The wind began to whistle through the windows. Phin glanced out. He could see the circular motion of the wind whipping up the debris and sand from the front yard.

A small hand grabbed his. "Come on, mister. It ain't safe."

Phineas looked down at the little one, with her chocolate-brown eyes and her nappy hair tied up in braids. She pulled again.

"Where are we going?" he asked.

"In the shelter. Come on." She pulled him toward the kitchen and through a door leading to a set of stairs that brought them into a cellar. A couple of oil lamps burned. At least twenty sets of white eyes peered at him. "Sit," the little one ordered.

Two minutes later Miss Edwards came down the same stairs. She glanced in his direction and settled across the room next to Mammy.

The house creaked. The older slaves broke out in song. His southern roots knew the old Negro spiritual, "Hold the Wind." Very appropriate for the moment.

The distant rumble of a train echoed through the basement. The older man, who was the first to enter the house, stood and worked his way up the stairs. Phin knew full well it wasn't a train. "Be careful," he cautioned.

"I's be careful, sir."

Mammy spoke up, "My Jimmy, he knows what he's doing. He's been workin' this here land fer all his life."

Phineas nodded. Jimmy and Mammy were married. He wondered which, if any, of the others were related to them.

The door creaked open again, and everyone looked at Jimmy. "She's blowin' away from the houses and barn. We's be safe soon."

Growing up in Savannah, Phin had never encountered a tornado before. That wasn't to say that some small ones hadn't been spotted a time or two, but he personally had never been through one. He didn't like the feeling of apprehension that came over him. On the other hand, the former slaves singing "Hold the Wind" seemed mighty powerful. Had God spared them and their plantation simply because they asked in song? Phin questioned what he knew of God. Did he have the faith to move the mountains, or wind, in this case?

Adeline Edwards stood up and brushed off her pants. "Well now, I say we get to cleaning up whatever mess this storm brought our way." She narrowed her gaze on him.

Phin's heart pounded in his chest. Was he the tornado coming to destroy their home? He stood with the others, waited his turn, and climbed out of the cellar. He'd locate his horse and be gone as soon as possible. He certainly didn't want to be a tornado in Adeline Edwards's life.

Chapter 3

Adeline couldn't believe how efficient Phineas Hamilton was in collecting his horse and fastening it to his buggy. He paused for an instant, giving the impression he wanted to say something, but climbed into his buggy and headed back toward town.

The next two days passed with everyone working to put the plantation back in order. She lost a large oak tree in the pasture, a water oak that had started to rot from the inside out. She preferred the natural hammocks that grew in the area. Two acres of the plantation grew orange trees, three grapefruit trees, two lemon trees, and one lime tree. They were winter fruit, but she loved their freshness when in season. Mammy would can the juice for drinks during the rest of the year. They even learned how to wrap the oranges in Spanish moss to preserve them for a long time.

Some of the other fruit plants were fig trees and muscadine grapes. But the fruit and nut trees were only for personal use on the plantation. They weren't a cash crop. Her cash came from the cattle. Thankfully, she only lost one during the storm. Unfortunately, it was a pregnant cow, which meant she'd lost two.

"Addy," Mammy called from the kitchen.

"Coming." She left the office and headed toward the kitchen.

"I thought you might like to know that the Mosleys lost their plantation," Mammy said when Adeline came through the doorway.

Adeline groaned in dismay. "They sold out?"

Mammy shook her head. "I's heard the other day they didn't sell. Mr. Willis bought it from the bank."

"But he used to work at the bank. How did he come to buy it?"

"Don't know, but I's certain it ain't legal. Mr. Willis, he bought several farms before he resigned from the bank."

"How do you know this?"

"Well, my friend Ginny, she was a slave for the Mosleys, stayed on like Jimmy and me did. And she overheard Mr. Mosley cussin' up a blue streak about Mr. Willis, sayin' he robbed 'em and all." Mammy shrugged. "I's figure with all the trouble ya be havin' with the bank ya might wanna knows."

"Thank you, Mammy." Adeline felt her temper rise. Was Phineas George Hamilton III trying to steal her plantation out from under her? "I'll be out this afternoon. Do you know where I can find the Mosleys?"

"He be stayin' with his kin, Alexander."

"Thank you, Mammy. I'll be home late." First thing she needed to do was change into appropriate clothing. She knew the ruckus she caused when she wore men's clothing when going to town. If she didn't want to offend Mr. Mosley's sensitivities, she would have to wear the proper visiting attire.

An hour later she was properly dressed and in the buggy. Alexander Mosley lived a good two and a half hours from her plantation. "Miss Edwards," Mammy's son Caleb called out just before she left the yard.

Caleb was her age, but he was already married and had fathered a child. "Yes, Caleb."

"Mom sent me out with this for ya." He held up a small basket.

Adeline smiled. Mammy must have prepared some food for the long journey. "Thank her for me."

"Yes, ma'am."

She jiggled the reins and headed toward town, to exit the opposite side and meet with the Mosleys. Hopefully, she could find some answers there.

When she arrived at the Mosleys' she walked up the front steps of the veranda to where Alexander was sitting with his brother W.D., smoking a cigar. "Good afternoon, gentlemen."

"Afternoon," W.D. said with a smile.

"I'm wondering if I might ask you a few questions, Mr. Mosley. As you probably know, I've inherited my family's plantation."

W.D. nodded, and Alexander stood up. "Excuse me," he said, and went into the house.

"Well, I'm having some issues with the bank, and I heard you did too."

W.D. nodded. "That's right. Mr. Willis, he's a wily one. He gave me a loan and set a ridiculously inflated mortgage payment. I couldn't meet it, and the bank ended up with my place. Which I agree was my own fault for not reading over the paperwork, but the weasel Willis bought my place from the bank for a tenth of the amount on the loan. Ain't right, I'm telling ya. Course, that new man at the bank, he agrees with me. Ain't seen anything like that before. He isn't certain he can get my place back, but he's given me hope."

Adeline's head swam. What new man at the bank? "Phineas George Hamilton III?"

"He's the one. Strangest thing, he came round yesterday and asked me all kinds of questions. Unfortunately, I didn't have a copy of my loan papers. Threw them out when the bank took my place." He shrugged. "Phineas, he said he'd look into it." W.D. leaned toward her. "Between you and me, I believe him. Willis and Ferguson, they're from the North. Can't trust no Yankee."

"Willis has family here."

W.D. grunted. "Maybe, but he acts like he's from the North. Came to the bank after the northern bank bought it in '64 or '65."

Adeline had never paid much attention to business and banking before she'd been put in charge of the plantation, so she never knew who owned or ran the bank. Now, she was paying attention. And she needed to pay more attention if she was going to save her plantation. "Thank you, Mr. Mosley."

"Pleasure is all mine. I hear you're running your plantation real fine. Your daddy, he'd be real proud."

"Thank you, Mr. Mosley." But she knew her father never expected her to be running the plantation. One of her brothers, yes, but not her. He'd planned to marry her off to one of the wealthier plantation owners. She headed back to her buggy and started the long trek home. Could she trust Mr. Phineas George Hamilton III? Should she?

Phineas rode to the former plantation of W. D. Mosley and knocked on the door. All seemed quiet. The sound of slow footfalls approached. The door creaked open. "Hello?" A woman no higher than four and a half feet, with weathered features, greeted him. "Can I help you?"

"Good morning, ma'am. I'm looking for Mr. Willis. Is he home?"

"No, sir."

"Do you know where I might find him?"

"No, sir. My husband and I bought this place from him last month."

"Last month?"

The woman smiled. "Bought it for a song. Took our entire savings, but it was worth it."

"Ah, well, my name is Phineas George Hamilton III. I work for the bank."

Her eyes went wide. "Harold," she hollered. "I told you there was something wrong."

"Come in, come in." She waved him in.

An older gentleman came in from the parlor. "What ya hollerin' 'bout now, Mildred?"

"This here gentleman is from the bank. I told you that Willis character wasn't on the up-and-up."

Harold paled. "What happened? Are we in trouble? Oh Lord, our money?"

"Let's calm down and sit for a moment, please," Phineas encouraged.

"Come on to the parlor; I'll fix us some tea," Mildred said as she headed farther back into the house.

"Tell me what's happening," Harold said as he led the way to the parlor.

"It appears Mr. Willis was involved in some sort of a scam with y'all."

Harold sighed. "Mildred said it was too good to be true."

Phineas sat down. "I'm not certain what the legal ramifications are, but I believe, since Mr. Willis falsified the report to the bank, and since Mr. Mosley should not have lost the plantation to the bank, the property will revert back to him. As for your money, legally, it is lost. However, since Mr. Willis was working for the bank at the time of the misrepresentation to Mr. Mosley, I'd say it would be in the bank's best interest to replace most, if not all, of your money."

Harold sat back. Mildred nearly dropped the silver tray she was carrying. "Are ya sayin' we might get our money back?"

"I'm hopeful." Phineas shifted in his seat. He hadn't spoken with the owners in Boston, but he wagered they wouldn't want to be part of a scandal. Although they did know something wasn't right here in Palatka. His next visit would be with the sheriff to put out an arrest warrant for Willis. So far, he'd found five accounts with fraud done by Jeremiah Willis. Unfortunately, Adeline Edwards's plantation was not one of them.

"Miss Addy, y'all got to eat, child." Mammy stood in the doorway with her hands on her hips.

Addy glanced up at the mantel and the clock. Seven thirty. "I'll be in in a few minutes." She scanned the ledgers in front of her for the umpteenth time. There had to be some kind of evidence that her father borrowed ten thousand dollars. But there was nothing. She added and readded figures from all the purchases in 1863. Nothing came close to even a thousand dollars, let alone ten.

Mammy placed her hand on Addy's shoulder. "Come, child. Ain't no tellin' those here numbers to jump up and confess thems money, no sir. Ifin your father borrowed the money, he had a purpose."

"But don't you see, I'll lose the plantation to the bank. I can't pay ten thousand dollars."

"Child, ya knows the good Lord, He take care of his own. Look at us, my people, we was slaves for generation after generation. Ain't no different than the Jews in Egypt. We's worked from sunup to sundown. We's prayed for freedom year after year. And it came, yes sir, the good Lord gave us freedom. And He'll figure out what ya got to do to save this here land, or not. But y'all have a roof and food. Y'all will rise up again. Yer a good woman with a smart brain. Y'all are better than most white folk. Ya will be blessed. Now come and eat."

Adeline nodded and left the journals. Was she not trusting the good Lord to provide for her future? Granted, she had responsibilities, and the twenty former slaves who stayed on the plantation would need jobs and places to live too. Silently she prayed for guidance, for the Lord to help her remain in control and help these people. Phineas George Hamilton III stood in the forefront of her mind. Was he her helper or executioner?

Mammy sat her down at the table, went to the stove, and pulled off a plate she had been keeping warm. "Here ya go, Addy, eat up." She removed her apron and placed it in the laundry bin. "I'll see ya in the mornin'."

Adeline watched as Mammy walked toward her house, silhouetted by the crimson sky. Jimmy came out to meet his wife, and the two embraced. A warmth flowed through Adeline, seeing the love between them. She never had seen the slaves as livestock, like her father and brothers had. She'd always seen them as people with their own lives and minds.

Adeline closed her eyes and prayed. "Father, You understand the needs of this plantation, my responsibilities and those of our former slaves. The changes since the war have cost so many people their homes and livelihood. I suppose it might be selfish on my part, but I don't want to see these people displaced. And I certainly don't want to see my home taken by a Yankee banker. Show me what to do?"

Mammy's words of waiting and trusting the Lord came back. "I'll try, Lord. I'll try."

She picked up her knife and fork and cut into the stuffed pork chop. The rich butter and garlic flavored the meat so well. Her taste buds watered in anticipation. The apple-and-raisin stuffing melted in her mouth, and Adeline groaned with pleasure. She'd never learned to cook. Perhaps she should have Mammy start giving her lessons. The day might come when Mammy would no longer be here, or she herself might no longer live on this plantation with Jimmy and Mammy. She'd learned how to rustle up the cattle. She could learn to cook too.

For the rest of the evening she left the books in the office and picked up a needlepoint she had long neglected. Working the plantation didn't allow for such pleasantries. Perhaps she should just walk away from the plantation, give it to the bank for the debt. It wasn't like she could pass it on to future generations. Her brothers were gone. They'd had no wives, no children.

No. She had twenty people who counted on her for their income. She couldn't just give up.

She set the needlepoint aside and went back to the office. So much for trusting the Lord. She needed to find that money, or where her father spent it, so she could figure out how to pay off the debt to the bank. She had no other choice. She was no longer a society girl, attending fancy balls, being doted on by gentlemen callers. She was a hardworking cracker, a woman who wore men's clothing and whose hands were as strong as most of her workers. In her mind's eye, she glanced back at the needlepoint. Another thing of the past. "Dear God, I wish Father was still here."

Phin went over the bank ledgers one more time. If he had found them all, Jeremiah Willis had done a similar scam on at least a dozen home and plantation owners, accounting for a large portion of the money missing from the bank. He composed his letter with the detailed accounting of monies and scams that Mr. Willis performed. When he gathered the papers and put them in order, they piled an inch thick. He wrapped them in a sheet of vellum and sealed all the seams with wax. He had found most of the missing money. He would have the correspondence shipped out to Boston in the morning on the first steamer leaving port. He'd talked to the sheriff, who issued a warrant for Jeremiah Willis's arrest. He'd done all he could do. The sheriff was working on a sketch for the wanted poster.

However, this did not solve Adeline Edwards's problem. Phin pulled out her father's loan papers again and scanned them. After a couple of minutes he tossed them back in the drawer. Somehow he needed to convince Miss Edwards to allow him to look over the plantation ledgers. But how?

He stood and grabbed the package for J. C. Wild of Old Boston Bank and headed for the wharf. Several paddleboats were tied up for the evening. The *Hiawatha* sat silent, tied to the dock. With her three decks, she seemed a bit ungainly. She made the trip from Palatka down the Ocklawaha River daily, which was in the opposite direction of Jacksonville. A three-masted schooner with a black hull was anchored out in the St. John's.

He spotted a man he'd been doing business with recently. "Captain Brock," Phin called out.

The captain turned. He was a pleasant character and had been working hard to restore what he'd lost during the war. His inn, the Brock House, was finished, and his ship the *Enterprise* was running regularly back and forth to Jacksonville, as was the newly refitted *Hattie Brock*, named after his daughter. "Good evening, Mr. Hamilton, how may I help you?"

"I'm wondering if you have a vessel sailing in the morning to Jacksonville."

"The *Enterprise* is about to leave in an hour and will arrive by morning. Do you need passage?"

"No, sir. I have a package that needs to go to Boston in quick order."

Captain Brock smoothed his goatee with his hand. "I'd be happy to accommodate. I take it this has some urgency."

"Yes." Phin didn't want to elaborate.

"Word has it you're looking into some recent issues with the bank and that you yourself hail from Savannah."

"Yes, sir. My family has lived in Savannah for five generations."

A smile broadened the captain's face. "I'll be happy to take your package, and I'll make certain it goes to Savannah on the next steamer. From there it can ship out to Boston."

"Thank you, I appreciate it."

"You're welcome." The captain leaned in. "Mosley is a friend. Ain't right what happened to his place."

"You understand I cannot speak on the matter."

Captain Brock placed his hand on Phin's shoulder. "Don't fret, son. W. D. and I go way back. I'm just glad you're able to fix the problem."

"I'm working on it."

The captain slapped Phin's shoulder and took the package. "I believe you are. I'm happy to help. I can assure you I'll have the package safely in

Savannah in the morning."

"Thank you, Captain."

"You're welcome." He turned toward the *Enterprise*. "Light those bowls," he ordered. Two large flames whooshed up as the bowls on either side of the ship ignited, giving light to the men in the bow to help navigate out of the harbor and into the St. John's.

Phineas watched as the ship pulled out under the night sky. Small lights emanated from the passengers' windows as they made ready for sleep. *Not a bad way to travel,* Phin mused. He turned back toward the bank, and rather than return there, he headed to his room at the Brock House. Soon he would need to rent an apartment or small house. From all indications he'd be in Palatka for a year or more while he settled accounts and dealt with the thievery of Jeremiah Willis.

If only Willis were responsible for Adeline Edwards's troubles.

Chapter 4

Phin worked through all the morning chores at the bank as he set up Ferguson for the day. "You're going out again?" Randall asked him.

"More customers to see." Phin paused. Should he tell Ferguson about the investigation? "It appears Mr. Willis was less than honest with some of our clients. I am going to try and repair the damage." He narrowed his gaze on Ferguson. He didn't trust the man, and yet there was no reaction.

Ferguson shook his head. "I'm sorry to hear that. Can I help?"

"No. I sent my evidence to Mr. Wild in Boston. I'm waiting to hear from him."

"Very well. But as I said, if I can help, I'd be happy to."

Phin nodded. He needed to find the facts impartially. "Have a good day." He prayed Ferguson would not cheat or make a mistake with any of their customers today.

He arrived at the Edwards Plantation by midmorning. "Lord, guide my words today." One thing he didn't want to do was anger Miss Edwards again.

She opened the front door as he stepped down from his buggy. She crossed her arms. Today her dark brown hair was not hidden by a bonnet or hat. Instead, it bobbed down to her chin. He didn't know many women who had short hair, but it fit her, framing her face like trees around a pale moon. "Good morning, Miss Edwards."

"Why are you here?"

No pleasantries. He couldn't blame her. "I'm here to plead with you once again to allow me the privilege of going over your books. It is my goal not to steal from you but to perhaps help you find the missing funds."

"I have gone over them. I cannot find where my father spent the money you claim he borrowed from the bank. And I still have concerns over the fact that it was Confederate dollars. How could a northern bank expect a person to pay full value on a Confederate dollar that is worth no more than five cents? You do realize that if my father borrowed ten thousand dollars, the most I should owe is five hundred." Which was still more than she could pay at the moment. After she sold her cattle, it would be a manageable amount.

He smiled.

"What?"

"I have pleaded such a case on your behalf with Mr. Wild, the owner of Old Boston."

She turned away, but not before he saw her tears. He hurried to her side, ready to hold her or offer words of comfort. But Miss Adeline Edwards would never allow such a thing. He knew she was southern bred, and a woman of such strong convictions would never swoon into the arms of a man whom she viewed as the enemy. "Please," he pleaded. He lowered his voice to a smidge more than a whisper. "I would like to try and help you."

She looked down at the floorboards of the front porch and gave a nod. He wouldn't push for more. "Thank you."

Adeline turned toward the front door and led him into the grand entryway of the old southern plantation, which sported a wonderfully polished staircase that fanned across the back wall above a small table and two chairs. The staircase was completely plastered below the banister with hand-carved wooden molding varnished to perfection. No doubt her father had money before the war. Two doorways framed the left and right side of the foyer. "Follow me." She led him toward the left doorway.

He scanned the fine craftsmanship on the hand-carved molding. It was exceptionally well done. They moved through a front parlor and headed through another doorway into a library of sorts. "Father's office is in here." She turned the glass knob of another door and swung the door open. The heavy mahogany furniture didn't quite fit Miss Edwards but said volumes about her father. "You'll find all the ledgers from 1863 right there." She pointed to the desktop. "I want to trust you, Mr. Hamilton, but I can't. So if you don't mind, I'll ask Mammy's youngest son, Jimmy John, to watch you. He won't understand facts and figures, but he'll be able to see if you take a page out of the ledgers."

"That is acceptable. Thank you for trusting me this much."

"I'll be back in an hour. I have some business to deal with, and then I'll be able to assist you in your search."

He smiled in spite of himself. The idea of the feisty Miss Edwards sitting beside him going over numbers thrilled him in a way he'd never experienced before.

Phin sat down at the desk and sorted the ledgers. A young black boy around eight or ten came in and stood by the door. "Hi, what's your name?" Phin asked.

"JJ," the boy answered.

"Pleasure to meet you JJ. I'm Phin."

"No sir, y'all is Mr. Hamilton. Momma would not appreciate me not usin' my manners."

Phin nodded. "Very well, I understand." He glanced back at the books and pulled out a blank sheet of paper and a pencil. Working with numbers and reading ledgers was a God-given talent and one he enjoyed. Delivering harsh news to clients who had overextended themselves and their funds at the bank was his least favorite aspect of the job. Helping Mr. Mosley regain his property gave him deeper satisfaction. If only he could help Miss Edwards. But from everything he'd found, she owed the money and would likely lose her plantation to the bank. There was still the issue of Confederate dollars being converted to the debt's bottom line, and he was praying for that outcome. Although with all the other losses the bank had incurred, he had serious doubts Mr. Wild would agree.

He scanned the first column of figures: expenses and income for January 1863. There was no income, only expenditures. He knew far too many folks who were never paid or only paid a fraction of the value on goods sold to the armies. He knew the North had taken control of Palatka in the spring of '63 when the town was shelled. No doubt that act influenced Liam Edwards to join the fight against the North.

No income for February, March, or April. . .expenses seemed moderate. . . nothing that shouted why the man would need a loan for ten thousand dollars. Was there another set of books? Did Liam Edwards have another life? With all the investigations Phin had conducted over the years, hiding money from family members was something he'd seen before. But why so much money?

He went back to the ledger and found May was the same. June had no recorded income or expenses. Then the handwriting changed. A cleaner pen stroke, easier to read. He smiled. He knew this was Adeline's penmanship. He went over her figures. They were clean and precise. Where her father would merely put "Feed," she'd break it down to the various oats and grains, how much she'd purchased and the price of each. No doubt she knew she would have to give a full account to her father when he returned. Phin paused for a moment, realizing he had not returned. But not only had he not returned, neither had her brothers. To have lost so many members of her family to the war must have been hard, and yet she fought and worked harder than most. She turned the losses into profits. She changed the direction the plantation was going. Incredible.

He glanced at JJ, who had taken a seat and was now asleep, and then looked at the clock on the mantel. Adeline would be returning soon. Phin went back to work scanning the ledgers in front of him. With each line item and every page, his confidence in Adeline Edwards's abilities grew.

Unfortunately, it took two hours before Adeline returned to her father's office. Jimmy John was asleep on the sofa while Phineas worked tirelessly over the books. She stood in the doorway and watched. He was scratching out figures on another sheet of paper. He paused then looked up at her. "Hi. I didn't see you return."

"I wasn't certain if I should interrupt." She glanced at Jimmy John and stepped over to him. She laid a hand on his shoulder. "I'm here. You can go see Mammy."

He bounced off the sofa as if he had been wide awake.

"How long did he last?"

Phineas shrugged. "I don't know. He sat down after ten or fifteen minutes."

"Have you found anything?"

"Lots."

She paled.

"Not related to the debt, but you are incredible, very detail oriented and precise. I love it." His blue eyes sparkled. "You don't know how refreshing it is to go over a set of books that. . .well, suffice it to say, you do good work."

She didn't tend to be vain, but his compliments made her spirit soar. For years she'd been dealing with all kinds of curious stares and comments about her running the plantation. To be acknowledged as having done a good job was priceless, absolutely priceless. "Thank you."

"I don't mean to be indelicate, but did your father have a gambling issue, or anything else that he would have borrowed so much money for? Also, I don't understand why the bank would give your father that much money after the North had already taken over Palatka."

"I don't know. To the best of my knowledge, Father did not have a gambling issue. Nor did my brothers. But if he borrowed that money, he had to spend it on something that had no relation to the plantation. I can't imagine Father putting the plantation up for collateral knowing he was going off to fight in the war. On the other hand, we had received word that my brother Brian had been killed shortly before Father went off to fight."

Addy closed her eyes and held off the memories of receiving the news, not only of her brother Brian but of her father and Liam Jr. She swallowed and turned away. "It was a horrible time."

"I can imagine." Phineas George Hamilton III's voice cracked.

Addy cleared her throat. "Let's get to work." She grabbed the smaller ledger from the pile. "This one reports the transactions from the local merchants. . . ."

They continued going over the books until the clock struck five. Mr. Hamilton jumped up. "Forgive my intrusion; I didn't mean to stay so long."

Adeline chuckled. "You do get lost in your work."

"I'm afraid so. Forgive me, and I'll be on my way."

"Nonsense, Phineas." They had stopped calling one another by their formal names hours ago. "Stay for dinner. Mammy is quite the culinary expert."

"Do you know how to cook, Adeline?"

"No, I'm afraid my training was in manners, needlepoint, and being a hostess. However, I've decided I'll need to learn, if I'm about to lose my home."

He reached over and placed his hand on top of hers. "Not if I can help it. In the pit of my stomach I know something is wrong with this loan. Even if I can't prove it, I certainly can have the bank make arrangements to extend the loan for a more satisfactory payment plan."

"Thank you." Relief washed over her. "I'm responsible for the livelihood of twenty souls. I couldn't imagine not providing for them."

He squeezed her hand. "I know."

She glanced into his blue eyes. A flutter went through her. "Please, stay for dinner. There is more than enough."

"I'd be honored," Phineas said. He stood up and offered his hand, as any southern gentleman of society would have been taught.

"Tell me about your home, your family?" she asked as she led him from the office to the front parlor.

"There isn't much to tell. I grew up in Savannah. My family hails from that area and South Carolina. I went into finance because I have an affinity with numbers."

"Well, that is boring. Did you play with numbers growing up?"

"Funny. No, well yes, in a way. I would work on numerical problems from a very young age for entertainment. I also liked to fish, hunt, play ball, and all the other pastimes for a boy."

"Did you serve?"

Phineas lowered his head and folded his hands. "No, I was in the North studying business finance in Boston when the war broke out. I could understand the viewpoints of both sides and decided the best way to serve was to finish my education and return to Savannah. I did, but then, Old Boston Bank, where I worked in college, started buying up southern banks, and I've been going from one situation to another for the past three years."

"What about your family?"

"My parents live in Savannah. They're happy I am a dedicated worker and have earned the respect of Mr. Wild, Old Boston's president. But I think they believe I have become too Northern in my thinking."

"Ah, I understand."

"It wasn't about the slavery issues for my parents. It was about the rights of the individual states to make decisions for themselves."

Adeline leaned back in her chair. "Truly, I understand. I'm not all that fond of Northerners using children in mills and giving them nothing for wages, owning their homes and. . ." She waved her arms. "We don't need to hash out all the reasons for the war. I'm hopeful we'll be able to rebuild the country stronger than it was."

"My prayer as well." He paused. "Tell me about yourself."

"As you can see, I was your typical southern belle. My mother passed away when I was thirteen and so, while I met all the benchmarks of a proper young lady in society, I also was more interested in the horses and cattle. I spent a bit of time learning some basic understandings of profit and loss from my father. Which is why I'm having a hard time believing he would go into debt for such a great amount of money when the war was progressing badly for the South." Adeline glanced up at the portrait of her father. "He was conservative in his purchases. I have never found one loan from the bank. In any of his dealings. He was a cash-and-carry kind of a man. Oh, he didn't mind keeping some money in the bank but not all—"

Phineas jumped up. "Where did he hide—"

Adeline jumped to her feet at the same time. "This way." She led him upstairs, to her parents' private bedchamber, which had a sitting room as well as two walk-in closets and a bathroom. The windows opened from floor to ceiling, allowing the outside air to help cool off the rooms. There was also a balcony off the back of their bedroom where Father would sometimes sleep on the hottest of days.

"My goodness, my parents have a large bedroom, but nothing like this," Phin said as he spun around, taking in the entire room.

Adeline shrugged. "It's what I grew up with. I don't know anything different. However, I don't use this room. I'm still sleeping in my own room, which isn't large, but has a huge walk-in closet. Momma said that, being a lady, I would need extra room for my gowns. Father complied, and they built my room within a few weeks after I was born."

"What you two doin' up there?" Mammy called up from the bottom of the stairs.

"I'm fetching something from my parents' room."

"Dinner is ready whenever you are. The crew's been fed. Y'all come down soon, ya hear."

Phineas smiled. "She looks after you."

"Yes." Adeline smiled back at him. "And I look after them. It's the way of the—"

"South," he said.

She went down on her hands and knees and rolled up the carpet that was in front of her mother's dresser. She pulled the iron ring that lay flush with the floor and lifted the floorboards that made a door to her father's secret savings. The old tin box was there. She opened the box and found a stack of Confederate bills. She knew by sight it would not be ten thousand dollars, but. . .

"May I?"

She handed him the pile of bills. He knelt on the floor and began to count out the money. Adeline looked back into the box. Seeing nothing, she lifted the box out of the hiding place. Her heart beat faster. Three gold dollars pointed toward the nightstand. She remembered her father's words. *"Baby girl, if something happens to me, these coins will point the way to help you and your brothers. Remember, Addy, they will point the way. You'll remember, won't you, baby girl?"*

"Yes, Daddy, I'll remember."

He'd kissed her forehead and held her close. She was only six at the time. She glanced over at the nightstand. Was there another hidden box under the nightstand? Should she tell Phineas? *No, I better wait.*

"There's five hundred and thirty-two Confederate dollars here," Phineas said. "Not even a tenth of the loan."

"So the current value is twenty-five dollars, not nearly enough." Adeline placed the box back over the gold coins, hiding them from Phineas. She was beginning to trust Mr. Phineas George Hamilton III, but not completely.

"Would you like me to take this to the bank and cash it in?"

"That would be nice, thank you."

"You're welcome." His stomach grumbled.

Adeline chuckled. "Let's go take care of that before we do anything else."

"I must say, the delightful aromas coming from the kitchen have my stomach crying for mercy."

Adeline laughed. "You won't be disappointed." But would she? Would she find the missing ten thousand dollars in the nightstand? Would she lose the plantation because her father made a bad choice before he went off to fight? *Please, Lord, don't let it be true.*

Chapter 5

Phin didn't want to leave Adeline's. He stayed well past the dinner hour, enjoying her company and some of the best peach cobbler he ever tasted, which was saying something, coming from Georgia where peach trees abounded. He'd seen plenty of citrus trees in Florida, a few nut trees, but only one or two peach trees. "Do y'all grow these peaches?"

"We have a tree but it doesn't produce much, at least not to Mammy's requirements. We purchase fifty cases of peaches from Georgia every year, and Mammy and a few of the other ladies get to canning. I lost count of how many jars of peaches get put up each year, but we always run out before the next harvest. However, about that time the strawberries and blueberries come in around here and we grow a mess of them. Although one year the pigs got into the strawberry patch." Adeline laughed. "Mammy was fit to be tied. It was amazing that the entire herd didn't become bacon the next week. Mammy loves her fruit, and I'll admit I love what she does with it."

"I hope you'll be able to stay on the plantation, but. . ." Phin hesitated. He didn't want to make false promises. "I want to say you won't lose the plantation. But I can't. I can say I will do my best to help you not lose it, but I cannot guarantee it. I'm sorry, I wish I could do more."

"You've already spent a day hunting and searching with me." A gentle pink flush swept across her cheeks. A flutter of awareness of her beauty filled him. He wanted to wrap her in his arms and protect her.

He looked away. Mr. Wild would have his head for mixing business with pleasure. He closed his eyes. "I must be going." He stood up. "It is getting late."

"Yes, yes it is. Mammy?" she called out.

"Yes, miss." Mammy came into the front parlor, wiping her hands on a dish towel. "Would you ask Jimmy to hitch up Mr. Hamilton's buggy?"

"Yes'm."

"I can do that."

"I know, but Jimmy and Mammy will be more at ease when they know you've left."

Phin smiled. "They look after you and your honor?"

"Yes, and don't you forget it. Jimmy can hit a flea off a deer's behind from two hundred yards."

Phineas laughed. "I won't forget it." He took her hand in his, bent down, and kissed the top of it. "You have my word of honor, Adeline. I will never disrespect you personally or financially."

Tears welled in her hazel eyes. "Thank you."

He fought every desire to pull her into his arms. How was he falling in love with this odd but brilliant woman? Who fell in love with a woman who wore men's clothing? And yet they seemed right on her. "Good night, Adeline."

"Good night, Phineas."

The cool night air hit him as he stepped out the door. The front porch was as wide as a room, shading the front of the house from the heat of the Florida sun. The house also sat on pillars. Every four feet a pillar held the house up, allowing the wind to blow underneath. It wasn't the popular shotgun style of a house where the front and back doors were located one behind the other. But for such a large house, it wasn't as stuffy and hot as some homes in the South could be.

He grinned as he stepped toward his carriage. In a way, Adeline's home was a lot like her, strong, beautiful, and not stuffy. He needed to get to the bottom of this mystery. He had to help save her land and home.

The former slaves nodded to him as they passed by on their way to their cabins. They seemed well fed, in good health, and happy, very happy. That too spoke to Adeline's character.

Adeline flew upstairs to her parents' room and went straight to work scrounging to find her father's hidden storage. The three gold coins had pointed to the nightstand on the left side of his bed. She lifted it. It was heavy. The large chunky wood design somehow matched her father. Once she had the nightstand set aside, she pulled back the carpet. But there wasn't a hidden door to a hidden cubby below the floorboards. She reached down and tried to pry the boards loose. Nothing budged. *Father must have glued the boards down for safekeeping,* she reasoned. She stood and glanced out the window toward the barn. It was late. She probably shouldn't go fumbling around tonight for a crowbar or other tool to lift the floorboards.

Her eyes flittered back to the floorboards where the nightstand had stood. "Tomorrow I'll find it." Contentment and calm filled her, something that hadn't been a part of her days for quite a while. The image of Phineas George Hamilton III scouring over the books came back to mind. He worked hard, he was thorough, and for some strange reason she trusted him. Oh, she knew it had something to do with him working to help Mosley get back his plantation. But it was more than that. Her stomach fluttered in anticipation of seeing him again. But when?

She went to bed and slept well, waking in the morning refreshed.

"Y'all looks mighty good this morning," Mammy said as Adeline walked into the kitchen.

"Thank you. Smells wonderful." The aroma of fresh bacon swirled with a berry cobbler or something. "What did you make?"

"Raspberry, blueberry, and black raspberry syrup for the pancakes."

"Yum." Adeline's stomach grumbled in anticipation. "I can't wait to taste it."

"Honey, I'm afraid y'all can't have it until tomorrow. The melted sugar will burn your tongue."

Adeline pouted as if she were six years old.

Mammy laughed. "Ain't gonna work, child, y'all are too old."

Adeline smiled. "I'll get some ice from the icehouse so we can cool it down."

"No ma'am, that's not what it's for. We's got some hot days left before it cools down. Uh-uh, no ma'am, y'all are goin' to have to wait."

Adeline fought the desire to stomp her foot. She knew Mammy was right, and with the heat of the day, she'd be wanting iced tea more than sweet berry syrup on pancakes. "I'm ordering an extra block of ice for next year."

Mammy's laughter died down. "Ifin's there is a next year. Jimmy and I's been talkin'. He might have to set out and find some work soon. We's ain't got much saved, and we's sure 'nough don't wanna be movin', but that bank man, he don't look like he can finds the money."

"I know." Adeline grabbed a corn muffin and cup of juice. "Tell Jimmy to start the day without me. I need to work on something at the house."

"Yes'm, I's do that." Mammy stirred the berry syrup.

Adeline knew she needed to find the money, and somehow she *was* going to find it. She couldn't let Mammy, Jimmy, and the others down. She'd find a way. "Phineas said he thinks the bank will renegotiate the loan and that will give me time to pay it off."

Mammy placed her hands on her hips. Her brown eyes focused on Adeline. "Ain't right to have to pay for you's father, but I's suppose y'all wouldn't be who you is if y'all didn't pay it back."

Adeline smiled and hugged the woman who had been such a vital part of her life. "Thank you, Mammy." She had to save their home. She couldn't imagine life without Mammy.

Father, help me find the money, she prayed. She excused herself and went out to the barn and picked up a hammer and crowbar.

"Miss Edwards," John Black called as he jogged over to her.

"Yes, John," she answered, setting the tools back on the workbench.

"Beggin' yer pardon, ma'am, but we've heard a rumor that you're goin' to lose the plantation because of a bank loan come due."

She frowned at him. *How'd the news travel through Palatka so quickly?* "I doubt I will." She hoped she wasn't lying. She was hoping Phineas would be able to renegotiate the loan with the bank. "Why do you ask?"

"Well," he stammered. "Me and a couple of the other crackers are thinkin' y'all won't be able to pay us and we should move on."

Adeline clenched her fists. "Suit yourself, but if y'all leave now, you'll lose your bonus, and I'll be compelled to tell whoever asks about your references that you left me in the lurch."

John squared his shoulders. "Ain't wantin' to do that, ma'am. We just need to put ourselves first, you understand."

"Actually, I don't. You said 'you've heard,' meaning you've been listening to gossip. I have not given you or the others any indication that I'm having trouble paying your salary, and yet you come to me believing rumors. I've taken care of this plantation and my cattle for the better part of three years now. You've never been hungry and never lost one day's pay." She turned from John. "Go, be gone, I don't need you working here."

"I didn't mean any harm, Miss Edwards. I've got bills to pay."

She spun around. "John, you've got gambling debts to pay, and you know it. So, go, gamble on another boss to pay and feed you well. I won't abide a man who doesn't respect me." The other men were gathering around. "That goes for each and every one of you. If you don't trust me to pay your salary, the gate's over there." She pointed toward the main entrance. "I've always treated each of you well, whether former slave or cracker. If I run into financial issues,

I'll be the first to tell you and give you as much notice as I can. But—"Adeline stopped and took a deep breath. "Get to work. We've got a long day ahead. See me in the office, John. I'll give you what's due you before you leave."

Phin couldn't get Adeline off his mind. Not only her debt to the bank, but the way she managed her plantation and her concern for her former slaves. He was drawn to her like cheese and grits. The question was, how could he help her?

"Phin!" Sheriff Brill hollered as he walked into the bank.

Phineas walked out of his office. "What's the matter, Sheriff?"

"All good, I'm happy to report. We apprehended Mr. Willis last night. He's locked in my cell. I figure you'll want to speak with him."

Phin grabbed his overcoat. "Lead the way." He glanced over to Ferguson. "I'll be back."

After they left the bank, he asked. "Where'd you find him?"

"Hiding out at his brother-in-law's mother's farm."

Phin raised his brows. "He has family in the area?"

"More or less. But I found that he never left town by ship or train, so I started visiting with all the kin I knew of in the area."

"Thank you, thank you, Sheriff. Mr. Wild will be very happy to hear that you apprehended him."

The sheriff escorted Phin to his office and the holding cell. Mr. Willis sat huddled in a corner.

"Mr. Willis," Phineas called out. The man's head came up, deep bags hanging under his dark eyes. "I'm Phineas George Hamilton III."

"I know who you are," Willis mumbled.

"So, you understand why I'm here. Do you wish to make restitution?"

Willis shrugged. "Money's in the satchel the sheriff took off me." He paused. "Most of it."

"I think I figured out all the transactions. Will you confirm that for me? I promise to ask the judge for leniency for your sentence."

"Law says ten years for each offense. I'll be going to jail for forty years."

"Four offenses, that's all?"

Willis lifted his head. "What do you mean is that all?"

"The Mosley place, the Joneses, Edith Sims's savings after she passed, and John Henry's orange grove. Nothing else?" Phin closed his eyes. He figured Willis wasn't responsible for the Edwards loan, but couldn't help but wonder if he had a hand in it. "What about the Braxton place?"

"No, sir. They forfeited the house because they couldn't make their payment. I sold the place for fifty cents on the dollar, just as I reported in the ledger."

They continued to go over everything Phineas had found questionable in the books. "That's it," Willis said.

"I have one more concern." Phin paused. "Mr. Liam Edwards borrowed some money in '64 just before he headed off to fight."

Willis closed his eyes and bobbed his head up and down.

Phin's stomach knotted. He hoped. . .honestly, he didn't know what he hoped for. "Why would you loan ten thousand dollars to a man who is leaving to fight in the war?"

Willis stood up. "What? I didn't loan him that much money. If memory serves, it was a hundred Confederate. That's all. Some cash to have on hand while he fought. He never should've gone. He was so distraught at the loss of his son. . . ." Willis shook his head. "But after them Yankees shelled the town, it was too much. Liam had to go fight. No one could stop him. I never bothered to tell his daughter about the debt. I figured we could write it off. Then y'all started writing letters from Boston sayin' how much of a failure I was and I thought, why not take some money from those high-and-mighty bankers. I thought I gave myself enough time. But apparently you can wade through ledgers with a fine eye and speed."

Phin's ears still rang. Willis said he had only loaned Liam a hundred dollars, not ten thousand. That meant someone else was tinkering with the books. And that someone else could only be Randall Ferguson. Phin's temper was rising. Had Ferguson witnessed Willis's deceit and decided to capitalize on it as well? "It's my job. Please put in writing all that you've told me, and I'll see what I can say to the judge."

Willis sighed and bowed his head. Phin stepped away. He stretched his neck and tried to work out the tension building within him. "Sheriff, come with me," he ordered.

Sheriff Brill coughed.

"I'm sorry, please come with me. We have another arrest to make."

The sheriff stood up from behind his desk and put his hat on his head. He and Phin worked their way back to the bank.

Randall Ferguson stood behind the counter. He took out his handkerchief and mopped his forehead. "Sheriff!" His voice quivered.

"Tell me the truth, Ferguson," Phin said.

The man gave a weak smile. "About what?"

Phin curled his fingers into a fist. "Excuse me for a moment, Sheriff," he said as he walked into his office and pulled the Edwards folder from his desk. He reexamined the note. Sure enough, if he looked closely, he could see where two zeros had been added to the original debt. He brought the paper out of his office and merely held it in the air. Randall Ferguson collapsed on the floor.

The sheriff ran behind the teller's window and leaned over Ferguson, placing a finger below the fallen man's nose. "He's still breathing."

Relief washed over Phin. When Ferguson came to, he'd fire him and then the sheriff would arrest him. Phin told the sheriff about the debt, the deception, and the other issues he suspected Randall was responsible for.

Ferguson moaned and sat up. "How much have you stolen?" the sheriff asked.

"Two dollars a day for sixty days," Randall confessed.

"And this?" Phin held up Liam Edwards's loan papers.

"I saw what Willis did with the Mosley place and figured I could do the same." Ferguson looked away. "Am I still guilty if I didn't get the money?"

Phin pounded his hand on the desk. "You miserable sot. Do you know the agony you've caused Adeline Edwards? Sheriff, take him out of here, or you'll have to arrest me."

Sheriff Brill slipped on the handcuffs and pulled Ferguson to his feet. "But I didn't steal the plantation," Ferguson protested.

"You stole over a hundred and twenty dollars from our bank. That is grand larceny in this state, and that means you're going to prison for ten years."

Ferguson's feet fumbled. The sheriff held on to him and pulled him toward the door. With every bit of his being Phin wanted to meet up with Adeline and let her know the good news. But the bank was open for business. He had reports to write, and responsibility had to come before pleasure. Sometimes he wished he didn't have such a strong work ethic.

Adeline worked hard all day, trying to keep up with the loss of John Black. Fortunately, no one else chose to quit. But she knew that day was coming if she couldn't come up with the money or if Phineas wasn't able to renegotiate the loan. She never did get back to the barn to get the tools she'd planned to work on her parents' floor with. But the money would have to wait because tonight, Adeline needed a bath. The men carried up the hot water for her after dinner. Admittedly, it was one of the holdovers from her old life, a hot bath.

An hour later, cleaned and refreshed, she took the time to put on a simple housedress. She wanted the freedom her legs would feel without being dressed in heavy trouser fabric.

"Don't you look pretty tonight, Addy," Mammy said as she walked into the kitchen.

"Thank you. The loose fit of a dress seemed like a welcome relief tonight."

"Yes'm. Pants, they make sense riding a horse and working a ranch, but y'all knows I'm partial to my work dresses. How 'bout some of that leftover peach cobbler from yesterday?"

"I'd love it."

"Good. I'll whip up some cream and join ya."

Adeline smiled. "Wonderful. I'll be right back. I left a couple tools in the barn I need."

"Yes'm, I'll have it ready when ya come back."

Adeline ran out to the barn. Memories of the morning and her confrontation with John Black came rushing back as she entered the barn. She'd been angry, upset, probably more hurt than she'd like to admit when he'd confronted her. She'd also been feeling a bit guilty about not telling Phineas about her father's promise.

"What can I git fer ya, Miss Addy?" Jimmy asked.

"I've got the tools right here." She paused for a moment. "Jimmy, would you please hook up my buggy and make certain the lamps have oil in them."

"Beggin' yer pardon, miss, but I's not too keen on y'all drivin' at night alone. I'll go's with ya. I's need to tell Mammy first."

"Thank you but. . ." She let her words fall off. John Black had been fit to be tied this morning. No telling who or what might be waiting out in the shadows for her. If she had to drive all the way to town to apologize and confess keeping the knowledge of the hiding spot from Phineas, it was probably wise to have Jimmy with her. "Thank you, I appreciate your offer."

"Yes'm. I's be back real soon." He ambled out of the barn, not running as he would have done during the slavery years. Addy smiled. She really did have a good relationship with her former slaves and most of the crackers. Perhaps she should rehire John Black. She pondered the thought for a moment then decided to pray about it, rather than act impulsively like she'd done this morning.

She closed her eyes and prayed for the Lord's guidance and for Phineas George Hamilton III whom, regardless of his job with the bank and possibly being the one to kick her off her land, she realized she had grown to respect. She especially loved how he respected her for her knowledge of bookwork and figures, not to mention the praise he'd given her more than once about how she'd made a profit on the plantation each year. She'd never met anyone, not even her father or brothers, who appreciated her intelligence.

"Miss Addy, what do y'all mean by goin' off in the middle of the night? What can't wait until mornin'?" Mammy had her hands on her hips, huffing and puffing as she walked into the barn.

Adeline smiled. "I need to make amends. And you know the Bible says not to let the sun go down on your anger."

"He ain't talkin' 'bout with everyone, He's just talkin' about y'all's spouse, and y'all ain't got no spouse. So, I's sayin' it can wait till mornin'."

"Mammy, you're not—"

"No, I ain't," Mammy interrupted. "But I's know when y'all are thinkin' of doin' something foolish. And this here is foolish."

How could she convince Mammy this was important, and not foolish?

"John Black is prob'ly drunk by now. Y'all best stay here and wait till mornin'."

"I don't need to speak with John Black. Well, maybe I do, but he isn't the one I need to speak with tonight." She could feel the heat rise on her cheeks.

"I's don't know who. . ." Mammy stepped back. "What did y'all say to Mr. Hamilton?"

By this time a small group had gathered around the barn. Adeline remembered enough of her cultured upbringing to know that a lady didn't argue in such settings. "Fix up the buggy, Jimmy," she ordered. "I'll finish our discussion in the house, Mammy." She marched up to Mammy and wrapped an arm across her back and led her to the kitchen.

They walked in silence. "I'm sorry to gather a crowd, Miss Addy."

"I know. I'm not at liberty to share what it is I said or did regarding my need to apologize, but suffice it to say I do need to speak with him. I'll take Jimmy with me, and we'll be safe."

"I'm not worried about that. It ain't like John Black knows y'all are goin' into town. It's dangerous drivin' at night when y'all live so far from the town. It's an hour in daylight, it will be at least two at night."

Adeline sighed in defeat. "You're right. I'll wait until morning. I'll go tell Jimmy."

Mammy went on to the kitchen. Adeline turned and saw Jimmy leaning against the doorway to the barn. Adeline continued toward him. "I'll be staying."

"I knows. Ain't no arguin' with my woman when she gets all excited."

Adeline laughed. "Good night, Jimmy."

"Night, miss. I's will take you's into town in the mornin'."

"No, I'll manage. I need you to finish with the branding."

"Yes'm." He reached for the lamp to turn it down.

"Hold up. I forgot my tools." She hustled back to the barn. She might not be able to speak with Phineas tonight, but she could certainly try and find out how much, if any, money her father left behind for her.

Phin locked the door of the bank an hour later than he'd anticipated. Word had spread like wildfire that Willis and Ferguson had been arrested. It seemed that everyone had come in to check on the balance of their accounts. Relief washed over Phin. He couldn't wait to ride out to Adeline's and tell her the good news.

A wire had come from Mr. Wild and the bank officers, telling Phin how pleased they were that he'd found the problem and was working with the sheriff. Before he left for the Edwards Plantation, he needed to send a wire that Willis had been captured, that he'd confessed, and that Ferguson had been arrested as well. He would send a more detailed letter in the morning.

Sending the telegram took no time. Within thirty minutes he was heading out toward Adeline. He smiled just thinking about her. She was a lovely woman. Any man would be blessed to have her for a wife, except for the cooking. Phin did love food prepared well. Of course, now Adeline would be able to keep Mammy and her family employed at the plantation.

A vision of him sitting on the front porch with Adeline and their children emerged in his mind's eye. *Lord?* Phin grabbed the reins. He always saw himself returning to Savannah and working in the banking industry there. He shook off the pleasant vision. *She wouldn't be interested in me. . .would she? Could she?*

He liked her. He respected her. But did he love her? Could he love her? Well, that would be the easy part. She was easy on the eyes. She had a confidence that was lacking in most women. But his business required attending social functions. How would a woman who wore men's clothing and rustled cattle be accepted in such settings?

These questions and more rattled around in his brain for the entire trip. By the time he arrived at the ranch, he saw the light being shut down at the barn and several dim lights on in individual houses and the plantation bunkhouse. The lights were on in the big house on the lower floor.

"Wonderful, she'll still be up." He continued to the house and pulled the horse to a gentle halt.

The front door of the house opened, and Adeline stood there in a dress. His mouth went dry. His pulse quickened.

"What are you doing here?" she asked.

"I have some important news to tell you. May I come in?"

She stepped back and opened the door wider. "Yes, of course."

He jumped down from the buggy. Jimmy slid out from behind Adeline. "I's take care of yer horses."

"I tolls ya." Mammy laughed.

"What?" Phineas asked.

"Don't ask," Adeline said. "We were just sitting down to some of Mammy's peach cobbler. Would you like some?"

"Absolutely. I'm starving. I haven't eaten all day."

"Why?"

"Busy, busy day at the bank." He stood beside her. The fresh scent of rose filled his nostrils. He had smelled it last night. He liked it. It fit her. The idea of coming home to Adeline every night after a long day at the bank felt good.

"I'm sorry to hear that. I'm certain Mammy has some leftovers from dinner we could heat up, or we could cook up some bacon and eggs."

"I'd love to be polite and refuse, but I'm too hungry. Thank you, anything would be glorious."

"Come in." She looped her arm around his and led him to the kitchen.

He loved the touch, the feel of her beside him. *Goodness,* he marveled. Could he fall in love so quickly? Was it wise? "You're beautiful," he whispered.

"Thank you. You're a fine sight yourself."

He stopped. She stopped. He reached up and brushed her hair from her face with the back of his fingers. "Adeline, I'm quite sincere. You're really spectacularly beautiful."

"Phin," she whispered. "There's something I need to tell you. I was less than honest with you last night."

He felt his back straighten. His jaw tightened. He'd allowed himself to dream about a future with Adeline, and yet she had not been truthful. Did she know about the debt? Ten thousand dollars. . .no, that wasn't true. He relaxed. "What?" His voice warbled.

"Last night when we went searching, I discovered some gold coins and remembered something my father once told me about where he would hide money. I should have told you, but I couldn't. That's not to say—" She fumbled over her words. "That I would have kept the money from the bank. . .I don't know, I guess I just wanted to see if it were true, if he had borrowed ten thousand dollars and hid it for the family."

"He didn't."

"What do you mean? The three gold coins were pointing—"

He placed a finger to her lips. "The reason I came so late was that I discovered this morning that your father didn't borrow ten thousand dollars. He only borrowed one hundred dollars."

"What?" She took a step back.

"Come, sit. I want to explain this fully to you." He led her to the sofa. She sat, and he settled down beside her. "As you know, I was sent here by Old Boston Bank to find out why this branch was losing so much money. Much more than other southern banks that were struggling after the war. It turns out that Mr. Willis falsified records and put together quite a not-so-little nest egg. Unfortunately, your father's debt wasn't one of his sins. Sheriff Brill captured Willis and brought him to jail this morning. I discovered the truth on all the accounts, except yours. He told me your father only borrowed a hundred dollars and he was not inclined to pester you for it."

"A hundred dollars? But the papers say ten thousand."

"Let me finish, please."

"Sorry."

Phin smiled and held her hands in his. "I have been suspicious of Mr. Ferguson for some time now. He's been making mistakes, is regularly late on his payments to the bank, and there's a few other incidents that have me concerned. Anyway, the sheriff and I confronted him, and he too confessed. Your father borrowed a hundred Confederate dollars from Willis before he left for the war. Ferguson saw how Willis finagled Mosley out of his plantation, and he got the wild idea of stealing yours from you. He figured it was a foolproof plan. Your father was dead and couldn't dispute the loan. Willis no longer worked at the bank and, well, Ferguson added two zeros to the amount owed, and voilà! Ten thousand dollars."

"Why? I mean does he hate me so much?"

Phineas caressed the top of her hands with his thumbs. "It isn't hate, Adeline. It's self-centeredness and greed. Something I've never seen in you. You're a remarkable woman. Your concern for your former slaves and crackers leaped ahead of your concern about your own needs. Remarkable, truly remarkable." His pulse quickened, and without thought, he leaned forward to kiss her.

Chapter 6

His soft, warm lips touched hers. She closed her eyes and drank in the moment. Realization of the boldness of his gesture ripped through her addled brain. She pulled away.

He sat there stunned, but she imagined he wasn't as stunned as she was. Her father hadn't borrowed ten thousand dollars. "I'm not going to lose the plantation?" It was the only thing she could think of to say when she'd rather be in his embrace and thinking soft romantic thoughts.

"No."

Mammy cleared her throat, and Adeline skirted away from Phineas. "Cobbler's gettin' cold."

Adeline jumped up. "Come on, you haven't eaten all day."

"Food. Yes, food is good. I was getting rather light-headed." Phin stood and whispered in her ear, "Forgive me."

She took his hand and squeezed it. "Let's get some of Mammy's good food in that belly of yours."

"Yes, ma'am." He smiled.

As they walked past Mammy, Adeline said, "We aren't going to lose the plantation. Father didn't borrow ten thousand dollars, only a hundred."

"Praise Ya, Jesus, and hallelujah!" Mammy zipped around Adeline and ran out the door.

"Where'd she go?"

"To tell Jimmy, I imagine. Sit down, and I'll see what we have to fill your belly."

"Sit with me. We won't have many minutes alone." Phineas sat down in front of a bowl of peach cobbler. "This looks wonderful. I'm sorry for kissing you, but not sorry for kissing you. I'm sorry that I didn't ask permission. I am overwhelmed with feelings for you, Adeline. Strong feelings. They've hit me over the head like a hurricane pounds the coastline."

What could she say? "Phineas, you've been helpful to me. . . ." Adeline paused. She'd not always had kind thoughts toward him. "You've changed my first impression of you but—"

"I know it's sudden. I'm surprised as much as you must be."

"What are you saying?"

"Right about now, if your father were alive, I'd ask to court you. However, I don't have that opportunity, so I guess I'll just ask you. Would you be interested?"

"I don't know. . . ."

Mammy walked in. "Goodness, child. There's been a lot of commotion goin' on tonight. Jimmy and I are goin' to take our cobbler to the house."

"That's fine. Mr. Hamilton hasn't eaten. What can I give him?"

Mammy put on her apron. "A man needs to eat. I'll fix 'im up a steak and reheats some hash browns."

Phineas stood up. "I'm quite capable of fending for myself. Just tell me where the ingredients are."

"You cook?" Mammy snickered and removed her apron. She set out the various items Phineas would need to cook a steak, eggs, and hash brown potatoes. "Good night, I'll see y'all in the mornin'."

Thankfully, Phineas was Southern and knew Mammy wasn't saying she'd see the both of them in the morning. She would have said "all y'all" if she'd meant that.

"Thank you, Mammy." Phineas winked.

He did tend to treat people—all people—well.

After Mammy left, Adeline spoke up. "Phineas, I'm not saying no. I guess I'm just saying I need more time. Not even a week ago you came to my home demanding payment."

"And for that I apologize. I was unaware of the false transactions. You saw that document and you know it was official. Upon further investigation I saw the slight difference in the color of the ink. But Ferguson did a good job falsifying the debt."

Adeline nibbled her lower lip. "Don't misunderstand me, I am. . ." She glanced down at the floor.

"Attracted?" he filled in for her.

She nodded.

He dropped what he was doing and came beside her. His touch was gentle. Warmth surged through her. She hadn't felt this much calm and peace since before the war.

"You feel it too, don't you?" he asked.

She acknowledged his question with a slight bob of her head.

He wrapped her in his arms. "Honey, I'll wait whatever amount of time you need to get accustomed to the thought of courting me. However, I will be extremely busy for the next month or so. I may not have any time to come see you. Will that be enough time to pray and think about whether or not you'd like to court me?"

"Yes, thank you."

"Wonderful." He kissed the top of her hands and went back to work making his dinner. "So, tell me about this hiding place."

"How much money do I still owe?"

"None. You're in the positive now, after the money we found last night. Was it only last night?" Phineas shook his head in disbelief.

"But that was only twenty-five dollars we found, and you said the debt was for a hundred."

"Yup." He turned the searing steak in the frying pan. "Confederate dollars. That's only five dollars with the current value. So you're twenty ahead." He wiggled his eyebrows.

Adeline giggled. "So if there is any more hidden money, it's all mine?"

"Absolutely. Where is this hidden money?"

"Daddy showed me that under the money box there were three gold coins. He said to see where they were pointing to, which last night was the floor under my father's nightstand. After you left, I moved the nightstand and carpet but couldn't pry the boards loose. Which is why I have this hammer and crowbar." She pointed to the tools leaning by the back door.

"I'll be happy to help you look, after I eat of course. I really am starving."

"I'd enjoy the company. What is going to keep you so busy for a month at the bank?"

"I have to write up the case against Willis and Ferguson, return all the monies owed, et cetera. I'll be in constant communication with Boston. They might send a senior officer down to help me."

"Aren't you a senior officer?"

"I'm a problem solver. I go from this place to that. . . ." He paused. "We will have to discuss my job and our future if we do consider marriage. I know your home is on the plantation."

"How often would you have to travel?"

"At the moment I haven't been home for more than a week or two a year."

Adeline shook her head. "That would never work."

"Agreed." He pulled his steak out of the pan and placed it on a plate then added the leftover hash browns to the frying pan. "Which means I would have to change my career and find a full-time job here in Palatka."

"Would you be allowed to keep working at the bank?"

Phineas shrugged. "I don't see why not. They'll be disappointed, but they'll also be content that this branch will be well taken care of."

"And you should gain people's trust if you are able to restore Mr. Mosley's plantation back to him."

"I hope so. But that one will be difficult. He freely admits he agreed to Willis's assessment. However, I should be able to prove to the judge that Mr. Mosley was given false information from Willis. The problem is he didn't keep as good a record as you have."

The more he talked, the more Adeline was attracted to him. He was a good man, with a sound sense of right and wrong as well as a good head on his shoulders. She wondered what he might suggest to help the plantation grow in the future. She also imagined them having talks like this in the future. It was an enjoyable promise, just like the kiss they shared.

They continued to talk easily through his dinner then sequestered themselves up in her parents' bedroom. He pulled the floorboards up with ease, but there was nothing. "Well, that's a disappointment," he said with a chuckle.

"Too good to be true, I suppose."

"Did you move the coins?"

"No. Do you want to see them?"

"Yes, please."

She opened the hidden compartment as she had the night before then pulled out the money box. He lay down on the floor and eyed the gold coins. He pushed himself up. "You're right, we've looked where the coins are pointing."

"Perhaps he never got around to hiding any money there. At least I have three gold dollars." She picked up the coins.

"Yes, you do."

The grandfather clock in the hallway chimed ten. "I would love to spend more time with you, Adeline, but I have an hour's drive ahead of me. I'll correspond by messenger, or I'll leave sealed messages with the general store. You can pick them up there."

"And I'll do the same. I'll be busy too."

They worked their way downstairs and to the front door. "I'll see you in a month, then, if not sooner. Good night, Adeline."

"Good night, Phineas."

He smiled. Her heart fluttered. How was it possible to feel so connected with someone you didn't know?

He left. He didn't kiss her, squeeze her hand, or show any sign of physical affection, and she realized she wished he had. *Goodness, Lord, what is wrong with me?* She shut the door. Perhaps in a month she'd be able to answer that question.

Chapter 7

It had been a week since Phineas had visited Adeline and proclaimed his intentions. The entire town was buzzing with Willis's and Ferguson's arrests. The judge was set to hear their case in a couple of weeks. She couldn't help but wonder if Phineas had managed to organize all the paperwork for the trial. Thankfully, both men were confessing to their greed, hoping the judge would go easier on them. Willis was looking at forty years in prison with the maximum sentence of ten years for each forgery. Ferguson was looking at ten. Adeline still fought her anger toward Randall Ferguson and what he'd attempted to do with her plantation, her life, and the lives of the people she employed.

Phineas's courting proposal was constantly on her mind. His letters were windows into who he was. He held nothing back. She in turn found herself telling him some of her dreams and desires. The idea of Phineas helping her run the plantation grew on her hour by hour. He was a good man, a kind man, and, most importantly, a sharp man with regard to business. Beyond all that, he was a handsome man. And she couldn't forget the way she felt calm and content in his arms.

She knew that according to social norms, the approved length for a courtship was a year, but she couldn't see waiting that long. When had she ever done anything in a conventional manner? She was certain she would cause yet another scandal, but folks should be expecting that from her now. Adeline chuckled at the thought.

"What's on y'all's mind?" Mammy asked. Today she was teaching Adeline how to make a pot roast dinner. It was high time she learned to cook. If Phineas could do it, surely she could learn.

"I was just thinking what folks in town would say if I up and married Phineas without a full year of courting."

Mammy laughed. "We simply jumped the broom. Owners didn't care if we married or not, they just wanted us to keep breeding like them cattle out there. But I's was fortunate. Jimmy and me, we's fell in love, and your father didn't have an issue with it."

Adeline's memories flickered back to her father. She missed him and her brothers. Granted, they believed in slavery and she did not, but they were good men overall, and they were kin. She missed being wrapped in her father's embrace at the end of the day when they would sit in the parlor before retiring for the evening. She was glad that he hadn't objected to Jimmy and Mammy getting married. "How long after you and Jimmy met did you 'jump the broom'?"

"A week or two, wasn't long. I's knew I'd be bred soon if I's didn't hook up with a man of my own choosin'. Jimmy, he was kind. We grew in love. But we's always had a certain, hmm, what's a delicate way of sayin' this. . ." Mammy paused peeling a potato. "A certain attraction for one another. You's got that for Mr. Hamilton?"

Adeline felt the warmth of a blush cross her cheeks, and she nodded.

"Good, 'cause that's how the good Lord designed us. If y'all love each other, marry whenever you's want to."

Adeline leaned over and kissed Mammy's cheek. "Thank you."

"You're headin' to town and fixin' on skippin' the rest o' this here lesson, ain't ya?"

"Yes'm."

Mammy laughed. "Young love, it does a body good."

Adeline paused. "After I check on something first." She ran up to her father's bedroom and studied the small table on the side of the bed. When she'd moved it before, it was heavy. She looked at the one on the other side of the bed. It wasn't a matching set, which she had never given much thought to, but today. . .

Adeline marched to her father's nightstand and lifted it. Its weight caused her to strain more than one should for such a simple piece. Granted, the wood was thick and not delicate like Mother's table. She tapped the wood and pulled out the drawer. Nothing! She placed her hands on her hips. She bent down and looked at the underside of the table. Nothing! The legs were thick and less refined than the other pieces of furniture in the bedroom.

She flipped the table upside down. Nothing seemed out of place. Then she noticed a slit in the leg just below the undercarriage of the drawer. It was like that on all four legs. The opening was large enough for a coin to be slipped in. *Could it be?*

There had to be a way to open the legs if they were indeed banks for Father's gold coins. The smooth, painted finish was unmarred. Adeline huffed. Did it really matter? She owned the plantation. She didn't need the money. Of course, it wouldn't hurt to have additional resources, and Father was always careful with his funds. He harped on her brothers over and over again to save for a rainy day. Adeline was more like her father in that regard, always cautious and careful with her funds.

She looked more closely at the table legs and noticed that the feet had steel tacks at the bottom larger than a silver dollar. "I wonder. . ." She looked around the room for something to pry them off. Seeing nothing, she grabbed one with her fingernails. It took a bit of doing, but finally she was able to pry it off. Her pulse quickened. Bright polished gold sparkled in the sunlight. She laughed. "Thank you, Daddy. I'll take real good care of it."

She checked all four legs, and all four were filled with gold coins. She didn't want to take the time to count them. She'd hold off on that and share the moment with Phineas. Phineas. . . She sighed as another course of excitement sped through her veins. The gold was exciting, but it paled in comparison with her love for Phineas.

Adeline up-righted the table and put it back in place then ran to the barn and had the buggy ready in record time. As she climbed on board she realized she was still dressed in her working clothes. She hurried back into the house, up the stairs, and dressed in a casual dress.

Heads turned an hour later as she drove into town. Folks that would often criticize her for wearing men's clothing gawked as she drove down the street. She ignored them and went straight to the bank.

"Adeline." Phineas beamed. "What brings you into town?"

"You." She blushed.

He turned the bank sign to say Closed, walked her to the chairs in the lobby, and sat her down. "What's the matter?"

"You," she teased.

"Me? What have I done? I've written every day. I haven't come to visit even though I've wanted to. I promised to give you a month."

"That's just it. I don't want a month."

"You don't?" The look on his face was priceless, a combination of confusion and fearful anticipation.

"Nope, I've decided—that is, if you still want me—I'd like us to get married."

His blue eyes sparkled. "I'd like that too. Should we plan a year from now?"

She shook her head.

"No?" The puzzled look came over his face once again. Then, as if for the first time, he noticed she was wearing a dress, not her usual attire that he'd grown accustomed to. "You mean now? Today?"

She shrugged.

"Darling, I'm flattered. But don't you want a fancy wedding, white gown, me dressed in a formal suit, flowers. . .the works?"

She shook her head again. "I only want you."

"And I you." He wrung his hands. "Forgive me, but I always saw my parents and family at my wedding." He stood up and paced.

"I'm sorry. Of course we can wait for your parents to come here."

He came beside her and went down on one knee. "I want to marry you today. I'd love to marry you today. But I would be a horrible husband. I've been working twelve hours a day. I'll have the new man trained in three weeks. Can we wait until then?"

"Of course. I can wait."

"Good." He pulled her into his arms. "May I kiss you?"

Warmth circled her heart. She leaned in as his lips brushed hers. First soft and gentle, then she met his kiss and it deepened. His love for her and her love for him mingled together in her soul. Oh yes, she'd made the right choice.

He pulled away and held her in his arms.

Adeline relaxed in his embrace.

He took her hands in his. "Let's go to the jewelry store and pick out some rings. And if you'd like, I'd love for you to pick out a wedding dress."

"I can try on my mother's," she volunteered.

"Oh, honey, that would be wonderful. To have your parents a part of our day, even though they can't be there in person, I love that idea."

Suddenly Adeline knew Phineas was right for them to wait. "Do you think your parents could join us? Is three weeks enough time?"

"I'll send a telegram and we'll know soon." He took her in his arms again. "Adeline, you've made me the happiest man. I'm looking forward to romancing you the rest of our lives. I haven't had a chance to do it beforehand, so you'll be getting a lifelong romance from me, I promise."

Adeline giggled. Life would be interesting with this man. "I love you, Phineas."

"I love you too."

Epilogue

"Hold still, Addy," Mammy said as she fastened the last of the fifty buttons on the back of Adeline's wedding gown. Her mother's gown fit well. A few tucks and alterations, and it was perfect. "Goodness, you're so pretty, child. Your mama is looking down from heaven and smilin', I's just knows it."

"I think so too," Adeline said. Phineas's parents had arrived a week earlier to help with the wedding preparations. Adeline loved them already, knowing that Phineas owed much of his character to their good example.

Mammy came around and pulled down the veil. "Jimmy is real honored y'all asked him to give ya away. You's knows folks are goin' to talk."

"Frankly, Mammy, I don't care. You and Jimmy are the closest I have to family. If folks have a problem with that, too bad."

Tears welled in Mammy's eyes. "We love you too."

Mammy aligned the train of Adeline's gown then opened the sanctuary doors for her to begin her walk down the aisle. When Mammy sat down up in front, Adeline could hear the whispers. Jimmy held out his arm. The music began. Jimmy took the first step. "You's a beautiful bride, Miss Addy."

"Thank you, Jimmy." She cupped his elbow, and he led her down the aisle.

Phineas's smile brightened. Adeline felt the tears forming in her eyes. She owed this man a debt of love. He'd saved her from financial ruin and, more importantly, he'd saved her from the loss of a lifetime of family. Together they were going to build the next generation. Together their love would overflow. A calming peace swept through her.

Phineas took her hand. She stepped up to face the preacher. She looked into Phineas's precious blue eyes and vowed to spend the rest of her life loving him, as he vowed the same to her.

Lynn A. Coleman is an award-winning and bestselling author of *Key West* and other books. She began her writing and speaking career with how to utilize the internet. Since October 1998 when her first fiction novel sold, she's sold thirty-eight books and novellas. Lynn is also the founder of American Christian Fiction Writers Inc. and served as the group's first president for two years and two years on the Advisory Board. One of her primary reasons for starting ACFW was to help writers to develop their writing skills and to encourage others to go deeper in their relationship with God. "God has given me a gift, but it is my responsibility to develop that gift." Some of her other interests are photography, camping, cooking, and boating. Having grown up on Martha's Vineyard, she finds water to be very exciting and soothing. She can sit and watch the waves for hours. If time permitted she would like to travel. She makes her home in Keystone Heights, Florida, where her husband of forty-two years serves as pastor of Friendship Bible Church. Together they are blessed with three children, two living and one in glory, and eight grandchildren.

Hometown Bride

by Patty Smith Hall

Chapter 1

I detest black."

Jillian Chastain picked at the edges of the thick veil coming to rest on her shoulders and grimaced. "I can barely see my hand in front of my face through all this lace."

"At least you won't have to wear it for long," Ruthie Peabody said, staring into the mirror beside her. "Though I do have a question. How long is the mourning period for a make-believe husband?"

Shoving the heavy material away from her face, Jilly met her friend's gaze. "I'm not the one who came up with the idea of a pretend funeral."

"I never thought you'd actually do it. Why not just tell everyone the truth?" Ruthie combed an errant curl into place. "You've never had a problem being honest before."

Jilly pressed her lips together. "You know why I can't do that."

"Not really." She turned and took Jilly's gloved hand in hers. "So your mother told everyone you'd married Gray before he left town. People will understand."

Jilly wasn't so sure. Since her father's death almost a year ago, his will, particularly how it pertained to ownership of the family farm, had been called into question. One thing everyone seemed to agree on was that unless Jilly married within a year of Papa's death, Greenhaven would go on the auction block.

She hadn't corrected the tale going around town because to do so would malign her mother's character. Since Jilly's father died, Mama hadn't been herself. She tended to forget things more often, and at times, she was almost childlike. Jilly attributed it to her concern over their perilous financial situation. But lately she'd had reason to consider it was something far worse, because even though Mr. Crawford at the bank was satisfied that the terms of the will had been met, Mama was not getting any better. Still, she refused to embarrass her mother by calling her a liar in front of the whole town. "At least it satisfied the stipulations in Papa's will. Now I'm the rightful owner of Greenhaven, just as I should be."

"Well, I can't fault you there. Why your father drew up his will requiring you be married before you could inherit is beyond me."

"Me too." But she knew why. Papa had thought she'd never marry, not after the heartache she'd endured. He was right. Giving even a tiny part of her heart to any other man but Gray felt wrong.

Which was how she'd landed in this situation in the first place. Closing her eyes, she drew in a deep breath. "I'm glad this will all be over soon, and we can get things back to normal."

"Things haven't been normal since the war ended, not with all those Yankee carpetbaggers coming into town looking for cheap land." Ruthie leaned closer to her. "I overheard Papa say that a group of them are buying out most of Marietta Square."

"Mr. Gilbert and the Lacys are selling out?"

Ruthie shook her head. "They were charged a business tax twenty times more than what they usually pay. Mr. Gilbert told Papa he would go bankrupt before letting those men buy his store out from under him."

That didn't surprise Jilly. Mr. Gilbert had always been a man of deep convictions. "I don't blame him. The thought of losing Greenhaven is the reason why I went along with this fabrication in the first place." She smoothed her skirts. "I only wish Mama would have picked a more suitable groom."

"Like who?" The corners of Ruthie's mouth turned up into a knowing smile. "Grayson Hancock is the only beau you've ever had."

"I could have had other beaus."

Her friend shot her an unconvinced look. "Really?"

Jilly scrambled for a name but drew a blank. "I haven't been out in society much since Daddy died."

"You weren't out much before." Ruthie removed the veil from Jilly's head. "But then you and Grayson had an understanding."

"You mean until he wanted to move to Texas." But Ruthie was right. No one had ever measured up to Gray in her eyes. He had been her knight in shining armor since the day he'd punched Marcus Avery for breaking her slate back in third grade. Gray had claimed her heart in that moment and held it until he'd proposed the impossible.

"There's nothing wrong with loving someone like you did Gray." Ruthie released a soft sigh. "I think it's kind of sweet."

"There was nothing sweet about how it ended." The pain and heartache of the day he'd left swept through her as if it had just happened yesterday. Five long years, and Jilly still grieved over what might have been. But she couldn't think about that now. Her mother needed her as well as Greenhaven. "I don't even think about Gray anymore."

Ruthie huffed out a chuckle. "And you say you don't lie."

Jilly wanted to stamp her booted foot. "All right, I think of him every once in a while, like when I go to the dentist." Though in all honesty, he'd invaded her thoughts more since her mother's lie had spread around town. The blue green of his eyes when he'd listen to her talk about her worries. The way he made her laugh.

When he wasn't making her cry. "Seems to me, marriage is nothing but trouble." Jilly straightened her shoulders as she glanced into the mirror once more. "Guess it's a good thing I never want to get married."

"Women never want to get married until they want to."

Jilly stared at her friend. "What does that mean?"

Ruthie shrugged. "I'm not sure. It's something Mama always says, but it seems to fit this situation."

Jilly shook her head. No matter what Mrs. Peabody said, she was certain of one thing. She would never marry.

Not in a thousand years.

"Are you going out to get a wife, Uncle Gray?"

Grayson Hancock looked down at the three young girls staring back at him from the floor of their hotel room and felt his heart contract. His nieces had become his life since his sister and brother-in-law had died from the influenza a few years ago. Back then, the things he knew about raising little girls wouldn't have filled a thimble. Yet they'd managed and become a family along the way.

But it wasn't enough. The girls needed a mother, someone who could teach them how to wear a dress or mend a sock. Someone who could help them grow into the women their mother would have wanted them to be. Coming back to his hometown of Marietta was the first step in finding such a woman. "Maybe not today," he answered Frannie. "I've got to find us a place to stay while we're here."

"Aren't we staying here in the hotel?" Marty frowned up at him.

Gray straightened his neckcloth. "We were, but. . ."

The girl glared at her two younger sisters. "Are we being kicked out again?"

"You were just as much the reason for us being run out of Mr. Godwin's store as we were." Charlie, the youngest at six, spat back. "If you hadn't punched me, I wouldn't have knocked over the jar of gum balls."

"You were stealing!" Marty barked.

"I was not!" Charlie looked up at Gray with those pleading blue eyes that always meant trouble was brewing. "I just wanted to see how it tasted before I spent my penny on it."

"That's not how it works," Frannie piped in quietly. "You have to pay before you can chew it."

Charlie's bowed mouth turned down at the corners. "Why would I spend my money on something I don't even like?"

Marty was about to answer when Gray cut in. "I need to find us a house to live in while I find a woman to court."

"I don't know why you couldn't have found someone to marry back home," Marty said, not for the first time. "What about our teacher, Miss Simmons? She's not married."

"She smells like one of the pigs." Charlie scrunched up her nose. "And she's older than dirt."

"That's for sure. What if Gray wants kids of his own?" Frannie clasped her hands together at the thought. "Are you and your new wife going to have a baby, Uncle Gray?"

"No." And if he had any say, it would be a long time before anything like that happened. Marty, Frannie, and Charlie needed him, and would for the foreseeable future. He had no intention of letting them down. A marriage of convenience was what he needed, not more children.

"Uncle Gray, why did you bring us here to find a wife?" Marty asked. "You always told Mama you were never going back home."

"That was a long time ago." When he'd been young and foolish, and thought that the one certainty in his world after four years of fighting the Yankees was Jillian Chastain. He'd loved her since the moment he saw her, all knobby knees and luminous blue eyes. Her kiss—an innocent press of her lips against his—had helped him survive the war. Two weeks after he returned, he got down on bended knee and asked her to be his wife.

She said no.

Gray's gut tightened at the memory, the shock still a deep wound to his heart. She'd said she couldn't leave Marietta, but if she'd loved him enough, she would have found a way.

But that was in the past. For now, there were three little girls who desperately needed a mama. He glanced at their downcast faces. "You may not understand this, but I believe your mama would have wanted me to find someone from our hometown to be your new mama. Even if it's just so that you can know where your mama and I came from."

Talk of their mother brought a hush over the room. Finally, Marty touched his arm. "Mama always said Marietta was the nicest place she'd ever lived."

"I want to see the beautiful piano in the church she always talked about." Frannie stole a peek at him. "She said it sounded like angels singing whenever someone played it."

"Can we go to Sweetwater Creek? Mama said you can make the best mud pies there." Charlie tugged at his sleeve. "So can we go, Uncle Gray? Please?"

Bending down, Gray scooped the little girl up and looked into her big blue eyes. She'd only been a few months old when her parents died. "How do you know about those mud pies?"

She leaned her head against his shoulder. "Marty must have mentioned it."

Gray nodded, concern clouding his thoughts. He knew that Marty still struggled with her parents' death. He'd prayed for years she could come to terms with her loss. "Once I get us settled, I'll take you to all the places your mama liked when she was a girl. Is that a deal?"

"Yes!" all three girls cried out in unison.

"Good." He met Charlie's gaze. "I expect to hear that you behaved like a little lady when I get back. Is that understood?"

She ducked her head. "Yes sir."

"Good." He lowered her to the ground then bent to kiss Fran and Marty. Another tug at his shirt. "Yes, Charlie?"

"Will you bring us each a peppermint stick? It might make it easier to behave."

He smiled as he pressed a kiss into the nest of golden curls at her brow. "I'll see what I can do."

She gave him an impish grin then turned and plopped down on the floor, pulling a small hand-stitched sack from her pants pocket. Gray grimaced. The last time the girls played jacks, he'd found them tussling in the front yard, Marty with a torn shirt while Fran and Charlie both sported shiners.

Hopefully, they wouldn't break anything this time.

Opening the door, he hurried out into the hall, torn between leaving the girls by themselves or bundling them up and catching the next train back to Houston. But what other options did he have? It had been five years since he'd dusted the memories of war off his boots and headed west. There were few familiar faces in Marietta now, even fewer friendly ones. He wouldn't even be here now if it weren't for the promise he'd made May as she lay sick.

"When you marry, go back home to find a wife."

He hadn't counted on her dying, but then May always had to have the last word.

Gray slowed as he walked down the hotel hallway. He'd keep his word, but who would want him? He owned a little bit of land, had a few dollars in his bank account. His house wasn't much in the way of fancy frills, but whoever he married could do whatever she wanted to do with it, all within reason, of course. It went without saying he needed a good Christian woman, someone who would mother the girls and be a helpmate to him. It might not be a love match, but he offered kindness and respect. Who knew? Maybe love would come over time.

If only he could find someone willing to pull up roots and move to Houston.

Taking the stairs to the lobby, Gray walked toward the front desk where a tall, lanky man stood going through yesterday's receipts. As he came closer, the man, a Mr. Slattery if he remembered correctly, lifted his head and smiled. "Good morning, Mr. Hancock. Is there anything I can do for you today?"

"Maybe." Gray braced himself against the desk. "I'm looking for a place to stay for the next month while I conduct some business in town. Do you have any suggestions?"

"Not right off the top of my head." The hotel owner reached toward a stack of newspapers, picked one up, and handed it to Gray. "Most folks advertise rentals in the want ads these days. You might find something in there."

"Thank you, Mr. Slattery." Gray reached in his pocket to fish out two pennies.

"There's no charge."

"Thank you." Slipping the coins back into his pocket, Gray tucked the paper under his arm and crossed the lobby to a small seating area off to the right. Sinking down into a comfortable leather chair, he relaxed for the first time since Miss Simmons had informed him that until he had the girls under control, they were no longer welcome in her classroom. Gray smirked as he pulled open the paper. The old crone had overreacted. Maybe Charlie shouldn't have slipped a tadpole down the back of the woman's dress, but that wasn't a reason to keep all the girls from getting a proper education. They needed book learning just like any other children. A bit of understanding would have gone a long way.

Gray's lips twitched. The way Charlie had described it, he would have paid good money to see the woman dance up and down the aisle.

He sighed. Which was why the girls needed a mother. May wouldn't have put up with the girls behaving like that. On the way home from the school that day, he'd stopped by the train station and bought four tickets home.

The left-hand corner of the page caught his attention. GRAYSON HANCOCK read the headline. Gray folded the paper in half then quartered it. He'd only been in Marietta for little more than a day, and there was already an article in the papers about him? Did it mention the girls and the episode in Mr. Godwin's store? Boy, that would send the town gossips' tongues to wagging. His chances of courting a God-fearing woman would be the same as roping a wild stallion.

It was only when he read the larger print above his name that his heart stumbled to a halt. LOCAL DEATHS. He pulled the newspaper closer and began reading.

GRAYSON ADAM HANCOCK, BELOVED HUSBAND OF JILLIAN CHASTAIN HANCOCK.

He read it again. Beloved husband of Jillian? Somebody down at the newspaper office had made a mistake. Jillian would never claim him as her husband. But as he continued to read, he found himself growing angrier by the second. What if Jilly had done this? Why would she go to all the bother of holding a funeral? Gray skimmed over the article to an address just down the street, then stood.

Finding a woman to court would have to wait.

Chapter 2

The small parlor in the front corner of the Chastains' house on Church Street had become Jilly's favorite hiding place these past few years. With its pale rose wallpaper and comfortable Queen Anne chairs, it provided her solace from the war's casualty reports and the heavy tax notices that plagued her waking moments. In recent months, with her mother's mental decline, it had become the place where she met God.

But today, all those little touches that had given her such peace were stripped away. Black crepe draped the mantel and covered the windows, casting a somber tone over the cheery area. Kerosene lanterns provided what little light there was, the lamps turned so low, it was as if the flames themselves were in mourning. A blanket of roses, carnations, and lilies from various friends and county leaders almost choked her with their heavy fragrance.

Still, there was no way to mask the odor.

Holding her breath, Jilly grabbed a vase of lilies and headed for the hall. Who knew Gray still had so many friends in Marietta? Of course, he'd been a war hero, having fought to protect the town during the Battle of Kennesaw. But he'd deserted all of them for a spread outside of Houston a long time ago.

She sucked in a breath, her nose twitching as she caught the heavy scent of the flowers. *Oh no.* Stopping midstep, she pressed her lips tightly together, moisture gathering behind her eyelids as she fought for control, but the sneeze continued to build until she couldn't hold it in any longer.

"Ah-choo!"

The vase jerked in her grasp, sloshing water over the sides and down the front of Jilly's dress. The cold water soaked through the heavy lace all the way down to her chemise. Sucking in another breath, she realized her mistake as she took a step toward the hall table, only to have her foot slip out from under her.

"Ah-choo!"

"Jillian Snow Chastain, what do you think you're doing, sliding around the hallway like that?" Her mother's skirts rustled as she hurried down the stairs. "Anyone who saw you would think you don't mourn Grayson's passing."

Setting the vase on the table, Jilly shoved it as far away from her nose as she could. "Mother, how many times do I have to tell you? Gray isn't dead."

"I know, dear." Mama gave her a soft smile meant to comfort, but it only made Jilly more frustrated. "The Good Book says that to be absent in the body is to be present with the Lord."

"Mama, Gray isn't. . ." Jilly closed her eyes. What was the use in trying to explain? Mama had always been a bit flighty, but now—the tales she'd told around town! It was surprising no one had called her out on them. How Jilly wished her mother would come back to her, especially now when there was so much to be decided about Greenhaven. But that didn't seem likely. Picking at her lace bodice, Jilly headed toward the stairs. "I need to change."

The front bell rang. Mama turned to the door. "I'll send Clarice up after I see to our guests."

"Mama." Jilly caught her by the hand and pressed it against her cheek. "Clarice has lived in Atlanta for the past five years, remember?"

Her mother looked at her as if Jilly had gone crazy. "Why, I just saw her out in the kitchen not five minutes ago! Why don't I go and find her while you answer the door?"

"But my dress—"

"You look lovely, dear." Mama took a step back. "Now, it's rude to keep our guests waiting on the front porch. They'll think we're not home."

"We wouldn't want that." Jilly drew in an aggravated breath as she watched her mother hurry toward the kitchen. Her flightiness was getting worse with each passing day. Dr. Mabry had said to give Mama time, that people grieved in different ways, but Jilly was worried. Mama had already told one whopper of a lie about her. What would she say next? That there was a baby on the way?

Which is why this funeral is necessary, she told herself as she walked to the door. Once she "buried" Gray, she would take her mama back to Greenhaven where they would quietly live out the rest of their days.

The doorbell gave an impatient trill. Someone needed to learn to hold their horses. Grabbing the handle, Jilly threw the door open. "For Pete's sake, we're in mourning!"

"Yes, I know."

His voice thundered through her like the loudest thunderclap. *No, it can't be.* Jerking her head up, she met blue-green eyes that still possessed the power to haunt her dreams. Jilly swallowed against the words lodged in her throat, then finally spoke. "Gray?"

Gray swallowed hard against the lump in his throat. Jilly had always been a pretty girl, with hair the color of ripe pecans and luminous blue eyes that a man could lose himself in. This woman. Even in heavy black widow's weeds, she could turn a dead man's head.

Just not this man.

Gray touched the brim of his hat. "Jillian."

"What are you. . ." The muscles in her slender throat worked frantically. "Why are you here?"

Good. She was as befuddled as he was. Taking her arm, he pushed open the door and stepped inside. "I was reading the newspaper this morning and was surprised to find out I'd recently died. Care to explain?"

Pushing him into the hall, Jilly peeked outside, looking left and right before slamming the door shut and leaning back against it. "You're supposed to be in Texas."

"You mean instead of in a casket sitting in your parlor right now." Some of the anger he'd felt when he'd read the newspaper article returned. "And I don't remember us getting married, but that's what it says in the article."

She drew in a sharp breath, as if his words had punched her in the gut, then grabbed his hand and tried to pull him toward a small side room. "Please, before my mother sees you."

Gray stood rooted to the floor. "I want an explanation, Jilly."

"I'll explain the whole sorry mess if you'll just give me a minute."

Gray knew he shouldn't do it. If he had the sense the good Lord gave him, he'd go out on the front porch and call to every neighbor that walked down the street until he got the truth. But the desperation in her eyes, the way she held on to his arm, almost as if her very life depended on it, gave him pause. He'd never been able to tell Jilly no. The only time he had, he'd wound up alone in Houston, nursing a broken heart. A few minutes wouldn't make a difference either way.

He stepped into the small sitting room off the front hallway and suddenly wished he hadn't. This is where he'd courted Jilly. Had held her hand on that couch in front of the fireplace, had given her her first kiss next to the bookcase. How many times had they stolen away in here, planning a life of children and cattle? A life she never intended to live with him.

The door closed behind him. Maybe this was something that needed to be done. Once they cleared the air, he could find a nice woman to help him raise the girls and move on with his life. Maybe then, he might even fall in love again. He turned to face her. "Well?"

Jilly drew a deep breath. "Why are you back home?"

Not what he wanted to discuss with her, but if it got her closer to giving him an explanation, he'd comply. "I'm here on personal business."

A tiny line between her brows that he'd kissed away many times in the past formed. "What kind of business would you have in Marietta after all these years?"

She was evading his question. Well, two could play that game. "Why don't you tell me why people are going to my funeral this afternoon when I'm very much alive?"

Her skirts rustled as she walked deeper into the room, her delicate hands clenched into a tight ball at her waist. "It's a long story, Gray."

Long or not, Jilly wasn't going to get out of this mess that easy. Walking over to the couch where they'd made so many memories, he tossed his hat onto a nearby chair and sat down, resting one booted foot on his knee. "I've always liked a good story."

"There's not time right now." She rubbed her gloved fingers against her forehead. "The whole town is going to be here any minute to pay their respects."

"To me." His mouth twisted into a smirk. "The dearly departed."

She stamped her foot. "Why can't you be a gentleman about this?"

He chuckled. "At least I didn't lie to the whole town."

"This isn't funny."

"I don't know about that. I mean, who holds a funeral for a husband who didn't know he was a husband, and a dead one at that?"

"At least this time they'll get the opportunity to say goodbye."

"Ouch! I'd forgotten what a sharp tongue you have when provoked." But oh, how sweet her kisses were when she apologized. "So you decided to throw a funeral?"

"You wouldn't understand." She stalked around the room like a caged bear. "I never intended for any of this to happen."

"Then how did you think this was going to play out?"

She wrung her hands. "I don't know. Just not like this."

Jilly may have thought this was a lark, but on the way over to her house the ramifications of what she'd done began to sink in. Everyone in town thought he'd died married to Jilly. How would he find a wife now? And what about a place for him and the girls? He couldn't very well rent a house with his obituary in the newspaper. This situation had to be straightened out sooner rather than later.

Yet when he looked at her, he couldn't help thinking she looked as upset as he felt. Maybe if he knew her reasons behind this, he might understand. "How did this happen, Jilly?"

She mashed her lips together—a sign she was nervous—before meeting his gaze. "Mama's been worried about us losing Greenhaven so she told Mr. Crawford over at the bank that you and I got married before you left for Texas."

He scrubbed the back of his aching neck. "I don't understand."

"Papa's will says that unless I marry within a year of his death, we'll lose the farm."

"That doesn't sound like your papa. He always intended to give you Greenhaven."

She shook her head, candlelight making the pale streaks of gold shine bright. "He'd always intended to give it to us as a wedding present, but when you left, he changed the will."

Gray's head snapped back. "I didn't leave. You sent me away."

"Because you wanted me to leave everything I'd ever known and follow you to some backwater town outside of Houston."

"There was nothing left. . ." Gray paused, drawing in a breath, then wrinkling his nose. "What is that?"

"What's what?"

He took another breath then shook his head. "You don't smell that?"

Jilly took a delicate sniff then pulled a handkerchief from her pocket and swiped at her nose. "It's probably just all these flowers. I've been sneezing all morning."

"It smells like. . ." Gray's eyes watered as he took another deep breath. "You're not burying a body, are you?"

"You know me better than that!" Tears trickled down her face. "That's just mean that you would think such a thing. And as for the smell, I think it's all these lilies. I think I might have an allergy to them."

"You should come up with something better than that. As I recall, you had quite a hankering for lilies when we were courting, and I never remember you sneezing, not once." Gray moved toward the door, sniffing around each corner as if on a treasure hunt.

"I developed it after you left for Texas."

"Really?" He opened the door and walked out into the hall. Goodness gracious, the odor was even stronger out here. "It seems to be coming from the front parlor."

"Gray, I promise you, it's just the flowers," Jilly called out from behind him as he marched over to the parlor entrance.

Well, he wouldn't take her word for a grain of salt, not when his nose disagreed. Gray glanced around at the black crepe then turned back to her. "You went all out for my funeral."

She grimaced. "It was more Mama's doing than mine."

He glanced at the casket. "A pine box?"

"It seemed wasteful to bury a nice casket with those fancy brass handles. Plus, I told everyone you died of dysentery." She gave him a halfhearted smile. "It felt appropriate."

Another little dig. Why was Jilly so perturbed with him? She was the one caught in a fib. "If you have what I think you have in that box, it could be dangerous."

Her luminous blue eyes turned hard. "Just because you're mad doesn't mean you have the right to try and scare me."

Gray took a step closer, his pant leg brushing up against her skirts. "You still haven't told me why you did this in the first place."

"Gray." She pressed trembling lips together, and for the first time, he noticed how pale she was. "I never would have involved you in this mess, but I wasn't left with any choice."

He studied her for a long moment. She seemed sincere, yet why had she lied in the first place? "Everyone has a choice, Jilly."

She flinched as his words hit their mark. When she finally looked up at him, there was a pain in her expression he didn't understand. "Not always, but if you're determined to have the whole story..."

The doorbell rang, followed by the sound of her mother's voice. "Jilly, could you get that? I'm going over the refreshments with Mrs. Culpepper."

"Mrs. Culpepper?" He glanced toward the hallway. "I thought your father freed her before the war."

"I guess she's returned for the day." Jilly looked toward the front door as the bell rang again. "I know I owe you answers, and I'll give them to you, just not right now. Maybe we can meet back here after the service?"

"My funeral is this afternoon?"

She nodded. "I thought you read the newspaper article."

"I didn't get to that part." Or much of anything after reading that Jilly was his wife. "What time is the service?"

"Three." She blinked up at him. "Why?"

Gray gave her a wicked wink. "It's not every day a man can go to his own funeral."

Chapter 3

The grind of the accordion, its shrill notes befitting for such a farce, greeted Jilly as she stood at the head of the long aisle leading into the cavernous sanctuary. Her mother stood beside her, one hand at Jilly's waist as if in comfort while the other lifted a large, snowy-white handkerchief to her nose. Rows of people, using hymnbooks and loose paper to beat back the scorching heat, sat waiting for the spectacle to begin.

Please, Lord, let this be over soon.

Mama leaned into her. "Gray was well liked. Look at all these folks coming to pay their respects."

Jilly nodded. Everyone in Marietta had always thought a lot of Gray. She had too, until she hadn't. After five years, she'd never expected him to show up on her doorstep this morning. *And just as irritating as ever.* Well, not irritating exactly. He had every right to know why he'd not only found himself being mourned but married to her, and she would have told him. But Gray had always been too handsome for his own good—hers too, if she were truly honest. The only thought her brain could hold the entire time he was there was how much she'd missed the sight of him.

Of course, then he had to open his mouth and tease her about this whole mess. Wouldn't he feel the fool when he heard why she was having his funeral in the first place?

Beneath her dark veil, Jilly took a quick peek around the sanctuary. Surely Gray had been teasing her about showing up today. Didn't he know how embarrassing that would be? Every person in town looked to be here. Someone had lined chairs along the back wall for the latecomers. Even the choir loft brimmed with people.

Jilly swayed slightly as she started down the aisle. This was awful, much worse than she'd imagined. What would happen if Gray *did* show up and someone in the crowd recognized him? What if, after the funeral, someone saw him around town? Her reputation would be in tatters, and Mama would be branded a liar. Worse than that, she would lose her inheritance to the highest bidder on the courthouse steps.

"Are you all right, dearest?" Mama asked.

Jilly drew in a deep breath and wished she hadn't, the stench coming from the casket enough to make her eyes water. There was no turning back now. She nodded. "I'm fine, Mama. Really, I am."

Mama patted her hand. "This will all be over soon."

Not soon enough. Not until she met with Gray and explained how all this had happened. Would he believe her mother had been the one to start this farce? He had to, just like he had to see why he had to leave town as soon as possible. For some odd reason, that last thought made her heart ache.

A few seconds later, Mama gently pushed her toward the pew directly in front of the casket. Glancing around, she noticed the first few pews in the center aisle were empty, save one or two latecomers. She didn't have to wonder why. The smell coming from the coffin could choke a horse. Hopefully, the story about Gray's death from dysentery would explain the odor.

Before taking her seat, Mama sniffed. "Good heavens, it smells like a pigsty in here."

Not pig, chicken. Gently grabbing her mother's wrist, Jilly pulled her mother down next to her. "Please, Mama. I just want to get this over with."

Mama's face screwed up as she got another whiff. "It smells like sh—"

"Mama!" Jilly interrupted before she could embarrass them any further. Another symptom Lydia Chastain had picked up recently—language that could give a sailor a run for his money. "Pastor Quinn is ready to start the service."

"Oh." Mama blotted her face once more before covering her nose and mouth. She leaned over so that only Jilly could hear her. "Poor Gray, dying from the grippe like that. It must have been pretty bad if he still smells like that."

"I wouldn't know." Jilly pressed her lips together to keep from snorting. The situation was becoming altogether too much—a dead fake husband, Gray's sudden arrival in town. These kinds of things only happened to other people, not plain old Jilly Chastain.

The congregation grew quiet as Pastor Quinn took to the pulpit. "Friends, we are gathered here today to say goodbye to one of our own, a man who fought bravely alongside his fellow soldiers to save our fair town against the oppressive Yankees. A son of the South, Grayson Hancock."

People on both sides of Jilly nodded, their makeshift fans flapping furiously in the stifling heat. The stillness of the moment was broken by the sound of a young girl's voice. "Why is the preacher talking as if you were dead or something?"

Jilly froze. Had Gray brought his wife and child to witness her humiliation? And just how old was his daughter? She sounded older than the five years he'd been gone. She shifted, barely turned from one side to the other. He must have snuck in after her. Rude as usual. Didn't he know that once the family of the deceased was seated, the doors of the church were closed?

Only he was the supposed deceased.

She straightened, her temper rising. Well, if Gray wanted to break the rules of etiquette, that was no skin off her nose. But to bring his child? You would've thought he would have mentioned her this morning when he came by the house. He'd barely been gone five years, hardly time to have a daughter who could talk in full sentences. Must have married the first woman that would have him if the child was old enough to be walking around, asking questions.

"Grayson was a good man, a rarity these days," the pastor continued. "He believed in the Bible and was saved by Christ's blood. He didn't deserve to die so young, but though he is dead to this world, he's alive and walking in Glory! Praise the Lord!"

"Amen!" a woman behind Jilly shouted. "He's walking those streets of gold!"

Not likely, Jilly thought. Though if he were, it would solve all of her problems. Not that she wished him ill, just away from here, where his presence made her nerves all jumpy and her heart thump like a drum in her chest. The boy she'd sent away all those years ago was gone, replaced by a handsome, virile man, a man who could prove very dangerous to her heart.

She stared at the casket. Hadn't she always hoped Gray would come back to her? Hadn't she always wanted to right the terrible wrong she'd done when she'd sent him away? Now it was too late. He had a wife and, from the sound of things, a child.

A scraping noise pulled her out of her thoughts.

"Did you see that? It looked like the casket moved."

Jilly stole a glance at her mother. Was her mother hallucinating now? Seeing things that couldn't possibly happen? She opened her mouth to reassure her but broke off when movement out of the corner of her eye caught her attention. The coffin had moved, just a hair. It couldn't be. Had this whole incident made her go crazy too?

In the pulpit, Pastor Quinn caught his second wind. "Because Grayson gave his life to Christ, he won't be consumed by the lake of fire and brimstone on judgment day!"

The arrangement of roses that sat atop the casket wobbled, then fell, the pungent smell from the pine box growing stronger with each passing second. The wall shook, and for a moment, Jilly wondered if it was one of those earthquakes she'd read about. Catastrophic, the books had called them.

Or was it something far worse?

Jilly grabbed her mother's arm. "Mama, we need to get everyone out to the street."

"But the pastor isn't finished yet." Her mother smiled up at the man. "He always does such a good job at preaching funerals."

"Yes, but—" Jilly stopped at the high-pitched squeal as one by one the penny nails holding the casket lid in place exploded from their bearings. A man in the choir loft ducked as one flew by his head and lodged in the wall behind him. One board then another broke free, jumping and twitching like water on a hot skillet. People in the pews beside theirs fell to the floor, peeking occasionally, their expressions a mixture of confusion and expectation. Even Pastor Quinn had gone silent, his gaze transfixed on the wooden box before him, almost as if he expected Gray to rise up out of the coffin like a modern-day Lazarus.

A loud boom rent the air around her, the odor so bad she could barely breathe. Small clumps of chicken manure and grass rained down on her, sticking to her clothes and skin, washing over her like the lie that had set this farce into motion.

She was ruined. Completely and totally. No one in town would ever take her at her word again. This incident would be carved into the town's history alongside the Battle of Kennesaw Mountain. It couldn't get any worse.

"Is Gray on fire?"

Jilly's eyes shot open just as a plume of dark smoke rose up from the casket like a storm cloud. A spark flickered then flamed to life deep within what was left of the chicken manure. Dear heavens, she'd set the church on fire!

She stood, only to be shoved back into her seat by a strong hand. "Stay with your mother."

"Gray?"

He didn't answer her, only took the wooden bucket he held in his hand, hurried over to the casket, and dumped the contents into the pine box. "Marty, hand me the other one."

A girl, no more than eight or nine, dragged another bucket across the floor to Gray while off in the corner, a pair of girls stood watching, their young faces a mirror image of the older girl. Just how many children did Gray have? Jilly glanced around. And where was his wife?

"The fire's out," Gray announced to no one in particular. "You can all relax."

"Gray, is that you?" a man asked above the mumbling and whispers behind her.

Her ruination was complete. Jilly threw back her veil and stood, turning long enough to see everyone making their way to the aisle, one or two looking back as if to make sure Gray was still there. She charged up to him. "What are you doing here?"

His lips twitched up in a wicked smile that left her breathless for a moment. "Saving the town, it seems. You can thank me later."

"Thank you?" Her voice rose a notch. "For what? Embarrassing me and my mother in front of all our friends?"

He chuckled as he flicked a piece of grass from her shoulder. "What was I supposed to do, let the church burn to the ground? What possessed you to put chicken dung in a closed wooden box in the first place?"

"It seemed fitting, considering who was supposed to be in the coffin!"

"You're funny." He smiled. "And as far as your reputation goes, you've lived through worse. Remember the time you decided to swim naked and the Wilson boys took off with your clothes? By the time I found you, you'd been in the water so long, you were wrinkled up like a prune. Gave you the shirt off my back just so you'd be covered up when you walked home."

Some men behind her snickered, and Jilly felt herself go crimson. "You swore you'd never mention that again."

"And I never did." His gaze turned warm. "Until now."

She sucked in a shuddering breath, surprised at the conflicting emotions she found in the depths of his blue-green eyes. Teasing, yes, but she also found concern as well as some odd emotion she couldn't quite put her finger on. It made her wonder. *Why did I ever send him away?*

"Gray?"

The word broke over Jilly like a bucket of cold water.

Chapter 4

Whatever sweet feelings they had shared in that look were snuffed out at that one word, though Gray wasn't sure why. Jilly had to know she would have never gotten away with this farce, especially with him in town searching for a wife. Or had she expected him to leave and save her the embarrassment? Well, she was sadly mistaken. He had no intention of leaving Marietta until he was good and ready.

"Gray, it *is* you!"

He turned around to find Robert Muster, an old friend from his days in the army. Beside him stood a pretty young woman who was stealing glances at Jilly. "Bob, I haven't seen you in a coon's age! How have you been?"

Bob glanced at the smoldering casket. "A lot better than I thought you were."

"Yes, well." Gray chuckled as he waved the girls toward him. "Let me introduce you to my nieces. This here is Marty, Frannie, and Charlie. Girls, this is an old friend of mine, Robert Muster." He turned back to Bob. "And I'm sure you remember Jillian Chastain and her mother, Miss Lydia."

Bob nodded to them then turned to the young woman beside him. "This is my wife, Sarah."

Jillian held out her gloved hand. "It's very nice to meet you, Mrs. Muster."

"We were so sorry to hear. . . ," the woman started then darted a nervous glance at her husband. "What I mean is. . ."

"It's all right, Mrs. Muster." Jilly smiled. "It's a unique situation."

The woman nodded shyly. "Yes, I guess it is."

There was a pause; then Bob took his wife's arm. "We'd better be going. Miss Chastain, I wished we'd met under better circumstances."

Jilly nodded as she slipped down into the pew.

"Girls, it was nice to meet you," Sarah said as she started up the aisle. "Mr. Hancock."

"Mrs. Muster." Gray tipped his head then gave Bob a friendly pat on the back. "You've got yourself a sweet lady there."

"And yours is everything you described and more."

"We ought to catch up while I'm in town. I don't know when the next time I'll get this way will be."

"Maybe you and the missus could come over for supper." Bob leaned in closer. "Now that you're back among the living."

"Uncle Gray and that woman ain't—" Charlie started.

No sense making it any worse for Jilly than it already was. Gray jumped in. "I'm not sure what Jilly has planned this week." He thought for a moment. "How about Sunday after church?"

"I'm not sure we'll be having church anytime soon." Bob glanced around, and Gray followed his gaze. Little bits of manure, dirt, and grass stuck to the walls and ceilings, and the pulpit and floor around the casket were scorched by small embers. The smoke had dissipated, but the noxious odor hung in the air.

"Don't worry, Mr. Muster. If I have to scrub every inch of this sanctuary myself, I'll make sure we have church on Sunday," Jilly said, shucking off her gloves.

Bob nodded. "Well, then we'll see you on Sunday."

As the couple followed the others out into the street, Charlie tugged on his sleeve. "Who was that?"

"A friend of mine I fought beside in the war."

"And them?" Charlie pointed her thumb toward Jilly and her mother. "How do you know them?"

Gray met Jillian's gaze. "Miss Jilly and I have known each other since we were about Marty's age."

Marty gave both ladies a stern look. "They look like they've taken a roll in the pigpen."

He flinched. Why did the girls have to be so mouthy? "Martha Jo, apologize to the ladies right now."

The girl looked up at him with innocent blue eyes. "But they do, Uncle Gray."

"You don't say it to their faces, stupid." Charlie frantically fanned the air in front of her face. "Though they do smell mighty ripe."

"Girls!"

"At least make her take a bath before you ask her to marry you," Charlie continued. "We'd appreciate it."

Of course Charlie would say what was on her mind. She always did. "Little girl, what have I told you about spouting off everything that comes into your head?"

"What is she talking about?" Jilly asked. "Didn't you bring your wife?"

"Oh, Uncle Gray ain't married," Frannie answered as she joined her sisters. "That's why we're here."

"But we should get a say in picking a new mother." Marty gave Jilly an unimpressed look. "We wouldn't want to make a mistake."

"But he has to find a wife soon or Miss Simmons won't let us back in school." Frannie nudged her sister.

"I never liked school much anyway," Charlie chirped.

"Me neither," Miss Lydia added.

"Ladies, please!"

Gray and the girls glanced up at Jilly's quiet admonishment. She pressed her lips together, a sign she was nervous, then pushed ahead. "Your uncle and I are old friends, that's all."

Friends. Gray didn't like that word when it came to Jilly, not with everything she'd meant to him. But now wasn't the time to confront the past. For the moment, Jilly's somewhat calm assurances had settled the girls.

"Then why did the preacher say Gray was your husband?"

"Charlie," Gray warned. He really should put a muzzle on that kid.

"That's a very good question, child." Pastor Quinn came walking up the aisle, his gaze sliding over each of them before finally coming to rest on Jilly. "And one I'd like to hear the answer to myself."

"You don't know?" Charlie asked.

Pastor Quinn shook his head.

Charlie looked up at the man. "I thought preachers knew everything."

The preacher gave her an encouraging smile. "Where did you hear that?"

"Rusty. He's one of our cowhands back home in Houston," Charlie answered. "He says preachers know it all."

Frannie tugged her little sister's braid. "That's not what Rusty meant."

Gray knew exactly what the young cowpoke had meant, and from the comical look on the preacher's face, so did he. "I'm sorry, Pastor. You know how these young people can be at times."

The man nodded. "Which is why they need to be in church, studying the Word."

"I couldn't agree with you more." Rusty would be warming the front pew when Gray and the girls made it back home. Gray held his hand out to the man. "Fine service. You preached a good funeral, Pastor."

"Thank you." He took Gray's hand and shook it. "And you are?"

Gray and Jilly exchanged glances before she gave him a little nod. Well, the cat couldn't stay in the bag forever. "Grayson Hancock, sir."

"Grayson Han. . ." Quinn eyed Jilly's downturned face. "The deceased husband?"

Jilly nodded.

"I don't understand." The pastor ruffled a hand through his hair. "Why did you tell everyone in town that Grayson was dead?"

"I'd like to hear the answer to that one myself," Gray said, crossing his arms over his chest. Beside him, the girls stared at Jilly expectantly.

She glanced back at her mother as if waiting for an answer then turned, her gaze shifting from one to another. Finally, she closed her eyes. "It was the only way I could think of to get out of this mess."

Pastor Quinn chewed on that news before answering. "Jillian, you do understand that marriage is a sacred covenant between a man, woman, and God, not something to be thrown away lightly. Even if you feel the need to dissolve the marriage, you could have done that without burning down the church."

"I'm so sorry about that, Pastor. I thought about using sand to weigh down the casket, but do you know how difficult it is to find around here?" Jilly was babbling now. "And I almost broke my foot trying to dig some red clay up. That's why I used chicken manure to weigh down the casket. I mean, I couldn't have the pallbearers carrying an empty casket into the church, now could I?"

Poor woman. She really was floundering. Gray couldn't stand to see her like this, no matter how much she deserved it. "I think what Jilly is saying, Pastor, is that she's very sorry about the whole thing."

"I understand, but Jillian, if you and Gray are having troubles with your marriage, I could counsel you. Maybe help you through this hard time." He gave them a sympathetic smile. "Be encouraged by the fact that every marriage has its rough spots."

"But Gray and I aren't married." The words burst out of Jillian's mouth like a steam engine plowing across the snowy plains, a slight tremor in her voice that made him want to fold her into his arms and keep her safe. "We have never been. Mama made the whole thing up."

Why? Gray glanced back at Mrs. Chastain, who seemed preoccupied with one of the hymnals. What reason would Jilly's mother have to lie about such a thing? "I don't understand."

"Mama hasn't been herself in a while now. I guess it made her feel better to think that I was married, and she's always been fond of Gray." That worried look she'd worn this morning flooded her features. "So she told Mr. Crawford over at the bank that Gray and I had a secret wedding before he left for Texas."

Gray wasn't sure why, but he believed her. Mrs. Chastain had always been as sweet as sugar when he'd come to call on Jilly, but even then, she suffered bouts of melancholy that worried Jilly and her father. Still, why had she dragged him into this situation after all these years? Wasn't there another man her mother could have married Jilly off to? And why did it fill him with pleasure to know she'd chosen him?

"I see," the preacher responded. "Though I think the situation presents us with a whole new kettle of problems."

What was the preacher talking about? "What kind of problems?"

Pastor Quinn shot a glance at the girls. "It might be best if we spoke in private."

"Wait one cotton-pickin' minute." Marty shoved past Jilly to face the preacher. "Uncle Gray don't keep secrets from us. Do you, Uncle Gray?"

"No." But the wariness Gray saw in the older man's expression made him uneasy. Whatever the man had to say wasn't going to be good. Gray pulled some change out of his pocket and handed it to Marty. "Take the girls down to the drugstore and get them that candy I promised them, okay?"

"But—"

Bending down to meet Marty's gaze, Gray rested his hands on her shoulders. "We'll talk about this later, I promise."

With one last disapproving look at Jilly, she nodded then herded her siblings down the church aisle without so much as a goodbye. Gray stood. One female in a snit at a time. That was all he could handle.

"You might want to take a seat," the pastor started once the girls were out of earshot. "Because what I'm about to tell you might knock you off your feet."

Gray glanced at Jilly, who looked about as confused as he felt. He sat down beside her in the pew then watched as she unpinned her hat and threw it down on the cushion beside her. Even with bits and pieces of grass and manure stuck to her, she managed to give the impression of delicate femininity.

His hands behind his back, Pastor Quinn came to stand in front of them. "Jillian, I'm not sure you know this, but I studied law before God called me into the ministry."

Jilly glanced over at Gray then turned back to the preacher. "That's lovely, Pastor, but I'm not sure what that has to do with us."

"Quite a bit, I'm afraid." He drew in a deep breath then grimaced as he glanced at the charred casket. "You see, when you submitted Grayson's obituary to the newspaper, you declared to the entire county that he was your husband. Because no objections were publicly made, it's considered a contract of sorts. In the state of Georgia, a public declaration is as binding as a wedding ceremony."

Gray's body tensed. Quinn couldn't mean what he thought he meant, that he and Jilly were. . . "What are you trying to say, Preacher?"

He slid them an apologetic glance. "That whether you want to be or not, you're legally married in the eyes of the law."

Chapter 5

"Can I help you with anything?" Gray asked for what felt like the hundredth time since they'd arrived at Greenhaven a few hours ago. "Maybe make some coffee? Or set the table?"

"No, I'm fine." Jilly pushed a thick wave of dark hair out of her eyes then went back to work on the carrots. "I've almost got everything done."

Gray stood at the table and watched as she took a handful of diced carrots and threw them in the boiling stew she'd insisted on making for lunch tomorrow. Jilly had said next to nothing since they'd pulled up in the front yard. Almost as soon as he set the brake, she jumped out of the wagon and rushed toward the house, jerking her veiled bonnet off her head as she walked. After he'd rubbed down the horses and fixed his bunk for the night, he'd found her in the kitchen, punching a ball of dough as if her life depended on it, flour covering her dark dress like stars in the desert sky.

Now she was attacking a pot of boiled potatoes. Gray leaned forward and covered her hand with his. "Those spuds never did anything to hurt you."

"For Pete's sake, I'm mashing potatoes." Her fingers tensed beneath his.

Gray chuckled. "You keep at it like that, and we'll be eating potato soup."

Jilly lifted her gaze to meet his. Heaven help him, she had the prettiest eyes, blue with splashes of violet that matched the evening horizon just as the sun dipped low. Those eyes had filled his nights during his first year in Texas until backbreaking work and worry over the girls obliterated what was left of his dreams. Now those eyes were filled with frustration as well as. . .regret?

She straightened. "I'm not used to cooking for this many people, so if you don't mind. . ." She nodded toward the kitchen door.

She wasn't going to get rid of him that easily. "Which means you should accept help when it's offered." He took the potato masher from her hand and laid it on the table. "I do know my way around the kitchen."

Jilly gave him a skeptical look. "You learned how to cook?"

"What do you think we eat back home? Dust?"

"I don't know." Her warm chuckle startled him slightly until he realized it was the first time she'd laughed today. "I figured you hired someone to cook for you and the girls."

Gray added salt and pepper to the potatoes then picked up the masher. "I barely had two cents to rub together when the girls came to live with me, and those I needed to reinvest in the ranch."

She took a stack of plates from the cupboard and began to set the table. "Is it terribly difficult? Starting a ranch?"

"It still is." He cut off some butter and put it into the pot. "There were times in those first few years I wanted to turn tail and come home."

She mumbled something as she walked over to the stove.

Did she just say she wished I had? He couldn't have heard her correctly. "Did you say something?"

"No. Why?"

He watched her carefully. "I just thought I heard you say something."

The nape of her neck turned red. "I talk to myself at times."

"I do too." He chuckled. "Sometimes it's the only adult conversation I have for days. Ranching and raising the girls keeps me so busy, I don't have many friends in town."

Carrying bowls of green beans and creamed corn, Jilly hurried to the table. "Not even a young lady?"

"The spread takes up most of my time." But, he admitted to himself, none of the women he'd met could hold a candle to Jilly. He might have drummed her out of his mind, but she still held tight to his heart. "I promised May when it came time to find a wife, I'd come back home."

"Well, you did that. Not even in town a full day and you find yourself married to me." The tiny lines around her eyes and mouth deepened, and her face went pale. "This is all my fault."

Gray hurried around the table and grabbed the bowls before she dropped them. "Hey, it's okay. We're going to get through this."

She glanced up at him, her lashes heavy with unshed tears. "You must hate me."

"No." He drew her into his arms. Good gracious, but she felt wonderful curled into his chest, her head resting against his shoulder so that he could feel every breath she took. He tightened his arms around her and rested his chin against her forehead. "I could never hate you, Jilly. Not in a million years."

"I couldn't bear it if you did." She pressed even closer, and Gray thought he'd flown to heaven. This was how he'd always seen his life, with Jilly, building a home and family.

"I'm hungry."

The announcement from the door made Jilly jump out of his embrace. Of course it would be Charlie, though her sisters flanked her on either side. Probably put her up to it. "Girls, what have I told you about sneaking up on people?"

"But we haven't eaten since this morning," Charlie wailed. "So we came to find out when dinner was. We didn't expect to find y'all huggin' each other."

"Why were you hugging each other anyway?" Marty barked, eyeing Jilly's pink cheeks and frowning.

Gray stiffened. "That's enough. Remember your manners."

"Miss Simmons says we don't have no manners," Marty answered, taking in the different dishes littering the table.

Jilly glanced at him. "Miss Simmons?"

"Our teacher." Charlie punched her sister on the arm. "Though she don't know nothin'. The only reason she's a teacher is because nobody will marry her."

Gray cringed. The children were in rare form tonight. "Girls—"

"I felt the same way about my teacher." Jilly interrupted him as she finished laying out the silverware. "I got so mad one time, I found a snake and put it in her desk drawer."

The girls giggled behind him, but Gray simply stared at her. "That was you? But Henry Mathis got in trouble for that."

"And he deserved it, cheating off my slate all the time." Jilly turned to smile at the girls. "Still, looking back, I probably shouldn't have done it."

"Did it bite her?" Frannie asked.

"No, it was just a little rat snake. But she did scream loud enough for the sheriff to come running from across the street to see what had happened." She untied her apron and hung it on a peg near the door. "All right, y'all sit down while I go wake Mama. But don't eat yet. We need to bless the food first."

As Jilly hurried out of the room, the girls scrambled into their seats.

"I like Miss Jilly," Frannie said as she tucked her napkin into the neck of her shirt. "She's nice and she smells good when she's not covered in chicken manure."

"So?" Marty answered, reaching for the milk pitcher. "She lied to the whole town about being married to Gray and about him being dead."

"Why don't you court her, Uncle Gray?" Charlie reached for the peas only to have her hand swatted away by Frannie.

Gracious gravy, were the girls playing matchmaker now? "I thought y'all didn't like the idea of me getting married."

The two youngest girls looked at each other while Marty sank down in her chair across the table. "Well, once we heard about the evil stepmother...," Frannie answered.

Evil stepmother? "Who put such an idea into your heads?"

"She did!" Charlie pointed at her oldest sister. "I already have two sisters who smack me around. Don't want an evil stepmother too."

For Pete's sake, no wonder the girls had fought the idea of a new mother so hard. "Martha Jo, what have you got to say for yourself?"

"I was just reading to them like you told me to," Marty replied, wrapping her arms around her waist. "What do we need a mother for?"

Marty's attitude shouldn't surprise him. She'd been the lead hen in their household since she was five. Maybe all she needed was more time to get used to the idea. He turned his attention to the younger girls. "What changed your minds?"

Frannie fiddled with her fork. "Marty and Charlie might not like it, but I want to go back to school. I like learning how to read and playing with my friends. If the only way we can go is to get a mother, then I'm okay with it."

"That's a stupid reason for Uncle Gray to go and get himself hitched," Marty muttered.

He chose to ignore her for now. "What about you, Charlie? What changed your mind?"

The little girl glanced at her sisters before answering. "Because I'd like to know what it's like to have a mother."

Marty sprang from her chair. "You had one. We all did."

"But I don't remember her like you do. I don't even know what she looked like." Charlie looked up at Gray with serious eyes. "Is it bad that I can't remember what Ma looked like?"

Leaning over, Gray scooped her up and set her on his lap. "No, darling girl. You were a wee little thing when your ma and pa died. Too young to make any memories with them."

"I wished I had." Charlie nuzzled against his shoulder. "That's why I like the idea of Miss Jilly being my ma. I mean, y'all seem to like each other."

Gray glanced toward the door. Any second, Jilly would return with her mother. "It's a bit more complicated than that."

"So it's true."

Gray glanced across the table at Marty. "What are you talking about? What's true?"

Marty glared at him. "On the way here, Miss Lydia told the preacher that it was about time you two were married, said you've been sweet on each other since you were in school." Her cheeks flushed with anger. "Is that why you wouldn't find a mother for us back home? Because of her?"

Yes, but he'd never thought much about it until he saw Jilly today. Now that they were "married," he needed to tell the girls the truth. "It's true. Jilly was my sweetheart, and we had planned on getting married. But when I returned from the war and asked her to marry me, she turned me down."

The room fell silent for a moment; then Charlie spoke. "Did you do something wrong?"

"Of course he didn't." Frannie elbowed her in the gut. "You didn't, did you?"

"Why did she say no?" Marty asked. What temper she had flared out.

Gray lifted his shoulders in a shrug. "I wish I knew."

"Why don't you ask her?"

Gray stared at his youngest niece. Such a simple question, yet one he wasn't any closer to knowing the truth to than he was a few years ago. Maybe it was time he asked her why she'd thrown away their chance at happiness. Jilly wouldn't be able to elude the question so easily this time. They were married—maybe not the way he'd hoped, but still, it was legally binding. In the eyes of the law, she belonged to him as he did her. The way it was always meant to be.

Married. There was a sense of rightness about it, as if they had finally come full circle. But could he convince Jilly of that?

Gray smiled. Until Pastor Quinn said he wasn't married anymore, he was going to woo his wife.

Chapter 6

"Why do I have to wear this?" Charlie ruffled the skirt of the cotton dress in irritation. "It's itchy."

Frannie ran her fingers down the crisp lines of her sleeve. "I kind of like it myself. It makes me feel all pretty inside."

"Cows don't care if we look pretty as long as they get milked and fed." Marty eyed herself in the mirror. "Don't know why we're bothering with all this in the first place. We're not going to be here that long."

"Now, girls." Jilly gave them each a once-over, tugging at a collar here, a hem there. After a long day of cleaning the sanctuary, she'd turned her attention to sewing dresses for the girls to wear to church. It had taken several late nights and early mornings, but even she was surprised at how well the dresses had turned out. "You all look lovely."

Frannie beamed while the other two smirked at her in the mirror. Jilly turned to gather the ribbons she'd found in her sewing chest and held them out to the girls. "These will look so pretty in your hair."

"I don't know why we have to wear these things in the first place," Marty said again, fiddling with her cuffed sleeves as Frannie grabbed the ribbons. "Uncle Gray says it shouldn't matter what you wear to church as long as you go there to worship."

Jilly couldn't argue with that. "Gray is right. God looks inside your heart, not at what you're wearing on the outside. But you want to make a good impression, don't you?"

"Why's that?" Charlie asked, tugging at her collar as she swatted her older sister away from her hair.

"Because Uncle is looking for a wife." Marty glared up at Jilly in the mirror. "Well, he was looking until the other day."

Jilly reached for the small velvet bag that held what little jewelry she had left and opened it. It was easy to understand why Marty disliked her so much.

She'd pretended to kill off her uncle and then she'd managed to trick him into marrying her. But whether it was her or another woman, Gray would marry one day.

But he's already married to me.

"Well, the people in this town can take me as I am or not at all." Marty struggled with the buttons at her wrist.

Poor girl. If she didn't make some changes soon, she was going to find herself alone a great deal. Jilly studied Marty in the mirror. "Don't you want someone to help you as you grow up?"

The girl shook her head. "I'm doing all right so far. Why would I need a mother now?"

"If we're doing so good, why did Miss Simmons kick us out of school?" Frannie asked.

A thundercloud exploded across Marty's face, and she glared at Frannie.

"Besides, I told you, I like wearing a dress." Frannie tugged at her collar. "I think we look real nice."

"That's neither here nor there," Marty snapped. "Why do we want to look nice? We want to be cowboys like Uncle Gray."

"I don't," Frannie replied, wrapping a blue ribbon around one braid. "I want to learn how to play the piano in church."

"Why, Frannie, that's a lovely idea." Jilly turned to find Charlie reaching behind her for the buttons. "What about you, Charlie? What do you want to do when you grow up?"

"I want to have a family with a mama and a daddy."

Jilly nodded. Gray was right. The girls desperately needed a mother, and until the preacher found out more about the legality of her marriage to Gray, she would have to do. But how? She didn't know anything about raising children. She'd have to learn fast, as much for her sake as for the girls'.

Pick your battles. How many times had she heard her mother say that very thing during her childhood? Jilly hadn't understood it then, but now, with the girls bickering about dresses, it made all the sense in the world.

She took a deep breath. "Marty, as long as your clothes are clean, you can wear your dungarees to church. All the Lord cares about is that your heart is ready for worship."

Marty threw her a suspicious glare. "Won't you be embarrassed in front of all your friends?"

Jilly shook her head. "I've embarrassed myself enough in the last week that no one will notice you wearing pants."

"Does that go for me too?" Charlie asked, pulling the skirts up to her waist.

"Yes, Charlie." Jilly unhooked the buttons on the back of Marty's dress. Maybe this hadn't been her best idea, but forcing them before they were ready wasn't the best way to go to church either.

"What about you, Frannie?" Marty gave Jilly a triumphant smile.

The younger girl busied herself with undoing her braids and brushing her hair out. Finally, she laid down the brush and glanced up at them in the mirror. "I'm going to wear my dress, especially after all the trouble Miss Jilly went to to make it."

"The only reason she made it for you is because she tricked Uncle Gray."

Frannie whipped her head around. "Marty! Don't you remember? Gray asked her first!"

Marty glared at Jilly. "And she turned him down!"

Oh dear. What had Gray told the girls about her? Why in the world would he do that? "What exactly has Gray said about us?"

Marty shook her head. "Not much. But Miss Lydia told the preacher the other day that she was glad you two were finally married. That y'all had been sweet on each other for years."

No wonder the girl was upset. "I'm so sorry, but Mama gets mixed up at times. That's why she told everyone Gray and I were married."

"So you ain't married?"

Jilly tried to tame her annoyance. The child didn't have to look so happy about it. "It's a little bit more complicated than that, dear. The truth is, I don't know. Pastor Quinn is looking into it."

"But Uncle Gray did ask you to marry him, didn't he?" Frannie asked, her blue-green eyes—so much like Gray's—staring up at her. "And you turned him down."

"Don't you love him?" Charlie asked.

"Of course I love him." She always had, and if she was truthful, she always would. Which was why Papa had changed his will so that she had to marry to inherit Greenhaven. Jilly pulled a handkerchief from her pocket and blotted her face. "Didn't Gray explain any of this to you?"

Charlie shook her head. "He looked about as confused as you do right now."

"Did he propose to you wrong?" Frannie asked.

Jilly smiled, remembering that evening. "No, it was really quite lovely.

He took me to dinner at the restaurant in town then drove us out to the old schoolhouse where we first met. The leaves were turning, so every time the wind blew, they would rain down on us like colorful pieces of confetti. It was as if there was no one else in the world but us."

"That doesn't sound like Uncle Gray." Marty sniffed.

"Did he get down on one knee?" Frannie asked wistfully.

So the girl was a romantic! Jilly stifled a smile. *Gray better keep an eye on that one.* "Yes, he eventually got down on one knee."

"And you broke his heart?"

All the sweet memories of that moment disappeared, leaving a bitter taste in her mouth. "Yes, but it's a little more complicated than that."

"That's the second time you've said that. What's that mean?" Charlie asked, looking confused.

"It's what grown-ups say when they don't understand something themselves," Frannie answered.

"If you love him, why did you turn him down?"

Jilly's head spun at Marty's question. How could she explain that she loved Gray too much to saddle him with her problems? That even now, all these years later, she still loved him so. But he had gone to Texas to fulfill his lifelong dream. She wouldn't take that from him.

It was time to get this conversation on to other matters and away from the heartache of the past. She shook her head and plumped Frannie's sleeves. "So is everyone set for tomorrow morning?"

"If I wear this dress," Charlie said, turning from side to side, looking this way and that, "can I take it off when I get home?"

"Charlie!" Marty cried out.

"Of course." Jilly sighed. Two down, one to go. But Marty was an uphill battle. It was time to change the subject. "What kinds of things do you like to do back home in Texas?"

The girls looked at each other then looked back at her, perplexed.

"You know," she continued. "Something like dolls or playing jacks or skipping rope. I used to love to do those things."

"I like to climb trees," Charlie answered excitedly. "The higher, the better. I like looking out over the whole world."

"Really? I've been afraid of heights since your uncle and I climbed Kennesaw Mountain one summer when school was out." Of course, she left out the part where Gray had hung off a cliff, barely holding on by his fingertips.

"What else do you like to do?"

"Well. . ." Marty had the bodice of her dress down around her feet. "Slim taught us how to spit."

"Slim?"

"He works at the ranch," Charlie said. "He showed us how to outspit every boy in our school."

Jilly bit her lip to keep from laughing. "How did he do that?"

"We started practicing with watermelon seeds." The child's face lit up. "Why? You want to learn how?"

"Why would she want to learn how to do that?" Marty scolded. "She's a lady."

"Well, ladies do fun stuff every now and then." Charlie stuck out her tongue.

Boy, these girls sure knew how to bicker. "I may be all grown up, but I've spit my fair share of watermelon seeds when I was about your age. I was pretty good at it too."

"You were?" Frannie's eyes widened. "Did you ever beat any of the boys at school?"

Jilly nodded. "One. Your uncle Gray."

"Uncle Gray is too good to lose," Marty scoffed. "He let you win."

Jilly patted her hair into place. "Is that why he refused to talk to me for a whole week after I beat him? He said he needed a few days to himself after losing to a girl."

Charlie giggled. "Really?"

Marty blew a raspberry. "You're bluffing."

Why hadn't she thought of this before? There was more than one way to herd cats, or in this case, convince Marty to at least try wearing a dress. "There's one way to find out."

A wide smile blossomed on Marty's face, giving a glimpse of the lovely woman to come. "Are you challenging us, Miss Jilly? Because we will whup you."

Jilly grinned at her. "I'll wager you won't."

"What do we get if we win?" Charlie asked.

Jilly would have to offer something the girls wanted and pray she'd win. "I don't know. What would you like?"

Marty's smile turned sinister. "You'll wear a pair of pants and a shirt to church tomorrow."

"Marty!" Frannie slapped her older sister on the arm. "Miss Jilly probably doesn't own any of those things."

The girl glanced down at her dress on the floor. "She's pretty good with a needle. I'm sure she could make do."

Jilly caught a flash of sympathy in the younger girls' eyes. Well, if that was how Marty wanted it, she'd play along. "And if I win, you'll wear your dress every Sunday without any complaints. Does that sound fair to you?"

The girls exchanged an excited glance, victory shining in their eyes. Marty held out her hand. "You've got yourself a deal."

Chapter 7

Ll right, ladies. Here are the rules. Each one of you will get three seeds that are the same size. You will go up to the line and take your turn. You'll be disqualified if you cross over the line. Whoever spits the watermelon seed the farthest wins."

Good gracious. Charlie sounded like a barker at the county fair. Jilly glanced down at the dark oval-shaped seeds in her hand and prayed, *Lord, help me with these girls, even if it means embarrassing myself again.*

"What are you girls up to now?"

Jilly glanced over her shoulder to find Gray walking across the yard, his clothes dusty from working on a broken fence at the back of the property. Her lungs refused to work as he came closer. How could a man look so good after a day of hauling logs?

Charlie's voice startled her out of her thoughts. "We're going to see who can spit a watermelon seed the farthest."

He came up alongside Jilly, the scent of fresh-cut pine and hardworking male tickling her senses. "How did they rope you into that?"

She swallowed. "It was a wager I couldn't refuse."

"A wager?" His voice bubbled with laughter. "Good Christian women like you don't go around making bets."

She used to laugh as much as he did, but the last few years had left her sober and serious. Well, not today. "They do if it will get your girls into dresses Sunday morning."

"Really?" His brows rose as if she'd amazed him. "Did you happen to tell them you are the reigning seed-spitting champion of the Marietta School District?"

Jilly felt her lips twitch. "I'm sure someone has beat my old record by now."

"I don't know." He took off his cowboy hat and hit it against his thigh. A cloud of dust formed around his knees. "You were pretty lucky back then."

"Lucky? I beat you fair and square."

"Like I said. Lucky."

"The girls seem to think you let me win." She hesitated for a moment. "Did you?"

The eyes that looked back at her were brimmed with innocence. "Did I what?"

"You're infuriating. Do you know that?"

"You are too." He leaned in close until she felt his breath against her ear. "I've always liked that about you."

Her breath caught, and she turned to stare out over the front yard. "Stop flirting with me."

Gray's warm, husky laugh sent a spark of awareness through her. "But you're so much fun to flirt with." Raised voices drew his attention to the girls. "I'd better go referee if we want to get this contest started. Good luck." Gray turned then stopped, took her hand in his, and lifted it to his lips. He placed a soft kiss on her knuckles. "Thank you for caring about my girls."

Jilly swallowed hard against the emotions knotting in her throat. "Anything I can do to help."

As Gray walked toward the gaggle of little girls, Jilly slumped slightly. What was she doing, laughing and flirting with Gray like old times? They might be married, but her situation with her mother was no better than when he'd left five years ago. In fact, Mama needed Jilly now more than ever. She had to stop this before both of them ended up getting hurt.

"Marty, take your place on the line."

It had been decided that as the oldest, Marty would represent her sisters during the contest. Looking confident, the tall, coltish girl took her place on the dusty line, digging the toe of her boot in the dirt for more leverage. Popping the first seed in her mouth, she swirled it around like it was a lemon drop while she drew in several controlled breaths through her nose. One more deep breath, then she puckered her lips and let the seed fly. It hung in the air for long seconds before finally hitting the ground with a plop.

"Mercy sakes!" Charlie whipped off her hat and gave a short whoop. "You almost spit that seed into the next county!"

Jilly leaned forward to get a better look. Goodness gracious! She might have been good in her day, but Marty could give Old Man Jenkins down at the mercantile a run for his money.

Marty glanced back at her and gave her a smug smile. "What will everyone in town say when you show up wearing pants at church tomorrow?"

"Pants?" Gray stared at her. "Why did you bet that?"

"Because she's not going to lose, are you, Jilly?"

Jilly glanced down at Frannie. The girl was putting all her faith in her, even when it meant going against her sister. For that alone, she had to try. "The contest isn't over yet."

"Suit yourself." Marty stepped up to the line again. As the girl went through her preparations, Jilly chanced a glance at Gray, only to find him watching her. He smiled, and she forgot all her good intentions and smiled back, which earned her a wink. Good gracious, they were flirting again, and in front of the children. Turning back, she caught Marty's second attempt.

"You went over the line," Frannie announced to no one in particular.

Marty turned and gave her a hard stare. "Did not."

"Did too." Frannie pointed to the ground. "Look at where you're standing."

Charlie crouched down for a better look then nodded. "Yep, you were over the line."

"Fine." The girl dug the toe of her boot deep into the ground. "Don't matter anyway. I always do best on my last seed."

"We'll see," Jilly replied, though she didn't doubt the girl's word. Her second attempt had passed her first by a good six inches. Jilly would be fortunate to make it half that distance.

Marty went through her ritual for the third time, but just as she took a deep breath, Frannie coughed. Loud. So loud, it startled Jilly.

It must have caught Marty off guard because she gulped, then stared back at them. "I swallowed my seed."

"That's too bad." Frannie couldn't suppress the grin on her face.

Marty took off after her sister. "You did that on purpose!"

"I did not." Frannie ran, screeching, until she found a safe haven behind Gray's back.

"You coughed on purpose!" The older girl tried to grab her arm, but Gray held her firmly in place. "You like wearing dresses and fixing your hair up in ribbons and stuff like that."

Charlie pointed an accusing finger at Frannie. "I've seen the way you gawk at the dresses in Mrs. Hawkins's store. You look at them like they were made of spun sugar or somethin'."

Frannie buried her face in Gray's waist. "What's wrong with that?"

It was time to step in before the bickering turned into a brawl. She looked to Gray. "May I?"

He gave her a brief nod. "They're all yours."

Jilly took Frannie's hand and pulled her out of her hiding place, crouching down beside her. "There is nothing wrong with liking dresses and ribbons and all those other girlie things, dear. But you didn't need to sabotage your sister's last attempt either."

"But she could have won."

Jilly couldn't argue with her there. "Maybe, but it's better to lose in a fair fight than win by cheating."

"You honestly believe that?" Marty asked, her anger tempered at the moment.

All three girls looked up at her intently, as if her words held meaning for them. These girls needed a woman in their lives to teach them how to be the people God wanted them to be, and for the moment, that was her. She might not ever get them all in dresses without a fight, but maybe she could teach them something more important. "I believe if you do your best, it's all right to lose sometimes."

Charlie grimaced. "I hate to lose."

"But you're so good at it, cow pie." Marty laughed.

"We don't call each other names either." Jilly looked over at Charlie. "I don't like to lose either. In fact, I hate it. But when I win, I want to know that everyone has tried their very best. When I win that way, it feels wonderful. Like a job well done."

"But I never win," Charlie moaned, kicking the dirt in front of her. "And I try really hard."

"Keep trying." She brushed unruly curls off Charlie's forehead. "Because the more you practice, the better you'll get, until one day, you'll surprise yourself and win."

"Is that true, Uncle Gray?"

Gray nodded. "Jilly's right. You just have to keep on trying."

"See, your uncle Gray agrees with me." She gave Charlie one last smile then tuned back to Frannie. "Now, apologize to your sister, please."

"Do I have to?" she whined.

Gray certainly had his hands full, and for now, she did too. "Yes."

Jilly wasn't sure the child would obey until she sighed and turned to face her sister. "I'm sorry, Marty. I shouldn't have made you swallow your watermelon seed."

"It's all right." The older girl grimaced. "And if you want to wear a dress, that's all right with me, even if I don't understand it."

"Me neither." Charlie walked over to Gray and anchored herself against his side. "How do you fish or climb a tree in all those petticoats and skirts?"

Frannie met Jilly's gaze. "I don't have to wear dresses all the time, do I?"

Jilly tried not to smile. It was a start. "I tell you what. When you want to go out and climb trees, you don't have to wear a dress. How does that sound?"

The girls exchanged glances, each nodding before Marty spoke. "That seems fair enough."

She glanced up at Gray. "Are you all right with that?"

He glanced at each of his nieces then back at her, respect warming his gaze. "That sounds like a fine plan."

"I think we ought to shake on it." Charlie spit into her palm and held her hand out to Jilly.

What was it with these girls and spittle? Another habit they needed to break, but not today. Jilly stole a quick glance at Gray, only to find his lips twitching from suppressed laughter. Jilly pretended to spit into her palm then grasped Charlie's hand. The other two followed suit. When the handshakes were done, the girls headed off toward the barn to see the animals.

Gray walked over to her. "I can't believe you talked the girls into doing that. It's like a miracle."

"I guess." Jilly stared down at her wet palm, trying to decide where to wipe it when Gray's fingers closed around her wrist and drew her hand to his chest. "Gray?"

"What's a little spit? My shirt is already dirty."

Jilly sighed. Of course, he just wanted to dry her hand. "Thank you."

"Thank you." His heart beat out a strong rhythm beneath her hand, a rhythm she knew matched her own. "You won the bet without popping the first seed in your mouth."

She smiled up at him. "Lucky, I guess."

Chapter 8

"You're teaching the girls how to sew? How did that happen?" Gray asked Jilly as they walked along a stand of trees near the edge of the Chastains' property.

She gifted him with a soft smile as her fingertips played against the tops of a tall stand of dandelions. "Charlie caught her shirt on a tree branch, and she wanted me to fix it for her. When I told the girls I knew how to sew by Charlie's age, they decided they wanted to learn."

"You deserve a medal." Since the spitting contest almost a week ago, the girls had held true to their agreement, only returning to their dungarees when they went outside to play. Today, he'd found them all in the front parlor, working quietly on old pieces of material. Jilly's successes with the girls were piling up.

Which was the reason behind this planned picnic today. A small token of his appreciation, or at least that's what he'd told her. In truth, he wanted her all to himself just for a little while.

"So what do you have planned for this afternoon? I hope we're going to have lunch."

He held up a small hamper. "You like chicken and peach cobbler? That's what I found in the icebox." He'd also managed to find some bread and cheese, a jar of sweet pickles, and lemonade to add to the meal.

"My favorites." She stopped to pick a handful of daisies. "Lunch and dessert. It doesn't get much better than that. And the fishing poles?"

"What do you think?"

"Really?" The flowers scattered as Jilly clapped her hands. "I haven't been fishing since Papa caught us that time right before I turned sixteen. Do you remember?"

Of course Gray remembered. Mr. Chastain had given him a good talking-to about the risk he'd taken with Jilly's reputation. "Your dad was so angry, he wouldn't let me see you for the rest of the summer. The longest two months of my life."

Jilly stopped and stared at him. "I didn't know that. I spent the whole rest of the summer thinking you were mad that I got you in trouble."

Had he been angry? Maybe, but he hadn't understood the damage the innocent outing could do to Jilly. Mr. Chastain had been right. Now, with nieces of his own, he could see the wisdom in the man's response. He would feel the same way if any one of his girls were put in a situation that would sully her reputation. "The next time I saw you, you were walking into the mercantile with your mother. I hardly recognized you with your hair turned up and skirts brushing the ground." He met her gaze. "You stole the breath right out of my chest."

Her lips parted on a soft sigh. "You never told me that either."

"Maybe I should have." He stepped closer. Mercy, how he wanted to pull her close and simply forget about the past in her embrace. Kiss her as he used to when their love lit up the skies like firecrackers on the Fourth of July. Over the last two weeks, the feelings he'd fought so hard to ignore had come back stronger than ever. The only wife he wanted was Jilly, but he'd need to tread lightly if he wanted to turn this pretend marriage into a real one. Drawing in a deep breath, he stepped away. "This looks like a good place for a picnic."

Jilly looked around at the green mossy bank along the edge of the creek. Large water oaks provided a refreshing shade from the afternoon sun. "I'd forgotten how pretty it was here."

"You don't come here anymore?"

She shook her head. "Pepper Creek is so much closer to the house."

Does this place hold too many memories for her too? "Would you like to find another place?"

"No. It seems right being here with you. This was our place, after all."

Flushed, she stepped back, catching a root that threw her off balance. Gray lunged for her, rolling under her so that he would take the brunt of the fall while his arms wrapped around her. When they finally came to rest, Jilly lay on top of him, her hands fisted in his shirt, her warm breath fanned against his neck. For several long seconds, the world faded away, leaving just the two of them, holding fast to each other, as it should be.

Jilly lifted her head, her nose brushing against his, her eyes filled with such longing, he could barely breathe. He finally managed to form words.

"Are you okay?"

She didn't answer, instead palming his face in her hands, her delicate fingers setting off sparks as she traced his jaw. She studied him for a long moment then brushed her lips against his. "Please kiss me."

He didn't need any further encouragement. With one arm wrapped around her waist, he feathered his fingers through the soft curls at the base of her neck, anchoring her head as his lips met hers. On a soft sigh, she wrapped her arms around his neck and kissed him back.

Holding Jilly like this almost made him mindless, but somewhere deep inside, he knew they had to stop. They may be legally married because of some technicality, but it wasn't real, at least not for him. When he made his vows to Jilly, he wanted it to be before God and man.

Gently, he released her and got to his feet. "Your papa was right. We shouldn't be out here alone."

Jilly sat up, her skirts splayed around her like petals of a flower in full bloom. Her fingers trailed across her lips. "I shouldn't have kissed you like that. You must think—"

"That that kiss was worth the wait." Gray smiled as she turned a deeper shade of pink. "Though I have to say I enjoyed all of your kisses equally as much."

"Now you're teasing me."

Gray held out his hand to help her to her feet. "I always thought kissing you would be my favorite pastime after we got married. And of course, teasing you, making you laugh, and watching you smile."

"Only we never married."

"No, we didn't."

Instead of taking his hand, Jilly stared out over the water. "Oh, Gray. How did I mess things up so badly?"

What was she talking about? Gray crouched down beside her. "Honey, if you're talking about the funeral and everything, it'll work out."

"No, I'm talking about us."

Was she finally ready to tell him what had changed her mind about marrying him? And was he ready to listen? Gray sat down beside her. "Talk to me, Jilly."

She hesitated for a long moment, to the point he wondered if she had changed her mind. Then she spoke. "It almost killed me to send you away. I couldn't eat. I couldn't sleep. Everything that seemed so wonderful about life suddenly turned dull. But I thought I was doing the right thing, letting you go so you could go to Texas. You had so many dreams about owning your own ranch." She took a shaky breath. "I couldn't burden you with my problems. It wouldn't have been right."

Jilly had had problems? Why hadn't she told him? Gray took her hand in his. "Nothing would have kept me from marrying you, Jilly. Do you understand? Nothing."

"You say that now, but—"

"No." Gray wanted to shake some sense into her. "Do you think my love was so fragile, anything could have destroyed it?"

She met his gaze. "You're the best man I've ever known, Grayson Hancock, but I know you. You would have put your dreams on the back burner because of me. I couldn't let you do it."

Gray's temper flared to life. "So you made the decision for me?"

She shook her head. "You don't understand."

"Then why don't you explain it to me and let me make my own decision?"

"All right." Rising to her feet, she brushed the dirt from her hands before clenching them behind her back. "The war wasn't kind to us, Gray. Papa lost most of his money investing in the Confederacy, and what little he had left, he wouldn't touch, in case Mama and I needed it. The only thing of true value we had left was Greenhaven."

His anger simmered. "You think I wouldn't marry you because you'd lost your money?"

"No!" Jilly cried out. "I know you never cared about my family's money. But it made life difficult. Papa gave up after the war ended. So when the doctor told us that his heart was giving out, I almost think he was relieved. And Mama. . ."

"But Miss Lydia's always been a little forgetful. I'm sure she'll get better. . . ."

Jilly shook her head. "She's different. She forgets to do things like brush her hair or pay a bill. I thought it would pass, but she's only gotten worse. When Papa died, I worried Mama would lose what little mind she has left."

And she had borne this all alone. "Isn't there something the doctors can do?" he inquired. "Medicine or some kind of treatment?"

"Papa took her to Atlanta to see a specialist in brain diseases, but he suggested we put her in an institution." Jilly's curls bounced violently as she shook her head. "We could never do that. So Papa brought her home. The doctor did say that any kind of change might make her worse. That's why I couldn't leave, not with Papa so sick and Mama. . .the way she is." Moisture glistened in her dark lashes. "That's why I turned down your proposal."

He squeezed her hand. "If I'd known, I would have—"

"I know." She nodded. "But you've dreamed of owning your own ranch since we were children. My own dreams might have been lost, but I couldn't take yours away from you too. I couldn't have lived with that."

Anger coursed through him. "So you decided our future without consulting me?"

"Didn't you hear what I said? Mama would have gotten worse if we'd moved to Texas."

"I heard you." Gray jumped to his feet, anger so wild and reckless pounding through him, only movement would offer any peace. "Did you ever think that I could have helped you? That we could have taken care of your mother together?"

"What about your ranch, Gray? What about all those dreams you had?"

He pushed his fingers into his hair and pulled at the roots. "Mercy, woman. Those dreams didn't mean anything without you there to share them."

"I didn't think—"

"No, you didn't." Now that the truth was out, he wasn't certain that he was better off knowing the truth. He wondered if she had ever trusted him. But she was sharing the truth with him now. That had to count for something. "I'm sorry. I shouldn't have barked at you like that."

"I never meant to hurt you. Saying no to you broke my heart into so many pieces, I'll spend the rest of my life trying to find them."

He knew the feeling well. Only one thing remained to be asked. "Do you still love me?"

"Gray. . ."

He closed the distance between them. "You owe me that much, Jilly."

A tear escaped and slid down her cheek. Without thinking, he took his thumb and gently stroked the moisture away. She closed her eyes then, and more tears fell. "Of course I love you. I always will, but—"

Gray didn't let her finish, instead settling his lips on hers. She tasted warm and womanly, a heady combination that soon had them both gasping for air. When Jilly stepped out of his arms, Gray knew he'd move heaven and earth to make this woman his wife. Not because of some silly obituary, but because he wanted to commit himself to her in front of God and everyone.

Because a life without Jilly was no life at all.

Chapter 9

Jilly slid a glance at the man beside her as they walked back to the house in an uneasy silence. Tension radiated off Gray like a clock that had been wound a bit too tight. She didn't blame him for being angry. Even as she explained her reasons for turning down his proposal, it sounded weak in her own ears, as if she didn't trust him with the sorrows of her mother's diagnosis.

She trusted Gray, with everything that was inside her. It was herself she had questions about. How many times had she wished she could stay in bed or read a book without worrying what Mama was doing? Hadn't she thought of running away when another one of Mama's "stories" reached her ears? Why couldn't life be easier than this?

Something her mother used to say flashed through her mind. *"God never promised you a rose garden, but work hard enough and He'll give you a beautiful bloom now and then."*

Gray was like that, always looking at the best side of things. He would have figured out a way to make their lives work together. His dream might have changed, but he would have found another one that included her.

She sighed. What a mess!

As they walked under a large dogwood tree at the edge of the backyard, a voice came from above. "Where have you two been?"

Shielding her eyes from the afternoon sun, Jilly glanced up and found Charlie dangling from a limb near the top of the tree. Gray stepped closer, his head thrown back so that he could get a better look. "Maybe the bigger question is what are you doing all the way up there?"

The child stood on the branch and reached for the next one. "I hadn't climbed this tree yet, so I figured I better get to it."

Her uncle spoke sternly. "What about the chores I left for you?"

Her childish giggle floated softly in the air. "I'm taking a little break."

"A little break," Gray muttered then leaned back against the tree trunk.

"It took her at least a half hour to climb up that high."

"Longer than that," Charlie called out. "I started around the time the preacher got here."

Jilly exchanged a look with Gray. Pastor Quinn had been here. Did he have news about their marriage? "Did he say why he was here?"

Even from this distance, she could see the girl shake her head. "Isn't that what preachers do? Drop in on folks when they don't expect them?"

Jilly bit her lip. Out of the mouths of babes. "Where did you hear such a thing?"

"Miss Lydia. She said most preachers wait until suppertime looking for a free meal, but Preacher Quinn ain't like that. He's better than most." The girl straddled the branch and looked over the terrain. "What is that mountain over there?"

Gray snorted. "I told you they were a mouthy bunch."

Jilly gave him an encouraging smile. "Another thing we'll have to work on."

"That list is getting mighty long."

"We have time."

He nodded then turned his attention back to Charlie. "Where are your sisters?"

"Marty is probably still down at the pond. That's where we all were before the preacher showed up." Childish laughter tinged the air. "Who would have thought Miss Lydia could swim like a trout!"

Alarm rang through Jilly. "Mama was with you?"

"She was the one who showed us the pond." Jilly's heart lurched as Charlie scooted out to the end of the branch. "She said it was too hot to be doing chores and thought a cool dip in the pond was what we needed."

"Charlotte Grace, come down from that tree right now before Jilly faints," Gray called out, his voice edged with worry. "She's afraid you're going to break your fool neck."

"But Uncle Gray—" Charlie whined.

"No buts, young lady."

"Yes sir." The girl shimmied down the tree like a circus acrobat, swinging from limb to limb with a confidence and ease of someone much older. It was only as she drew closer to the bottom that Jilly realized something was missing. "Where is your dress?"

"Down by the pond," she answered, standing on a limb just above them. "You said I didn't have to wear it when I climb trees."

"I didn't expect for you to go running around in your undergarments either. Why didn't you change into your dungarees?"

"I didn't have time. And when Marty mentioned something about swimming, Miss Lydia said all of us could swim in our unmentionables."

Dear heavens, the girls had been splashing around in their undergarments for all the world to see? And the preacher! What would the man think of the girls' immodest behavior?

Gray glanced at Jilly then caught his niece as she lowered herself to the ground. "What do you mean by 'all of us'?"

"You know. Me, Frannie, Marty." She paused, eyeing Jilly. "And Miss Lydia."

Mercy sakes alive! Mama walking around in only her chemise and pantaloons where anyone could see her? Surely she put her clothes back on before Pastor Quinn arrived, because if she hadn't. . . Jilly's cheeks flamed. Maybe Charlie was mistaken. Maybe it wasn't the pastor. "How did you know the pastor was at the house?"

"Miss Lydia saw his wagon in the front yard. She told us to go play so we could dry out while she entertained the preacher until you got home." Charlie glanced up at the two of them. "Where were you two?"

Sweet sugar, if this wasn't the icing on the cake. No one in town would ever speak to them again. Jilly crouched down in front of the child. "Miss Lydia got dressed before she went up to the house to meet the preacher, didn't she?"

Charlie shook her head. "She didn't want to keep him waiting so she just threw her dress over her shoulder and walked up to meet him."

Jilly felt the blood drain from her face. What had Mama been thinking, carrying on like that? That was the trouble—she didn't think clearly anymore, and Jilly wasn't sure what she could do about it.

A pair of strong hands reached down and pulled her to her feet. *Gray.* At least now he'd understand why she'd done what she had done. "This isn't the end of the world, sweetheart. We'll get through this. Why don't you go up to the house and check on your mother while I round up the girls and help them get dressed?"

"Yes." Without thinking she leaned up and gave him a swift kiss before picking up her skirts and racing toward the house.

Gray had never seen a woman run so fast, though he had to admit he admired Jilly's trim legs.

"Well, that wasn't very ladylike," Charlie said as she wiggled out of his arms. "Jilly said a young lady must never run but take her time when she walks anywhere. It's supposed to give a feeling of serenity." She scrunched up her nose. "Whatever that means."

Serenity was probably the very last emotion Jilly felt at the moment. Poor darling, her mother had always been an example of manners and modesty. *It must be difficult to watch a person you love slip away like this and there's nothing you can do.* But he was here now. She wouldn't face this situation alone. "It was an emergency."

"You mean because the preacher's here?"

"Yes." And because her mother was entertaining the man in her unmentionables. The girls needed to know what was behind Lydia Chastain's strange behavior. "You see, Charlie, Miss Lydia is sick."

The girl thought for a moment. "She doesn't look sick."

"It's like that sometimes." Gray laid his hand on her small shoulder. "Miss Lydia's brain isn't working like it should."

"Uncle Gray, did I get her in trouble?"

He glanced down at the worried expression on Charlie's face. "No. Why would you think that?"

"It's just I'd hate to think I caused her any problems." She played with the pink ribbon on her chemise. "She may not be right in the head, but I like her. So do Marty and Frannie."

"You do?"

"Did you know she likes to fish too? And play games and sing songs." The girl smiled. "She's like a crazy old grandma to us, though I wouldn't ever tell her that to her face. It might hurt her feelings."

Gray smiled. Jilly's lessons were bearing fruit. "What do you think about Jilly?"

"She's pretty and smart, and even though I haven't seen her do it, I'm betting she's a good seed spitter. She seems to know how to handle us, even Marty when she's giving everyone fits." Her tiny brow furrowed. "Though I can't see her taking a swim in her underwear, can you?"

Gray pressed his lips together. No, but maybe after they were married, he might coax her down to the pond. He cleared his throat. "No, I guess not."

"But me and Frannie, we like her," she continued. "We think she'd be a good mother to us, and you love each other and stuff." She rolled her eyes. "The way you two make cow eyes at each other? *Blech.*"

"What about Marty?"

"You know how she is, but she's coming around." Charlie waved him down as if to tell him a secret. "Did you know I caught her putting ribbons in her hair the other day?"

That sounded promising. Still, there was one more hurdle to jump. "With Miss Lydia being so sick, Jilly couldn't move back home with us."

The child thought for a moment. "So why don't we move here?"

"What?" He hadn't expected her to be so agreeable.

The girl cupped her hands around her mouth and yelled loud enough to be heard three counties over. "Why don't we move here?"

Gray rubbed his ears. "I can hear you just fine."

"I wasn't sure. I thought you might be going deaf in your old age." Charlie snorted. "Can you see yourself with two of those horns Old Lady Hawkins uses? You'd look like a confused goat!"

"Very funny." He tugged her braid. "But why would you want to move here?"

"Well. . ." Charlie stepped on the bottom step of the front porch. "I like this place and Miss Lydia and Jilly, even when she's trying to make us into young ladies." She glanced up at him. "You smile more here."

"You think I'm a grump?"

"You are a grump!" She giggled. "Well, sometimes. But you laugh more when you're around Jilly, and that makes us happy." Charlie slipped her small hand in his. "Why stay in Texas when we all could be happy here?"

Gray stood for a long moment. There was a lot of wisdom in his youngest niece's words. Life was too short not to have the joy of family. What if they could have it here?

His decision made, Gray gently pushed Charlie up the stairs. "Let's go find your sisters then get back to the house. Jilly might need our help with Grandma Lydia."

"Grandma." Charlie fell into step beside him, a smile lifting her voice. "I sure like the sound of that."

Chapter 10

S he was barely holding herself together.

Jilly took another sip of her tepid tea and stole a glance at her mother. Though the buttons had been slipped into the wrong loops, leaving gaps at her neck and waist, Frannie had somehow managed to get Mama back into her dress. Her hair hung limp in a mess of gray curls around her shoulders, and Jilly couldn't be certain, but she thought she saw her mother's bare toes peek out from under the muddy hem.

"I'm sorry I came by unannounced, but I thought you and Grayson might be interested in what I learned down at the state house." Pastor Quinn glanced at Mama then gave Jilly an understanding smile.

She'd been dreading this moment. Maybe not at first, but then that was before she'd spent the last two weeks with Gray and the girls, before childlike laughter had filled the quiet places in her life. Before she'd fallen in love with Gray all over again. Whatever the preacher had to say meant that her time with Gray and the girls was coming to an end. Jilly replaced her cup on its saucer and placed them on the table. "Of course. I know Gray is as anxious as I am to get this cleared up." Brushing the wrinkles out of her skirt, she stood. "Let me go see what is keeping him."

"No need." Gray walked into the room, his wide smile as he shook the pastor's hand causing her heart to twist painfully in her chest. Their talk today had shown her how much she'd hurt him—how much she'd hurt herself by not trusting him with the truth about her parents. If he never forgave her, she'd understand. She'd never forgive herself.

"Son, why don't you come over here and sit by me?" Mama patted the cushions beside her then turned to the pastor. "You should see these two when they're together. All those longing looks and stolen kisses! It makes an old woman like me wish for her younger years again!"

Jilly's face caught fire. "Mama! We've done no such thing!"

Mama gave Gray's knee a motherly pat as he settled in beside her. "How was your picnic this afternoon? I know you've been looking forward to spending some time alone with Jilly."

"It was fine, but...," Jilly sputtered. If Mama kept on like this, she'd die of embarrassment. She could see the tombstone now. *Here lies Jillian Chastain who was crushed by the rock she crawled underneath.*

"There's no need to be embarrassed, dear." Mama gave the preacher one of her biggest smiles. "It's a blessing to share time with your husband. Isn't that right, Preacher?"

Pastor Quinn's lips twitched. "Yes, ma'am. It certainly is."

Goodness gracious, word of this visit would be talked about for years to come. And if they weren't married? Jilly knew a few women who'd be calling her a Jezebel behind her back. Well, let them. It didn't say much about them if they spread gossip around like manure.

"You know, I have three granddaughters now, so I'm hoping for a grandson next year, but in God's own time."

Jilly slammed her eyes shut, suddenly unable to breathe. A child with Gray? She used to dream of a little boy with Gray's blue-green eyes and stubbornness. But she'd locked those dreams away when he left for Texas. If only Gray could forgive her, maybe then they might have a future together.

"Miss Lydia, would you like to freshen up a bit while Jilly and I talk to the pastor about a private matter?"

Jilly opened her eyes to find Gray standing, holding his arm out to her mother with all the patience and understanding in the world. Mama stood, clutched his arm, and smiled up at him. "You always were such a good boy, Gray. So kind and respectful to my daughter. I'm glad you're my son."

"I feel the same way about you too, Miss Lydia." He bent and pressed a tender kiss to her wrinkled cheek. "Now, if I can just convince your daughter."

"*Psh.* My daughter doesn't need convincing." She patted his arm. "She's loved you all of her life. Just like you've loved her."

"Let me help you get settled, Mama."

Jilly started to stand, but her mother waved her off. "My son is quite capable of walking me to my room. Just sit and visit with the pastor." She glanced over to where the girls fidgeted on the couch. "I have some penny candy in my room if you all would like some."

They nodded then turned to Jilly. "Can we, Miss Jilly?" Frannie asked.

"Yes, you may."

Gray met her gaze. "I'll be back in a minute."

She wasn't sure how to respond. Jilly had never asked for help with Mama, yet Gray had stepped in and taken care of the situation when she'd been overwhelmed. Was that how it would be if they were married? Bearing each other's burdens no matter how heavy they were? Her problems with her mother felt like too much at times, but with Gray, with his natural patience and kindness, maybe the burden wouldn't be so much to bear.

"It's a heavy load to bear," the pastor said quietly. "It must be difficult carrying the burden all by yourself."

Had the preacher read her thoughts? Jilly shrugged. "She's my mother and I love her."

"The church would like to help."

"Really." She chuckled. "Even after I lied to them and almost set fire to the sanctuary?"

He smiled. "It wasn't that bad. In fact, I ought to thank you. The sanctuary looks better than it has in years. And folks are a lot more understanding than you give them credit for." He sat forward in his chair, his elbows on his knees. "You know, you're not the only person going through a tough time."

"No, but. . ." How could she explain this fear that she'd be asking too much? "I don't want to burden people with my problems."

Pastor Quinn gave her a gentle smile. "Isn't that what the church is for, to bear one another's burdens?"

"But what if a burden is too much to bear?" The question escaped her lips.

"Then we bear it together." Gray answered from the doorway, his gaze fixed on her. "That way, it's lighter for the both of us."

"Oh, Gray. I hate the thought of doing this to you," she said as he took the seat beside her. "I mean, look at what you'd have to give up."

"But look what I'd get," he whispered, taking her hand in his. "A wife I love with every breath in my body, watching our girls become women who take after their mama. A mother-in-law who loves me like a son. What more can a man ask for?"

"But my mother—"

"Won't be our only problem." He nodded to the door where Marty, Frannie, and Charlie stood. "We've got those three and no telling how many more children to raise over our life together, but that's the thing. We'll do it together, with God's help."

"And the ranch?"

He gave her a crooked grin. "Someone very wise reminded me that home is where the people you love are. You're my home, Jilly."

Was it possible? Could they have their happily ever after? She wouldn't know until she tried. "You make a very strong argument."

Gray smiled, and for the moment, the world faded away. "Does that mean you'll marry me? Even if we're already married, I want it blessed by God."

Pastor Quinn laughed. "As it is, a ceremony would be in order. I could perform it while I'm here today."

Married to Gray! Today! Her heart threatened to burst out of her breast.

"Wonderful, Pastor. I appreciate it." Jilly heard the joy in Gray's voice, and it matched her own.

"Good grief, you're doing it wrong," Charlie called from the door.

Both she and Gray turned toward the door. "What do you mean?"

Marty rolled her eyes. "You asked her, but you didn't give her a chance to answer your question."

They exchanged a glance; then Gray stood and went down on one knee. Taking Jilly's hand, he gazed up at her, love shining in his eyes. "Will you marry me, Jillian? Help me raise these three hooligans? Let me lighten your load? Be the mother of my children, but most importantly, be my friend and wife until our days on this earth are through?"

It was the most perfect proposal she'd ever heard. She threw herself into his arms. "Yes!"

A multipublished author with Love Inspired Historical and Barbour, **Patty Smith Hall** lives in north Georgia with her husband of over thirty years, Danny, two gorgeous daughters, her son-in-love, and a grandboy who has her wrapped around his tiny finger. When she's not writing on her back porch, she's spending time with her family or reading on her front porch swing.

Miss Beaumont's Companion

by Grace Hitchcock

Dedication

To Mama, my Italian southern belle.

Acknowledgments

To my husband, Dakota, for his encouragement and loving support; to my wonderful beta and critique partners for always being there for a "quick" question; to Tamela Hancock Murray, for being the best agent a writer could ever dream of having; and to the Lord, for His provision.

"Look at the birds of the air; they do not sow or reap or store away in barns, and yet your heavenly Father feeds them. Are you not much more valuable than they?"
MATTHEW 6:26 NIV

Chapter 1

B reathe. Just breathe," Aria whispered as she adjusted the ribbons on her mask, ensuring that her identity was kept safe.

"Now, you know what you must do, Miss St. Angelo," her employer reminded her as the carriage wheels crunched to a halt on the gravel drive in front of the governor's mansion.

"Smile, dance, and make small talk with the politicians." She smoothed the royal-blue replica of a Marie Antoinette gown she was wearing.

"*And* get an introduction with Byron Roderick to secure a call," Mr. Beaumont reiterated. "My daughter is going to pay for disappearing with her aunt this afternoon. Mildred knows how much I need her at Governor Foster's masquerade ball to meet the state senator's son." He turned his dark eyes to her. "If I weren't so concerned about making an inferior impression by being tardy, I would have dragged her back by her coiffure," he growled. "It's imperative for my political future that no one discovers you're not Mildred. If you ruin this night for me, I needn't remind you of the repercussions to your future."

"Yes, sir," she whispered. As the granddaughter of reduced aristocratic Italian immigrants, her options for a respectable living were limited. Even though she cringed at the idea of pretending to be her employer's daughter at the ball, she knew that if she didn't execute this task, Mr. Beaumont would be true to his word and throw her out. She also knew that his daughter could do little to stop it, especially since she was the one who created this ridiculous situation in the first place by sneaking off without a word.

His eyes narrowed at her powdered skin, disguising her olive complexion, and pile of powdered hair. "Straighten your wig. One glimpse of your black hair and the facade is shattered. You're wearing heeled shoes, I hope?"

She nodded. *It's only a little fib. Who will it hurt?* With one hand steadying her wig, Aria gathered her skirts in the other and descended the carriage, stepping into Mildred Beaumont's identity as she crossed the threshold of the governor's mansion. The dark-skinned butler at the door, dressed in Revolutionary-era breeches, coat, and tricornered hat, bowed and removed her cloak. She gave him a small smile of thanks before falling into step behind Mr. Beaumont. At her employer's pointed stare, she realized her blunder and awkwardly threaded her arm through his as if they were truly father and daughter.

Her breath caught at the sight of the masked ladies and gentlemen on the ballroom floor, whirling in the light of hundreds of candles flickering in the chandeliers, candelabras, and sconces. Some of the gentlemen around her wore pirate trappings, animal heads, and bandit costumes, but most of them merely wore masks. *Probably just to appease their wives,* she surmised by the sullen press of their lips. There were a few women in bold Regency gowns, some in Civil War attire, and far too many Marie Antoinette costumes roaming about. She felt a giggle rise within, knowing how furious Mildred would be to know her costly "unique" costume was donned by at least nine other women. Her exquisite gown had become positively average.

Mr. Beaumont snatched an appetizer from the silver tray of a passing maskless footman who was dressed in the same breeches attire as the butler to distinguish himself from the guests. She reached for a miniature crab cake, but Mr. Beaumont squeezed her elbow.

"Too smelly," he muttered under his breath as she reluctantly drew back her hand. "Smile brightly and be engaging."

He pulled her toward a group and introduced her to diplomat after senator after representative, making her head dance. She bravely made small talk until her stomach rumbled. Her eyes grew wide as she discreetly pushed a hand against her corset stays and silently begged for the tête-à-tête to end when her stomach rumbled again. Blushing, she quietly excused herself to find the banquet table.

She scanned the room for food but, feeling eyes upon her, turned to see the distinct flash of white-blond hair belonging to Mildred's former beau, Joel Branson, who was staring at her from across the room with his soon-to-be fiancée draped over his arm and the banquet room behind them. Her heart stopped as recognition lit his eyes. She touched the corner of her mask. *Millie must've told him what her gown looked like before he broke their relationship off to be with Fiona,* she thought as he leaned down and whispered into Fiona's ear. Sensing he was about to seek her out, Aria settled for an Italian pastry from one of the dessert tables. Then, before he could make his way through the ballroom, she ducked into an unlit hallway for a bit of privacy. *No wonder Millie decided to escape tonight if she knew that horrid man would be here.* She stepped into the dark recesses of the hallway and stole a bite of cannoli.

Byron Roderick hated the politics behind attending a masquerade ball, but as the son of an influential state senator, he smiled and supported his father as expected. After all, everyone knew he was being groomed for the office himself.

"Don't you think so, Mr. Roderick?" the overeager mother questioned.

"Uh, yes," he replied as he tugged the coat of his costume, hoping his response was the correct answer to the question he hadn't heard. He had attempted to be Paul Revere, but to his amusement, he matched the servants, which was why he'd discarded his mask and put on his wire-rimmed spectacles so he could at least be recognized. But now with the mothers circling him with their single daughters in tow, he began to wish he had left it in place.

Before the current predator could ask yet another question, he excused himself and headed for the dark hallway. *I'll probably pay for that later.* He sighed, rubbing his hands over his eyes as he stepped on something soft and heard a muffled squeal. Startled, he looked down into a pair of dark eyes behind an elaborate Venetian mask. The petite lady, dressed in a cloud of royal blue, stumbled away from his boot and back into a column.

"I'm so sorry, miss!" He grabbed her by the elbows to steady her, spying a half-eaten cannoli in her hand.

"No, it's my fault." She held her hand over her mouth as she talked around a mouthful of pastry, quickly swallowing. "How could you expect to see me in such a dark space?"

"Were you hiding from someone too?" he asked, adjusting his glasses.

Laughing, she nodded and lifted up her dessert plate. "I haven't had a bite to eat all evening. I was trying to consume this before my, uh, father finds that last politician, or future politician, he wants me to meet. A Mr. Byron Roderick. Have you met him? He's probably just another overweight, red-faced man twenty years my senior." She glanced at the pastry, obviously wishing to finish the treat.

"Ah, I believe I might know whom you are speaking of." He struggled to swallow back his amusement at her candor as he motioned for her to continue eating. "Tell me, what would you rather be doing on a night like this?"

She leaned forward in a conspiratorial whisper. "Honestly? I'd like to finish my book tonight, but my father insisted I go husband hunting instead."

Biting back his laughter at this refreshing young lady, Byron smiled, and with a flourished bow, introduced himself as she took another mouthful.

Aria choked on her pastry, and the man dressed in the servant's costume gently slapped her on the back. "I am so sorry," she croaked into her napkin. "I thought you were one of the staff as you weren't wearing a mask! I never would have spoken so outrageously if I thought—"

He laughed, taking her empty plate and setting it aside on a vacant chair. "But then I wouldn't have gotten to know you quite so well, now would I, Miss. . . ?"

"Beaumont." She dipped into a curtsy. "Millie, I mean, Mildred Beaumont," she added in a fuller southern lilt, as Millie might. *How do I fix this? If Mr. Beaumont finds out I've insulted the very man he wishes Millie to marry, he will relieve me of my position.* "So, who were you attempting to run away from?" She took in his towering height, broad shoulders, and chestnut hair and gave him what she hoped was a captivating smile.

"A horde of mothers and their single daughters." He peeked around the column. "But as they seem to be occupied at present, it may be safe to reappear." He turned back to her, extending his hand. "Miss Beaumont, would you do this lawyer the honor of being his partner for the next dance even if he isn't a politician twenty years your senior?"

Feeling her cheeks burn, she let out a shaky laugh as she surrendered her hand to him and then realized that the next dance was still a few minutes away from beginning. Yet, he didn't seem to mind having her hand threaded through his arm.

"So, tell me. What do you like to read when you're not husband hunting?"

She stumbled to answer as Millie would. All she could remember Millie reading was the latest fashion magazines, but as that hardly seemed like a good enough answer to incline his interest to calling, she answered truthfully as herself. "Charles Dickens. My favorite of his works is *Little Dorrit*."

Mr. Roderick's brows rose, and he began another line of questioning that sent her scrambling for Millie-approved answers when the music concluded. *Thank goodness the dance is starting.* She held back a sigh, grateful to be free from fibbing for the moment. Over the next few minutes, she learned that he was an excellent dance partner, and as she dearly loved a waltz but rarely had the opportunity to dance, she allowed herself to get lost in the dips of the violins as he guided her about the room and she hummed along with the music.

"You sing," he stated rather than asked.

She nodded. "My mother is quite accomplished and taught me as a small child."

"Is Mrs. Beaumont with you this evening?"

Realizing her blunder a little too late, she cringed. "I mean *was* accomplished. She still seems so near," she lied, thinking how her perfectly healthy mother was living with their large family in the French Quarter where her father worked as a clerk.

"I'm so sorry to hear that," he replied, mistaking her expression for grief.

Aria dipped her head as she imagined Mildred might. "Thank you."

"May I cut in?"

Aria snapped her head up to find her gaze met by Joel Branson's.

Mr. Roderick bowed to her, giving her an apologetic smile as Joel stepped in, placing his hand about her waist. "You've become quite slim," he commented.

Aria's eyes flared at the inappropriate comment, but she knew if she answered, he would guess her secret.

"I suppose you're still angry with me for breaking things off with you and forming an attachment with Fiona?"

Not daring to reply, she shook her head.

"Then why have you been avoiding me?" Joel whispered. "I know you want me. You know I only started courting Fiona to show your father I was serious about the dowry's importance. I still love you. All you have to do is convince your father to give you a larger dowry, enough to tempt me away from Fiona's fortune."

She kept her gaze averted as anger rippled through her veins. *Is this what poor Millie had to endure? She said Joel was manipulative, but to use her love for him as a means to obtain wealth? Despicable.*

"Do you really want to take a chance with one of these ancient bachelors or widowers when you know I would adore you as my wife?" He twirled her in his arms as the final notes played. "You have one month before I ask for Fiona's hand. Think carefully, my dear," he whispered as he bowed and left her on the floor, alone.

Mr. Roderick returned to her side, concerned lines etched between his eyes as he escorted her off the floor. "I'm sorry. If I had known you didn't wish to dance with him, I wouldn't have allowed him to cut in."

She shook her head and tried to return a smile to her face. "I didn't know I had let my feelings show so. I was a little uncomfortable, yes, but thankfully it was only for a moment." *Flirt with him.* She turned a sparkling smile up to him. "And now I'm back with you and perfectly content."

He stopped by the refreshment table. Handing her a glass of lemonade, he said, "This may be a bit presumptuous, but I would love to see you again. Would you allow me to call on you tomorrow?"

Her heart skipped a beat at the thought of spending more time with him, but then sank as she realized he wouldn't actually be calling on *her*. Mr. Roderick would be seeing Millie, the youngest daughter of a politician. . .someone of status, not a poor immigrant with weak ties to Italian royalty. She took a quick sip and gave him a bold wink. "As long as it doesn't interfere with my reading, that would be marvelous."

Chapter 2

At breakfast the next morning, Mildred thrust back her chair and stood with such force it nearly toppled over. "I shouldn't be surprised anymore at the lengths you will go to protect your career, Daddy, but"—she turned her fiery gaze on Aria—"I cannot believe *you* would go along with his scheming."

Ignoring her protests, Mr. Beaumont picked up his newspaper and snapped it open. "Nonetheless, I expect you to receive Mr. Roderick this morning and to be not only cordial, but *interested*. And, as I said, Miss St. Angelo had no choice in the matter."

"One *always* has a choice." Mildred threw down her napkin and stormed out of the room in a flurry of skirts.

Mr. Beaumont looked up from his paper to Aria and raised his brows. "Well, what are you waiting for? Go to her."

With a sigh, Aria set aside her nearly untouched breakfast and, with a rumbling stomach, followed her charge to the parlor. Mildred sat with her feet curled under her, viciously flipping through the latest edition of *Harper's Bazaar*.

"Millie," Aria began softly, crossing the room and touching a hand to Millie's puffed sleeve, "I'm sorry I had to pretend to be you last night, but my position was in jeopardy if I refused your father." She cracked a smile. "And I have to admit that I did think that if you had thought of this plan instead of your father, you would've done it in an instant."

Millie set aside her magazine and rubbed her face, a soft laugh bubbling from her lips. "You are quite right." She dropped her hands and met Aria's gaze. "I'm sorry I was cross when I should be thanking you for stepping into my shoes and sparing me from being humiliated." She bit her lip and asked quietly, "Did you see him?"

Aria fidgeted with her deep cuffs of ivory lace. "He cut in while I was dancing with Mr. Roderick and tried to speak with me, or rather you, on a delicate matter."

"He did?" Hope filled her voice as she swept her feet off the settee. She tossed her long, flowing caftan behind her velvet skirts and made her way to the window in true Mildred theatrical fashion. "Did he apologize? Is he releasing Fiona from their understanding?"

Aria's fingers traced the simple coral beads around her neck, and she slowly shook her head. "He spoke to me about your dowry. He acted as if that was the only impediment."

"It is." Millie's shoulders drooped with her voice. "Daddy refused to give him a dime more. If only Joel had more connections, Daddy wouldn't blink at a larger amount. When my sisters were courted by key politicians, Daddy offered them more. He didn't even wait to be asked, Aria. And now that I am asking, he refuses."

"If money is all that is keeping you two apart, you're lucky to be rid of him," she replied softly, stroking Millie's arm.

Millie pressed her palm to her chest. "My head realizes this, but my heart. . .loves him."

Aria draped her arm about her friend's shoulders. "They say that time helps heal all wounds."

"We are nearing twenty-two years of age and are practically old maids! We don't have time for wounds to heal. Besides, this is a wound that need not be if only Daddy would yield and increase my dowry by a few thousand dollars." Her brows furrowed as she planted her hands on her hips. "If Mother were here, she would talk some reason into him."

"I know, but another way to heal quickly is by meeting a very handsome man. When you see Mr. Roderick today, you will forget all about Joel Branson," Aria said, grinning.

"Handsome?" A hint of a smile appeared on Millie's pouting lips. "What kind of man is he? Please tell me he is not stiff and dull like every other suitor Daddy has brought to my door."

"Far from it. You're fortunate to have such a viable option in the place of Mr. Branson. I quite enjoyed my conversation with Mr. Roderick, who seems kindhearted and enjoys a laugh." She smiled, thinking of the merriment she'd spotted in the corners of his mouth. *If only he were calling on me instead of you.* Her smile froze. She could not afford such thoughts. "Now, I know you don't care much for spectacles on a man, but on him. . ." Aria's voice drifted off as she lost herself in the dream of last night. *Stop it! He's meant for Millie.*

"He wears spectacles?" Millie wrinkled her nose.

"Honestly, I think they only add to his handsomeness," she murmured as she heard gravel crunching under wheels. She peeked through the curtain to see Mr. Roderick step down from the carriage, and her heart picked up speed with every stride he took toward the front door.

"Hello? Aria, I asked you what we should talk about." Millie tapped her on the shoulder, breaking her reverie.

The butler appeared at the door and, bowing, announced, "Mr. Byron Roderick to see you, Miss Beaumont."

"*Already?*" Millie nearly squeaked.

"Show him to the parlor and offer him some refreshments, Newton," Aria instructed. She turned to pat down Millie's golden hair, pulling a single curl over her shoulder.

Millie inhaled through her teeth with a moan. "Why didn't you wake me sooner this morning to prepare me? How am I to keep up the charade if you haven't even told me what you two spoke about? He will know that I'm not the masked lady from last night. Quick, give me a topic!"

"Books," Aria replied, straightening Millie's brooch.

"Well, that is no help whatsoever." She rolled her eyes and peered into the looking glass above the mantel, giving her cheeks a generous pinch.

"I'm sorry to rush away, but I better take my leave of you for fear he may recognize me," Aria said as she cracked open the door and glanced down the hallway to ensure she wouldn't be spotted.

"Oh no you don't." Millie whirled to face Aria. "You cannot give me little to no notice that I have a caller and then run off moments before he appears. How could you throw me to the wolves like that?"

"Mr. Roderick is hardly a wolf. Mr. Beaumont informed me last night that while the memory of me is fresh in Mr. Roderick's mind, he must only see and hear you on his first call. Tomorrow he can see me after you have convinced him that it was you he met last night and not me."

"But the topics!" Millie grasped her by the arm, halting her flight. "What books?"

"You'll be fine. Just speak of the classics and ask him about his work."

"His work? You know how much I hate the political realm," she muttered.

"He is a lawyer," Aria returned, slipping into the hallway.

"See?" Millie hissed after her. "I didn't even know that! This mission is doomed. Please don't leave me," she begged.

"I'm sorry. You know I have to listen to your father." Aria gave her a smile of encouragement. "Besides, you've always wanted to be an actress, so pretend you are on the stage and give the performance of your life."

Mildred exhaled and dropped her shoulders. "I suppose that any great actress must be ready to perform even if she has no lines to read from."

"That's the spirit." Aria grinned and quietly retrieved her shawl. She made her way out to the back gardens, hoping the blossoms would keep her mind preoccupied.

She could not allow herself to think of his hazel eyes, or to remember how it felt to dance in his arms. Plucking an orange-and-yellow lantana, she inhaled its sweet scent and thought of how refreshing it had been conversing with Mr. Roderick as an equal. She tucked the flower into her low coiffure and sighed, reaching for a pink camellia. It had been so long since someone from Millie's set had treated her as anything other than a servant. As a lady's companion, she had a foot in both worlds. She wasn't part of the downstairs staff, and yet she wasn't considered a member of the family. She was paid to be a friend and chaperone.

Hearing voices, she paused in gathering her bouquet to silence the crunch of the leaves underfoot and listened. She gazed through the evergreen hedge that led to the side garden and found Mr. Roderick conversing with Mildred on one of the benches. The sunlight fell on Mildred's locks, bathing her in a heavenly glow, but judging from the look on his face and the angle of his brows, she felt Byron Roderick appeared less animated than he'd been with her last night. *I wonder if he can tell that Millie isn't me? I was so covered in that wig, mask, and powder that it speaks of his character that he should ask to call on a woman who may have been hiding her flaws.* She prayed he would not suspect Millie.

Watching them converse, she again found herself wishing she could be in Millie's pretty shoes as she was last night, but at the thought of her large family who would go without if she lost her position, she again shook her head, attempting to dispel any thought of Byron. *He must be Mr. Roderick to me.* Though they had only met last night, she felt herself inexplicably drawn to him. She would not risk the stability of her family or her brother's future tuition funds for the sake of one man's handsome eyes.

Her stomach flipped as he bent down to bid Millie farewell and kissed her on the hand, an action that disturbed Aria more than it should. She turned away, unable to witness him falling in love with her pretty charge. Aria slowly yanked away the petals from a camellia as she ambled back inside and away from the couple. Depositing half of the bouquet in a large vase, she kept the rest for arranging in Mildred's hair. Turning the corner of the hallway, she collided into a broad chest, knocking her flowers to the floor.

Hands reached out to steady her shoulders, and she found herself once again face-to-face with Byron Roderick. She dropped her gaze, praying he would not recognize her. "I am so sorry, sir," she mumbled, stepping away from his touch as she bent to retrieve her flowers.

He beat her to them and handed the colorful bunch back to her and straightened his hat. "The fault is mine," he assured her. "Are you quite well?"

She nodded and risked a glance through her lashes up at him as she accepted the flowers and met his eyes, her heart hammering. "Please excuse me," she whispered and darted upstairs. He had not recognized her.

Byron tugged his hat over his eyes and hunched his shoulders against the autumn chill as he marched back to his law practice. Something wasn't right about Mildred Beaumont. The spark he witnessed in her last night no longer lit her dark eyes, which seemed less radiant in the daylight. He shook his head at the uncharitable thought. *It was most likely the candlelight that enchanted me rather than her eyes. That and the fact she was the only woman who didn't throw herself into my arms all night.* He had secured another call with her for the following afternoon, but if it went anything like today, he wasn't sure if he would continue his pursuit.

He let himself in through the side door, nodding to his associates as he made his way to the back of the office to his private room. *She was probably nervous. . .but last night, she was so full of confidence and genuineness. Today, she seemed like she was reading from a script and was afraid of reading a line incorrectly.*

Byron shrugged out of his coat, sank down at his desk, and tried to focus on the day's work. He shifted through a handful of files of potential clients seeking legal representation, eager to select his next couple of cases. His glance fell on a pro bono case of a young family of Irish immigrants, and he flipped through the file.

His father didn't approve of this less glamorous aspect of his work, but Byron relished helping the working man, even if it didn't pay as well as the gentlemen or parvenu cases brought to the law firm. Almost every Sunday over dinner, the elder Mr. Roderick tried to convince Byron that he could do so much more for the people in the political realm, but Byron loved the hands-on work of being a guardian angel to someone who felt that all hope was lost. He felt it was his calling to come to the aid of the less fortunate ones in society: the widows, the orphans, the poor, and those without a voice. One day, he hoped to have his own practice and dedicate more of his cases to the lower class. Until then, he could not allow this Irish family to be taken advantage of by those who knew better. Adjusting his glasses, he got to work.

Chapter 3

Aria stayed a few paces behind the couple and remained silent. Mr. Beaumont strictly forbade her from getting too involved, for he didn't want her to become a distraction. She was accompanying Millie and Mr. Roderick on their walk by the river to chaperone only. After spending the entire morning instructing Millie on how to keep Mr. Roderick's interest, she couldn't help but smile with approval as Millie gave all the proper responses. Yet Aria sensed the theatricality behind them and hoped Mr. Roderick didn't think her charge insincere. It would take a lot more than a handsome face to make Millie forget Joel Branson.

She shifted her reticule to the other arm. The weight of the new novel she had bought for her little brother called to her, but she knew it would be awhile before they reached the coffeehouse and she could finally indulge in the book. Mildred was too fond of the river walk to hurry. To take her mind off her anticipation of reading Arthur Conan Doyle's book, Aria brought her attention back to the couple ahead of her.

Mr. Roderick commented on Millie's singing ability, and Millie gave a nervous laugh. She looked over her shoulder at Aria, her widening eyes silently begging for help.

"I would love to hear you sing sometime, Miss Beaumont," he continued.

Aria threaded her arm through Millie's, rescuing her. "Miss Beaumont shouldn't be singing anytime soon." She turned her gaze to her friend. "I'm sure your father wishes you to rest your voice after your cold last week," she added, which wasn't entirely a falsehood.

Millie's smile brightened. "Oh yes, he told me he wants me to sing at Mrs. Foster's musicale in two weeks and wishes for me to sound my best."

"He did?" Aria's jaw dropped. *What is he thinking?*

Mildred gave her a furtive wink. "Yes! Of course he did."

Aria hid her grimace behind a gritted smile. *Why are you adding to the lie?* Mildred could carry a tune, but she was no songbird, and no amount of practicing would change that in two short weeks. "Forgive me. How could I have forgotten when I've heard you practice your piece about a dozen times." *A dozen times in two years.*

Mr. Roderick's gaze met hers, and she quickly broke their connection before he could recognize her. "Oh! I see that taffy cart you like so much, Miss Beaumont. I'll get us some chocolate taffy sticks." She hurried away so not to bring any more attention to herself than necessary.

Out of the corner of his eye, Byron noticed Miss St. Angelo watching him and Miss Beaumont from three tables down. She sat near the front of the coffeehouse, appearing to enjoy her steaming café au lait and vanilla crème brûlée as she silently giggled into the pages of her novel whenever Mildred came up for air in her long-winded narratives, allowing him a rare moment to inject a sentence before she began her endless chatter again.

"Why, there's Fanny Branson!" Mildred slipped from her chair. "If you'll excuse me for one moment, I need to speak with her."

Byron rose, dropping his napkin in his haste, but she was already halfway across the room before he could reply.

Miss St. Angelo caught her arm in passing, whispering, "Are you sure that is wise?"

"Of course." Miss Beaumont scowled. "I'll return in a minute."

Byron stifled a sigh of relief for a moment's respite and turned his attention to Miss Beaumont's companion, who, returning to her novel, took a generous spoonful of her vanilla custard. He stepped over to her table and tilting his head, read the spine. "*The Adventures of Sherlock Holmes*, eh?"

She lurched, dropping her spoon into her lap. "Blast," she murmured, and wiped her napkin over the stain on her gray frock.

"I'm sorry I startled you." Heat suffused Byron's face as he stood, helpless to repair the situation.

She waved a dismissive hand. "It matters not. No one will notice, and I shall work the stain away when we return."

His gaze fell on the considerable smear on her skirt, and remorse smote him. "So." He cleared his throat and glanced over toward Miss Beaumont, who was deep into her conversation with Miss Branson. "You enjoy mysteries?"

She smiled, setting her book on the table. "Not usually, but I know that if I gift this to my younger brother, my mama will ask me about its content to ensure that it is proper and I can't rightly say it is when I haven't read it." She tapped the cover. "My hope is that my brother will take to reading for his adventures again rather than finding mischief with his questionable friends. He's been longing to attend Louisiana State University since he was a small boy, but now I fear his rough companions will discourage him from seeking higher education." She shook her head and smiled at him as she rose. "I'm sorry. I'm rambling." She emitted a soft laugh. "I should see if Miss Beaumont needs me. So, if you'll excuse me. . ."

Her laugh rippled in his mind. He looked from her to Miss Beaumont and then back to Miss St. Angelo. An uncomfortable lump formed in his chest. *Why does the companion remind me more of the masked lady than Miss Beaumont does?* Byron studied the curve of Miss Beaumont's lips and the way she carried herself. The longer he stared at her, the more he came to suspect that something was amiss. *Why would Miss St. Angelo pretend to be Miss Beaumont?* But, looking at Miss St. Angelo's olive complexion, he shook his head, dispelling the foolish thought.

Aria perched on the edge of Millie's four-poster bed as the maid brushed Millie's hair, readying her for bed. "So, after spending the afternoon with Mr. Roderick, what do you think?"

"That's all for tonight, Louise." Millie waved the maid off and set to plaiting her own hair. When Louise closed the door behind her, Millie sighed. "I'd rather not risk Louise repeating our conversation to Daddy. I think Roderick is nice enough, but really, Aria, how could you think that he could ever compare to Joel Branson?"

Because Byron Roderick is twice the man Branson will ever become, not to mention he is kind and considerate. Aria bit back her reply. "I thought you would find him handsome and his company enjoyable."

"I didn't say he wasn't handsome." Millie finished her braid with a red silk ribbon to match her dressing robe. "And while he's not your typical politician's son, I found him quite lackluster. I as much as told Fanny Branson that so she would relay it to her brother, but the girl is practically voting for Fiona." She shook her head and tossed her braid over her shoulder, scowling. "I thought we were friends."

Aria rolled her eyes and laughed. "I can't believe you told her that! Did you forget I was merely yards away during your outing? You barely allowed the poor man to get a word in edgewise. How could you possibly think Mr.

Roderick is boring if he didn't even get the chance to speak?"

Millie smirked. "Well, maybe I did monopolize the conversation. But I think you should know that I only plan to let him court me until I can figure out how to convince Daddy to increase my dowry to make a marriage with Joel possible."

Aria's heart lurched. *Mr. Roderick doesn't deserve to be anyone's second choice.* "And if your father doesn't concede, will you keep stringing Mr. Roderick along?"

With a dramatic sigh, Millie flopped onto the bed, jostling Aria. "If I can't have Joel Branson for my husband, then I suppose Mr. Roderick will have to do."

Chapter 4

With her train ticket tucked in her reticule, Aria boarded the train for New Orleans, ready for a break from Millie's courtship. While Millie allowed Mr. Roderick to keep calling and seemed to enjoy his company, Aria knew Millie's heart wasn't in it. She still hoped against all to return to Mr. Branson's arms. After a painful two weeks of watching Mr. Roderick court Millie, Aria was more than grateful when Millie announced she was spending the weekend with a friend from school and that Aria could have a couple of days off to visit her family in New Orleans if she wished.

And she did wish it, for she had begun to long for the moments when Mr. Roderick would inevitably turn to her during his calls for their daily, brief conversations when Millie grew distracted. She drank in her stolen moments with him, knowing he would never belong to her, but with each passing week, she grew more and more tempted to break her silence. Yet she feared if she did indeed speak the truth about the night they met, she would not only lose her position but also Byron's friendship for her deception. Again and again, she resigned herself to being Millie's shadow. Even if Byron could forgive her for masquerading as Millie, he would most certainly never consider Aria for his wife when he could have the American heiress with all the political privileges that would come with such a union. Aria's heritage would bring him nothing but strife. She sighed. A little distance would do her good.

With her carpetbag tucked by her feet, Aria settled back into the tufted seats of the train, eager to see her family, whom she missed terribly. It had been far too long, and after an exhausting week of running after Millie and her endless trips to the shops and her portrait-sitting with the famous photographer Andrew Lytle, Aria looked forward to her book, or rather Millie's book. Mr. Roderick had given Millie a copy of a classic with plans to discuss it with her at a later date, but Millie, having no interest in *The Scarlet Letter*, gave the book to Aria to study and to tell her about it later.

Aria was deep into the pages of her book and sucking on a hard candy when she heard a throat clearing above her. Expecting the conductor, she reluctantly paused, marked her place in her book with a candy wrapper, and dug around her reticule for her ticket before looking up. She snapped her book shut and gasped, nearly choking on her sweet. "Mr. Roderick! What are you doing here?" She worked the question around the lump of candy, immediately wishing she hadn't indulged in a piece from the little bag she had brought for her brother and sisters. *How do I get rid of this?* she thought frantically, as she was still a good twenty minutes from it dissolving. *Why am I always eating when he catches me unawares?*

"I have business in New Orleans." His smile widened. "Are you visiting your family?"

"Why, yes." She blinked, surprised that he remembered. "But what are you doing back here? Why aren't you in first class?"

"I always travel coach when alone. There's no need for me to take first."

"No need?" *If I had the option, I would always take first.* Forgetting herself, she almost chuckled, but the candy in her mouth stopped any expression of mirth. *Time for desperate measures.* Thinking quickly, she knocked her book from her lap. When he bent down to retrieve it as she knew he would, she quickly disposed of the candy into her handkerchief and stuffed it behind her. Smiling up at him, she uttered her thanks when he returned her book. "Why, how clumsy of me. *Grazie.*"

His hazel eyes sparked at her Italian, and she blushed. She was usually so careful not to slip into the comfortable language while away from home, but he unnerved her in the best of ways.

Spying the title, his brows rose. "*The Scarlet Letter?* Did Miss Beaumont finish it already?"

Not wanting to lie, Aria dusted the book cover and slowly replied, "No. Miss Beaumont graciously allowed me to take it with me to read. We are going to discuss its contents at great length later." *There, that wasn't a lie.*

"Are you enjoying it as much as *Sherlock?*" he asked, his eyes shining behind his polished glasses.

She gestured to the seat across from her. "Well, if you aren't traveling with anyone, why don't you take a seat and I'll tell you." She knew she probably shouldn't offer, but at this point in their conversation, it seemed rather rude not to invite him to sit down. Although she had to admit, it wasn't just courtesy that prompted her to offer him the empty seat.

Aria was instantly drawn into their conversation, and when the conductor announced they were pulling into New Orleans Union Station, she looked out the window and was shocked to find herself in the city already. She reluctantly packed the book into her satchel and rose to leave, but Byron immediately relieved her of her burden and gestured for her to precede him off the train.

He walked with her outside and paused, checking his pocket watch before clicking it shut as if he too was surprised at how fast their journey seemed. "Is anyone meeting you?" he asked, looking up and down the platform.

A rare breeze cooled her hot cheeks from the stifling train car and their riveting conversation. "No, I never let them know when I'm coming, as Millie almost never plans ahead," she explained as they descended the platform steps to the busy street.

"Oh, well, I'll hail a carriage for you then." He started to raise his arm.

She quickly reached out and grasped his sleeve before he signaled a driver. "Please don't concern yourself with a carriage for me. I'm not far from my parents' home. It's only thirty minutes on foot and I could use the walk. Miss Beaumont usually isn't one for long walks, so I quite enjoy taking in the city on foot."

"Then you must allow me to see you home." He extended his arm to her. "I can't have you wandering off on your own."

Mr. Beaumont would be livid if we were seen together. "It's really not necessary," she reassured him. "I know you have a meeting soon, and I do this often enough and have never had any trouble. You seem to forget that I grew up here."

"There is no way around it, Miss St. Angelo. If you do not take a carriage, then I will escort you. What if something happens to you and Miss Beaumont discovers I was here and allowed you to leave unattended?" He offered Aria his arm again and grinned. "It is futile to argue. I'm a lawyer, you know, and I will win."

Aria's heart stopped at the sight of his smile. *This is getting quite out of control. If someone saw us walking arm in arm in the city and word got back to Mr. Beaumont, I could very easily lose my position.* But again, not wishing to seem rude, she slowly nodded and accepted his arm. *I suppose I could always just tell Mr. Beaumont the truth and pray that he believes me.*

While it may have been a short stroll from the station to the Commercial Hotel where he was staying, the walk to her family's apartment across from

Jackson Square was nearly a half hour's walk away, and Byron was once again thankful he accompanied Aria to keep her from harm's way. Even though she claimed it was safe, New Orleans was no place for a pretty woman to walk about unescorted. He tried to remember Mildred's smile and comely face, yet he kept losing her features in Aria's smile that illuminated her dark eyes as well as her lovely face.

Cutting through the square and around the Andrew Jackson equestrian statue, Aria paused at St. Ann Street in front of a four-story redbrick building with French doors lining the first floor and wrought-iron lace balconies wrapping the second and third floors. Judging from the exterior, it had once been a grand apartment building but had fallen into disrepair.

"Well, we have arrived." Her smile looked forced as she added, "I would ask you up to offer you a refreshment, but I know you have to return to the hotel to freshen up before you meet with your client."

Catching the hint that she did not wish for him to continue with her, he bowed and was about to offer his goodbye when two little girls squealed as they barreled into Aria and threw their gangly arms around her waist.

"Aria! You're home!" they shouted.

He watched as Aria's enthusiasm filled her countenance. No longer was she the proper lady's companion. She was a sister who missed her family. Kissing each of them atop their dark brown hair, she exclaimed how they were growing prettier by the day.

When they turned their curious gazes to him, Aria straightened, and with a hand on each of their shoulders, she said, "Mr. Roderick, allow me to introduce you to my sisters Gemma and Teodora."

Byron grinned at the miniature Arias and bowed, sending the girls into a fit of giggles to which Aria rolled her eyes and rubbed her brows with her thumb and forefinger. "It is an honor to meet you two ladies."

Teodora dipped into a wobbly curtsy while Gemma popped her thumb out of her mouth and asked, "Are you our sister's beau?"

Aria winced and dipped her chin as she chided them. "What a question to ask. Of course not. He is courting the lady I work for, Miss Beaumont. We happened by each other on the train from Baton Rouge."

Byron hid his smile behind his hand, laughing inside at her chagrin, when a soft voice called her name. Turning, he saw two more young ladies crossing the street with baskets loaded with laundry balanced against their hips.

"What are you doing here? Did Mr. Beaumont finally convince Millie to let you go?" the taller of the two teased, giving Aria a quick embrace before they both examined him. "And who is this gentleman? Have you finally brought home a caller?"

"Bianca, please." Aria shushed her, and ignoring her questions, she continued, "Mr. Roderick, please excuse my sisters. This is Miss Bianca and"— she turned and gestured to the shorter sister—"Miss Caterina St. Angelo."

Before he could even tip his hat, Bianca asked him, "Won't you come up and join us for dinner? Mama is making meatballs and spaghetti."

"He is busy, I'm sure," Aria interjected, looking up at him when the upstairs window opened and a heavyset woman leaned out. "Aria, don't keep your guest standing outside. Bring him up!"

Aria returned her wave and turned to him with eyes sparkling with mirth as a giggle escaped her lips. "I'm so glad that practically the whole family is here to greet you. I hope you aren't too overwhelmed."

"*Practically* the whole family? How many more of you are there?" He laughed.

"Well, there's still Palo, my brother, and my papa, and, of course, my aunts and uncles and their children, but they live one apartment down from ours. I know you are busy, so please don't feel like you have to stay."

Not wanting to intrude, he tipped his hat to her. "Please tell your mother that I am honored for her invitation, but business keeps me from having the privilege of dining with you all tonight."

She reached for her reticule. "Thank you for accompanying me. It made the time pass quite quickly."

"And for me as well," he admitted with a smile, surrendering the bag to her. Bowing, he left Aria to the endearing chatter of her sisters, thinking how adored she was by her family. . .and by him. He sighed. *Lord, help me to honor my word to my father, for my heart seems to be leaving my head behind for Miss St. Angelo and her enchanting eyes.*

Chapter 5

until I've
never had a

The next morning Byron stopped by the bustling French market on his way back from seeing his clients. He bent down and selected a ripe pear from one of the vendor's crates. Squeezing it to test its tenderness, he decided to purchase a couple and have them for breakfast when he spotted Aria in a powder-blue gown with her sister Bianca near a vegetable vendor, their hands waving wildly as their Italian escalated. While he didn't understand their words, he became worried as their tones grew more and more hostile. Paying the vendor, he tucked the pears into his pocket and wove through the crowded stalls to Aria's side. "Is there a problem here?"

At his voice, Aria jumped and immediately dropped her hands. "Byron!" She stumbled to correct herself. "I mean, Mr. Roderick."

His heart skipped at the sound of his Christian name on her lips. "Is everything all right?" he asked again.

She scowled at the vendor and said something in Italian to him in a reproachful tone, wagging her finger at him before turning to Byron. "It will be," she said with a smile. "Our vendor was trying to charge us *twice* the usual amount. He says figs are in high demand this weekend." With her hands planted on her hips, she looked over her shoulder at the vendor and raised her voice. "Does he think we can be taken advantage of so easily?"

"You aren't the only vendor here," Bianca added to the man, nodding in agreement. "Aria, I'm going across the market to finish Mama's list. Come find me if you see a *reasonable* price for figs, but can you get the pecans?"

Aria nodded and marched over to the next stall.

Byron grinned. Gone was the timid companion. Being home brought a confidence to Aria's shoulders that he quite enjoyed. "So, figs. What are you preparing?"

"Fig cookies for the neighborhood children." She shifted her basket on her arm as she perused the vendors. "It's not much, but we enjoy baking them, and the children have come to look forward to late October because they know that's when Mama's fig cookies will be made."

Byron couldn't help smiling down at her. For a family who obviously struggled to make ends meet, he admired their generosity. He removed the basket from her arm, surprised at its weight. "That sounds delightful. I've never had a fig cookie."

She awarded him a small smile of her own and a nod of thanks. "Grazie. Maybe I can set a few aside for you. We are baking them this afternoon." She paused at a cart and popped a pecan sample into her mouth, nodding with approval. "I'll take two pounds of pecans," she said, counting out the amount as the vendor weighed the nuts. "So, tell me, what are you doing out so early?" She paid the man and set the sack of pecans in the basket.

He laughed, rubbing his eyes under his spectacles. "Well, it's been a long night."

"Long night? You haven't gone to sleep yet?" She lifted her brow.

"I was helping my clients build their case. Normally, I would have come to New Orleans to meet with a client sooner, but the office had me tied up with other cases. They didn't deem Mr. and Mrs. O'Neal's claim against their landlord worth the office's time, especially since they live so far away. Apparently, none of the law offices here would take their case, so they were forced to seek help in Baton Rouge. I was barely able to slip away." He lifted his hat and ran his fingers through his hair, self-conscious of his unkempt state. "Hence the late night. I was on my way back to the hotel to freshen up before I represent them in court."

"How kind of you," she replied as they approached Bianca, who was filling her basket with figs.

Byron shuffled, feeling uncomfortable. "Please don't think I told you that for praise. I was only trying to explain my disheveled appearance."

"You don't need to explain anything to me. Miss Beaumont knows you are a good man." Aria gave him a sweet smile. "And from the sound of it, your clients think so too."

Something about the corner of her lips seemed familiar. He shook himself as he joined their small party, walking back toward Jackson Square. *Why would her lips seem familiar?* To distract himself, he retrieved the fruit from his pocket and offered the ladies one of the pears. Bianca politely refused, but Aria accepted it.

"Pears are a weakness of mine." She turned her head to take a discreet bite of her fruit.

As you are a weakness of mine. The thought almost stopped him in his tracks. He was enjoying her company far more than Mildred's. *Maybe I am calling on the wrong lady at the Beaumont residence.* With a bow, he left the sisters at the door at the bottom of the Pontalba apartments and returned to the Commercial Hotel.

Aria's siblings were relentless in their teasing as she chopped up figs for the cookie filling. Just when she felt they were through and she could have a moment's peace, her mama finished sifting five pounds of flour into her large bowl and turned to her.

"So, who is this man whom we've seen for the past two days? Should we be inviting him to dinner?" Her thick brows rose, her meaning clear as she measured out the white sugar.

"As I told you before, he is Miss Beaumont's gentleman." Aria finished with the figs and began working on pitting the dates.

"He may be Miss Beaumont's young man, but only in Miss Beaumont's mind. He likes you, daughter. Why else would he escort you 'safely' home twice in two days?" Mama laughed, shaking her head. "In my day, a young man walking a girl home was a sign of courtship."

"It's not like that," Aria retorted, thumping her knife against the chopping block and sweeping the minced figs, dates, pecans, and raisins into the wooden bowl of spices, sugar, and water before stirring it into a fine paste.

"Mmm-hmm." Her mother humored her as she cracked open the eggs with one hand and kept the other splayed on her lower back, clearly not believing her.

Aria opened her mouth to protest, but the sound of someone pounding on the door intruded. She met her mother's worried gaze and, wiping her hands on her apron, followed her down the stairs. Family and friends would never pound. Peering around Mama's shoulder, Aria stifled a gasp at the sight of a police officer. Seeing a lawman at the Pontalba buildings was never a good sign.

The policeman scowled. "Is Palo St. Angelo here?"

"Why?" Anxiety clouded Mama's voice. "Is something wrong?"

"We received a complaint from one of the merchants that shortly after Palo and his friends left the man's shop, a gold watch was missing from the case where Palo had been lingering."

Mama blanched and reached back for Aria's hand. "Are you accusing my son of theft?"

The officer raised his brow as if it was obvious. "The merchant had a witness."

"That is ridiculous," Aria interjected. "Palo would never rob anyone." *But those boys he keeps company with might. . . .* She pressed her lips into a grim line.

"My son is a good boy. He wants to go to the university and wouldn't dream of—"

"I am only doing my job. I was told to bring in Palo St. Angelo, and I plan to follow through with my orders. Now, will you fetch him, or do I need to come inside and drag him out myself?"

"He's not here." Mama's voice shook.

The officer frowned. "You're only making this more difficult on yourself, ma'am."

"She's telling the truth. He's down the street at a friend's house." Aria rested a hand on her mother's shoulder, lending her strength. "I'll take you to him." She turned to her mother and whispered, "The officer is only doing his job. There has been some terrible mistake, but it will come out all right. Don't worry, Mama."

"You know that it won't turn out right. It never does for our sort. This will ruin Palo's chances for acceptance at the university, and you've been saving for so long." Mama whimpered into her hands, sinking down on the door-step. She lifted her apron and hid under the checkered cloth, as if seeking a moment's privacy to gather herself.

Aria knew, as did all the St. Angelo children, not to disturb her when the apron was lifted. She motioned for the officer to walk ahead of her down the sidewalk. "He is right around the corner, sir."

Chapter 6

Dressed in her ivory traveling gown, Aria stood in front of the daunting wooden gates with windows of iron bars. She'd promised Mama to take a tin of fig cookies to the jail before boarding her train to Baton Rouge. Straightening her shoulders, she reminded herself of her plan, swallowed, pulled the bell cord, and waited. She could hardly believe that her little brother could be accused of theft much less be held in New Orleans Parish Prison. She would have to be strong for Palo even if she felt like wallowing in despair.

The gates creaked open as if the jail did not receive many visitors or release many prisoners. She shivered, clutching her tin and the Doyle novel in one hand and her carpetbag in the other and prayed, *Lord, help him be pardoned quickly.*

The guard waved her inside and quickly closed the gate behind her, barring it from the inside with a large plank. "What's a comely little thing like you doing in a place like this?" His eyes roved over her, causing a blush to creep up her neck.

She lifted her head and, as if daring him to keep his vulgar gaze upon her a moment longer, narrowed her eyes and answered in what she hoped was a clear, strong voice. "I've come to visit my brother, Palo St. Angelo."

"Brought him something, did you?" He nodded to the pretty blue tin with flowers curving around the container. "Let's see it."

Hesitant, she handed him the tin, his calloused, dirty fingers brushing against her kid gloves and leaving smudges as she jerked her hands away from his touch. He popped open the tin Mama had so lovingly prepared. Aria knew it had been a sacrifice for Mama to come up with the extra ingredients to send Palo two dozen cookies to lift his spirits, but the guard seemed uninterested in the care that went into making the treat as he dug his filthy hand into the tin, breaking the crescent-shaped cookies and raking them between his fingers until they became like gooey bread crumbs.

Aria gasped. "Wh–what are you doing?" she sputtered.

Not even bothering to replace the lid, he took the one cookie left unharmed before shoving the tin back into her hands, spilling a few crumbs onto her immaculate gown. "I had to check it for a file or a knife. Don't really trust you Italians since one of your kind murdered Chief Hennessy two years ago."

A knife or a file? Was he jesting? They're just cookies, she wanted to scream. *And we don't particularly trust the people of New Orleans because of what happened afterward either.* She thought of the mob lynching that resulted in so many Italian men's deaths, but she knew to speak of such things wouldn't do any good. "You could have just cut them open instead of destroying two dozen cookies."

The guard's brows rose at her tart reply. "A cookie will taste the same if it looks like a crescent moon or mash." His yellow teeth flashed as he popped the cookie into his mouth and smacked his lips. "Now," he said, sucking his fingers one by one, "if you want to see your brother, I suggest you keep it civil. Leave your bags up front. You can get them on the way out."

Aria clamped her lips shut, wishing she wasn't at this man's mercy, but she swallowed her pride for her brother's sake and dipped her head.

Taking her bowed head as a sign of submission, he grinned and motioned for her to follow him. In the common room, he instructed her to take a seat at one of the tables while he fetched Palo. Perched on the edge of a grimy chair, Aria watched as an enormous cockroach crawled across the ceiling and dropped dangerously close to her. She stifled a scream as she lifted her skirts to keep the disgusting creature from scuttling up her clothes and shivered as it disappeared into a hole in the wall.

The dank, dark room reeked of hopelessness. Through her lashes, she discreetly observed two other couples with their heads bent together, visiting at the small tables dotting the room. Judging from the simple gold bands on the women's fingers and the men's soft, sorrowful gazes, she supposed they were married. *How awful to be separated from the one you love.*

Unwillingly, her thoughts drifted to Byron and his kindness in walking her home. She could only pray that he would answer her petition for help. It would be difficult to get a letter to him with Mr. Beaumont's watchful eye on the post. She would have to wait for a moment when Mildred left the room to ask him to represent Palo. Remembering how compassionate his voice became when he spoke of his pro bono work, she felt confident that he would come to her aid.

The moment Palo appeared in the doorway, all else faded away except the stricken, wide-eyed gaze on her brother's face. She longed to run to him, but with the guard standing by and scowling at her every move, she simply rose from her seat and waited as he shuffled toward her, encumbered by the heavy chains binding his ankles. Tears closed her throat at the sight of his filthy face and torn shirt pocket. *They are treating him like an animal. He is only fifteen, and he hasn't even been found guilty yet. Oh, why didn't I encourage him sooner to give up those rowdy boys? He wouldn't be here if I did. I knew they would get him into trouble.*

Instead of giving into her grief over his loss of innocence, she plastered on a brave smile. "Palo," she whispered, her voice cracking. *No, I must do better.* She embraced him and gave him a peck on the cheek, and for once, he did not shy away from her affections. "How are you doing?"

He shrugged, the chains on his ankles clanking as he took the seat opposite her at the table. "I don't think there's much hope for me. There are boys here that have been awaiting trial for six months." He looked up at her, his eyes brimming. "Most of them are pretty sick, and I doubt they will make it to see their day in court."

"But you didn't do anything wrong. Surely that counts for something?" She reached across the table and took his hand in hers.

"The merchant at Brooks and Brooks doesn't care who gets locked up as long as someone does, and we don't have money for a lawyer, unless you use the money you set aside for my college fund," he mumbled. His tone exuded misery as his Adam's apple bobbed.

"It won't come to that. That's partly why I came today, to bring you cookies and some reassurance," she said, lifting the tin. "I know someone who is a lawyer, and I will be seeing him in a couple of days, if not sooner. I'm sure he will be sympathetic to your situation and will see to it that your court date is moved up."

"That's an awful good connection for a lady's companion," he replied, a teasing lilt reappearing in his voice at the prospect of being represented. "It was that fellow who escorted you home yesterday, wasn't it?" He grinned at Aria's blush but didn't press the matter further and nodded toward the tin. "I'll take those cookies now."

She handed him the tin, but before she could explain its state, he popped it open. At the sight of the crumbled mess, his jaw tightened. He knew the sacrifice it cost to make so many cookies for one person. "No respect," he said through gritted teeth.

"It will still taste the same." She dimly echoed the guard's cruel words. "It will taste of love." She reached out and stroked his cheek, his patchy stubble pricking her fingers. "I wish I could stay longer, little brother, but I have to catch my train." She pressed the book into his hands. "Maybe this will help pass the time. I hope you will enjoy it as much as I did."

A small smile played at the corner of his lips. "Sherlock Holmes? That's quite the switch for you. Thanks. I'll be waiting for your lawyer beau to come for a visit."

Aria blushed again. "His name is Byron Roderick and he is Miss Beaumont's suitor." Despite her gentle chide, she couldn't help but smile at his ability to tease even when in prison.

"Will this Mr. Roderick be able to clear my record? I doubt Louisiana State University will accept a convict."

She squeezed his arm. "Your dream won't die in here. I won't let it."

The guard approached their table with his arms crossed. "Time's up."

The hope in Palo's eyes faded. Aria grabbed him in a fierce hug and bid him farewell. "*Ciao*, Palo. Remember the verse in Joshua. 'Have not I commanded thee? Be strong and of a good courage; be not afraid, neither be thou dismayed: for the Lord thy God is with thee whithersoever thou goest.' The Lord will not abandon you in here, and neither will I."

Palo nodded as the guard grabbed him by the arm and pulled him away. "Hurry," he called over his shoulder.

With the gates closing behind her, Aria strode across the street toward the train station, determined to make her little brother safe once again.

"I hope your journey was fruitful?" Father asked as he sank into his favorite leather wing-back chair by the fireplace.

Byron removed his coat and stretched his hands toward the fire to take away the chill from his ride over from the station. "I was able to save my clients' lifework and managed to get their rent reduced for a year as recompense for the landlord's actions."

"That's not what I meant and you know it." Father struck a match and lit his cigar. "You were supposed to meet with my friend to discuss that high-profile case. If you take his case and win, your career will be set for life."

Byron sighed. *Are we really going to have this discussion again?* He took the chair opposite his father. "I did meet with him, and while I appreciate the business, I've told you before, Father, that I don't care about having *all* high-profile cases, especially when I don't believe the client is innocent."

"But you should care. I can't be responsible for your finances forever and besides, you need to have experience that will actually *impress* influential voters. A pro bono case here and there is fine, but not every other case can be charity work. I've been grooming you for my seat all these years and it's about time that you show some gratitude and use that law degree I paid for and actually take some prestigious cases that will *pay*."

"I am very grateful to have had your support in school, but since I graduated nearly five years ago, I've offered many times to completely cover my costs so that I may pursue my preferred line of work, but you continually line my pockets."

"That's because we have an image to uphold, son." With his cigar between two fingers, Byron's father rubbed his forehead. "I am thankful you are at least doing something right for your future by courting Miss Beaumont, but promise me that you will stop this nonsense of taking on so many pro bono cases and take some real clients."

They are real clients, Byron wanted to retort, but he swallowed and tried to remain respectful. "I wish I could promise you, sir, but my passions lie with the people. And I assure you, I do not work for free on a majority of the cases."

"A chicken or a basket of baked goods is not what I consider payment. Besides, I keep trying to tell you that you don't have to surrender your passions for the people if you take the state senate seat." He leaned forward, his elbows resting on his thighs. "You will have more power to help those people from that seat than down in the ditches with the rabble."

Byron nodded. "I understand you, sir, and while I agree that the state senate could offer a better foothold to help the poor, I feel that my calling is to help the people by serving them in the ditches, as you put it."

Mr. Roderick grunted and waved him off. "There you go with that 'calling' nonsense. Ever since you started going to that church, you've been impossible. If only your younger brother were finished with his schooling, I'm sure he wouldn't be as ungrateful as his elder brother."

"I know Tom is passionate about politics. If you could wait a little while longer, you will have another Roderick ready to follow in your footsteps, and I will be free to run my practice."

"I don't have any more time! You know as well as I that the time to begin campaigning is now."

Byron gritted his teeth. Their conversation always seemed to go in circles, never ending. He tried to be respectful to his father, but it was getting harder as time went on and the day for announcing a new candidate approached. "I don't know how to say this, Father, but I don't want to be a state senator."

"Do you think I don't know that?" His father puffed on his cigar, scowling into the embers. "For years, I've dreamt of a dynasty, a legacy of Roderick men in the political world. Your grandfather clawed this family up society's ladder, yet you seem determined to throw our name in the gutter. You keep this up and Mr. Beaumont's daughter won't have you, and then where will I be? Completely abandoned by my own son."

Byron bowed his head, the weight of his father's expectations and disappointment pressing on him. "I'm sorry you feel that way, sir. I would never intentionally harm our family's name. I think that working in the French Quarter, though not as well paid, is just as honorable as a job at the capitol."

Without a word, his father flicked his cigar into the fire, shoved back his chair, and stomped out.

Byron sighed and leaned back in his chair and stared into the flames. Maybe his father was right. Perhaps he should relinquish his dream and pour his efforts into marrying well and winning the seat. He could still make a difference. . .only not in the way he had hoped, or with whom he hoped.

Chapter 7

It was too glamorous. Ordinarily, Aria looked forward to attending a musicale for weeks, but with Palo in prison, all she could see was the opulence. How could she pretend to enjoy the quartet, the singing, and the decadent refreshments when all she could think of was Palo, shivering in a damp cell? The letter in her handbag, explaining his situation, weighed on her, but with Mr. Beaumont near, she would have to wait for the right moment to slip it into Byron's hand.

She longed for the songs to transport her to a happier time, but try as she might, every note reminded her that she was out of her class. This group knew nothing of the hardships of her people. The only reason she was here was because of Millie, and even then, Mr. Beaumont had barely approved of hiring her. He had only relented when he'd discovered her very distant ties to the Italian aristocracy. While she looked the part of a fine lady, under the refashioned pink ruffles of Millie's discarded gowns, she was still that little girl from St. Ann Street, living in a run-down apartment hand to mouth after her father lost his job. She was the first and the last of her family to attend the fine school where she had met Millie. If Mr. Beaumont ever saw her family's home, she was certain she would be released at once. She glanced out of the corner of her eye at Byron. He had seen where she was from, and yet she knew that he would not hesitate in coming to her aid.

"Aria," Millie whispered to her behind her fan, "I'm not feeling well. I'm supposed to sing in a moment, but I feel as if there is a frog lodged in my throat." She wrapped her gloved fingers around her ivory neck. "I can't possibly go on in my state."

Aria followed Millie's gaze to where Joel Branson stood in the corner of the room without the infamous Fiona on his arm. "Are you sure it isn't just nerves? You've practiced over and over for two weeks. And you know your father would be quite upset if you deferred, especially since Governor Foster's wife is hosting the event."

"I know, but I'm sure I will croak if I go up there now." Mildred's eyes widened. "I've never sung in front of Jo—I mean, anyone before." She flapped her fan to cool her burning cheeks. "I wish you could sing for me. If only you could pretend to be me once more."

"The only way we could pull that off is if I stood behind the curtain and sang while you mouthed the words." Aria giggled into her hand at the ludicrous notion.

"That's it!" Millie gripped both of Aria's hands in her own, giving them a little shake.

"What's it?" Aria blinked, not following her friend.

"You'll sing for me from behind the curtain." Millie squealed, grabbing Aria's wrist and pulling her toward the makeshift stage that resembled a miniature of the one in the opera house.

Aria jerked them to a halt. "You can't be serious. I was completely jesting, Millie. We would be caught after two lines!"

"We could completely pull it off. You know the words. You've heard me practice it about five thousand times," she said, pushing Aria behind the curtain. "Now, you wait here and when you hear them announce me, be ready and listen for the opening notes."

Before Aria could protest further, Millie disappeared. Aria rubbed her forehead. "How on earth do I get roped into these things?" she muttered to herself as the current soloist finished her ballad.

Aria peered through a sliver in the curtain and caught sight of Mr. Beaumont in the front row with a vacant seat to his right, giving Millie an encouraging smile as she took the stage. The pianist began the introduction, and taking a deep breath, Aria prayed that Millie knew what she was doing and wouldn't get her fired for this ridiculous scheme.

As she sang, the lyrics of "The Song That Reached My Heart" enveloped her, and she nearly lost herself in their beauty, her eyes finding Byron as he took his seat next to Mr. Beaumont. Her heart burned as she watched his gaze transform as her voice filled the room and she caught the first hint of love cross his face. He was falling for Mildred's voice. . .*her* voice. She returned her gaze to Millie's lips, determined not to fail. At the more difficult parts, Millie flicked her fan in front of her face, conveniently hiding her lips.

When the song concluded, the room erupted in applause. Aria couldn't help but smile at Millie's performance as she curtsied and bowed her head to the audience while they tossed flowers at her feet. Mrs. Foster walked onto the stage to personally congratulate her and announce intermission.

Aria quietly slipped away from the curtain, and once she was as far away from the stage as possible, she made certain that she was seen to allay any suspicion as Byron rose and escorted a beaming Millie from the stage. Aria caught Millie glancing out of the corner of her eye toward Mr. Branson in the corner, a satisfied smirk playing on her lips as if she could sense his jealousy at seeing Byron dote upon her.

Good. She deserves his attention, Aria thought, and followed behind as Byron escorted Millie to the refreshment table for a glass of punch, praising her performance all the while.

"You are fortunate that came off well," Mr. Beaumont murmured into his glass of punch, appearing at her elbow.

Aria paled. *Of course he would know.*

"Calm yourself, Miss St. Angelo. No one else caught on to your little ruse or else Mildred wouldn't have been so well received. But, as it seems Mr. Roderick is quite smitten with her so-called voice, I suggest that you give up singing for the remainder of your time under my roof. We cannot risk him discovering the truth prior to their marriage," he added before stepping away to speak with Governor and Mrs. Foster.

Aria took a deep breath and joined Byron and Millie, overhearing him say, "When you mentioned you could sing, I had no idea that you were such a songbird, Miss Beaumont."

Millie flicked open her fan, dipping her head in false modesty at his praise. "It was nothing. I hardly practiced at all."

Aria refrained from rolling her eyes as she stood behind Millie with her hands folded in front of her skirt, waiting for her chance to speak with Byron alone.

Millie's fan fluttered fiercely. "Would you mind fetching us some pastries, Mr. Roderick? I'm feeling a bit famished from all the excitement."

"Of course." He bowed, excusing himself, but not before his eyes met Aria's, sending a shiver down her spine.

In his gaze, everything around her faded as it had that first night they met. Millie drew Aria to her side, breaking her trance, and nodded toward the other side of the room. Aria followed her gaze to see Joel grinning at Millie. *Oh no.* "Would you like me to ask him to leave you be?" Aria asked, knowing how sensitive she was about seeing Joel Branson after their separation.

"No," she said, downing the last of her punch. "I'm determined to speak with him."

"You're what? Are you sure that's a good idea, Millie?" She looked over her shoulder to Byron. "People know of your past with him, and if you are seen with Mr. Branson, there will be talk."

Millie shoved her glass into Aria's hands. "Of course it's a good idea. I heard that his latest triumph, *Fiona*,"—she dragged out the name as if it disgusted her—"is in the powder room. With a face like hers, she'll be in there awhile, so what better time is there to speak with him alone without Daddy or that girl watching our every move?"

"But, you are here with—"

"Distract Byron. I'll only be gone for ten minutes." Millie waltzed across the room and tapped Mr. Branson's arm with her fan, whispering something up to him. Aria watched as his eyes grew wide and he nodded, escorting Millie out to the veranda for a private tête-à-tête.

Aria shook her head and finished her punch, setting the empty glass aside when she felt a hand grasp her elbow. She turned to find Byron returning with napkins and a small dessert plate holding three cannolis dipped in dark chocolate, starting her mouth to watering.

"Where is Miss Beaumont? I brought the refreshments she requested," he said, lifting his plate in offering.

"She had to speak with someone." She hoped the vague answer would suffice, knowing Millie would end her employment if she revealed Millie's secret tryst.

He nodded but didn't appear vexed as he handed her a napkin for her pastry. "Then let's enjoy these before the music begins again."

Not caring that a cannoli was a tad too messy for public consumption, she prayed for the courage to ask for his help and bit into the treat.

Byron couldn't believe it when he had discovered Aria behind the curtain. He had been searching for a program when he overheard Millie's song announced and Aria's voice filled the air. He could have listened and observed her sing for hours, but knowing Mr. Beaumont was waiting, he hurried to his seat to watch Millie's performance of a lifetime, thinking it was little wonder why he didn't have a connection with Millie. She had never been the one behind the mask.

To test his theory, he retrieved the one thing he knew would solidify the masked woman's identity and watched as Aria ate the cannoli. No other lady besides the one woman he met that first night weeks ago would chomp into a pastry with such fervor.

Aria handed the soiled napkin to a passing waiter and kept speaking, but all he could think of was, why would she lie to him? He knew that Miss Beaumont's father only wanted him for his daughter because of his connections, so perhaps he was the one behind Aria's masquerade. While he felt that he should be angry learning the truth, he only felt a sense of relief, for it explained why he didn't feel drawn to Mildred and why he was so attracted to Aria. Miss Beaumont's companion was the masked songbird.

With this revelation, he knew that trouble would follow. Because of Mildred's budding friendship with the governor's wife, he had told his father he was seeing a woman who would help his father's political career, but now, he discovered he was in love with Mildred's companion. He drew up abruptly at the thought. *Am I in love with her?* He contemplated all the times his thoughts drifted to Beaumont Manor not because of Mildred, but because of Aria and her smiling eyes. His father would not be happy, but now that Byron had found her, he would not let her go.

"Mr. Roderick?" Aria looked up to him, confusion in her gaze. "Are you quite well?"

He blinked. "I'm sorry, did you ask me a question? I'm afraid I was deep in thought."

"Yes, but, um, I can ask you again tomorrow if you, um. . ." Aria bit her lip and looked down at her hands before smoothing the front of her pink skirt and glancing at nearby guests.

The concerned lines above her brow stirred him. "Pardon my distraction. What is it that you needed to ask?"

She dipped her head and picked at the lace trim on her fan. "I'm sorry to bother you during the musicale, but I didn't know when I might be able to catch you alone again, and the delicate matter I wish to discuss cannot wait."

The tremble in her voice alarmed him. He gently took her elbow and guided her to the corner of the room near a floor-length window. "Please, continue."

"I had hoped to catch you outside of the courthouse last week, but you hailed a carriage so quickly I wasn't able to catch your attention." A pretty blush crept over her cheeks. "And by the time I reached the hotel, you had already left for dinner. The hotel desk clerk wasn't willing to disclose at which restaurant you were dining, but when I told them you were courting my employer, they told me to leave a note." She babbled all in a rush, her voice wavering and eyes on the brink of overflowing with suppressed tears.

"I didn't receive any note."

"That's because I have it here." She dug into her reticule and handed him a folded and sealed note. "It was too sensitive to leave with just anyone."

He thought of the dark alleyways surrounding her home in the French Quarter, and his blood ran cold. "Did something happen to you while you were home?" He pocketed the note and motioned for her to take one of the chairs lining the wall, aching to help her in any way he could.

"No, it's my brother." She twisted a handkerchief between her hands and glanced over her shoulder. "You can read about it later. I don't want to bother you with it now."

"It's no bother. Please, let's sit so you can tell me what's wrong. You look positively ill." He ran his hands through his hair at the sight of her tears.

Aria sank into the seat, her fingers curled around her handkerchief as if she were petrified of it being ripped away from her. "I'm afraid my employer would not look kindly on what I'm about to disclose, so I beg for your discretion."

"Of course." He set his plate on the vacant seat next to him.

She looked up at him, her eyes wide and bottom lip trembling. "I can't paint this into a pretty picture. All I can say is that there's been a horrible misunderstanding." She lowered her head. "My brother, Palo, was accused of theft," she whispered.

No wonder she is so distressed. He knew how much she adored her brother. Leaning back in his chair, he pressed his fingers together into a steeple and lifted them to his lips, tapping contemplatively. "Is he guilty?"

Indignation filled her features at his audacious question. "No."

She half rose as if to leave, but he placed his hand on hers, staying her. "Please, it's my job to ask." She returned to her seat, her eyes dropping to his hand holding her own. He quickly released her and settled back, quite aware of the impropriety of touching in public, much less at an event to which he had escorted another woman. The clink of crystal glasses and laughter shook him out of his reverie and, clearing his throat, he leaned toward her. "Tell me everything you know."

Chapter 8

A ria barely finished her tale when Fanny Branson appeared in front of them with her hands on her hips.

"There you are!" She lifted one brow at the sight of the two of them seated together. "I have been looking for Miss Beaumont for nearly a quarter of an hour. Do you know where your charge is, Miss St. Angelo?"

Reluctantly, she rose and Byron followed suit. "I believe she was speaking with someone on the veranda," Aria admitted.

"Well, you shouldn't keep Mr. Roderick a moment longer, as intermission is nearly over and he should fetch her." Fanny pursed her lips at him. "After all, you did escort her, did you not?"

"Of course." A hint of annoyance clouded Byron's voice.

Aria's heart thudded with dread, as he hadn't given her an answer yet. She longed to have more time with him to discuss Palo's fate, but she knew she had to maintain a calm facade in front of Miss Branson or risk being discovered and losing her position. *So many secrets. First my deception with Byron at the masquerade and now I have to keep this from Mr. Beaumont.*

"I shall see to your request, Miss St. Angelo." He gave her a short bow before slipping away to find Millie.

"Do you not care about Miss Beaumont's reputation?" Fanny hissed.

Aria's stomach dropped. *Surely, she didn't overhear us?* "Pardon?"

"How could you allow her to venture out onto the veranda alone? She is obviously speaking with my brother, who is as good as engaged. Do your duty and go to her this instant or I shall inform Mr. Beaumont of your tête-à-tête with Mr. Roderick. Regardless, I'll be warning Miss Beaumont."

Aria lifted her head. "We spoke of nothing flirtatious, I assure you."

"Miss Beaumont is my friend, and I won't sit idly by and allow you to throw yourself at her beau. You are a distraction, and she needs to be put on her guard."

As long as it's not Mr. Beaumont, tell the world, Aria wanted to retort. Instead, she answered, "As you wish. Please excuse me." She hurried toward the French doors when she spotted Millie returning from the veranda with flushed cheeks.

Instead of heading toward Byron, who had been intercepted by Mr. Beaumont, Millie twisted around until her eyes found Aria's. With brisk steps, she crossed the floor and snagged Aria by the elbow, whispering, "We need to go. *Now.*"

Confused, Aria scrunched her eyebrows. "Now? Is something wrong? Did you tear your dress again?" She glanced at Millie's emerald gown and only found a tiny smear on her glove. "Did your father wish for us to leave early?"

"It's nothing like that, and no, Daddy doesn't know. Trust me and come. We are done here for the night." Millie pulled her toward the front room.

"But what about Byron? You can't leave your escort, especially at the governor's mansion," Aria protested.

"Watch me."

"Mildred!" Aria yanked her arm away, halting them both. She gritted her teeth, and with a smile meant to keep others from suspecting an argument, she added softly, "Mr. Roderick has been nothing but kind to both of us, and I can't allow you to do that. You can at least spare two minutes while I tell him that we are leaving and you bid Mrs. Foster a proper farewell. Your father will have my hide if you do not."

Millie sighed and rolled her eyes. "Fine, but please do hurry. We don't have much time. I'll explain at home."

Aria slipped away and, scanning the room, spied Byron speaking with an elderly gentleman. Not wanting to interrupt, but not daring to be caught in a drawn-out conversation, she waved him to her, praying he would come before the two minutes were up. "I'm sorry," she whispered when he reached her, "but Millie and I must leave."

"Is she unwell?"

"I'm not exactly sure what is going on, but it seems that she wishes for a bit of privacy, so we will take Mr. Beaumont's carriage and have it sent back for him." Aria glanced over her shoulder to ensure that Millie was distracted. "Will I see you soon about. . . ?"

He gently touched his lips to her glove, sending a jolt to her spine. "Yes, I'd like to discuss how to proceed with your brother's case in a more private setting. Perhaps we could meet at the coffeehouse tomorrow morning, say, nine o'clock?"

Aria blushed and quickly withdrew her hand, hoping he did not feel her trembling. Though she knew she shouldn't risk being seen with him in public, she had to for Palo. And if she were honest with herself, she secretly ached to spend more time alone with him even if society considered him as good as promised to Millie. "Perfect." She dipped into a curtsy and rushed away for fear Millie would ask what was taking so long.

"Finally," Millie grunted, pushing Aria through the doors and into a waiting carriage. "Hurry now, before Daddy tries to follow."

"What is with all this cloak-and-dagger nonsense?" Aria asked as she settled her skirts around her on the seat. "Why do we have to leave so suddenly?"

Millie waved her off, her eyes alight with excitement and her cheeks flushed as she peeled off her gloves and lowered the window. "Is it hot in here to you?"

"It's November," Aria said, her voice flat. Something wasn't right. *Did Mr. Branson ask for her hand in marriage? And is she rushing home to avoid her father stopping her from doing something foolish?* Aria wanted to inquire further, but she knew Millie wouldn't reveal even a smidgen of her plan until it was too late to give her any form of advice. So Aria remained silent, staring out the window and trying unsuccessfully to not think of a certain pair of hazel eyes.

Lord, I know I cannot have him, but now that he has agreed to help Palo, I fear my heart is lost to him forever. Unbidden, tears streaked down her cheeks, but before Millie could notice, she brushed away any trace as the carriage halted in front of Beaumont Manor.

When they were about halfway up the main stairs, Mr. Beaumont hailed them from the front door.

"Girls! Get down here," he barked, tearing off his top hat and handing it and a riding crop to the butler.

Millie's cheeks paled. "How did he find out? And how did he catch up with us?" she whispered more to herself than to her companion as they followed him into the cold parlor.

Spying Mr. Beaumont's red face under his furrowed brows, Aria cringed. *He must have followed us with alarming speed to match his temper, which does not bode well for you, Millie.* She slipped into the room behind Millie with her head bowed slightly and hands folded, waiting for his wrath to descend upon Millie for whatever crime she had been scheming.

"When were you going to tell me about your brother?" Mr. Beaumont's angry gaze burned into Aria, startling her. "When the scandal was laid at our doorstep? It's bad enough to have you here with your. . .background, but I had to find out at the *governor's* musicale from my colleague that his daughter overheard you mention your brother's conviction."

Her heart hammered in her chest. *Fanny.* She gripped the back of the settee to steady herself.

Mildred whipped around, her mouth ajar. "What is he talking about?"

Ignoring his daughter, Mr. Beaumont continued. "And when I went to find you, Mr. Roderick informed me that you had both left in *my* carriage, forcing me to borrow a steed." He threw his arms up. "Honestly, if you wished to keep this from me, did you not think that *someone* would overhear you if you confessed his transgressions in a crowded room?"

Aria managed to meet his gaze even as her knees quaked beneath her skirts. "I'm sorry, sir. I thought discretion was best suited for this situation, as my brother is innocent. He merely needs to have his name cleared."

"And how could you afford for him to be found innocent? A good lawyer is the only thing that stands between him and prison. I cannot have my daughter's companion related to a convict," he shouted, jabbing his finger at Aria.

Millie gasped, pressing a handkerchief to her eyes. "Daddy, you can't. I'm sure—"

"Palo will not be a convict. Mr. Roderick has agreed to represent him," Aria said, desperate for the chance to save her position.

"You approached Byron Roderick? That's whom you were telling?" The vein in his forehead rose. "Impudent girl! How dare you address my daughter's suitor under the governor's roof! If Foster catches wind of this, which he will, he will think I have no authority over my employees. What made you think that Roderick would even help you? You've never said more than two sentences to him."

She swallowed back her fear and hastened to explain. "We met quite by chance on the train to New Orleans and—"

"So, you got a taste of the high life at the masquerade ball and now you think you can waltz in and steal a lad from the upper crust because you managed to get him to call on 'you' after the ball." He let out a short laugh. "I would have you remember that he wasn't calling on you. He was calling on *Mildred's* position, *her* wealth and *her* connections."

His words couldn't have stung more if he had slapped her. "I wasn't trying to usurp Millie's beau." *How could I? I have nothing to offer him.*

"I won't stand for it." He huffed. "I was prepared to let you go with a reference even after the scandal you've brought into our house, but now to discover that you were attempting to steal my Mildred's love—"

"He's not my love. She's welcome to him," Millie interjected, threading her arm around Aria's waist, offering her strength. "I was going to call it off after tonight anyway."

Her father held up a hand, halting her once again. "You don't have to defend her, my dear girl. Miss St. Angelo, you have put my daughter's future in jeopardy. She is nothing without her reputation. You are to leave here at once."

Aria dipped her head. "I understand, sir. I will leave first thing in the morning."

"No." He scowled, his brows nearly meeting. "I mean tonight."

"But Daddy, it's far too dark for a proper lady to leave a house unescorted." Millie's wide-eyed gaze darted to Aria.

"Tonight," he roared.

Aria clenched her fists. *After all I've done for him, he would throw me out on the street like a beggar.* "Mr. Beaumont, you can't possibly expect me to take public transportation at this time of night. It would be quite dangerous to take the last train out to New Orleans unaccompanied."

"I don't care. Your disregard of the boundaries set for a lady's companion makes you too dangerous to keep under my roof. Your very presence could ruin Mildred's reputation and her chances for a good match forever. Go pack at once." He stood by the door, motioning her to make her way through the threshold. "You are fortunate that I am being kind enough to even allow you time for packing."

Aria stiffened and, pressing her lips into a thin line, replied, "I will need my wages."

"Insolent—" he began.

Millie stepped in front of Aria. "Daddy, we owe her that much," she reprimanded him softly. "She cannot safely return home without her wages."

He dug into his pocket and, counting out an amount, tossed the bills onto the floor and brushed by the two girls, shouting, "Take it and get out of my house."

With a heated face, Aria stiffly retrieved the bills, folding them and tucking them into her reticule before Millie gently grasped her arm and led her up the stairs. "What am I to do?" Aria whispered to her friend.

"You will come with me," she answered emphatically, letting them into Aria's small blue room.

"What? Where are you going?"

Millie shut the bedroom door behind them and turned her excited gaze to Aria. "It's why we left the musicale early. Joel and I are eloping."

"Eloping? Millie, have you taken leave of the senses the good Lord gave you?"

Millie pressed her hand to her chest. "I have just generously offered to save you from a terrible fate. Don't insult me. Joel and I talked it out, and I can tell you about it on the way to meet him," she said, dragging Aria's trunk from the closet.

"I should tell your father." Aria sank onto the bed, too stunned to pack.

"Why? You see how he would do anything to protect our precious reputation. He will not stop until I'm married off like all my sisters." Millie began tossing Aria's clothes into the trunk. "You best hurry. Daddy won't allow you much more time."

"Except Byron is a good man." *And not to mention, the most handsome one I've ever met.* She stiffly began gathering her things as Millie went through the adjoining door.

"And you know Joel is a good man. He only ceased his courtship because he needs a little more money than what Daddy was intending to give us," Millie replied a bit too loudly from her room before carrying in an armload of dresses.

No, I don't know. Aria rubbed her temples. "But your father is still offering the same amount. So why would Joel suddenly change his mind?"

Millie grinned, dropping her garments onto Aria's bed. "You see, that's where we figured if we eloped, Daddy would have to give us more money or else we would say we wed without his blessing. Faced with such a scandal, he wouldn't balk at an extra few thousand."

"Mildred Eloise Beaumont!" Aria gasped, nearly dropping her small framed portrait of her family.

"Brilliant, isn't it? I've seen how Daddy plays his politician's game." She giggled. "I bet he never thought I'd be brazen enough to try something so daring, but he pushed us into a corner. What did he expect me to do?"

"I don't know, maybe marry Byron Roderick? He is a wonderful man.

And what if Mr. Branson decides *not* to go through with the wedding? He will ruin your reputation and any chance you have of a happy marriage." She cringed at echoing Mr. Beaumont's words but knew that despite his cruelty, he was right. Mildred's reputation must be protected.

"With you there to chaperone, it will be more than proper until our vows our spoken." Eyeing the clock, she flew between the two rooms, stuffing both of their things into Aria's trunks. At Aria's confused look, she explained, "I need to make it look like everything is yours and not mine. Daddy won't blink at you having an extra trunk, but three would raise brows, so I must stuff everything into two."

Aria felt torn on whether or not to notify Mr. Beaumont, but she knew that once Millie set her mind to something, she wouldn't change it even if she discovered halfway through that she was in over her head. If she didn't elope tonight, Millie would find another way into Joel's arms. At least this way, Aria could watch over her. As her lady's companion, or former companion, she felt duty-bound to protect Millie's reputation even if it meant going along with her harebrained scheme.

"Are you sure you want to go through with this? Once you leave with Mr. Branson, there is no returning," she warned.

"Why would I want to return?" Millie snorted, slamming the trunk lid shut.

Because you have a father who loves you and more wealth than I could ever imagine. "Then I will act as your chaperone this one last time and will not leave your side until the vows have been spoken and a ring is on your finger, declaring that you are legally Mrs. Joel Branson."

"Thank you!" Millie squealed and embraced her before giving a little twirl and sighing as she repeated, "Mrs. Joel Branson."

The footmen appeared at the door, and Henry, the shorter of the two, gave Aria a sad smile and announced, "It's time."

Aria tied on her cloak over her fine dress and gave Millie a hug.

"I'll see you soon," Millie whispered into her ear, giving Aria's elbow a squeeze.

With arms crossed and a biting remark, Mr. Beaumont surveyed Aria's shameful exodus from the manor. Knowing she wouldn't be allowed to say her farewells to the staff, she bid farewell to the two footmen carrying her things and nodded in passing to one of the maids. "Please give Cook and the rest my best wishes," she whispered.

The maid dipped her head but made no response, fear flickering in her eyes as Mr. Beaumont bellowed for Aria to move along.

"If you don't leave this instant, I won't allow you the use of my carriage to the station, young lady," he warned.

Aria squeezed the maid's arm and, with her satchel and reticule in hand, rustled out into the damp night. The footmen harnessed her two trunks stuffed with her and Millie's things onto the back of the carriage while Aria looked over her shoulder one last time at the manor that had been her home for the past five years. She had treasured her time under the Beaumont roof and the benefits that had come with being Millie's companion. With a sigh, she slipped inside the carriage and almost shrieked when she saw a form occupying the corner.

"Shh!" Millie whispered, pressing her gloved hand to Aria's mouth.

"I thought you were meeting me at the station later! How did you—?" Aria sputtered.

"I told the maids to tell Daddy I was going to bed early out of protest of your dismissal, so no one will miss me until morning and maybe not even until the afternoon since they think I'll be sulking." She grinned as they started toward the train station. "Maybe your being fired is really a blessing in disguise."

With each bump in the road, Aria silently questioned if going along with Millie's plan was the right thing to do, but Millie chatted so much about her upcoming nuptials that it was difficult to even formulate a sentence, much less an argument, for Millie to abandon her plan.

Reaching the station, Millie practically leaped out of the carriage and into the waiting arms of her intended. "Joel," she said with a sigh, resting her head against his chest.

"My darling, I was worried you wouldn't come," he whispered into her hair.

"Why wouldn't I?" She lifted her gaze to meet his, her love exuding from every feature.

"Well, for one, I thought you wouldn't be able to keep the secret and your companion would talk you out of it." He chortled and traced her chin with a curved finger.

"Believe me, I tried." Aria stepped out of the shadows as Mr. Branson bent to kiss Millie.

Mr. Branson jerked up, his gaze darkening. "What is *she* doing here?

Mildred, I thought I told you—"

"Daddy fired her and was determined to throw her out of the house this very night, so I thought I would bring her along as our chaperone until we're married. You aren't angry with me, are you, my darling?" Millie rubbed her hand up and down his arm as if to warm him to the idea of Aria joining them.

"I could never be vexed with you." To Millie, he gave a smile, but Aria could see beyond Millie's enchanted gaze that Mr. Branson was livid, and his anger made her suspicious.

If his intentions are honorable, why would he hesitate at protecting her reputation? She bit her lip as the porters carried the luggage to the train. *Because if they didn't wed before the morning and were unchaperoned. . .* She shuddered with the realization of what he had intended to pull on her naive charge. *Mr. Branson was going to use the scandal to pressure Mr. Beaumont into a ghastly amount.* She frowned at the back of his jacket as he purchased another first-class ticket. *Scoundrel. Mr. Beaumont was right to push him away from Millie.*

Aria clutched her satchel and reticule and marched up to Millie's side, determined to keep her eye on Mr. Branson. Instead of allowing him to sit beside Millie in the first-class compartment, she planted herself on the plush seat next to her charge. Mr. Branson raised a brow at her, but she returned his stare with a defiant one of her own, daring him to argue with her. She knew what he was up to and she would not allow him to get away with it. She would see to it that Millie's reputation was guarded until the very end.

Aria kept the corner of her eye trained on the couple and gazed out the window, wondering when she would ever see Byron Roderick again and if he would travel to New Orleans Parish Prison to see her brother even though she wouldn't be at the coffeehouse in the morning. *Dear Lord, have him help my brother despite all that I've done to him and what Millie's running away will do to his pride. Let me not have spoiled the only chance my brother has of being released from prison unscathed.*

Not seeming to sense the tension in the compartment, Millie kept the conversation flowing with bubbling excitement while Mr. Branson kindly nodded and replied whenever he could. While Aria thought his tone suggested that he did love Millie in his own way, his actions and flagrant disregard for her reputation proved his love of money was greater and that he would go to any extreme to see to it he was compensated for marrying Mildred Beaumont.

After a very long ride to New Orleans, they took a hired carriage to the church Mr. Branson had mentioned to Mildred, but as Aria had guessed, it was closed, and no amount of pounding on the parsonage door would wake the pastor.

"What are we going to do?" Millie's voice spiraled out of control along with her composure as the full weight of her circumstances overwhelmed her.

Aria squeezed her elbow. "Don't worry. We will return first thing in the morning, and until then, I'll see to it that you are taken care of so there will be no call for society to declare that you were caught in a compromising position." She turned to Mr. Branson and said with a clipped tone, "I suggest the Commercial Hotel. Let's be off before we are spotted."

Mr. Branson sighed and escorted the women back inside the waiting carriage. In a matter of minutes they were in the hotel lobby, standing at the front desk as Mr. Branson ordered three rooms.

Whenever they traveled in the past, Millie and Aria had separate rooms, but tonight, she would not let her charge out of her sight. Stepping forward, she whispered to Millie, "It will be best for your reputation if I stay with you the entirety of the night."

Overhearing her, Mr. Branson interjected, "I hardly think it is necessary."

Does he think I'm stupid? She scowled. "Do you care for Miss Beaumont so little? Protect your bride-to-be, Mr. Branson, and book two rooms instead of three," she demanded, staying all arguments.

The frazzled front desk clerk returned his gaze to Mr. Branson. "Sir?"

He sighed and flicked his hand, relenting. "We will take just the two rooms."

Aria leaned forward, adding, "And make them on *separate* floors."

Mr. Branson rolled his eyes, nearly growling as he paid the deposit.

It was going to be a long, restless night watching over Millie. *I will not fail Millie, not on my last night as her companion.*

Chapter 9

Byron checked his pocket watch for the tenth time. *Where is she?* His knee bounced as he tapped the worn wooden table with his spoon. He looked through the wavy windowpanes from his seat in the corner of the coffeehouse and sighed. At the throat clearing from the table next to him, he realized the three cups of coffee he'd downed without food was beginning to take a toll on him. He set aside his spoon and, instead, let his anxiety out by polishing his spectacles until they shone. It wasn't like Aria to not follow through with a promise. While he had never met with her before on his own, he knew that whenever Millie set an appointment, Aria was always there, strictly punctual, with her charge in tow.

Now that he knew he had spent that glorious first evening dancing with Aria and not with the politician's daughter, he had decided to break it off with Miss Beaumont. He only needed to confront Aria and find out once and for all why she lied to him even though he had a pretty fair idea Mr. Beaumont was behind the whole situation.

When the waiter came by for an embarrassing third time asking for his order, Byron decided that something must've come up and Aria couldn't get away, so he quickly paid for his cups of coffee and headed for Beaumont Manor with his hat in hand to find his masked lady and help rescue her brother. The thought that Aria had come to him in her need warmed him on the chilly walk as the last of the leaves crunched beneath his boots. With each stride, he grew more and more determined that no matter what Aria confessed, he would see this lad received justice. The only payment he desired was a dimpled smile from Palo's pretty sister.

Letting the knocker fall against the mahogany door, he stepped back and waited until one of the maids answered.

Upon seeing him, her eyes widened and she dropped into a curtsy. "Mr. Roderick! Please, do come in. I'll fetch the master." She showed him into the parlor, and in a matter of seconds, Mr. Beaumont came charging inside.

"Roderick." He rubbed his hand over his haggard face and sighed, gesturing for Byron to take a seat. "I have to admit, I am surprised to see you."

"Why would you be surprised to see me, sir? I know it's a bit early, but I usually call for Miss Beaumont on my lunch break." He rested his hat on his knee, as the frazzled maid had forgotten to take it from him.

Mr. Beaumont's shoulders slumped as he rested both hands on the back of the settee opposite Byron. "Well, I suppose word will spread to you soon enough. I awoke this morning to discover that Mildred has run off."

Byron's stomach dropped as he stood. "Miss Beaumont is gone? Did she leave a note?"

"A handful of her things are packed. I half hoped that she ran off with you, but I fear the worst." He tipped his head back, letting out a long breath. "She's gone, and no doubt so is that scoundrel, Joel Branson. If I get my hands on him—"

"What did Miss St. Angelo have to say? Did she know of Miss Beaumont's plans?" Byron gripped the rim of his hat. To pretend to be someone under duress was one thing, but to lie to a man about the whereabouts of his daughter was another. *She wouldn't. Not Aria.*

"I know not. She is gone as well." He dug his hands into his pockets and stared into the fireplace.

"Then Miss Beaumont's reputation is safe." He gave a breathless laugh. "Surely you have comfort in that, sir."

"I cannot say for certain that they left together," Mr. Beaumont replied, reaching for the pitcher of water on the side table and pouring himself a glass.

"Well, why would Miss St. Angelo leave without her charge? Unless maybe she was following her to stop Miss Beaumont?" He thought out loud, raking his hands through his hair at the thought of the two women leaving the protection of the manor.

"I cannot say for certain, because I fired Miss St. Angelo last night due to the shame she has brought upon our family by keeping her brother's plight a secret and further shame for including my daughter's beau in her nonsense. I sent her away the moment we returned from the musicale."

"You sent her away in the dark? You cannot be serious." Byron could not believe it of the man. Miss St. Angelo might be poor, but she was trained as a gentlewoman and besides, the night was not a safe time for any woman of character to be out alone.

"I lent her a carriage to the station." He shrugged, dismissing Byron's concern. "I'm done with her and have nothing further to say in regard to her well-being." His eyes narrowed. "Why do you care?"

Because if I have anything to do with it, the lady is my future wife. Byron made for the door.

"Where are you going?" Mr. Beaumont called after him, following him out into the hallway.

Byron tugged on his hat, pausing only to find his coat on the coatrack. "I'm going to find Miss St. Angelo. It seems you have Miss Beaumont's well-being in hand, and I must see to Aria's, as no one else in this house will."

" 'Aria,' is it?" His brows rose. "You care for my daughter's companion," he stated.

"Of course. She has become a dear friend during my time calling on your daughter. A time that has now come to a close," Byron added. He had intended to quietly end things with Mildred this morning, but if she had run off with another man, then she had saved him the trouble.

"Never fear. I'm sure Mildred's reputation is quite safe if she left with Miss St. Angelo. If she has tainted it in any way in your eyes, I will see to it that you are compensated accordingly." Mr. Beaumont crossed his arms, waiting for Byron to accept his terms.

Byron clenched his fists. "You act as if this is a business deal."

Mr. Beaumont gave a short laugh. "Don't act like it isn't for you as well. Everyone knows you are being groomed to take the office. Your father is benefiting from this union just as much as I am."

Byron scowled. "Consider any agreement terminated. If Miss Beaumont was here this morning, I would have ended my suit anyway. I know she wasn't the lady I met the first night."

His jaw dropped. "I don't believe my ears. You would give up my daughter for that little Italian woman?"

"That 'little woman' is a lady, and yes. Yes, I would."

Exhausted from her whirlwind morning of seeing Millie safely married to Branson, Aria gripped the wooden handle of her umbrella to keep it from flying off in the torrential downpour. She shuffled down the sidewalk toward her home, her spirits feeling as soaked as her skirts. *What am I to do now, Lord? How am I supposed to tell Mama I lost my position? Who will hire me when I don't even have a recommendation? What am I to do?*

Nearly in tears, she let herself inside to find the house abnormally quiet. Taking the stairs to the kitchen on the second floor, she peeked in to find her mother kneading bread on the wooden countertop.

"Mama?" she croaked.

Her mother whirled around with a rolling pin in hand. "Aria, what on earth?" Seeing her daughter's red eyes and wet skirts, she crossed the room and embraced her, paying no mind to the flour covering her apron or her sticky rolling pin. "Why, you are soaked through! I was just about to let this bread rise and make a café au lait. Come sit and I'll make us a cup." She fluttered to the stove as the milk began to boil.

"Where is everyone?" Aria sank into a wooden chair at the table.

"Bianca and Caterina are out delivering laundry, and the littles are at your aunt's house," her mother answered, pouring the hot milk over the fresh coffee before stirring in a generous spoonful of sugar. "But tell me why are you here and not with Miss Beaumont?" Setting the frothy coffees on the table, she retrieved a hardened loaf of narrow bread and sliced off two pieces.

"I've ruined everything." Aria buried her face in her arms.

"What are you talking about?"

"I was fired from my position. I am so sorry," she said through her sobs.

Mama came around her chair and wrapped her arms around Aria. "Oh, my sweet girl."

Aria wiped her eyes with the back of her hand. "How on earth are we going to make ends meet now that I've lost my income?"

Mama sank into the chair beside Aria and slid the coffee toward her. She handed her a piece of bread. "Now don't you go worrying. The Lord will provide."

"I was providing through my position, but now that's gone. What are we going to do? How is Palo supposed to go to college? How are the little girls going to get new dresses for school? Papa works so hard, and it's still not enough. The family needs my income."

"The Lord will provide whether you have a job or not. He wouldn't give me all these little children to take care of and not provide for them, or us. If He wants Palo to attend college, Palo will be given the means to do so whether you have a position or not." Mama gestured for Aria to take a sip. "Life is always easier to face with a cup of hot coffee and bread to bolster our strength," she said, dunking her bread into the steaming cup.

Aria followed suit. "How can you be sure He will provide?"

"The Bible says in Matthew chapter six, 'Behold the fowls of the air: for they sow not, neither do they reap, nor gather into barns; yet your heavenly Father feedeth them. Are ye not much better than they?' The Lord has provided for us all these years, so why would He stop now?"

Her mother paused, her finger tracing the rim of her cup, a faraway look in her eyes. "When your father was fired, it was hard for me to adjust. I asked why God would allow a father of six to be laid off from a wonderful position that would permit our children to attend a good school, and then make him a desk clerk at a struggling office where we can barely make ends meet. But every month ends *do* meet, and we even have money left over to bake fig cookies for the neighborhood children." Mama smiled. "He will always provide for His children, but it may not be in the manner we wish."

"But wasn't He providing for us through my position? Why did I have to lose it?" Once again, despair threatened to engulf Aria.

"It may not be clear now or ever, but take comfort in this, the Lord has your future and our family's future in His hands," Mama said, cupping Aria's face. "My little songbird. He treasures you far more than the birds of the air. Trust that He knows what is best."

"He treasures you far more than the birds of the air." Mama's words echoed through Aria's mind, bathing her in peace. *All this time, I've been acting as if I am the provider when it's You, Lord. It's only ever been You.* She bowed her head. *I give You this burden, Lord, a burden that I took. I know You will provide. Someday. Somehow. You will.* "Thank you, Mama," she whispered.

"I don't want you to catch your death, so why don't you go change and I'll make you a proper breakfast?" She bent and kissed Aria's cheek.

Aria nodded and, taking her cup with her, climbed the stairs to the third floor to her old bedroom that she shared with her four sisters. Before she stripped off her soiled dress, she stepped to the curtain to draw it for a bit of privacy and thought she spied a familiar figure below gazing up at her apartment building.

"Is that Byron?" she thought out loud, nearly pressing her face into the glass to get a better look. Her motion drew the figure's gaze, but she couldn't discern his identity through the rain. When he turned away without acknowledging her, she drew the curtain, dismissing her first impression as wishful thinking. If Palo was to be released from prison, it would be through divine intervention.

Chapter 10

Aria hung up the last of her freshly laundered dresses in the shared closet. After having a room to herself for so long, it felt quite crowded sleeping with her four sisters in one room. She turned to the floor-length window and gazed out onto St. Ann Street below and across to Jackson Square. She smiled as she watched her little sisters play on the green, dodging the fine folks parading about. Spying a couple with a young lady in a dowdy gray dress trailing behind them, she sighed and turned away, missing being a companion. It had only been three days since she had acted as a witness for Mildred and Mr. Branson's marriage, but those days felt like a lifetime while she waited for some word from Byron about Palo. Now that she had lost her position, she had even less money for a lawyer should Byron change his mind.

Aria bit her lip, trying not to worry about how she would help support her family now that she was unemployed and didn't have a reference for all her years of work. Tapping her chin, she thought maybe she could inquire after some of Millie's old friends and see if a younger sister needed a companion. *Whatever happens, I know You are in control, Lord.*

"Aria!" her mother called from the second floor, no doubt needing help preparing dinner.

She let the shabby curtain drop. "Coming, Mama," she called back, tying her apron over her powder-blue gown and making her way down to the kitchen area. "Where shall I start?"

"A gentleman is here to see you." Mama grinned, wiping her hands on her apron, leaving red streaks from the sauce she was preparing.

"Who?" Aria's breath caught.

"I think you know." Mama winked.

Aria stepped down the stairs with her skirts trailing behind her as her clammy hand stuck to the curved wooden stair rail. Peering through the glass of the worn French doors, she spied him waiting in the shared courtyard with his hands behind his back, staring up at the clotheslines crisscrossing from the upper levels, underclothes fluttering in the gentle breeze.

She grimaced as she smoothed her hair, wishing she hadn't worn it in a simple braid, but there was no time to fix it now. She took a deep breath and opened the door with a creak.

He turned toward her, the wrinkle in his brow easing as he caught sight of her. "Aria." His breath caught.

Her heart stopped at the sound of her name on his lips. The world around her quieted, and for a moment, nothing else existed as she stepped toward him, longing for more but not daring to hope. "Mr. Roderick." She dipped into a curtsy. "How did you know where to find me?"

"I was worried when you didn't show up at the coffeehouse, so I went to Beaumont Manor, only to find that you had been sent away." His hands traced the perimeter of his hat.

She felt the heat rise from her neck to her cheeks at the knowledge that he knew of her shameful dismissal. "I'm so sorry I kept you waiting for me at the coffeehouse. I would have sent you a note, but everything happened so fast and before I knew it, I was on the train to New Orleans with Millie and Mr. Branson and it was too late."

"So, you *were* with her." His lips pressed into a grim line. "Good. I feared the worst when I heard that she had run off with that rogue."

Aria nodded slowly, determining the soreness of the topic. "Millie made certain I arrived in New Orleans safe and sound, and in turn, I made certain she was good and married before I left her in Mr. Branson's care." She looked down at her hands. "I'm sorry if you're disappointed to hear that she is married."

"I'm not sorry in the least. In fact. . ." He took a step toward her, close enough that she could close the distance between them with a kiss if she wished. "I was going to speak with her and her father to let them know of my intent to break off the courtship."

"Oh?" She swallowed, trying not to focus on his lips. "And did you?"

"Yes. You see, I found myself in love with someone else," he whispered, tucking a wisp of hair behind her ear.

"Oh." Her heart lodged in her throat, and she had difficulty breathing.

"Now, I believe we had something to discuss," he said, dropping his hand and breaking her trance. "Your brother."

"You've seen him?" She pressed her hand to her heart.

He nodded. "Once I saw that you were safely home, I went to speak with him."

So that was him in the rain.

"And afterward, I did some investigation and found pretty indisputable evidence that your brother was not the one who stole from Brooks and Brooks." He grinned.

"Is it enough to get him released?" she asked breathlessly.

"I'd say so." Palo sauntered into the courtyard, hands in his pockets.

Aria squealed and ran to him, throwing her arms around his hard shoulders and pressing a kiss onto his bristly cheek. "Palo, thank the Lord! What happened?" She swiveled around to Byron and back to Palo.

"Mr. Roderick said he suspected the son of the shopkeeper was being underhanded, so he went all Sherlock Holmes on him!"

"Mr. Holmes, eh?" She turned to Byron, unable to stifle her grin.

Byron shrugged and returned her smile. "I merely visited every pawnshop in town until I found the watch described and discovered who pawned it."

She laughed. "You're jesting. The thief didn't use a pseudonym?"

He shook his head and chuckled. "Not very bright, that lad. I presented my findings to the elder Brooks, and all charges have been dropped. Your brother is a free man. If he does well on his entrance exams, he should have no problem getting accepted into Louisiana State University."

"I don't know how to thank you." Aria lifted her hands, unable to express all that was in her heart.

He waved her off. "I should be thanking you. Your brother's case has pushed me to finally commit to my plan of opening my own law practice in the French Quarter where I can be more useful."

"Here?" She couldn't stop the smile that flooded her face. "We will be neighbors."

"More than that, I hope," he replied so quietly that she wondered if she had heard him correctly.

He looked over her shoulder and smiled at the little faces pressed against the wavy windowpanes of the French doors.

"Come on out. We have a surprise for you," she called to them, motioning her little sisters and cousins outside. At Palo's greeting, they came tumbling out into the courtyard, bombarding him with embraces and questions. "With Palo's return, you will be a hero in the family's eyes." Aria smiled up to him, wishing again she could thank him, but any words felt inadequate.

"I'm glad I could help," he replied, his smile seeming only for her.

"Would you like to come up?" Aria managed to ask over the din.

"I'd love to, but how about we take a stroll first?" He offered her his arm as the children ushered Palo inside and Mama let out a cry that could be heard for miles.

As they walked, Aria's secret burned within her, and she longed for the truth to step into the light. *I could tell him now. I have no job to lose.* She looked at him out of the corner of her eye, admiring his broad shoulders, his confident stride, and prayed her lies would not take him from her.

Byron halted alongside the Mississippi River, the scent of the muddy water wafting up to them. He bent down, picked up a pebble, and tossed it into the river, the water swallowing it without a skip.

Taking a deep breath, she began to pour out the secrets she had kept hidden in the dark. "Mr. Roderick—"

"Please, call me Byron."

"Byron," she said, loving how perfect his name felt on her lips even amid her admission, "I have a confession to make."

"Before you say anything, I need to make a confession of my own." He turned to her, taking her small hands in his. His pale hand stood out against her olive skin. "I must confess that you captured my heart the moment I first beheld you, and every moment I've spent with you afterward has only confirmed your kind, unselfish nature."

She thought back to their collision in the garden. He had not seemed all that enchanted with her as he raced away. She stepped back from him, trying to clear her head. "I'm not as wholesome as all that. You see, I deceived you." She nearly choked as she rushed onward to explain. "Granted, I was forced into the situation by my employer, but that was no excuse for allowing you to continue to believe it was Millie you met that first night." She lifted her lashes and met his gaze. "I was the masked lady." At his silence, she grasped his sleeve. "Please, can you ever forgive me for the masquerade?"

"I knew you had a good reason for why you were pretending to be Miss Beaumont."

"You knew?" She blinked, confused. "Then why. . .for how long?"

He grinned. "Ever since I spied you singing behind Millie and I gave you that Italian pastry at the musicale. No woman other than my lady from the masquerade ball would consume a sweet like that." Kneeling, he took her hand in his. "Aria St. Angelo, will you do me the honor of becoming my wife?"

For her answer, she took a seat on his knee, wrapped her arms about his neck, and pulling him into an embrace, pressed her lips to his again and again.

Grace Hitchcock lives in Baton Rouge with her husband, Dakota, and son. She is a member of American Christian Fiction Writers and holds a Master's in Creative Writing. Her debut novella, *The Widow of St. Charles Avenue*, released in Barbour Publishing's *The Second Chance Brides Collection* in August 2017. Connect with her online at GraceHitchcock.com.

Above All
These Things

by Connie Stevens

Dedication

To Lauren, Chelsea, Victoria,
Robbie, and Tracy—
the nursing staff at
Northeast Georgia Diagnostic Clinic
where a good deal of this story was written
while these ladies cared for my husband
during his chemotherapy.
Colossians 3:12–14 says charity (love) is the greatest
of all the Christian characteristics we are
commanded to demonstrate.
Thank you for being such beautiful
examples of charity.

Chapter 1

Annulet, are you listening?"

Annulet Granville yanked her attention back to the guest list her mother flapped against the polished oak tea table.

"Yes, Mama, I heard you." She bit her lip to prevent resentment from coloring her voice.

Celeste Granville sighed and nudged the paper across the table, positioning it in front of Annulet. "I've put a star beside the names of the young men to whom you should pay the most attention." She poured more tea into her cup and stirred in a generous amount of sugar. "I hope you realize how important this ball is for your future. Have Polly arrange your hair in a more becoming style and pin some jasmine sprigs in the curls. That way, every man with whom you dance that night will remember your fragrance. Your gown should be ready by the day after tomorrow. We will go into Bethel Station Friday for your final fitting."

Annulet half listened as she scanned the list of wealthy, influential guests. Every detail of her mother's plans was focused on one thing: drawing the attention of affluent men.

She knew the reason. She wasn't completely ignorant of the unwise business investments her father had made over the years, even though Montgomery Granville never spoke of such things in her presence.

Her mother cleared her throat. "I hope you appreciate my efforts to make this ball a success. I'm doing this for you, darling."

Annulet rose and crossed to the open window where a soft spring breeze wafted into the parlor. "Auctioning me off to the highest bidder isn't done for me, Mama."

Her mother's audible gasp indicated her remark might have been a bit too pointed, but it was the heavy footstep at the door that sent a splinter of warning through her.

"Annulet Renee, what do you mean by making such a crass statement to your mother?" Papa's disapproval reverberated through the room.

Annulet turned and faced her father, her chin slightly uplifted. "In essence, that is what you're doing, Papa. Isn't this ball for the purpose of pairing me up with a rich man?" She stalked to the tea table and snatched up the guest list. "Every man on this list is wealthy."

"What's wrong with that?" Her father's scowl was undoubtedly meant to intimidate. "It is my responsibility to match you with a man who can provide for you in the manner to which you are accustomed."

He closed the gap between them and shook his finger in her face. "It is your duty to your family to enter into such a match, to strengthen the resources and ensure the legacy lives on."

Her mother sat primly with her hands in her lap, clearly not planning on coming to her daughter's defense. Annulet refrained from rolling her eyes but could no longer rein in her tongue.

"Legacy? To what legacy are you referring, Papa?" She spread her arms to indicate the lavishly appointed room. "Pretending we are rich and important? Am I to be on display for men to ogle and see which one meets your standards?" She waved the guest list. "How is this any different from the buying and selling of slaves? They are forced to stand up on a platform while people bid on them, and they have no say in—"

"That's quite enough, Annulet." His hardened tone sent a shiver through her. "Sit down and mind your manners."

She complied, but her agitation didn't retreat.

Papa paced to the cold fireplace and clasped his hands behind his back. "The fact is that you and your mother enjoy living comfortably." He shot a glance at Mama before returning his scrutiny to his daughter. "Neither of you mind how much money you spend. Marrying well will mean security."

Mama squirmed in her chair. "Montgomery, that's not quite fair. May I remind you of your investments? The steam engine that was touted to be safer but exploded on its maiden voyage, and the gold mine up near Dahlonega. What was that called again? Hydraulic mining? Your partner ran off with the investment money before you saw a single grain of gold. And what of that gambling house you bought into in Chattanooga? The one where your partner was convicted of running rigged gaming tables. Is he out of prison yet?"

Papa glared at Mama, but she didn't seem inclined to fall silent. She shook out and refolded her dainty handkerchief. "Most planters in Georgia do quite well, but then they stay home and run their plantations instead of going off—"

"My father and my grandfather always left the tiresome duties of running the plantation to Jacobson. I see no reason why I can't do the same." He turned his back, but not before Annulet caught a crease of regret between his eyes. "Dolf Jacobson was always trustworthy."

Mama turned in her chair. "But Dolf Jacobson's *son* is the overseer and manager now. Perhaps Rudd Jacobson isn't the man his father was."

Papa's shoulders slumped.

Annulet held her breath. Never before had she or Mama shown such defiance to Papa. Remorse spindled through her. She should apologize for speaking the way she did. Certainly Papa believed his investments would pay off just as he believed he could trust his overseer to supervise the operation of Thornwalk. But before she could open her mouth to express contrition for her words, Papa turned on his heel and strode out of the room.

She rose from her chair and started after him, but her mother called her back. "Leave him be, Annulet. His ill humor will abate after a while." She patted the chair beside her. "We must finish going over these lists."

Annulet dropped the guest list on the table and settled herself in the chair. Mama ran her finger down the list for what seemed like the hundredth time. "These are the three men who should garner most of your attention." Her finger paused at the first name with a star beside it. "Charles Templeton is the son of Spencer Templeton, a longtime friend of your father's and grandfather's. He and his father own a very prestigious law firm in Atlanta." Her finger slid down to the next star. "You remember Royce Forbes of Fair Groves Plantation in Oconee County, don't you?" She continued down the fine-grained stationery and came to a stop beside the last star. "Of course, Ramsay Wheeler of Meadowgold Plantation is one of the most eligible bachelors in this area. You are already acquainted with the Wheelers."

Annulet stared at the men's names. She'd never met Charles Templeton and scarcely recalled hearing her father mention Spencer Templeton's name in passing. She'd met Royce Forbes a few times—*isn't he more than fifteen years my senior?* She'd known Ramsay Wheeler for several years. He was certainly handsome enough, and could have his pick of all the girls for a hundred miles around.

"Ramsay Wheeler will inherit Meadowgold one day. It's one of the most diverse and prosperous plantations in this area." Her mother raised her eyebrows in a speculative manner. "Plus, he's good-looking and has a solid family background."

Annulet shrugged. "If Ramsay is one of the most eligible bachelors in the area, his attention is probably attracted elsewhere."

A tiny smile tipped the corners of Mama's lips. "The sweetest peaches on the tree are worth the climb."

"Mama!" Heat crept into Annulet's face. She didn't wish to pursue the topic. Or Ramsay Wheeler. In fact, she didn't wish to pursue any man.

Meadowgold Plantation

Discomfort threaded through Peyton Stafford. The obvious fear in the eyes of the Negro man doing his best to clean off the seat of the carriage kindled sympathy in Peyton's chest. Ramsay Wheeler, Peyton's old friend from college, growled a profane oath at the man.

"Why wasn't this done before you brought the carriage around? Hurry up!"

"Yassah, massah. I be done in jus'—"

But the poor man apparently didn't move fast enough for Ramsay, because he backhanded the servant, nearly knocking him to the ground.

"Get out of my way, you imbecile." Ramsay climbed into the carriage and slid across the seat, making room for Peyton. His demeanor changed quicker than the flutter of a hummingbird's wing. He grinned at Peyton and beckoned him into the carriage.

"There should be enough ladies at this soiree to show you some southern hospitality, if you know what I mean." Ramsay waggled his eyebrows up and down.

Peyton glanced at the slave scrambling to the driver's seat and then back to his friend. He positioned himself on the carriage seat and lowered his voice. "You were kind of hard on that man, weren't you?"

Puzzlement flitted across Ramsay's expression, as if he didn't know what Peyton was talking about. "You mean him?" He tipped his head toward the Negro. A puff of air blasted from his lips. "That's all they understand." With a dismissive flick of his fingers, he went on, rambling about the party, the lovely women they would encounter there, and upcoming social events on the calendar.

Peyton clenched his teeth. In the few days since he'd arrived at his college chum's home at Meadowgold Plantation, the few encounters he'd observed between his friend and the slaves disturbed him. From the time he was four-teen years old and first voiced questions to his teachers and then to his father about slave labor in the South, he'd never felt completely at ease with their responses.

"Cotton plantations in the South and textile mills in the North couldn't turn a profit without slave labor. Besides, slaves at the big southern plantations are fortu-nate to live at a place where they are taken care of."

Try as he might to set aside his disquietude, the troubled feeling nipped at him. He pulled in a deep breath. "So, what is the name of this plantation where we're going?"

"Thornwalk Manor." Ramsay brushed invisible lint from his cuff. "Mont-gomery Granville owns it. I'm sure you'll meet him this evening, if he's home. He travels a great deal." He stretched out his legs and crossed them at the ankle. "His daughter is Miss Annulet Granville."

Ramsay pronounced the name as if tasting every syllable, reminding Pey-ton of some of his friend's escapades in college with the young women from the Brandywine Academy for Young Ladies, situated across the lake from their dormitory. Another topic Peyton did not wish to pursue.

"Will planters be in attendance at this party? Other than Montgomery Granville, that is?" That was the purpose of Peyton's visit to Georgia, after all—to make business contacts for his father's textile mills. Not that he was opposed to meeting lovely young ladies. He just didn't appreciate Ramsay's carnal habits when it came to women.

"Undoubtedly." His friend arched one eyebrow and laughed. "Old man Granville will want to talk about his moneymaking schemes, especially if he has an audience."

Minutes later, the carriage rolled to a stop in front of an impressive-looking home. The slave whom Ramsay had treated so scornfully jumped down and hastened to open the door of the carriage. Ramsay stepped down and waited while Peyton disembarked.

The slave lowered his eyes, but Peyton paused. "Thank you, uh. . . What is your name?"

The black man jerked his head up, startled. His glance shifted sideways to Ramsay, then back to stare at Peyton's chest, as if he was afraid to look Peyton in the eye. "M–my name be J–Joseph, suh."

"Thank you, Joseph."

Ramsay scoffed. "You don't say thank you to a slave. Folks will know you're not from around here."

Peyton ignored his friend's admonition and preceded him up the steps to the massive front portico with its ornate white pillars. They paused in the open double doors leading to a lavish entryway. If he had to endure this party, he must find some planters in attendance and discuss business. From his vantage point, he located a number of men, some of whom seemed more interested in getting their names on the dance cards of preferred ladies. Others appeared engrossed in conversation with each other.

Beside him, Ramsay tugged on the lapels of his frock coat and straightened his silk cravat. "You see that vision of loveliness in the green dress standing over there under that archway? The one with a half dozen men around her?" A throaty chuckle rumbled from Ramsay. "That, my dear fellow, is Miss Annulet Granville. She is ripe for the picking, and if I don't miss my guess, this party is for the purpose of snagging her a rich husband."

Peyton looked in the direction Ramsay indicated. A lovely woman stood there, but she didn't appear to be enjoying the attention from the men. At least it seemed so to Peyton. The half smile she wore looked as if she'd painted it on, and her eyes bore a pained expression.

"Mm-mm, that is one fine woman." Ramsay laughed. "But I say why graft yourself to the tree when all you want to do is taste the fruit."

His friend's vulgar comment set Peyton's teeth on edge, and he wondered if this trip was worth the trouble.

Chapter 2

Peyton watched as Ramsay threaded his way through the crowd toward the object of his desire without looking back to see if Peyton followed. That suited him. Being introduced to a flock of strutting peacocks and their prey wasn't the reason he'd come to this gathering.

He scanned the room and tried to differentiate between the men who were of Ramsay's mind-set and the ones who were likely business targets. Peyton spied a few older gentlemen standing in a knot and engaged in conversation. Since he was already tiring of the obnoxious flirting going on in the ballroom, speaking with these men was far more appealing. He stepped around couples and navigated past the musicians. When he finally arrived at the place where the men had stood, a pair of open French doors beckoned. Perhaps they'd stepped out for a breath of air. He exited to the wide veranda but saw no sign of them. He heaved a sigh. Returning to the party held little appeal. He much preferred to catch a glimpse of the fields and assess the cotton production.

The sun grazing the treetops to the west threw long shadows as he walked across the lawn to a crushed shell path that led through the formal gardens and past a tall hedgerow. After walking several minutes, he came to the edge of the rolling fields. Halting his steps, he took in the sight before him. Sparse, scraggly plants, half the height they should be for this time of year and competing with weeds for space, held out meager hope for a good crop. He examined the stems and leaves and found them inferior. Had they planted new seed or let the perennial plants sprout up on their own? The condition of the plants suggested the latter. He saw no evidence of irrigation and speculated the soil hadn't been amended. Attempting to make a business connection with Granville wouldn't be worth his time.

There was nothing more to see, so he turned around to return to the manor house when he heard a man barking orders. The voice came from the other side of the hedgerow. He crept closer and pushed aside a cedar bough. A man who, judging by the coiled whip hanging from his belt, must be the overseer, ordered two slaves to unload a wagon full of crates and bundles and carry them into a cabin tucked into the trees—a cabin much nicer than the pitiful shacks lining the edges of the fields.

The overseer growled at one of the slaves, an elderly man he called Eli, threatening him to pick up the pace or face consequences. The slave named Eli lowered his eyes and did the overseer's bidding, despite the crates appearing too heavy for a man of his advanced years.

Peyton took a step closer, and Eli looked up. When he did so, the overseer turned to look as well.

Caught!

The overseer shoved Eli aside and stomped toward Peyton. "Who're you and what're you doin' here?"

Determined not to let this ill-mannered oaf think he could be intimidated, Peyton stood tall. "I am Peyton Stafford, a guest of the Granvilles."

The unkempt man didn't appear impressed. "Rudd Jacobson. I oversee this place."

Peyton lifted his chin in a brief nod. "I'm curious what Mr. Granville thinks about the condition of his fields and crop."

Animosity narrowed Jacobson's eyes. "Can't see as that's none of your business. 'Sides, old man Granville don't never come back here. He's too good to get his hands dirty." He flicked a glance up and down Peyton. "Best you head on back to the big house. You and your fancy clothes be a mite too delicate for this part of the plantation."

Peyton wished to ask Jacobson why the crop was so poor and why the supplies were being carried into the overseer's cabin. He couldn't claim knowledge of an overseer's job description. Did the job entail the dispersing of food as well as tools? He doubted it.

A bad taste lingered in Peyton's mouth as he returned to the path that led back to the manor house. Not only were the slaves obviously afraid of Jacobson, from all appearances, the overseer was taking advantage of Montgomery Granville. He shrugged off the thought. Why should he care?

The sun had sunk behind the trees on the western horizon, and shadows blended with each other as he headed back to the manor house. Dusky sky drew a curtain over the plantation. If Ramsay's earlier remarks were any indication, his friend planned to stay at the party much later than Peyton hoped.

He still wished to discuss mutually beneficial business agreements with the planters—if he could find them.

He made his way back through the gardens, following the curving path through heavily scented flowering shrubs and vines. Just beyond, he noticed a white structure peeking out from between the magnolias. Upon closer inspection, he realized it was an arbor with a swing.

And it wasn't unoccupied.

Annulet Granville sat there, swaying gently in the gathering twilight. She appeared annoyed that he'd interrupted her solitude, but since she'd seen him, the polite thing to do was at least greet her.

"Good evening, Miss Granville." He gestured to the cozy arbor surrounded by foliage. "This is a lovely spot."

She lowered her eyes and smoothed her skirt before looking up again. "I'm sorry, but we haven't been introduced."

He gave a slight bow. "Peyton Stafford. I apologize for intruding."

"Mr. Stafford." She gave him a cool appraisal. "You don't sound like you're from around here."

He tucked his hands behind him. "I'm from Boston. I'm here to meet with cotton planters for the purpose of establishing contracts for my family's textile mills."

Her lips pursed. "I see. I don't recall your name on the guest list."

Did she think him an interloper? "I've just arrived at Meadowgold Plantation to visit with Ramsay Wheeler. He and I go back to our college days."

She gave a noncommittal shrug. "I suppose it would have been rude of him to leave you behind." Her gaze wandered past him, in the direction of the gardens from where he'd come. "You were out exploring our grounds?"

His face warmed, and he glanced at his shoes. "I knew no one inside, and thought perhaps I could find some of the men with whom I could speak."

Her eyebrows arched. "About cotton contracts."

"That's right."

"The party didn't interest you?"

An odd question coming from the young woman who was supposed to be the hostess, but he'd found her sitting out in the arbor by herself. He took a straightforward approach. "No, but Ramsay insisted I come. He indicated on the way here that he anticipated dancing with you."

In the fading light, her expression turned defensive for a moment. Then she changed the subject. "What kind of contracts do you hope to initiate?"

Peyton clasped his hands behind him again. "My father would like to contract with a dozen or so planters for a guaranteed supply of fine quality cotton without having to negotiate with agents."

She sent her glance past him again. "May I assume you were inspecting the cotton crop at Thornwalk to see if it measures up to your standards?"

It certainly did not measure up, but he doubted Miss Granville was truly interested in his opinion. "I was curious why your father still plants long staple cotton when this area of Georgia has been having more success with short staple."

The moment the comment left his lips, she stiffened. Perhaps he should have worded his observation differently. "I wrote a series of articles three years ago for the *Southern Agricultural Journal* that were quite well received, in which I outlined the success of short staple cotton in Georgia."

She rose from the swing, arms akimbo. "Of course a man from Boston would know what type of cotton grows best in Georgia."

So, she wanted to debate? "I graduated with honors from the University of Georgia in Athens. Since they did not offer a major in agricultural science at the time, I focused my thesis on research the school could use to develop such a course of study. The department heads sent my collection of term papers to the *Southern Agricultural Journal*."

Even in the deepening shadows, her cheeks glowed pink. "Well, I suppose I've been put in my place."

Regret threaded through him. It wasn't his intention to embarrass her. "I was only trying to explain that I do know what I'm talking about when it comes to cotton cultivation and harvest in Georgia." He paused and glanced over his shoulder. "Miss Granville, forgive me for saying so, but I believe your overseer isn't doing his job—based on the evidence I saw of the crop and the soil. I wonder, is your father aware of the condition of his fields?"

Judging by the indignation he saw blooming in her eyes, he'd best keep the rest of his opinion regarding Thornwalk's overseer to himself.

Annulet bristled. How dare this man think he could come to her home and insinuate that her father was less than capable of running his plantation!

"I don't see that that's any of your business, sir. My father does not need your advice on the operation of his plantation." She bit back a demand that he leave at once. Since he was here with Ramsay Wheeler, Mr. Stafford had no means of transportation of his own. Besides, her mother would be livid if she offended the Wheelers, seeing as how Ramsay had a star next to his name on the guest list. But she most certainly would refuse to put Peyton Stafford's name on her dance card.

She folded her arms in a defensive posture. "My father is a third-generation planter."

Mr. Stafford mimicked her stance. "That may be so, but from what I saw, the fields have been neglected, and the cotton is not nearly what it should be by this time of year. I don't know what your—"

"That's right, Mr. Stafford, you don't know." Holding back her temper required all her self-control. Who did this man think he was?

"Look, it makes no difference to me." Mr. Stafford raised his upturned palms. "I have no intention of discussing a contract with your father. If you don't care that your overseer is taking advantage of him, that's entirely your business. I just thought your father should know."

Her thoughts came to an abrupt halt. What was he talking about—taking advantage of Papa? But if she asked, he'd assume he'd bested her, and she'd never allow that. "Then I would propose that if my father wishes to know your opinion, he'll ask for it. Until then, I assume that an *honor* graduate of a prestigious university will have acquired civility and refinement, and have the manners to know when to be silent."

He studied her a moment. "I have enough manners to extend a kindness where it is needed."

A kindness. "Why would you possibly think my father is in need of benevolence?"

Mr. Stafford tucked his hands into his pockets and leaned against the frame of the arbor. "Because I believe he is unaware of his overseer's activities. But your father isn't the only one to whom I referred. You too, Miss Granville, seem in need of rescue."

The audacity of the man! "I need rescue?"

Mr. Stafford stroked his chin. "I truly don't understand something, so perhaps you can enlighten me. I find the idea of your parents holding a party for the purpose of finding you a rich husband preposterous."

Mortification seethed through her. "You, sir, are no gentleman."

She picked up her skirts and marched back to the house, to the soiree she so resented. Mr. Stafford was right. This party was preposterous.

Chapter 3

Peyton trailed Annulet Granville at a distance. Clear blue eyes, sparking with anger, lingered in his memory and still hypnotized him long after she'd turned and stamped out of the arbor, pride intact. The lanterns along the path reflected off the pale green gown that swished with every determined stride. Chestnut hair fell down the back of her neck, silky tendrils inviting him to curl them around his fingers. Why would a woman as beautiful as Annulet Granville need help finding a husband?

He regretted that she'd misunderstood his statement. Should he apologize? If he approached her now, she'd likely throw the nearest heavy object at him. Unfamiliar as he was with the lady, he had no inkling of how long she might feed her indignation. He'd wait before making another attempt at conversation.

She disappeared through a back door. Peyton paused in the shadows where the lantern light didn't reach. He rubbed his fingers across his forehead. He'd never before been so mesmerized by a woman. Best he keep his mind on task.

Three men stood talking on the veranda, silhouetted in front of the windows aglow with candlelight. Peyton proceeded to the wide steps and approached them. They turned and greeted him, and he nodded in response. One of the men held out his hand.

"Good evening, sir. I don't believe I've had the pleasure. I'm Montgomery Granville." Light from the windows defined the silver streaks in the man's hair and beard.

Peyton gripped his hand and shook it. "Peyton Stafford."

Granville's eyes lit with recognition. "You're the young fellow Ramsay Wheeler told me about. I understand your family owns textile mills in Massachusetts."

"Yes, sir." What all had Ramsay told these gentlemen? He hoped Granville wasn't expecting to discuss a contract.

Instead, Granville introduced the men to his left. "This is George Murdock of Mockingbird Plantation, and Theodore Bartells of Dogwood Villa Plantation."

Murdock, the man in the gray frock coat and turquoise satin vest, shook Peyton's hand. "So how do you like our fair state? Must be a lot different than what you're used to."

"Different, to be sure. I've seen some very lovely sights." Peyton tailored his neutral reply so as to not indicate a guaranteed contract until he had an opportunity to assess the man's crop.

Bartells scratched his chin. "Didn't I read something in the *Southern Agricultural Journal* with your name on it?"

Peyton nodded. "Yes, sir. I wrote a series of articles for that publication. Southern cotton is essential to our mills, and we've found Georgia short staple cotton to be superior to other varieties. It's our first choice when it's available." He slid a surreptitious glance toward Granville to gauge his reaction. As expected, the man frowned and slid his thumbs up his suspenders.

"My grandfather and my father both grew long staple cotton." He looked to the other two men before aiming a pointed stare back at Peyton. "I never saw the need to change."

Peyton knew thin ice when he encountered it and took a moment to think carefully how to word his reply, but Murdock and Bartells beat him to it.

Bartells glanced at his companions. "We've been growing short staple for over thirty years."

"So have we." Murdock nodded. "Why, my father changed over from long staple to short staple back in 1820. Our crop has always done well."

Granville's face reddened, and his thick brows met in a deep furrow. "Excuse me. There is someone I need to see." He spun on his heel and stalked away.

Peyton watched him enter a side door and stride down a hallway. Murdock and Bartells spoke in low tones to each other.

"Is he still growing long staple cotton?"

Bartells shook his head. "I don't know, but if that's the case, he can't be doing very well. It might explain why he's trying to match up his daughter with old money."

Murdock grunted. "He's building castles in the air."

A pang of sympathy tugged at Peyton. It was a sad thing, indeed, to see a man of position and prestige lose influence among his peers. But the sympathy stopped there. He simply couldn't condone forcing one's daughter to marry for money in order to shore up the family finances.

He turned to Murdock and Bartells. "A pleasure meeting you gentlemen. I'd like to have the opportunity to see your operations, if I'm not being too presumptuous."

Murdock pumped Peyton's hand. "Not at all. Young Wheeler knows where my place is. He can give you directions. Stop by one day next week."

Bartells nodded. "You're welcome to come by Dogwood Villa and see how we do things. I think you'll be impressed with our crop. We produced four hundred and sixty bales of fine short staple last year."

Peyton shook Bartell's hand. "I look forward to it."

They parted company, and Peyton traced the steps taken by Montgomery Granville a few minutes earlier. The hallway Granville had taken was lined with what Peyton assumed were generations of family portraits. Why he felt the need to pacify Montgomery Granville, he couldn't say, other than his own conscience nudged him to reveal to the man what he'd observed earlier. He proceeded to the end of the hall where he found a door standing partially open.

Peyton peered inside. Granville stood at a desk pouring amber liquid from a flask into his cup of punch. Peyton tapped on the door.

"May I come in, sir?"

Granville harrumphed and gave a nod.

Peyton entered the plush study, his footsteps silenced by the thick carpets. Expensive tapestry covered the matching chairs facing the polished mahogany desk, and fine, tooled leather covered the desktop. Velvet drapes set off the windows, and cut-glass prisms hanging from the lampshades threw gossamer shimmers of light dancing on the walls.

Peyton tucked his hands in his pockets. "Mr. Granville, I didn't intend to offend with my comments. I hope you'll take what I said the way it was meant."

"Hmm." Granville held up the flask. "Can I offer you something stronger than that feeble, watered-down punch?"

"No thank you, sir." Peyton studied the pattern of the rug for a brief moment. "I hope you won't think me out of line, but I went for a short walk a little while ago and looked over your fields."

Granville fired a sharp glower at him. "Did you now?"

"Sir, the variety of cotton you choose to grow isn't why I've come to speak with you privately." Peyton swallowed. "I believe your man, Jacobson, is mismanaging your plantation. By the looks of your fields, the soil doesn't appear to have been amended, the crop is inferior, and I suspect no rotation has been done for years, nor have any fields been left to fallow. I saw no evidence of irrigation, and if I had to guess, I'd be willing to bet no new seed has been planted in a long while."

Storm clouds stirred across Granville's countenance, and he set his cup down on the desk with a clunk. "Is that so? You have no right to tell me how to run my plantation."

Peyton fingered the inside of his pockets and looked Granville in the eye. "I agree. But when Jacobson challenged my presence, I asked him what you thought of the condition of your fields and your crop. He said you never go back there to the fields, and he indicated he runs things the way *he* sees fit.

"Mr. Granville, I understand you are a third-generation planter, so I'm sure you know there are certain practices that should be followed to ensure a successful harvest. I don't believe Mr. Jacobson is following them. I just thought you ought to know."

An indignant lift of his chin defined Granville's feelings about Peyton's opinions. "Yes, well, you must excuse me while I get back to our guests." Without another word, he strode from the study.

Peyton heaved a sigh. He'd done what his conscience had told him. Now it was up to Granville to do whatever he wished with the information. Peyton followed the older man back toward the ballroom, but before he could walk the length of the hallway, Annulet Granville appeared around a corner and stopped short when they locked gazes.

The tempestuous look on her father's face sent shards of foreboding through Annulet. What could possibly have—

Her feet halted as she came around the corner. *Peyton Stafford.* She clenched her fists at the sight of him. Did that horrid man insult Papa? Did he spout his opinions in front of Papa's peers? She narrowed her eyes at him, her stomach tightening and her teeth clenching. How dare this man come into her home and humiliate her father!

He gave a slight nod. "Miss Granville." He moved past her, headed toward the ballroom.

She opened her mouth but could do nothing more than sputter. She picked up her skirts and called after him just as the musicians struck up a waltz, drowning out her words. But she was intent on confronting the man and insisting he leave at once. He'd done enough damage.

"Annulet."

Mama's voice rang with urgency. Annulet watched Mr. Stafford thread his way through the waltzing couples before turning to face her mother.

Mama grasped her by the hand and pulled her aside, lowering her voice to a conspiratorial whisper. "Daughter, I've just learned that Mr. Stafford—the man who arrived with Ramsay Wheeler—comes from a wealthy family that has owned textile mills in Massachusetts for five decades."

This wasn't news to Annulet. She pressed her lips together and searched the sea of people that had swallowed Mr. Stafford, praying she could find the man before he could embarrass her family any further.

Mama tugged her hand and leaned close. "Ramsay tells me he and Mr. Stafford attended the University of Georgia together, and that the university is forming a new study program based on Mr. Stafford's research." She held up two fingers. "The family has money, and Mr. Stafford has earned a standing at a prestigious university. Perhaps Peyton Stafford should be the target of your pursuit."

Mama's suggestion yanked cords of horror around Annulet's throat, and for several seconds she could neither breathe nor swallow. She pulled her trembling hand from her mother's grasp and backed away. Her lips opened and closed, groping for words to express her aversion to the man. "M–Mama, you don't—surely you can't be—" She sucked in a breath and reached for the wainscoting to steady herself. "Mama, Peyton Stafford is high-handed and arrogant, and I wouldn't marry him if he were the last man on earth. I'd rather marry someone I barely know than—"

At that moment, one of the men from Mama's guest list approached. Royce Forbes, with one hand on his paunchy middle, bestowed a broad smile on her. He bowed low, revealing a round bald spot surrounded by a thatch of graying hair.

"Miss Granville, I've been looking for you. I believe this is our dance." He held out his hand.

Annulet swallowed back the urge to be sick. She croaked words past her lips, unsure of how they might sound. "I'm s–s–sorry, I can't."

Every instinct within her told her to flee, and flee she did. She aimed her feet for the rear door at the far end of the hallway, unable to endure another minute of this fiasco.

Mama called after her. "Annulet! Annulet Renee! Come back at once and attend to your guests."

For the first time in her life, Annulet couldn't find it within herself to comply with her mother's wishes. The evening air engulfed her, stealing her breath momentarily. She ran through the gardens, pausing only long enough to grab one of the lanterns hanging on a post. The light flickered to and fro as the lantern swayed in her grip, but it was enough to illumine the pathway to the arbor—her sanctuary, her hiding place.

Chapter 4

The secluded arbor welcomed Annulet's return with soothing comfort. She recalled running here as a child, weeping with disconsolation over her father's departure for yet another journey. Her governess never looked for her here. The poor woman had loathed being outdoors among the trees, thinking a snake or spider might drop down on her at any moment. So the arbor became Annulet's haven when she craved solitude.

Nothing had changed.

She sank down on the swing for the second time this evening. Doubtless, Mama was furious, but if she'd stayed one more minute, she couldn't have controlled the tears any longer. She leaned back and closed her eyes, willing the cool evening air to soothe her face. Cicadas and whip-poor-wills tuned up for their evening concert, but the solace she usually found in their music rang hollow.

Muted strains of a waltz from the stringed ensemble floated on the encroaching darkness, an unrelenting reminder of her obligation to her parents. A number of men to whom she had promised a dance waited in the ballroom—men on her mother's list of selected prospects. Unshed tears burned her eyes. Oh, how she detested being made a spectacle.

Guilt nipped her. Was she being selfish? Her parents had not spoken plainly regarding the need, but she caught the underlying motive. They needed her to marry well. Her mother's biting comments about Papa's moneymaking schemes left little to the imagination. What had Papa said? It was her duty to her family. Of course, Papa had spouted some nonsense about the family's resources and legacy, or some such thing. He made it sound noble, like a warrior going into battle. But a warrior often died in battle. She was expected to live the rest of her life with a man solely based on his financial assets. The make-believe games she'd played as a child, and the dreams she'd dreamed as a girl of falling in love and living a fairy-tale life evaporated like the morning dew under a hot sun.

It wasn't as if she had no social life. Over the past few years, she'd had gentlemen callers and escorts to all the important events. Contrary to Mr. Stafford's rude assumption, she didn't need help to make the acquaintance of eligible young men. She opened her eyes and gazed at the stars—thousands of them—winking at her through the boughs of the magnolia trees, and wondered which of them was hers. How was a lady to know which man God picked out for her? Wouldn't that be like choosing one star?

Of all the young men who'd come calling over the past few years, two were now betrothed to others, one was attending West Point, and she'd heard another was traveling abroad. Ramsay Wheeler had acted as her escort a time or two, and she'd been flattered by his attention. She expected, since Mama had put a star next to his name on the guest list, that Mama would nudge her in Ramsay's direction. But now her mother seemed adamant she should pursue Mr. Stafford. The very idea caused her toes to curl in suppressed anger.

After dodging waltzing and flirting couples, Peyton finally located Ramsay standing near the open French doors, sipping punch.

"You aren't dancing?"

Ramsay scowled and downed the remainder of liquid in his glass that smelled suspiciously of rum. "Where've you been? Didn't see you on the dance floor."

Peyton shrugged. "I'm not much of a dancer, and what I really wanted was to speak to some of the other planters. Mr. Granville introduced me to a couple of area plantation owners."

"Hm." Ramsay looked past Peyton across the ballroom. "Have you seen Annulet Granville? Seems odd she's not present at her own party." A lecherous smile lifted one corner of his mouth. "Unless she and some young buck have sneaked off to get to know each other better, if you know what I mean. I wouldn't mind getting to know her better myself."

Peyton's disgust for his friend's implication fueled his impatience to leave. "Listen, Ramsay, I have a beastly headache. I think I'd like to call it a night. Would it be all right if I went on back to Meadowgold and sent the carriage back for you?"

He'd stretched the truth a mite, but if he stayed in this ballroom five more minutes the nagging pain in his head would surely mushroom into more than a simple annoyance. His purpose in coming didn't include enduring the nerve-grating nonsense going on around him at this moment. His father sent him here to form business connections. The two introductions with Murdock and Bartells would do for a start.

Ramsay clapped him on the shoulder. "Certainly." He tossed another searching look across the room. "I intend to get some time with the lovely Miss Granville, and I'm not leaving until I do."

Peyton gave him a brief nod. "Thanks. I'll see you later then."

He made his way out the door and pulled in a deep, cleansing breath of night air. Several of the drivers lounging against the carriages snapped upright when he approached. He found the Meadowgold carriage halfway down the drive with lantern light playing off the shiny trim. Ramsay's driver, Joseph, hopped down and opened the carriage door.

"Is Massah Ramsay comin', suh?"

Peyton lifted a hand to indicate the man didn't need to hurry. "No, Joseph. He's staying a while, but I'd like to go on back, if you don't mind."

Joseph's eyes widened. "Iffen I don't—" He gulped. "Yassah."

Peyton took a last look across the front portico of the lovely manor house and expansive yard, now dotted with lanterns. At the far end of the gardens, a pinpoint of light glimmered. Wasn't that where he saw Annulet Granville in the arbor earlier? Perhaps Ramsay was right. She might have returned there with a young man. He dismissed the image in his mind. It was none of his business. Peyton turned to climb into the carriage, but before he stepped all the way up, a thought occurred to him.

"Wait." He stared at the tiny gleam of light again. What if some man was forcing her into something against her will? He couldn't turn his back and leave her at the mercy of some cad.

He returned both feet to the ground. "Joseph, could you wait a few moments, please?" He picked his way across the yard to the gardens, the darkness impeding his progress. Guided only by the flickering lantern light, he found the secluded arbor. A soft sound reached him.

Someone was weeping.

He curled his fist, ready to teach the scoundrel who made the lady cry a lesson in manners. He pulled back a thick magnolia bough to reveal Annulet Granville sitting alone, dabbing her eyes and nose with her handkerchief.

He shot a glance to the right and left. "Miss Granville, are you all right?"

She gasped and leaped to her feet. "I–I'm perfectly f–fine." She fisted away the moisture from her cheeks and lifted her chin. "Hasn't anyone ever told you it's impolite to sneak up on people?"

The quiver in her voice told him she wasn't perfectly fine. "I'm sorry if I frightened you. I merely wanted to ensure you were safe."

He expected a prideful retort, but to his surprise, she relaxed her shoulders and sniffed. "As I said, I'm fine. I was just getting a breath of air."

One didn't weep when out enjoying the air, but contradicting the lady didn't seem the prudent thing to do. Instead, he clasped his hands behind him. "I'd like to apologize for making you angry earlier. It wasn't my intention."

She gave a mute nod.

He drew in a deep breath. "What else could I have done? If I saw someone galloping headlong down a road and I knew the bridge ahead had been washed out, and I didn't warn the person, wouldn't you consider that quite wrong of me?"

Miss Granville tipped her head to the side and folded her arms. Her narrowed eyes hinted she caught his analogy.

He fingered a smooth magnolia leaf. "I've done a great deal of research that proves short staple cotton is much more successful. It is quite evident from the lack of richness of the soil and the quality of the plants that your overseer isn't doing his job." He gentled his tone. "I don't wish to upset you or your father, but if he won't listen to the facts, I fear Thornwalk Manor is doomed, and your home along with it."

She pursed her lips into a bow and worked her jaw. "You presume to know a great deal, Mr. Stafford. You think spending a few years at the university entitles you to tell those of us who've lived here all our lives how to grow cotton." She took a bold step toward him. "Well, Mr. Stafford, my family has been growing cotton on this land for going on four generations. I don't think we need the advice of someone from Massachusetts to tell us how to—"

"You're missing my point."

"Am I?" She gestured toward the fields. "Didn't you inspect our cotton and declare it *inferior* to your high standards? When was the last time you planted a crop?"

"About three years ago, when I was conducting my research." If an argument was what she sought, he'd oblige her. "I planted fifteen acres myself. I had no help, no slaves, nobody but me tilling the soil. I sweated over the land and raised blisters on my hands. I planted different kinds of seeds in various conditions. I tested ways to amend the soil, and documented fields that were irrigated opposed to those that weren't. I measured the plants weekly, charted the growth and development, and monitored the progress to determine which variety produced not only the most cotton bolls per plant, but also the best quality. At harvest, I determined which varieties and which soil conditions produced the best crops."

"That hardly makes you an expert on running a plantation." Her steel-edged tone held a hint of desperation when her voice cracked ever so slightly. Did she truly grasp the dire condition of her family's plantation, or did she simply want to win the argument?

He pondered the question for a moment before forming a reply. "What if what I'm telling you has merit? Don't you owe it to yourself and your family to investigate it?"

Her shoulders straightened, and her chin lifted. "My father is a proud man."

"I understand. No man wants to be told he's going about his business in the wrong way. But what would be the consequences if he chooses not to listen?" He held out his hands, palms up, in an entreaty. "Don't you agree that withholding truth is more damaging than hurting your father's pride?"

When she offered no response, he took a step closer and inclined his head to catch her focus. "Your father can turn his plantation around and make it productive if he will listen to reason. I hope he will, for your sake."

Unease flickered across her face, but she didn't lash back at him. "What do you mean?"

Peyton turned toward the manor house where music lilted from the open doors. "Miss Granville, we both know the purpose of this party. No young woman should be forced to join herself in marriage to a rich man solely because of her father's imprudent business practices."

Chapter 5

Annulet forced down a gulp of tea past the lump in her throat. For three days she'd listened to Mama berate her for escaping to the arbor and leaving her to make excuses for her daughter's absence.

"Mama, I've said I'm sorry a hundred times." She set her delicate teacup in its matching saucer. "I wish you would try to understand."

"I will not listen to your whining anymore, Annulet." Mama slapped her napkin down on the table beside the teapot. "The gentlemen we invited—the men with whom you were supposed to socialize—were quite put out that you left your own party, not just once, but twice." She shook her head. "Charles Templeton expressed his disappointment that he only got one dance with you, and was resigned to dance with Genevieve Watson and Florence Taylor. He felt the trip all the way from Atlanta was hardly worth his time."

Mama's pointed frown made Annulet squirm. She cast her gaze to her lap. "I know. I'm sorry, but he and Genevieve seemed to enjoy each other's company."

"That's not the point, Annulet Renee, and you well know it." Mama wrung her fingers. "You knew the purpose of the ball and what was expected of you. Royce Forbes accused your father of misrepresenting you. He said your father led him to believe you were more mature and poised, and that he needs a wife in possession of better social graces than a young girl who runs away and cries because she's not getting her way." Mama's voice rose in volume and pitch with every word, until she finished her diatribe on a strident note.

Annulet winced. "Mama, Mr. Forbes is almost twenty years older than I am and has two children in their teens. He is completely correct. He *does* need a more mature woman, about twenty years more mature."

"That's nonsense." Mama pushed her chair back and stood. She smoothed her skirt and stepped to the window on the plush carpet. "Your father is several years older than I am, and we have a good marriage."

"Papa is only eight years your senior, and the two of you weren't thrown together. You love each other." Her parents had their fusses from time to time, but she'd never doubted their devotion to one another.

Mama turned and faced her, a softer expression in her eyes. "We do now, but we barely knew each other when we married. We grew into love."

Annulet's jaw dropped. "You...and Papa...I never knew that."

"Of course you didn't." Mama crossed back to the tea table and sat as regally as a queen. "My point is that regardless of whom you marry, if you determine to make your marriage work, it will."

Annulet didn't like the direction this conversation was going. Her only hope of bringing it to a close was finding a way to appease Mama. "I did dance with Ramsay Wheeler—a few times."

She didn't mention Ramsay's inappropriate suggestion that they go somewhere private and sip on something stronger than punch to "rid themselves of the cloak of archaic propriety." The invitation had made her breath catch, but not in a good way. She tugged at her sleeve to ensure the bruise left by Ramsay's fingers digging into her forearm was covered.

"Well—" Mama brushed her fingertips across her brow. "At least the Wheelers weren't offended by your childish behavior. I do recall, however, urging you to spend some time with Mr. Peyton Stafford, and he too left the party without so much as a notice from you."

If only Mama knew that she had, indeed, spent time with Mr. Stafford. She could recall every word of their conversation at the arbor, and each syllable both infuriated her and fascinated her in turn. How could that be? The last person by whom she wished to be fascinated was Peyton Stafford.

Polly, the Negro woman who waited on Annulet and her mother, came to the doorway. "Miz Granville, ma'am. Eli brung the mail."

Mama turned. "Come in, Polly." She held out her hand for the mail. "You may take the tea tray now."

"Yas'm." Polly picked up the tray and eyed the cookies left on the plate.

As the woman turned to leave, Annulet whispered. "Help yourself to the cookies, Polly."

A flicker of a smile lit Polly's eyes. "Thank ya, missy."

Mama passed two of the envelopes to Annulet. "These are for you." Her expression spoke of her hopeful expectation.

Annulet broke the wax seal on the first one and scanned the brief note from Elizabeth Reynolds, one of her acquaintances from whom she'd received an invitation three weeks ago for an upcoming ball. She blinked and reread the missive.

> *My sincerest apologies for any confusion or inconvenience, but I fear*
> *the invitation to the ball on May thirtieth was sent to you in error. The*
> *guest list does not include anyone with whom you are acquainted, and I*
> *wouldn't wish for you to feel uncomfortable in your attendance. . . .*

Elizabeth was rescinding her invitation? Heat rose into Annulet's face, and her stomach knotted.

"Who is it from, dear?" Mama's question jolted her.

Annulet drew in a slow, deep breath. "Elizabeth Reynolds."

Mama waited, no doubt for Annulet to read Elizabeth's note. Instead, she refolded the stationery and tucked it back into the envelope. She rose and held both envelopes against her waist.

She didn't wish to discuss the note, or Ramsay Wheeler, or Peyton Stafford. The solitude of the arbor called. "It's too lovely a day to spend indoors. I'm going for a walk." She scurried out before her mother had time to inquire what Elizabeth had said in her note. Humiliation over the rebuff fueled her gall and hastened her steps.

By the time she reached the arbor, perspiration dotted her brow. She sank to the swing, panting to catch her breath. Elizabeth's words echoed in her mind. It made no sense. She and Elizabeth had many mutual friends. Why would she think Annulet wouldn't know anyone at the ball? Even if she didn't, introductions could be made. Anger, hurt, and embarrassment collided in a hopeless tangle.

The second envelope lay unopened on her lap. She stared at it and fingered the seal. The envelope bore no indication as to the identity of the sender. After the sting of Elizabeth's snub, dare she open this one?

Reluctantly, she pushed her thumb against the seal and broke it. Two sentences.

> *The house party of June fifth is not for matchmaking purposes. In view*
> *of the scandalous behavior displayed at your party on Saturday last, the*
> *invitation you received must be retracted.*
>
> *Mrs. Rosalyn Powers*

Written by the mother of her friend Ruthanne, the penned words on the paper pointed an accusing finger at her. Word must be all over the county that Annulet Granville was on the hunt for a rich husband. An invisible fist punched her in the stomach.

It wasn't true. She'd despised the idea from the start. She only agreed to go along with the scheme for her parents' sake.

Her first impulse was to wave the two letters under Mama's nose and cast the blame for them at her feet. She crumpled the papers in her hand. Mama's plan had backfired, and Annulet was sure to catch the brunt of her mother's displeasure. Papa might even try to force her into an arranged marriage.

Whatever would she do?

The last time she sat on this swing, Mr. Stafford had come upon her and found her crying like a child. Despite the hint of comfort she'd experienced at his concern that evening, a growing sense of outrage seethed through her. His statement about her parents having a party for the purpose of finding her a husband reverberated in her head.

"It must have been him!" Of course. Peyton Stafford must be the one spreading the malicious rumor. A growl started in her toes, rose up through her belly, and emerged past her lips.

"Argh!"

God's Word stated she was to love her enemies. If Peyton Stafford was indeed responsible for proliferating the slanderous gossip, then he certainly qualified as an enemy.

Peyton slowed the gelding Ramsay had loaned him to a walk. Sorting through the information he'd collected since arriving at Meadowgold three weeks ago was proving a dilemma he hadn't sought. Each of the two plantations he'd visited used slave labor. That in itself wasn't a big surprise, but the startling revelation of his own ignorance distracted him from the very purpose of his visit.

How could he have attended the university a day's travel from here for four years and not have been aware of the reality faced by the slaves working on these plantations? While he'd attended a few functions hosted by planters during his college years, he'd never had occasion to see how the slaves lived or how they were treated. His questions had always been answered with vague accounts of how well the slaves were cared for.

Now, seeing for himself the true cost of a bale of cotton, he was sickened by his lack of comprehension. The very planters with whom his father wished him to contract for their cotton bought human beings and forced them into labor and often threatened them with brutality.

The slaves at the two plantations he'd visited this week seemed to be well fed, and their housing simple but adequate. The overseer didn't carry a whip like Jacobson at Thornwalk did, but it was still a distasteful business to buy and sell human beings like livestock. Memories of the other slaves he'd seen during the first week since his arrival still haunted him: the elderly slave at Thornwalk—Eli—forced to carry loads far too heavy for a man his age; and the condition of several other slaves at Thornwalk, some thin and sickly, others who bore open wounds on their backs, undoubtedly from Jacobson's whip. The disturbing images, the buying and selling of these people, the splitting up of their families, repulsed him.

He'd been told from his youth that slave labor in the South was necessary in order to turn a profit, but a profit taken at the expense of human flesh was plain evil. The contract with Mr. Wheeler, Ramsay's father, was already signed, much to Peyton's dismay after witnessing the way the slaves at Meadowgold were treated, but the paltry single contract wasn't going to meet his father's expectations.

Peyton nudged the gelding into a trot, heading down the road back toward Meadowgold. He wished he could simply return home and tell his father he wanted nothing more to do with this business deal. But something he remembered from his college days niggled at him. He still recalled one of his favorite professors making a pointed statement:

"If an injustice exists, and you become aware of it and do nothing to change it, you are as guilty as the one committing the injustice."

When Peyton had asked him the basis of his statement, the professor took a piece of paper, wrote something, and handed it to Peyton, telling him to look it up. On the paper, the professor had written "Colossians 3:12–14."

Over the past few years since Peyton had graduated from college, he'd reread those verses found in Colossians a number of times. The godly attributes listed—mercy, kindness, humbleness of mind, meekness, long-suffering—always stirred him to want to be a man who employed those qualities. But it was that last virtue—charity—that gave him pause, because according to the scripture, charity came first. *"Above all these things,"* it said.

Coming from an affluent background, he'd always assumed charity meant giving money to the poor. A light of understanding dawned within him. If charitable deeds were done only to soothe one's own conscience, then was it truly charity in the biblical sense? What if charity took on a different perspective, a new meaning, and became the basis of his convictions, like it was for his professor?

What, if anything, could he do to effect a change in the way the slaves lived and how they were treated? Perhaps not much, but even if he only caused a small change, it would be a change for the better for someone—maybe Eli, or Joseph, or one of the hundred others he'd seen in the past three weeks.

He nudged the horse to pick up the pace. He had a letter to write. The words began forming in his head: *Dear Father, I know you're not going to be happy about this. . . .*

Chapter 6

Peyton looped the reins around a hitching post. The city of Ridgefield wasn't anything like the cities in Massachusetts. Larger than Bethel Station, to be sure, and definitely more people. Its centralized location in the county made it convenient to use the Ridgefield bank and telegraph office on his travels to the outlying plantations.

He filed a document at the land office, met with the manager of the largest cotton mill in the area, and sent a couple of telegrams before stopping by the post office to mail the letter to his father. Until he received a reply, he'd continue to pursue the task he was sent to do, even though he had no doubt his father would replace him.

His last stop was the bank before heading back to Meadowgold. He approached a teller. "Excuse me, but I need to see the manager. Is he in?"

The mousy fellow with a receding hairline and double chin nodded. "Yessir, he's in. If you'll wait just over there, he'll be with you in a few minutes. He's got someone in his office right now."

Peyton thanked the man and moved to wait where he was directed. The bank manager's door was open, and Peyton saw Montgomery Granville sitting across the desk from the banker. Peyton sent a glance across the bank lobby. Was Annulet here with her father? Odd that Granville would use the Ridgefield bank instead of the one in Bethel Station. He shrugged it off. It was none of his business.

He sat in a chair just outside the banker's office and drummed his fingers on the armrest, waiting for the banker to finish his business with Granville. Through the open door, he couldn't help overhearing Granville's raised voice. The words *surety* and *mortgage* reached Peyton's ears, and he stiffened. He didn't want or need to hear this. As he rose to step away from the banker's office door, his boot caught the leg of the chair, sending it thudding into the wall. He glanced to see if either man had noticed, and the scene pulled a frown onto his face. Granville had laid a diamond-and-pearl necklace on the desk, and the banker shook his head. Peyton yanked his gaze away, but not before Granville looked up and saw him.

Peyton feigned looking through his pockets, pretending he didn't see or hear any part of the conversation. A grimace shuddered through him, and he turned his back to the open door. His thoughts swirled and tumbled.

Don't speculate, Peyton. You don't know any of the facts.

Even if he walked out of the bank now, he'd not be able to dismiss what he'd seen. He did know Thornwalk Manor Plantation was in trouble, so it wasn't surprising Granville was trying to persuade the banker to accept his wife's jewelry as a payment of some sort. The image of a once successful man begging the banker to acquiesce to his request was a sad picture indeed.

He berated himself again. Being a chess player had created a habit of thinking two or three steps ahead. The only basis he had for such conjecture was his knowledge of the condition of Thornwalk's crop and fields, and Ramsay's theory that the party was nothing more than recruitment for a rich husband for Annulet.

He positioned himself across the lobby, ensuring he would hear no more of what should be a private conversation. If Granville was indeed in financial trouble, Peyton suspected it stemmed from more than just the poor crop. He'd not been able to dismiss the memory of Rudd Jacobson directing old Eli to carry those crates into the overseer's cabin. Shouldn't they have been delivered to the manor house kitchen? If they'd contained tools or seed, they should have been taken to the barn. Even if the crates contained food for the slaves, why store it in Jacobson's cabin?

Since he didn't plan to contract with Granville, he shouldn't care about the man's financial troubles. But what he'd been trying to shrug off kept nudging him. Try as he might, he couldn't forget about the way Rudd Jacobson treated the slaves and, truth be told, he couldn't forget about Annulet and her destiny to be married off to a man not of her choosing.

He pulled his watch from his pocket. He didn't have to meet with George Murdock for another two hours. There was time for a quick errand before he transacted his business at the bank. He slipped out the door and headed down the street toward the courthouse.

The plump, gray-haired woman at the front desk directed him to the records department. Peyton pushed away the nagging guilt of what he was about to do. Another clerk, a younger man, looked up as he stepped into the records room.

"Help ya?"

Tax records were public. He wasn't invading Granville's privacy. Peyton nodded. "I'm looking for property tax records for the past year."

The young fellow straightened his spectacles and pulled an unwieldy volume from the shelf. "Alphabetized by property owner. Leave the book on the table there when you're done."

Peyton thanked him and began turning pages. He found the *G* section and ran his finger down the page. *Granville, Montgomery; Thornwalk Manor.* Just as he'd thought. The record showed the taxes were in arrears, and not only from the present year. There was a balance owing from last year as well.

The next two days were taken up with meeting other planters and touring their plantations. Only one met all of his father's criteria, but reluctance over the appearance of the slaves and the harshness of the overseer held Peyton back from offering a contract. He told the man he'd be in touch. Another plantation didn't produce as much cotton, but it was fine quality. Not only that, the man and his four sons worked the fields alongside a half dozen slaves who appeared healthy and well treated. Peyton and the planter shook hands on a tentative deal.

He turned his gelding into the long drive at Meadowgold and rode to the stable. A young boy came out to take the animal, and Peyton asked the child's name. Fear filled the boy's eyes for a moment until Peyton smiled at him and produced some licorice from his pocket.

"My name be Toby."

"Well, Toby, you take real good care of this horse now." Peyton patted Toby's shoulder. "Enjoy that licorice."

Toby beamed. "Yes, suh!"

Peyton pulled his satchel from the saddle and headed toward the manor house. Ramsay called to him from the side veranda.

"Come and join me. Mother is hosting a bunch of women for some kind of hen party, so I'm having lunch out here on the veranda." He snapped his fingers at one of the servants. "Bring a place setting for Mr. Stafford."

Peyton pulled up a chair across from Ramsay while his friend inquired about his trip.

"I certainly found some quality cotton. I think Father will be pleased."

While they ate, the slave Peyton remembered as Joseph brought a letter on a small tray. "Mistah Stafford, suh. This just come fo' you."

Peyton took the envelope and turned it over but did not recognize the seal. "Thank you, Joseph."

Ramsay snorted. "There you go again. He's only doing what he's supposed to do."

Peyton glanced up. "It's never wrong to use good manners." He broke the seal and opened the letter. His gaze scanned down to the bottom of the page. The letter was from Montgomery Granville.

Enduring the luncheon given by Mrs. Wheeler on behalf of the Ladies' Missionary Society was excruciating enough, not knowing whether or not Ramsay would make an appearance. But being seated across from Elizabeth Reynolds after having received her offensive note stung Annulet with embarrassment. Elizabeth eyed her with a smug smile. "So tell me, Annulet. How many proposals of marriage have you received since your party? It's been—what? Three weeks? Surely you must be inundated by now." A smirk punctuated the girl's catty statement.

Titters around the table accompanied the flames of mortification that burned Annulet's cheeks. Several other women hid their amusement behind their napkins.

The woman seated to Mrs. Wheeler's right flicked her gaze over Annulet with raised eyebrows, and Mrs. Rockwell, president of the Ladies' Missionary Society, gasped, fingertips covering her lips. If God could close the lions' mouths for Daniel, surely He could close Elizabeth's mouth as well.

A few murmurs rippled around the long table for what felt like an eternity. Then Mrs. Wheeler cleared her throat. "Why don't we all retire to the garden at this time. I've ordered our dessert and tea to be served there."

The ladies rose and exited the dining room one by one. Elizabeth and a couple of her friends cast taunting glances over their shoulders. Annulet held her head up but wished the floor would swallow her. If only she could slip out unnoticed.

Two maids entered the dining room and stopped short when they found Annulet standing there.

"I–I'm not feeling very well. Can one of you call for my carriage to be brought around?"

One of the maids bobbed her head. "Yes'm."

"Thank you." She glanced in the direction of the door the other guests had taken. "I'll wait on the side veranda where it's shadier."

The maid scurried off, and Annulet let herself out the French doors. She quietly closed the doors behind her and drew in a slow, deep breath. The sweet late spring air cleansed her lungs and calmed her spirit. The sooner she put Meadowgold Plantation and those ladies behind her, the better—

"Well, well. Good afternoon, Miss Granville."

Startled, Annulet sucked in a sharp breath and clutched her throat with one hand. She spun in the direction of the voice and found Ramsay and Mr. Stafford sitting at a wicker table enjoying their lunch.

Mr. Stafford rose, wiping his mouth on a napkin, but Ramsay remained seated, leaning back in his chair. He offered no apology for frightening her. "Wasn't Mother's luncheon menu to your liking?"

She lowered her hand to her chest in an attempt to slow the pounding of her heart. "It was fine, but I–I'm not feeling well."

Mr. Stafford stepped forward. "Please sit down, Miss Granville. Would you like a sip of water?"

With a fleeting glare at Ramsay, she sent Mr. Stafford a polite shake of her head. "No, thank you. My carriage will be here in a few moments."

A lecherous smile stretched Ramsay's face. "I'd certainly like more than a few moments with you, especially since we didn't have a chance to spend any time alone at your party. We must remedy that."

Her stomach tensed, and she narrowed her eyes. "I don't appreciate your inappropriate suggestions now any more than I did at the party."

His eyes traveled all the way to her toes and back up again. "If you want my opinion, you and your parents have tumbled from your pedestal, so you're no longer entitled to pick and choose suitors."

Mr. Stafford turned and stared at Ramsay. "That's no way to speak to a lady."

Ramsay snorted. "Maybe she will prefer you over me, old man. Does she think your family has more money than mine?" He pushed away from the table and strode past Annulet into the house, leaving her standing there reliving the humiliation she'd suffered inside with the women.

There was nowhere to run and hide, and there was still no sign of her carriage. She lowered her gaze to the toes of her slippers, heat rising from her belly.

She closed her eyes and made a wish that Mr. Stafford might disappear from her presence, but his voice broke the silence. "May I see you home?"

She jerked her head up. "No, thank you."

"I wish you'd allow me. It would be my honor to ensure you arrive home safely."

She cocked her head and hesitated. "Weren't you the one who spread the rumor, who told half the county that I was on the hunt for a rich husband?"

A tiny scowl knit his brows. "I assure you, Miss Granville, I have not, and would never speak so about a lady."

She studied him. A gentleness in his tone invited her to believe him. Was this the same man she considered rude at her party?

Her carriage rolled to a stop by the veranda steps. Mr. Stafford offered his arm going down the stairs, and he aided her stepping up into the conveyance. She settled on the seat and turned to him.

"Thank you, Mr. Stafford. I–I'm sure I will get home just fine without any help."

Chapter 7

Peyton pushed back his chair from the table and smiled at the black woman who had served him. "Breakfast was delicious. Thank you."

He still hadn't gotten accustomed to seeing disbelief in the eyes of the slaves whenever he spoke kindly to them or said thank you. Ramsay rolled his eyes but finally gave up ridiculing him for it.

Ramsay strutted out of the dining room. "Any more meetings for you today?"

Peyton nodded and checked his pocket to make sure he'd tucked the letter from Montgomery Granville inside. "Yes, if I can borrow a horse again, I need to see another planter today." After the way Ramsay had embarrassed Annulet yesterday, Peyton had no inclination to tell him he was going to Thornwalk.

"Of course, take any horse you like."

Peyton peered at the gray sky. "I think I'll get started so I can miss the rain. See you later this evening." They parted, and Joseph stepped up.

"Mistah Stafford, suh. You be needin' another hoss?"

"Good morning, Joseph." Peyton cast another glance at the sky. "Yes, but I sure hope the rain holds off until I can get to Thornwalk."

Joseph's eyes brightened a fleeting moment but then darkened as he bit his lip and lowered his gaze.

"What is it, Joseph?"

The man hesitated, but the deep frown across his brow prodded Peyton to encourage him. "It's all right, Joseph. You can speak freely."

Joseph slowly raised his chin until he looked Peyton in the eye. "My wife, Polly, be at Thornwalk. Massah Wheeler sell her a few years back. Her and me don't see each other much. Tried to see her that night when you an' Massah Ramsay go to that party, but she were servin'."

The pain in Joseph's eyes skewered Peyton, and he laid his hand on

Joseph's shoulder. "I've decided not to ride to Thornwalk today, since it might rain. Do you suppose you could bring a carriage around? Of course, I'll need a driver."

Pure joy washed over Joseph's dark eyes. "Yes, suh!"

While he waited for Joseph to bring the carriage, Peyton pulled out the letter from Granville and puzzled over it for the twentieth time. Why would the man ask him to come to Thornwalk to discuss business? Peyton had been careful not to give any indication at the Granvilles' party that he wished to enter into a business relationship with the man. He shook his head and tucked the missive back into his pocket.

Peyton was glad for the carriage when a misty rain began falling before they turned into the long drive at Thornwalk. Joseph held an umbrella over Peyton as he descended the carriage and hurried up the steps to the front door.

Peyton leaned close to Joseph. "I'm not sure how long I'll be, but I'll make certain it's enough for you to spend some time with your Polly. I'll send word when I'm ready to go back to Meadowgold."

Joseph beamed. "Thank ya, suh." He reached forward and thumped the knocker against the door.

A thin black woman in a plain blue dress and white apron opened the door. Her eyes widened, and a soft gasp escaped her lips. "Jo—"

Joseph's smile stretched across his face. "This here be Mistah Stafford to see Mistah Granville."

The woman nodded, moisture glistening in her eyes. "This way, suh. Iffen you jus' wait in the lib'ery, I tell Massah Granville you here."

She scurried out, and the hushed greeting taking place in the foyer fell sweetly on Peyton's ears. "Joseph, I miss you so."

A few minutes later, Montgomery Granville entered the library. "Mr. Stafford, thank you for coming." He shook Peyton's hand. "Please come to my study."

Without waiting for Peyton to reply, Granville turned and strode down the hallway that Peyton remembered leading to the man's study. The extravagantly appointed room spoke of Granville's love for prestige.

Peyton settled into one of the tapestry chairs facing the mahogany desk and waited for Granville to explain why he'd been summoned. Before either of them could speak, the door opened and the woman whose eyes had lit up at the sight of Joseph entered, carrying a coffee tray.

"Y' want me to pour da coffee, suh?" The timidity in her voice testified of her fear.

"No." He waved his hand in dismissal, and she wasted no time obeying.

Granville poured two cups of coffee and placed one on the desk in front of Peyton. "After our last meeting, I suppose you were surprised I wanted to see you."

Peyton gave a single, mute nod. Granville didn't appear to be in a hurry to reveal all that was on his mind—at least not yet. The man stirred sugar into his coffee and returned to his leather upholstered chair.

Finally, he cleared his throat. "I'll admit what you said a few weeks ago at the party made me angry. After I cooled down and had time to think about it, I decided to meet with my bookkeeper." He rubbed his chin whiskers and gestured to the open books on his desk. "I brought the ledgers home and tried to compare them with the invoices, but everything was in a state of disorganization and confusion. I've had difficulty trying to reconcile them."

Granville rubbed the back of his neck. "I've always let Wilbur Pembroke handle the business end of things. When I asked him to explain the figures in this column and that column, and numbers that don't seem to be justified, he hemmed and hawed. Couldn't give me a straight answer other than the crops haven't brought in the price he'd expected for the past few years."

Peyton remained silent, still unsure of what the man had in mind. Perhaps Granville just wished to get his advice about cotton varieties.

A disgruntled and indistinguishable mutter rumbled from Granville's lips. "We've enjoyed a very comfortable and expensive way of life for five decades. I do like my imported cigars and one-hundred-year-old brandy." He arched his brows and sent a pointed look at Peyton. "And my wife certainly does spend money." He leaned back in his chair. "I've not changed the way we've done things at Thornwalk since my father and grandfather's day."

Peyton picked up his coffee cup to stop himself from drumming his fingers. Granville certainly was beating around the bush. At least Joseph and Polly had a bit of time together while he waited for Granville to make his point. "Mr. Granville, I can't help wondering why you've asked me to come here."

Mr. Granville leaned forward and stacked his arms on the desk. "I know you saw me at the Ridgefield bank several days back, and you saw I was trying to use my wife's jewelry as a mortgage payment." He locked his unblinking stare on Peyton. "Stafford, you know we are in financial trouble here."

Granville rose and walked to the window and pushed the velvet drape aside. From where Peyton sat, the view overlooked fields that should be flourishing, but weren't.

"What steps do you think ought to be taken to make Thornwalk successful again?"

The question wasn't unexpected, so Peyton gave a brief description of amending the soil, improving the irrigation, and investing in a quality grade of short staple seed.

Granville turned from the window and faced him.

Peyton set his cup down. "Mr. Granville, please forgive me if my question is too bold, but how long have you been leaving the operation of Thornwalk completely up to your overseer and bookkeeper?"

A frown creased Granville's features. "I can't think of a time they didn't run things. Rudd Jacobson's father used to be our overseer, so he's the one who trained his son. As far as Wilbur Pembroke goes—" He lifted his shoulders. "He's been the bookkeeper for Thornwalk for as long as I can remember. At least fifty years. Why?"

Peyton crossed one leg over his knee. "Do you not examine the books regularly?"

Granville returned to his chair. "Numbers were never my strong suit—a truth to which my teachers could attest over the years. My father always trusted Mr. Pembroke, and I've never had reason not to do the same."

The picture forming in Peyton's mind was becoming clearer, and once again he thought of Annulet. Anger stirred his gut. How could this man leave the running of his plantation to others, and then when his own irresponsible habits proved imprudent, try to marry off his daughter to a rich man to bolster the family finances? He swallowed back the scathing diatribe he wanted to launch. Instead, he drew in a breath and prayed for patience.

"Mr. Granville, how old is your bookkeeper?"

Granville shrugged. "I suppose he must be. . ." He appeared to count on his fingers. "Around eighty or so. At least."

Peyton nodded. "I suppose that might be why the books are in a state of confusion. Have you spoken with Mr. Jacobson?"

Granville shook his head. "I went to his cabin to pay him a visit, but he wasn't there."

The puzzle pieces were falling together. Peyton hooked his knee with his linked fingers. "I believe I can tell you what you would have found. I witnessed a large number of crates filled with supplies being carried into the overseer's cabin."

"What?" Granville placed his palms on the desk. "Why would he do that?"

Peyton had a hard time feeling sorry for the man. Was he really that unenlightened over the operation of his own plantation? "I would suggest questioning the slaves. Jacobson ordered them to carry the crates into his cabin. One older slave in particular—he was called Eli—was carrying very heavy crates. He likely knows what Jacobson is doing with them." He leveled a look at Annulet's father. "I believe your overseer is robbing you blind, Mr. Granville, and your fields are so poorly maintained it's no wonder you haven't had a decent crop in what I suspect is several years."

The man sitting behind the desk narrowed his eyes, and Peyton half expected him to bark his indignation and order him out of his office. Instead, Granville studied Peyton for a long, silent minute. Finally, he spoke. "I have a proposal."

Peyton exited Granville's study and walked down the hallway. He found a servant and asked if Joseph could be notified he was ready to go.

He stared out across the expansive garden to the thick row of trees, beyond which lay the fields of substandard cotton. What had just happened? What had he done? He ran his hands over his face. How was he going to break the news to his father that he'd agreed to take over the position of overseer and manager of Thornwalk Manor Plantation?

After two straight days of rain, Annulet enjoyed getting out and traveling to Bethel Station to the dressmaker. Limiting her order to only one new gown didn't bother her. Polly was handy with a needle and thread and might be able to alter a few of her older gowns. That they were cutting back expenses didn't surprise her, but she wondered what had triggered this sudden display of good sense. "Tell me again, Mama, why we are tightening our belts, as you say."

Mama sighed. "Your father has fired Mr. Jacobson."

"The overseer?"

"Yes." Mama sat primly on the carriage seat. "Your father and the new man he's hired have employed a list of new policies, including cutting out any unnecessary spending." She shook her head. "I don't like it. It's going to make us appear destitute, and no respectable young man will want to give you a second glance."

"But, Mama, if this new man can figure out the cause of the financial setback, perhaps our situation will improve."

And I won't have to marry a man I barely know.

The carriage rolled to a stop behind another one at Thornwalk's front door. "Mama, whose carriage is that?"

Mama's eyebrows drew together, and she bit her lip. "It looks like Dr. Lunsford's carriage."

They disembarked the conveyance and hurried to the door. Polly met them in the entry hall. "Miz Granville, Massah took sick. We send fo' the doctor right off. He upstairs wid Massah Granville now."

Annulet's breath caught in her throat. Before she could grab handfuls of her skirt and hasten up the stairs, the doctor stepped onto the landing and descended the lower steps.

Annulet clutched Mama's arm. "Doctor, what is wrong with Papa?"

Telltale bags under the gray-haired man's eyes defined his weariness. "I'm afraid Mr. Granville has suffered an episode of apoplexy. He needs rest and quiet."

Annulet's knees quivered and nearly gave out. Her gaze traveled up the staircase to the wide balcony that led to her parents' bedroom. "How bad is it?"

The doctor's grave expression was all the answer she needed.

Chapter 8

Annulet blinked against the tears that burned her eyes, and Mama clasped both hands to her bodice, gasping as if she'd just run uphill. Papa was always so strong. To think of him stricken down and bedridden was unfathomable.

Mama wrung her hands. "I must go to him." She moved to maneuver around the doctor, but he stopped her.

"I've given him something to make him sleep, and I don't want him disturbed." The doctor sent a stern look first to Mama and then to Annulet. "When you go into his room, you must not agitate him or allow him to know you are distressed. I want him to remain completely calm. Is that understood?"

Annulet nodded, the thousand words that fought for release all strangled in her throat. Dr. Lunsford retraced his steps back up the staircase. Annulet took Mama's hand, and they stepped into the drawing room off the entry hall. When she knew her legs would not hold her up another moment, she sank into a chair.

"Miz Granville, ma'am?" The kitchen maid stood in the doorway. "The new ovahseah is here."

Mama shook her head, unmindful of the tendrils of hair coming loose from their pins. "I can't be bothered now, Betsy."

Betsy glanced down the hall and then back to Annulet and her mother. "Mistah Stafford say he need to see you and young missy."

Annulet blinked. Mr. Stafford? It couldn't possibly be the same—

Peyton Stafford stepped in behind Betsy. "Please accept my apology, Mrs. Granville, for intruding on you at this stressful time." He turned to Betsy. "Could you please bring a tea tray to the ladies."

"Yes, suh." The woman scurried out.

Annulet snapped her mouth closed and fixed an incredulous stare at Mr. Stafford. She tried to string words together in a coherent sentence, but the news of Papa's illness and now learning Peyton Stafford was the new overseer paralyzed her thinking ability. Fearing the shock could be Mama's undoing, Annulet reached out and tugged Mama's hand, coaxing her mother to sit on the settee beside her.

Mr. Stafford stood with his hands behind his back. "I had a meeting scheduled with Mr. Granville for this afternoon."

Protectiveness loosed Annulet's lips. "My father is not seeing anyone."

He lowered his eyes momentarily, but when he spoke again, his tone was gentle. "I understand. When I got word your father was ill, I knew I needed to speak with the both of you."

Annulet shook her head. "I don't understand this." She glanced at Mama, who didn't appear the least bit confused. "My mother informed me that Papa had hired a new overseer, but I, I never—"

"But you didn't expect it to be me." The kindness in his eyes belied the original impression she'd formed three weeks earlier.

She released the breath caught in her throat. "No, I didn't." She returned her accusatory gaze to Mama. *Mama knew the new overseer was Mr. Stafford. Why didn't she—*

Mama cleared her throat. "Mr. Stafford, I'm not sure I'm in any state of mind to participate in a conversation." Mama's dignity had returned, if not her honesty. "Learning my husband has been taken ill is a shock."

He sat and divided his focus between both women. "I know, and I'm truly sorry. What we need to discuss can't wait for a better time. I believe if we are all in agreement over the strategy for Thornwalk, it will be of great benefit to Mr. Granville."

At that moment, one of the older slaves appeared at the door. His white hair and beard gave him an almost angelic appearance. "Mistah Stafford, suh. Here be th' books you wanted."

"Thank you, Eli." Mr. Stafford stood to take the stack of ledgers.

Before the slave called Eli could turn to go, however, Annulet held up her hand. "Wait. Eli, is it? I'd like to ask you some questions."

The elderly black man hesitated and slid his gaze to Mr. Stafford, who gave him a silent nod.

"Can you tell me about Mr. Stafford's position here at the plantation?"

"Annulet." Mama's scolding tone chided her. "This is not necessary."

"It's all right, Mrs. Granville." Mr. Stafford set the books on the low table between them. "She has the right to know what is going on. Go ahead, Eli.

Answer Miss Granville's question."

Eli clasped his hands in front of him and dipped his head. "Mistah Stafford be the new ovahseah. He diff'runt from Mistah Jacobson."

Annulet tipped her head and studied the black man and then the new overseer. "What do you mean by 'different'?"

A trace of annoyance tiptoed through Annulet when Eli shifted his gaze to Mr. Stafford, as if asking for permission. It appeared Mr. Stafford had already established himself.

"It's all right to speak, Eli. You're not in trouble." Mr. Stafford slipped his hands into his pockets.

Eli's shoulders eased in response to Mr. Stafford's statement. "Mistah Stafford be a fair man. A honest man. An' he don' carry no whip. He take all dem supplies and foods Mistah Jacobson keep in the cabin and he give it all to th' slaves. Firs' time in a long time all th' young'uns go to bed with full bellies."

The slave sent a look of cautious respect to Mr. Stafford. "He pry open all dem crates and give new tools to the field workers—to the ones dat be lef'."

"The ones that are left?" Annulet furrowed her brow.

A conflicted look struck Eli's features, as if he didn't know whether the news was sorrowful or joyous. "Mistah Jacobson, he sell off 'bout a dozen slaves, and da money go in his own pocket. We don' know where dey is now."

Mr. Stafford spoke up. "Eli is the one who came running to tell me Mr. Granville was taken ill. It was he who rode to town for the doctor."

Annulet held up her hand to halt the avalanche of information. Sorting through the details could wait. "All I care about right now is my father."

"Of course." Mr. Stafford turned to the slave. "Thank you, Eli. Would you please stop by the kitchen and see if the cook needs anything special for Mr. Granville. If she does, please let me know."

"Yes, suh."

Annulet watched the man go, wondering why she never even knew his name before today. There were obviously a lot of things she didn't know, but she suspected she was about to learn.

Betsy returned with a tea tray. A bracing cup of tea was exactly what she and Mama needed. Her hands shook as she poured the beverage into china cups.

"Mr. Stafford, you mentioned a strategy."

Peyton took a sip of tea and put the cup aside so he could take up the ledger on top of the stack. "I know you must have a lot of questions. Let's begin with how I came to this position."

By the time the ladies had emptied their teacups, he had explained the letter he'd received from Mr. Granville, their discussion that day in Mr. Granville's study, and his own surprise over having been offered the position of overseer and manager of Thornwalk.

"I've spent the last two nights going over the books, and to the best of my knowledge—and my suspicions—I believe Mr. Jacobson was doubling and tripling supply orders and then selling the merchandise."

Miss Granville glanced at her mother and back to him. "Is that what Eli meant when he talked about the crates in the cabin?"

"Yes. There were stacks of full crates and bundles in the overseer's cabin." He turned several pages in the ledger on his lap. "This book has notations in it with initials. If my suspicions are correct, he was selling the goods."

"So our overseer was stealing from us?" Mama's indignation rang from her question.

"I'm afraid so." He still had a hard time conjuring up sympathy over the Granvilles' ignorance of how their plantation was being run, but in the light of Mr. Granville's sudden illness, he resolved he'd do what he could to help them.

He went on to describe the health and condition of many of the slaves—tangible proof they weren't getting adequate food, despite the record books stating regular food stores were purchased.

"Eli told me there was a man who came around about once a month or so, usually after dark. By the following day, all the crates of supplies stored in Jacobson's cabin would be gone." He tapped his finger on the page. "The initials BDK appear, as far as I can determine, about every four to five weeks."

Miss Granville set her teacup down with a clunk. "Who is this BDK, and where is Mr. Jacobson now?"

Peyton drew in a relieved breath. "I was going to inform your father today that Mr. Jacobson is in the custody of the Ridgefield sheriff, and a friend of Jacobson's—one Boots Kiellor—is sitting in jail in Dahlonega for theft. He will likely be charged in this case as well. The most important thing, however"—he set aside the ledger and opened another book—"is the way we are going to steer Thornwalk. By Mr. Granville's orders, I've devised a plan. It's not going to be easy, and it's going to take some time."

He turned the book so Mrs. Granville and her daughter could see the notes he'd made. "I have a plan for the fields and crops, as well as managing the workers. The men have already begun plowing under the crop presently in the fields. Truthfully, the quality is so inferior, it's not worth the labor required to harvest it. But we can replace it."

He glanced up and was immediately struck by Annulet's wide blue eyes, so earnest and curious. So attractive. So. . .mesmerizing. He pulled his focus back to the notes on the page. He had no right to think of her as Annulet, but in truth, she had become dear to him—at least in his private thoughts.

"The soil needs to be amended to better support a new crop." He kept his eyes on the book, fearing looking back at Annulet would be a distraction from which he might not recover his concentration. "I've spoken with Eli, and he and I have a plan to dig irrigation ditches that will bring water in from Mud Creek, which is fed by the Broad River. The fields will be divided into thirds. After the soil is amended, one-third of the fields will be planted with short staple cotton."

"Isn't it a bit late for planting now?" Annulet's voice pulled his gaze up.

A whiff of her perfume teased his senses. Violets, if he didn't miss his guess. He gulped. "It is, but we will still have time to harvest before the first frost." His pulse stepped up, and he forced his attention to the written plan. "The east section will be planted in vegetables—beans, okra, peppers, and tomatoes for the summer. Carrots, cabbage, sweet potatoes, and squash for the cool months. Vegetables are a cash crop. They can be harvested and sold sooner."

Mrs. Granville twisted her fingers. "I'm terribly sorry, Mr. Stafford. Your plan does sound wonderful, but I simply must go upstairs to my husband." She rose, and Peyton followed suit.

"I understand. I can finish mapping out the details with your daughter, and she can tell you the rest later." He stepped aside for the mistress of the manor. "Please know that I'm praying for Mr. Granville, and for both of you ladies as well."

"Thank you, Mr. Stafford." She hurried from the room.

Peyton lifted his hand toward the door and looked back at Annulet. "I will understand if you wish to accompany your mother."

She shook her head. "No. I'll let her have some time with Papa. I want to hear the rest of your plan."

He took his seat again. "There is a section of grassland at the far northern end of the property that I believe we can rent out for grazing livestock. I'll look into that."

"Well." Annulet lowered her gaze to her lap. "As my mother said, the plan sounds quite prudent."

Peyton scooted forward on his chair and rested his elbows on his knees. "Managing the fields and crops is only the beginning. As long as I am here, the workers will receive their full portions of food, and there will be no brutal treatment or intimidation used. In addition, I propose repairing the slave cabins. Some are in such poor condition, they have no doors, and the roofs appear ready to collapse."

Her expression turned reflective, and she gave a thoughtful nod. "I'm glad." She sent him a quizzical look. "You said something a few moments ago that showed a different side of you."

Peyton interlaced his fingers to prevent himself reaching for her hand. "What's that?"

"Are you. . .truly praying? For Papa?"

He gave a slow nod. "And for you."

Chapter 9

Five days and Papa had still not awakened. The doctor's face bore evidence of concern and weariness as Annulet walked him to the front door.

Dr. Lunsford retrieved his hat. "Until he awakens, we can't know how much damage was done. Talk to him. Perhaps your voice. . ."

Annulet bit her lip. "Does he hear us?"

"Who knows?" He patted her shoulder. "It certainly can't hurt. I'll be back tomorrow."

"Thank you, Doctor." She should try to talk Mama into lying down for a bit, but the beckoning of God in her spirit was too strong to resist. The solitude and sanctuary of the arbor drew her.

She settled into the swing and lifted her eyes heavenward. "Dear God, please look upon my father lying there on his bed." A sob caught in her throat. "God, I don't think Mama and I can go on without him. I beg You to bring him back to us."

The nearness of God overshadowed her as she spent a season in prayer. A tear slipped down her cheek, and she brushed it away with the back of her hand. "Lord, help me to be strong and courageous. How can I help Mama? I need wisdom to know what to do, how to make decisions. I feel like I'm falling."

God whispered to her spirit. *"Hold still, child. I won't let you go."*

She lingered in the arbor for a time, letting God comfort her heart. When she rose to go back to the house, faraway, muted voices carried from beyond the line of trees. She stopped and listened. More than one voice, but too far away to hear what they said. She ventured closer to the trees and pushed aside a thick bough.

Peyton Stafford, side by side with a half dozen slaves, toiled over the plowed soil. The elderly slave with the white hair, Eli, directed in the distribution of some sort of matter in a wagon. Even at this distance, the odor caused Annulet to wrinkle her nose.

The men appeared to be split into two teams in competition with each other. Two men on the wagon tossed shovelfuls of the stinky substance onto the furrows while Mr. Stafford and three other men used hoes to combine it with the soil. As she watched, the teams challenged each other with teasing and laughter until they reached the end of the rows.

Panting and wiping sweat, Mr. Stafford clapped each of the men on the back and shook Eli's hand. "If we work like this every day, we'll have this field planted in no time."

Disbelief dropped Annulet's jaw. Mr. Stafford labored over the land as if it were his own. Dirt-caked and sweaty, he worked as hard as any of the slaves. He was the son of a wealthy textile magnate. He didn't have to do this. Confusion and amazement stirred her alternately. What kind of man was he?

A nudge captured her attention. She'd asked God for wisdom. Perhaps He was opening her eyes to the direction He wanted her to go. She pushed past the trees and picked up her skirts, high-stepping across the furrows as she approached Mr. Stafford and the workers.

The moment he saw her, he pulled his hat off and self-consciously brushed at his shirt. "Miss Granville. I didn't expect to see you out here."

She regarded him with new respect. "Nor did I expect to see you out here." She allowed her gaze to sweep across the field, the newly cultivated rows, and the slaves. "What can I do to help?"

His eyebrows lifted. "I beg your pardon?"

"I want to do something." She spread her arms to indicate the land all around them. "This is my home, and I feel I should be participating in this plan of yours to save it—not only for myself, but for my father."

Mr. Stafford's features softened. "The best medicine for your father is to see the plantation financially stable."

"I agree." She met his gaze.

A tiny smile lifted one corner of his mouth. "All right. If you really want to help, take over managing the house. Keep track of spending, cut back expenses, make do with what you have, supervise the servants, oversee the kitchen garden, organize a group of women to sew and mend clothing for the slaves so they aren't dressed in rags, explore the attic and see if there is anything usable stored away."

She hoped the overwhelmed feeling didn't show on her face. She forced a nod. "I can do that."

"Good." Another smirk made his lips twitch. "We'll have to meet regularly to keep track of the accounts. What about your mother?"

She studied the dirt smudges on her shoes. She'd not been able to get Mama to leave Papa's bedside for more than a few minutes. "My mother is fully occupied caring for my father. I don't want to leave her out of the decision-making or supervising, but I believe she will appreciate those tasks being done so she can give my father her undivided attention."

Mr. Stafford wiped his hand on his trousers and held it out to her, and they shook hands as if sealing a business deal. His large fingers swallowed hers, and a strange—but not unwelcomed—sensation filled her. Mr. Stafford's touch wasn't anything like Ramsay Wheeler's.

Over the course of the next few weeks, Annulet began managing every aspect of the house, from working in the garden to balancing the household ledgers. She recruited Betsy and Polly to help her go through the attic, and they discovered trunks and crates of discarded clothing, rolled-up rugs, and a canvas bag filled with shoes she'd worn and outgrown as a child. They discovered more than a dozen old shutters in one barn, and stacks of lumber suitable for the cabin repairs in the loft of the second barn. The approval on Mr. Stafford's face when she showed him the treasures was worth every dusty sneeze.

Every day she watched him in the fields, directing the field laborers and working alongside them. One evening, in the fading light of dusk, he plowed an area for a garden for the slaves to grow their own vegetables. She smiled as he showed some of the young boys how to set snares to catch rabbits and grouse, and on two occasions he brought in a deer and wild turkey. His dedication to make his plan work moved her to realize she no longer viewed him as the enemy.

"That's wonderful news! The best news! Truly an answer to prayer." Joy welled up within Peyton when Annulet told him her father was awake.

Mrs. Granville joined them in the drawing room while Dr. Lunsford was with her husband. "He's still very weak and struggling to speak, but we're hopeful he will improve."

"We're grateful for your prayers." The expression on Annulet's face invited him to believe her sincerity. He was loath to break the connection by blinking.

She cleared her throat and shifted on her chair. "I read the newest entries in the ledger. It appears your cash crop of vegetables is doing well, and I'm impressed by the growth of the newly planted cotton."

Given her previous opinion of his research, her acknowledging the success of the short staple cotton was just short of miraculous. "I appreciate how you stepped up to run the household, freeing your mother to care for Mr. Granville."

Mrs. Granville bestowed a wobbly smile on her daughter. "She's done an excellent job."

He sent Annulet a short nod, hoping she saw it as more than simply approval, especially since he had a sensitive matter to bring before both of them—one they very well might resist.

He pressed his palms against the armrests and drew a fortifying breath. "I propose releasing some of the slaves—fourteen to be exact—four men, six women, and four children. With the changes we've made in the crop and field rotation, I believe we can get along fine with a reduced number of workers." He watched both ladies to gauge their reaction.

Mother and daughter looked at each other and then back at Peyton in unison.

Mrs. Granville pressed her fingertips together and studied him for a minute. "On what do you base this decision?"

Persuading Southerners to free their slaves might prove to be a monumental undertaking, but Peyton's convictions wouldn't let him keep silent. Taking a practical approach might be an easier way to circle around the subject. "For one thing, we would have fewer slaves to feed and care for and wouldn't need to make repairs and improvements to as many of the cabins."

He tried to read the woman's expression but found it conflicted. He hoped she wouldn't insist on letting her husband make the decision. It might be weeks, or even months, before Mr. Granville would be well enough to make such a ruling. On the other hand, Mrs. Granville might view the number of slaves as some kind of status symbol.

He waited.

Finally, she raised her eyes to meet his. "I will admit that I have avoided going to that part of Thornwalk for many years because of the way the slaves have to live, knowing it's our fault." She glanced at Annulet. "I know your father might disagree, but for now, we are the ones making these decisions." She arrowed an unwavering gaze back at Peyton. "So I agree with you."

"I know Papa would say it's financially more prudent to sell them." The uncertainty in Annulet's clear blue eyes and her questioning tone begged him to clarify his position.

He leaned forward, dipping his head for a moment. "I believe the buying and selling of human beings, holding them in bondage, and treating them like livestock is an egregious thing. The slaves suffered brutal treatment at the hand of Rudd Jacobson. They went without food and clean water. Some died for lack of medical care. There are young children—no more than five or six years of age—who were taken away from their mothers. Some of the young girls suffered unspeakable things.

"Did you know when Rudd Jacobson sold those slaves, he separated three families? Did you know one of the slaves at Meadowgold is married to one of your slaves here at Thornwalk, and they rarely get to see each other?"

Moisture pooled in Annulet's eyes, and she swallowed visibly. Her voice was a hushed whisper. "I never knew. . . ." She struggled for composure, and Peyton gave her a minute to collect herself.

She dabbed at her eyes with her napkin. "If this is the case, why don't you want to free all of them?"

He sent a silent prayer of thanks heavenward for Annulet's compassion. "I would like to see all of them free one day. But until that can happen, we can treat the ones here at Thornwalk with dignity and kindness."

Annulet studied him with such scrutiny, he feared he'd been wrong in discerning her reaction as compassion. He hurried to continue.

"There is a scripture, Colossians 3:12 through 14, that lists qualities we, as Christians, are to demonstrate and employ. Mercy, kindness, patience, forgiveness, to name a few. But the most important quality, above all these things, it says, is charity." His throat grew tight. "Charity is the practice of showing Christ's love to each other, and the scripture says it is 'perfect.'"

He watched Annulet's face as she turned over in her mind what he said. Her eyes softened, a slight wrinkle indented the space between her eyes, and a barely perceptible nod indicated her agreement.

"You've given me a lot to think about."

Peyton sat at the desk in his cabin and recorded the acts of freedom in the plantation record book. He wrote a document for each freed slave to carry, testifying of their freedom. Lastly, he arranged transportation for the released slaves on a train headed northbound to Ohio. The memory of their faces when he told them they were free would stay with him forever. Even those who hadn't been chosen looked at Peyton with respect. How he wished he could arrange for Joseph and Polly to live together as husband and wife. At least he could do his best to see to it they had more time together.

Eli had wept openly when his papers were pressed into his hand. When Peyton had offered him the choice of either accompanying the others north or taking the position of assistant overseer with a small stipend, the older man's eyes widened in amazement. *"Mistah Peyton, I be proud to work wi' you."* He had gestured to the gathering of the slaves standing around him. *"All us here respec' you. Yo' is a good man."*

Chapter 10

The land office agent's desk was cluttered with ledgers, documents, and disarrayed maps. The narrow table along one wall held a row of record books, and the single chair at the table was stacked higher than the armrests with folders and papers. How the agent could keep track of anything was a mystery to Peyton.

The bewhiskered land agent tugged at his sleeve garters. "Mr. Stafford, this here is Harold Wigham. He's the sheep farmer I told you might be interested in that grazing land y'all got at Thornwalk."

Peyton shook hands with Mr. Wigham. The man had a firm grip and dirt under his fingernails. "So Granville finally run off that Jacobson fella, did he?" Wigham shook his head. "He was a no-good rascal."

Peyton couldn't disagree with Wigham's assessment of the former overseer, but he didn't come here to discuss Rudd Jacobson. He steered the conversation in another direction. "I've been the overseer at Thornwalk for about five weeks now. Since Mr. Granville took ill several weeks ago, I am acting as his representative, but all transactions will have his approval."

Wigham nodded. "Tell me about this piece of land."

Peyton hooked his thumbs in his belt. "It's about seventy acres, and has lain fallow for about five years. I don't know why that section wasn't planted, but it's gone to grass and clover now. A narrow creek runs along the north border. We are seeking to lease it as grazing land."

Wigham stroked his chin. "Is it fenced?"

"Not yet, but we could discuss that under the terms of agreement." If Mr. Wigham wished to negotiate a contract, Eli and two or three men could plant posts and string wire. "I'd be happy to take you out there so you could look it over."

The sheep man nodded. "I'd like to see it. Not that I doubt your word, but my sheep can be mighty particular." He scratched his head. "Thing is, I ain't wantin' to lease. If the land suits me, I was lookin' to buy it outright."

The farmer's declaration took Peyton by surprise. "I see. Well, I will have to talk with Mr. Granville about that, as long as the doctor says he is up to such a conversation."

They agreed on a time frame and shook hands. As Peyton left the office and walked down the street toward the post office, he turned the conversation over in his mind. Annulet and her mother had agreed that leasing the land for grazing rights had been a fine idea, but they hadn't discussed selling any part of the plantation.

How would Annulet react? Thornwalk was her home, her legacy. Since she was an only child, she and her husband would inherit it one day, and he was about to propose selling off a chunk of it.

Her husband? The very idea created an uncomfortable tightness in his chest.

Just as he reached the post office, Ramsay Wheeler stepped out the door. His friend's fine linen shirt, silk cravat, and cassimere morning coat flaunted his position in the community. Peyton's own cotton duck trousers and striped muslin shirt, while clean and neat, made him feel dowdy by comparison. He lifted his chin. Why should he be embarrassed because he worked hard?

"Morning, Ramsay."

Peyton's greeting was met with a smirk. "Well, look who's in town. I figured you'd be too busy running Thornwalk to venture out among civilized people." Ramsay glanced up and down Peyton's attire. "I must say, I thought it was a joke when you told me you had taken the job of overseer, but you're actually serious, aren't you?" He guffawed. "You've lost your mind, Stafford."

Ramsay's shallowness wasn't a shock, but his ungracious behavior raised Peyton's eyebrows. He wouldn't waste his breath trying to explain his convictions to a prideful and arrogant man who'd never dirtied his hands, much less extended a humanitarian gesture to anyone he considered beneath him. Knowing Ramsay's attitude toward the slaves, Peyton tried to defuse the public confrontation, but Ramsay hung on to the subject like a terrier with a bone.

"What do you think your father is going to have to say about this idiotic playacting you're doing?"

The answer to that question hadn't been far from Peyton's thoughts since the day he shook hands with Montgomery Granville and agreed to take the job. The letter he'd written to his father had been sent before he accepted the overseer position, and Peyton had been waiting for a reply to gauge exactly how he should word any addendum regarding his new occupation.

Peyton slid his gaze past Ramsay to the door of the post office. "I sent him a letter some time ago and have not received word back yet. I keep hoping I'll get a letter soon."

Ramsay laughed, a sarcastic sneer pulling his lips. "You're about to get an earful from your father. He arrived just this morning at Meadowgold looking for you."

The breath in Peyton's lungs caught for a moment, and his stomach turned over, but he refused to allow his facial expression to show any reaction. He locked his steady gaze on Ramsay. "Well, I suppose you can give him directions to Thornwalk."

Peyton walked through the side door at Thornwalk and met Mrs. Granville heading toward the stairs with a small tray. "How is Mr. Granville this afternoon?"

A weary smile tugged at her lips. "Awake and cantankerous because he wants to get out of bed."

Peyton grinned. "Sounds like a good sign. Would it be all right if I speak with him briefly?"

"Of course." She smiled when he took the tray from her. "He will be happy to see someone else besides me."

They entered the room, and Mr. Granville brightened. Peyton greeted him and pulled up a chair close to the bed. He described the meeting with Harold Wigham. "Our plan was to lease those seventy acres as grazing land, but Mr. Wigham wants to purchase it. We didn't discuss price or terms. I wanted to speak with you first. What do you think?"

Granville rubbed his unshaven jaw and fixed his stony stare on Peyton. He didn't answer for a long minute, and Peyton feared he'd agitated the man. Finally, struggling with regaining his speech, he pushed out a few halting words.

"Make Th–Thornwalk. . .smaller. What about crop?"

"Switching out and rotating crops can be done with the acres we've currently planted and still turn a profit." Peyton gave a brief summary of the rotation plan and explained how the schedule would benefit the soil and produce successful results.

Granville gave Peyton a long, hard look before nodding. "Do what. . .you think best. Trust you. Get a good price."

"I will, sir. I'll bring you the bill of sale to sign." Peyton grasped Granville's hand and shook it.

He bid the Granvilles a good day and returned to his cabin, wondering what his father would say about such a decision. No doubt Father would have pushed for more acreage and bigger holdings, to be the most influential planter in the state. It was Father's way to do business.

Peyton shook his head. His mind-set was vastly different from his father's. His strategy was a carefully thought-out plan he could steer with a focus on rescuing Annulet's home, not garnering prominence and rank to overshadow every other plantation.

Thoughts of Annulet eased into his mind. What would she say about the reduction of the size of the plantation? His impression of her had changed over the past several weeks, and his initial belief that she was spoiled and pampered was inaccurate. No, Annulet Granville loved her home and her parents, even when they made decisions that distressed her. The fervor and determination with which she had given herself to the job of managing the household made his heart smile. On top of everything else, she was beautiful, inside and out.

Her image, the curve of her cheekbones with their pink blush, and her very scent filled his senses. Chestnut-brown hair gleaming in the sun, blue eyes that made him wish he had nothing else to do but lose himself in their depths. The sound of her voice and the music of her laughter sang to him. Beyond that, however—like the scripture said, *above all these things*, it was her compassion and giving heart that drew him and made him long to be in her presence. His pulse stepped up. Ordinarily, a young woman like Annulet wouldn't consider being courted by an overseer. Despite his family background, she still might not, especially if Father decided to cut Peyton off.

Ramsay's news of Father's arrival had lingered in the back of his mind all afternoon. He considered going to Meadowgold to see him, but Peyton didn't wish their reunion to be overheard or witnessed by anyone, most of all Ramsay. If Father had to come to Thornwalk, he'd be indignant, but this is where Peyton felt more at home.

Strange. The evening he'd spent here as a party guest almost three months ago hadn't left him feeling at home. On the contrary, he'd been most uncomfortable. When and how had that changed?

Annulet nudged the door of her father's room open and peeked in. Papa was sitting up in a chair beside the bed while Mama arranged a shawl over his shoulders. She tapped on the door before slipping in.

"I'm so happy to see you sitting up." She planted a kiss on Papa's forehead and sat on the edge of the bed.

His smile was lopsided, his movements awkward as he reached out to pat her hand. "Your mother s–says. . .y–you do fine job with house."

She blushed under his praise, but Mama clasped her hands to her chest. "Oh my, she has taken over everything, Montgomery. You should see the way she's managing the servants and taken over the household accounts, all so I can be here with you. I never knew our daughter possessed such skills."

Mama's comments surprised Annulet. "I'm not the only one working hard. Betsy and Polly have taught me much—in the garden, and the kitchen. Betsy is even teaching me to bake. Mr. Stafford has hunted venison, wild turkey, and duck. He butchered a wild hog that had gotten into one end of the vegetable crop. We haven't needed to purchase much at all from town, other than coffee and flour and the like. Cook has created some wonderful meals with the simplest resources."

She cast a furtive glance at Mama. "We've also canceled plans for entertaining for the remainder of the year. I know you don't like it, Mama, but it's necessary."

Her mother shrugged and slid a glance to Papa. "I'm beginning to understand the purpose, even though I fear withdrawing ourselves from the season's social events will damage Annulet's chances of marrying well."

Papa turned his watery eyes to Annulet. "You see any. . .men who came. . . to party? Ramsay Wheeler?"

The last person she wished to discuss was Ramsay Wheeler. The memory of his lewd suggestions and his uncouth manhandling sent a shudder through her. She tried to change the subject.

"I believe Cook is preparing a ham for supper from that wild boar Mr. Stafford shot. Ham has always been one of your favorites, Papa."

"Annulet, answer your father's question." Mama arrowed a look at her. "You said you saw Ramsay when you went to Meadowgold for the Ladies' Missionary Society luncheon given by Mrs. Wheeler."

Her teeth clamped tightly, Annulet studied her clasped fingers for a long, silent moment. "Only briefly."

"But why didn't you—"

"Mama, Ramsay Wheeler isn't the gentleman you think he is." She squared her shoulders and looked her mother in the eye. "I will not see him again."

Distress threaded her mother's tone. "I don't understand."

Papa leaned forward in his chair. "Why, daughter?"

Annulet didn't want to upset Papa. She gentled her tone. "Please understand. I know my own mind. I've prayed over the kind of man I want for a husband, and I'll settle for nothing less. The Bible says a man should be kind, tenderhearted, humble, and patient. He should bear with others when they stumble, and he should be forgiving. Above all, I want a man who loves—not just me, but others as well. A man who extends God's love to other people fulfills scripture, because God's Word says love is the bond of perfectness."

Her stomach tumbled, and she stopped to take a breath. "Papa, I promise I'll make you proud of me."

Papa's eyes glistened with unshed tears. "I am. . .proud. . .of you."

She slid off the edge of the bed. "I have several things I need to do." She scurried to the door and hastened down the stairway, heart pounding.

She'd just described Peyton Stafford.

Chapter 11

More than a day and a half since Ramsay Wheeler announced Peyton's father's presence at Meadowgold, the man had yet to make an appearance at Thornwalk. Peyton had tussled with whether or not to go to Meadowgold and face his father's wrath. In all likelihood, Ramsay wasted no time in telling Ellery Stafford he'd encountered his son in town, so his father knew Peyton was aware of his arrival.

Should he or shouldn't he?

What a ridiculous argument. It would take at least a half day. Peyton sent a sweeping look across the fields. He couldn't afford the time, especially after releasing a third of the slaves. Giving those people their freedom was the right thing to do—nothing would ever convince him otherwise. He doubted Father would see it that way, and thus would dispute Peyton's claim of not being able to take time away from his job.

Six of the men were busy working on the cabins. Four more had to look after livestock, the barns, and the grounds, as well as care for the kitchen garden. Since yesterday, Eli and five slaves were busy cutting fence posts and digging postholes for the grazing land, which meant Peyton had only a dozen slaves working with him in the cotton and vegetable fields. Keeping track of the work and seeing to it that everything was done properly made for a long day.

Their hard work was paying off. The beans and okra were thriving, the tomato plants bore a plethora of yellow blossoms, and the cotton was showing great promise. Weeds liked the amended soil as much as the crops did, however, so it required diligence to prevent the intruders from taking over. There was still a good deal of work to be done on the cabins, and to take the men away from the repairs meant the slave community would remain in the dilapidated quarters for an undetermined length of time. Peyton swung his hoe at a weed with more vigor than necessary. Even Annulet and Mrs.

Granville supported making the repairs.

The decision whether or not to go to Meadowgold wouldn't matter anyway—not truly. Father was going to be livid at Meadowgold or Thornwalk. The location wouldn't change his reaction to Peyton's letter or the revelation of his new job. Weighing all the options, Peyton only hoped he could manage to avoid an audience when the confrontation took place.

A soft rain began to fall as he paced slowly down each row in the field, examining the new cotton crop and chopping out weeds with his hoe. In the adjacent rows to his right and left, slaves worked alongside, none complaining about the cooling rain. They'd gotten a late start this season—planting usually took place in early spring. But if the weather held, they still hoped for a good crop before the first frost. The creamy blossoms had all turned to yellow, and then to pink, and many had already fallen off to reveal new green bolls.

Hope bubbled up within him, and his thoughts turned to Annulet—again. To his great relief, she was in favor of selling the seventy acres to Mr. Wigham. It was her suggestion they begin readying the posts for the fencing, but she insisted that Mr. Wigham should supply the wire. Her business acumen stretched a grin across Peyton's face.

He was anxious to tell her how the cotton was doing, to encourage her that their plan was slowly becoming reality. The healthy crop was worth all the work they'd done cultivating and amending the soil. In return, he looked forward to hearing the gladness in her voice when she described a project she'd finished, or a new idea she'd had. He chuckled every time he remembered her excitement over having baked bread for the first time. Spending time with her in the evening, sharing what they had accomplished or planning a new strategy, had become his favorite part of the day.

He paused midrow and let a memory wash over him. Last week, she'd mentioned she had been reading the scriptures to her father, and she read the selection Peyton had told her about in Colossians. Even now, the thought made his heart sing.

He cast a look up into the gray clouds weeping moisture and thanked God for the rain. It meant they could hold off digging the irrigation ditches for now. Water dripped from the brim of his hat as he swung his hoe, breaking up the clods of dirt to let the rain soak in.

Someone called his name. He looked up and saw Annulet at the edge of the field waving her handkerchief. Why in heaven's name was she out here in the rain? His chest tightened. Had her father taken a turn for the worse?

He gripped his hoe and strode toward her between the rows of cotton, his heart pounding out a rhythm to match his footsteps. Distress etched lines around her eyes.

"What is it? What's wrong?"

She dragged her hand over her face and wiped away the raindrops. "You have a visitor. He is most insistent upon seeing you. I told him you were in the fields, and he became quite indignant. When I asked his name, he simply said you would know who he was."

His gut twisted like a clenched fist. "Yes, I know who he is." He blew out a stiff breath. "It's my father, Ellery Stafford, and I've been expecting him. I'm so sorry if he was rude. I'd hoped to be the one to greet him so you could be spared his bluster and pomposity."

She waved away his concern. "I've dealt with pomposity before. He's waiting in the front parlor. I asked Betsy to bring a coffee tray and some of her special cookies."

He let his gaze slide to the hem of her gown and those dainty little slippers she wore, stained with mud. "I'm sorry I don't have anything to shield you from the rain."

Her charming face tipped up to meet his eyes, and the smile that lifted the corners of her mouth made him forget the falling rain, the mud, and even his father. "You must think I'm made of sugar frosting." Was that teasing in her voice?

He tossed his hoe aside. "I need to go and see him, but—" He looked down at his own wet clothing and muddy boots.

Annulet laid her hand on his. Her touch sent delicious tingles up his arm. "You go to your cabin and get cleaned up. I'll run back and have Polly help me change, after which I'll keep him entertained. Don't hurry. Your father will have some of Betsy's cookies while he's waiting for you."

Peyton turned his hand to curl his grimy fingers around hers and gave her a tight smile. "Waiting isn't something my father likes to do."

She squeezed his hand. "You leave him to me."

Annulet glanced at her reflection in the entryway mirror. Polly had made hasty work of twining her damp hair and pinning it in place, leaving a few tendrils to dangle by her ears. Her dress was one of last year's gowns, but she doubted Ellery Stafford would know the difference.

She gathered every bit of her gentility and tact and stepped into the parlor where their guest paced back and forth. "I'm terribly sorry to keep you waiting, Mr. Stafford. Peyton wasn't easy to find, as busy as he is. I just don't know what we'd do without him." She graced him with her most enchanting smile while at the same time realizing this was the first time she'd used Peyton's Christian name. She hoped his father didn't mind, because the name felt very right on her lips.

The stiffness in his neck and jaw appeared to relax momentarily, and he picked up his coffee cup. "I must say, I thought you'd forgotten me."

Annulet lowered her lashes. "Oh, no sir. We're delighted you've come to see us." She picked up the cookie plate and held it out to him. "Do have some of these wonderful cookies."

He narrowed his eyes at her. "How much longer do you plan to keep me waiting to see my son? I assume he told you I'm his father."

Peyton was right. His father didn't like to wait. She suspected the senior Stafford was accustomed to having everything his way, and when people didn't kowtow to him, his indignation spilled over. Time to add a measure of diplomacy. "He did, and I assure you, he will be here shortly." She gestured to the most comfortable chair in the room. "Please, have a seat."

She took the chair across from him and perched on the edge, her fingers clasped together. She'd need every bit of charm she could muster to mollify the man without letting him intimidate her.

Storm clouds swirled on Mr. Stafford's countenance. "Look, Miss Granville, you are a lovely hostess, but I have come a long way to meet with my son. He and I have business matters of utmost importance to discuss, so I would appreciate it if you'd go and tell him I'm still waiting." His ire ground out the last few words.

Another sweet smile. "Peyton is aware of your presence, Mr. Stafford, and he will be here as soon as he can be."

When the man heaved an impatient sigh, Annulet dug deeply for an extra whit of fortitude. She pasted her smile in place but allowed firmness to define her tone. "Furthermore, I told him not to hurry."

Peyton's father gripped the armrests and bristled like an angry cat. "You what?"

Annulet leaned forward and refilled his coffee cup. "I do treasure this time we have to get to know each other. Are you quite sure you wouldn't like another cookie?"

"No, I don't want—"

She looked at him with a demure tilt to her chin. "Perhaps you haven't been apprised of all that Peyton does for us. In addition to overseeing the workers, he has reworked the entire plan for our crops, organized a much more productive growing schedule, and has taken on repairs and maintenance of the slave quarters. He works side by side with the field laborers and has earned their trust and respect by doing so. Did I mention he was the one who brought to my father's attention the theft and misuse of accounts committed by our former overseer? When Thornwalk was teetering on the brink of disaster, Peyton's knowledge and levelheaded calculations, along with his proposals to redesign the strategy and purpose for our plantation, gave us a solid course to follow."

Ellery Stafford's mouth opened and closed like a trout on the riverbank breathing his last. Suspecting he was rarely rendered speechless, Annulet seized the opportunity. "Mr. Stafford, I hope you know and appreciate the kind of man your son is."

Stafford held up both palms in surrender. "Next you will try to tell me that he walks on water."

She laid her clasped hands in her lap, praying she was the picture of grace and hospitality on the outside, because on the inside passionate words were fighting for release. This man sitting in front of her had no idea what a wonderful son he had. Did he know that Peyton prayed for her father? Did he realize the depth of his son's faith, or the strength of his character, or the gentleness of his compassion? Peyton Stafford had taught her what true mercy and kindness, humbleness and forgiveness were, because he lived those qualities. Every day out in the fields he labored and sweated and gave of himself to save her family's home.

"Above all these things put on charity. . .the bond of perfectness."

Oh, how she longed to give freedom to the understanding dawning within her, and shout it from the rooftop. But Mr. Stafford wasn't the first person who should hear those words from her.

Peyton needed to hear them first.

Chapter 12

Peyton paused outside the double doors that led to the front parlor to breathe a prayer for wisdom and discernment in dealing with his father. He had no desire to engage in a shouting match, and he would not be disrespectful, but neither would he let Father coerce him into surrendering his values. He'd made his position clear in his letter.

He tapped the papers in his hand. Three tentative contracts. Not much to show for being in Georgia for almost three months, but it was all he'd been able—or willing—to negotiate before accepting Mr. Granville's proposal to take over Jacobson's position. He refused to contract with planters who treated their slaves like animals. He didn't care how many bales of cotton they produced.

No bellowing or demands rang from the parlor, so perhaps Annulet had him eating out of her hand. She'd best take care, however, that she didn't get bitten. Just as Peyton took a step toward the open door, his father's voice, uncharacteristically tender, reached him.

"You think a great deal of my son, don't you, young lady?"

Peyton froze and dared not move. In that heartbeat of time, Annulet's answer was more important than his own breath. A silent eternity passed. Dread spiraled through him. If she didn't reply soon, he'd explode.

A soft, feminine clearing of her throat preceded her words. "Yes. I do."

Yes? His trapped breath released in a whoosh, and his dread was replaced by a momentary flash of giddiness. Hearing her admit her feelings made his heart take flight.

Reality shook a mocking finger at him. *She didn't say she cares for you.* Father had merely asked if she thought well of him. His spirit plummeted back to earth. He shrugged. A couple of months ago, she could barely tolerate his presence.

He still had to face his father. Perhaps Father would refrain from turning the meeting into a clash of wills if Annulet was present. On the other hand, if she stayed in the room, she'd witness his father's anger and criticism.

Lord, this is in Your hands. Take control.

He quit procrastinating and entered the room. His father sat across from Annulet, leaned back and legs crossed in a relaxed manner. A pleasant expression eased his father's face as he chatted with Annulet. The moment Father looked up and connected his gaze with Peyton's, however, his brow creased into a scowl. He rose from his chair.

His father was never one for demonstrative shows of affection. Peyton extended his hand. "Father. Good to see you."

Father gripped his hand. "Son." Stiff politeness thickened the air.

Annulet rose. "Would you like some coffee?" Without waiting for Peyton to answer, she picked up the pot and jiggled it. "Oh my, it's nearly empty. I'll just go to the kitchen and refill it. There are plenty more cookies. Please excuse me, gentlemen."

As she stepped past Peyton he caught the meaningful look she sent him. An ember of hope glowed within him that they'd have a moment alone later to speak privately. The thought teased his pulse to trot a bit faster.

He watched Annulet's skirts swirl and disappear around the corner before crossing to sit across from his father.

"I assume you received my letter."

His father reached inside his frock coat and retrieved the missive. "Yes, I received it. I must say I was disappointed. In sending you here, my expectation was for you to prove yourself qualified to one day take over the position of president of the company when I get ready to retire. Instead"—he flapped Peyton's letter in the air—"you send me this epistle stating your convictions about the use of slaves, and the part our company plays in reinforcing the practice of slavery." He steeled his gaze. "Made me sound like some kind of greedy profiteer, making money from the blood of these people."

Peyton winced. "I don't recall putting it exactly that way." He pressed his fingers together. "Father, I do apologize for letting you down. I know you've been counting on me to establish contracts with the planters. That's what you sent me here to do."

His father did not reply, and Peyton drew in a deep breath. "I know I should have written to tell you I had taken this job. I kept telling myself I was still waiting for a reply to my first letter, but in hindsight, I realize now I owed you the courtesy of informing you. It must have been a shock to hear

Ramsay Wheeler tell you I was working as Thornwalk's overseer."

Father glowered. "I never had much use for Ramsay Wheeler when the two of you were in school together. He practically crowed like a jubilant rooster telling me that you took this job."

Peyton could just imagine. "I do apologize for not letting you know earlier." He unfolded the papers and laid them out for his father to examine. "Why don't we look at these potential contracts."

While his father looked over the information, Peyton went on to explain what he'd observed at each plantation, and why he felt they were good candidates for contracts. "Both George Murdock and Theodore Bartells are anxious to finalize the transactions, and of course, you have a contract with Meadowgold."

There was no mistaking the puzzlement in Father's expression as he dropped the papers on the low table and leaned back in his chair, fingertips drumming on the armrest. He studied Peyton with such scrutiny, Peyton felt a thousand eyes were watching him.

"What changed?"

Peyton didn't need to ask what his father meant. He weighed his answer carefully. "What I have observed since I've been visiting the different plantations doesn't confirm what I've been told for years about slavery. When I was younger, I believed the slaves were taken care of and that they were necessary to turn a profit, but nobody ever painted a true picture. When I was attending the university, I never had occasion to tour the fields except the acres where I worked near the school. I certainly never visited the slave quarters of any plantations. My studies took all my time."

Peyton closed his eyes briefly, pleading with God to make his father understand. "After witnessing the brutality, the living conditions, the separation of families, I cannot, in good conscience, recommend contracting many of the plantations I toured, regardless of the quality or quantity of their crop."

Father nodded. "I admit that I was aware of the ugly side of slavery, but didn't feel you needed to know. At the time we were discussing your coming here to contract planters, I wondered if it was a mistake to send you."

Annulet entered the room carrying the freshly filled coffeepot, and Father nodded his head toward her. "This young lady has filled me in on your new position here at Thornwalk Manor, and all that your job entails."

Annulet's wide blue eyes shifted first to Father and then to Peyton. "O-oh, I've forgotten to bring more sugar." She placed the pot on the table and turned back toward the door, but Peyton caught her hand.

"Please stay. You need to hear this."

She took a seat and fixed her gaze on him. He couldn't look away.

"When Mr. Granville offered me this job, I saw it as a challenge. I'd seen evidence of the mismanagement of Thornwalk, and I realized the family would be in dire straits if I didn't do something."

His senses drowned in the sight of her. "I couldn't let that happen."

Annulet drew in a sharp breath at Peyton's expression. She'd never noticed the gold flecks in his brown eyes before. Had they been there all along, or had his determined passion to communicate something for which he struggled to find words brought them out? Either way, they had a mesmerizing effect, and she had no desire to break the connection.

Peyton's explanation might be for his father's benefit, but she hung on every word.

"The crop in the field was so poor, I had no intention of contracting with Mr. Granville, but that night at the party, I attempted to meet other planters."

Her stomach tightened. She remembered back to the party. He'd paid more attention to the other men with whom he might do business than he did to her. Perhaps she should be insulted, but her mother had suggested pursuing Peyton because of his family's ties with northern textile mills. Their initial motivations weren't so very different. Shame heated her face, but she waited to hear all he had to say.

Peyton's tone pleaded with her to understand. "After I saw how the slaves were being treated, I felt sick. So when Mr. Granville offered me the job, stepping in to replace the man responsible for the mismanagement and the harsh treatment of the slaves felt noble." He lifted his shoulders. "I admit I relished the chance to show off my agricultural skills as well. But when Mr. Granville was taken ill, something happened"—he touched his fingertips to his chest—"in here. It no longer seemed important to be seen as the 'hero who saved Thornwalk.'"

Annulet wasn't sure when it happened, but something special had taken place within her as well.

Peyton finally dropped his gaze. "I had people depending on me."

Mr. Stafford harrumphed. "I was depending on you too."

A rush of defensiveness filled Annulet, and she bit her lip. She'd not been invited to join this conversation, but she suspected Peyton had a reason for asking her to stay.

Peyton cast an uncertain look at the man sitting across from him. "Father, you are a very successful man, and you're surrounded by people who are ready to do your bidding. Going in another direction doesn't mean I don't love and respect you."

Was it her imagination or did Mr. Stafford's eyes just soften?

Peyton's tone turned pensive. "Over the past several weeks, the people here. . ." He returned his gaze to her again. "Have grown quite dear to me."

Annulet's heart beat against her ribs like a hummingbird trying to break free. She leaned forward and pretended to fuss with the coffee tray so Peyton and his father wouldn't see her blush.

When Peyton spoke again, she couldn't refrain from looking up at him. The tenderness in his eyes was nearly her undoing.

"People became more important to me than the way I was perceived by associates or peers." He shifted his focus to Mr. Stafford. "Or even you, Father. God has called me to this, to let Him work through me to make changes in the lives of a handful of slaves."

When he looked back at Annulet, her breath caught. Peyton Stafford had already made a difference in her life. Only time would tell where those changes might lead.

"Well." Peyton's father rose. "Perhaps one day this week, you can introduce me to the planters with whom you've contracted on my behalf."

Mr. Stafford angled his head and looked at his son, as if seeing him for the first time. "At the end of the day, son, all a man can truly call his own are his convictions and principles." He turned to Annulet. "Miss Granville, would you mind retrieving my hat."

She scurried to the entry hall, and when she returned to the parlor, Peyton and his father were embracing. A tiny sob worked its way up her throat, and she swallowed several times to force it back.

Mr. Stafford smiled and took his hat. "Thank you, my dear, for being such a lovely and gracious hostess."

He leaned close to Peyton and whispered, just loudly enough for Annulet to hear, "If you're smart, you won't let this young lady get away."

Peyton shook his father's hand. "I will happily take that advice, Father." He turned and caught both of Annulet's hands in his. "If she'll have me."

Annulet stared at him, breath caught in her chest, astonishment rendering her speechless. Every vestige of poise and decorum vanished. Was he saying what she thought he was saying?

Apparently taking her shock for indecision, sorrow marred his features. "You're turning me down?"

Tears filled her eyes as she tightened her fingers around his. "I need to know. . ."

"If I love you?" He kept his grip on her hands as he lowered himself to one knee. "Oh, my sweet Annulet. I've only begun to love you, and I promise to love you for the rest of my life. Will you marry me?"

This was the moment she'd dreamed of as a girl, the one she'd made herself forget. She pulled one hand free and covered her mouth, tears slipping between her fingers as she nodded. "Yes, Peyton. Yes."

Connie Stevens lives with her husband of forty-plus years in north Georgia, within sight of her beloved mountains. She and her husband are both active in a variety of ministries at their church. A lifelong reader, Connie began creating stories by the time she was ten. Her office manager and writing muse is a cat, but she's never more than a phone call or email away from her critique partners. She enjoys gardening and quilting, but one of her favorite pastimes is browsing antique shops where story ideas often take root in her imagination. Connie has been a member of American Christian Fiction Writers since 2000.